ACTS OF THE VIGIL

Books by Joe Bergeron

The Endurian Universe

Other Books

For Jenni—an invisible girl who kept me company on many a night.

ACTS
OF THE
VIGIL

Book Seven of the Endurian Universe

JOE BERGERON

Endurian Press

Acts of the Vigil is a work of fiction. Names, places, and incidents either are products of the author's imagination or are used fictitiously.

Cover illustration by Joe Bergeron

Published by The Endurian Press

www.joebergeron.com

Chapter 1

Premier

A black-haired man calling himself Bob Paladin walked along a wooded path. Sunlight glowed in the leaves of the oaks and maples that lined it. Bob's gait was loose but still somehow constrained, as though he would ordinarily be dashing about in all directions were it not for his conscious decision to relax.

Despite the beauty of the day, despite the fact he was about to bamboozle someone in a benign and amusing way, Bob remained pensive and unhappy, aware that this visit was a waste of time, and an act of procrastination.

The campground didn't need his personal attention. The real duty that awaited him was a weight on his thoughts, something he wished he could ignore. He couldn't face it without first enjoying a few moments of simplicity among people who wore their cares more lightly.

Bob sauntered up to Ed Rhinebeck's RV, a vehicle so thoroughly in place that weeds poked up between the planks of the deck that fronted it. Party lights decorated the awning, while unlit tiki torches stood nearby. Ed himself, a balding, potbellied man, was comfortably sprawled in a green folding armchair.

"Hey there, Ed, how's it going?"

"Well, Bobby, howdy do. Nice to see you. Pick yourself a chair, why don't you."

Bob plopped down in a chaise lounge and regarded Ed with a wide, slightly goofy grin. Ed was one of his most loyal and amiable campers, and Bob wanted him to be satisfied.

"Hey Marian!" yelled Ed. "Bobby's here. Why don't you bring him out a beer."

Marian promptly appeared, a can of beer in hand, her smile as effusive as always. Bob added an extra twinkle to his blue eyes for her benefit.

"Oh, Bob, we don't hardly see enough of you! Sometimes I wonder how this campground of yours keeps going when you're never here to run it."

Bob waved that off with a laugh. "Oh, Marian, Daphne's a very good manager, and believe me, I do keep an eye on the place, from a distance. But I'm a busy man. I might wake up in Patagonia and go to sleep in Timbuktu. You just never know with me."

Marian gave a giddy laugh. "Oh Bob, you're such a braggart."

Bob chuckled. "True. Now, about this problem you mentioned to Daphne — ?"

"Goodness, it's those raccoons," said Marian. "They rattle and rustle all night long. This tin box we sleep in isn't very soundproof, you know. Is there anything you can do? I don't want you to shoot them or anything, but maybe you could trap them or scare them off somehow?"

"Well, that's a tough one, Marion. If I lived on site I could come by beating on a pie tin three or four times a night, but that's out. I might have a trick or two up my sleeve though. I'll see what I can do."

"Oh, I know you will, Bob. You're always so clever about everything."

"Shucks, Ma'am..." said Bob modestly. "Anyway folks, I can't stay long. I've got to go visit a friend of mine in the hospital."

"Oh, that's too bad," said Marian. "My mother just got out herself. Tests, tests, tests, new hip, colonoscopy, my goodness, there's just no end to it at her age."

At least your mother hasn't spent the last few months... forming... in a vat, thought Bob. He glanced at the roof of the RV. "How's that satellite dish working out for you, Ed?"

"It's mighty slick, Bob. Thanks for the recommendation. Now if only that damn Possum Perturbare would quit screwing around with all my shows!"

This sudden show of vehemence from the usually placid Ed Rhinebeck was enough to give Bob a start.

"Heh," said Marian. "Most TV is so stupid anyway. I think Doc Possum improves most of the shows he messes with."

"Well, when he crosses the President's eyes during the State of the Union address, that's going too far."

Bob attempted a grin. "How do you know they don't cross by themselves?"

"Well, Bob, it's okay if you prefer the other guys, but this isn't the time to be showing disrespect for our Commander in Chief. Not with alien freaks trying to take over the world, and those Vigil weirdoes sitting in their ivory tower up in Boston, and Perturbare running around loose..."

"So, you've never shown any disrespect to the president?"

"Sure I have, when it's the wrong guy in there."

Marian looked concerned. "Settle down, Ed."

But Ed didn't appear to be disposed to settling down. His face took on a truculent cast. "I tell you, if that damn terrorist ever came around here I'd greet him with that little Glock I got in the camper."

Marian laughed nervously. "Goodness, Bob, you've turned white as a sheet!"

"Terrorist?" said Bob in a small voice.

"Well, sure," said Ed. "Maybe he don't blow nothing up, but he's still trying to screw with everything people have worked so hard to build in this country. He's always trying to keep everyone on edge and scared. He doesn't like what's on TV? Fine, let him go read a book instead of messing with what I want to see. He's an elitist and a damn traitor."

"Traitor? Er...what makes you think he's even an American?" asked Bob.

"If he's not, I'd be even happier to see someone gun him down. But I'm pretty sure he's an American. What foreigner would be that smart?"

Bob saw no point in continuing this discussion. He excused himself, leaving the beer untouched; it would surely not go to waste. He wandered through the campground greeting other campers in a distracted manner, unable to enjoy the clean coolness of the Pennsylvania morning. This campground was the least of his enterprises, but usually it was one of the most enjoyable. The chance to hobnob with these feckless, cheerful, ridiculous people was priceless. After today's experience he did not think he would return anytime soon.

Leaving the campsites behind, he swallowed hard and said, "Okay then. Brainchild. Let's see what we can do about the raccoon rampage. Send a microflyer, and give those coons holy hell if they disturb the sleep of these fine folks again. Don't hurt the furry beggars though. And don't let anyone get even a glimpse of the microflyer. We mustn't give Ed and his fellow patriots anything more to complain about."

Somehow that didn't feel like enough. He stood there chewing his lip for a few moments.

"And also, Brainchild, close down the campground at the end of the season. It's no fun anymore. Does Daphne play the lottery?"

"Yes."

"Good, see that she wins a few million this fall. She's done a good job, and I like her. Then offer to sell her the campground, if she wants it."

A side path led to a clearing in the woods. Bob looked up. A curvaceous wasp-waisted flyer, its white surface gleaming, settled silently before him. The canopy rolled back and "Bob", who was of course more widely known as Doctor Possum Perturbare, stepped in, a little shakily. The vehicle sealed itself and ascended.

The computer Brainchild One spoke up in its usual tone of boyish, cheerful competence. "Doctor, as long as you devote yourself to discomfiting the world's population, it's unreasonable to hope that you'll never encounter anyone who is unhappy about it."

"Ah so. I suppose it's silly of me to resent them for it too. Are you implying I should change my ways?"

"Not at all. I'm merely pointing out how your expectations are at odds with your behavior in this regard."

"Remarks noted. Well, Brainchild, Ben Raintree Mark Two is about to be decanted. Let's go wish him a happy birthday."

"Yes, Doctor. On course for the Vigil's experimental station." In minutes the flyer was higher than any airplane could reach, flashing west across the continent.

Perturbare sat fretting over the strange fate of Raintree and his own sorry role in its unfolding.

"Doctor, I'm receiving the second satellite feed of the first episode of the new Vigil animated series. It's encrypted with a new interference-based algorithm which can only be deciphered by combining the current signal with the previous broadcast, which I have already noted and stored."

Perturbare perked up. "No kidding? Well, I guess they had to at least *try* to keep us out. Gee, my new favorite show. Let's see it. Slow down the flyer so I won't arrive before the show's over."

A display lit up on the console. Music throbbed in a grand fanfare. The announcer cried out, "Behold the Vigil! Defenders of Earth! Guardians of mankind! Heroes from space and time!"

Seven awesome figures flaunted themselves on the screen.

Perturbare laughed. "Those poor guys! So desperate for some good press that they don't even clamp down on this kind of exploitation."

The characters exploded onto the screen one by one.

"Fomalhaut! Mystery man from the future...or is he from the past?" A figure in glassy greenish armor, with a featureless sphere for a head, punched a hole in a wall and then fired lasers from his wrists.

"A fair question, as far as it goes," said Perturbare. "And this is *sooooo* like him. Always punching things, he is."

"Stingray! Aquatic avenger! A modern-day Captain Nemo!" A hulking blonde-haired figure burst out of a breaking wave and bowled over a squad of aliens on a beach. A bulbous submarine floated in the background.

"Yep, yep. Close enough. But he doesn't really look that smart."

"T'Ukudu! Awesome emissary of an alien race!" A gigantic blue-skinned humanoid lifted an immense boulder, flung it at a monster, then turned and winked at the camera.

Perturbare snickered. "I wish I could see him wink like that. Just once!"

"Aureus! Cosmic android devoted to justice!" A beam of white fire lanced out of the eyes of a golden muscleman, burning through a flying saucer.

"Oh, that's the worst yet! Aureus cares as much about justice as he does about quilting. Look how they've drawn him! And he's a robot, not an android. I guess they used up their research budget before they got to him."

"Tom Standing Crane! Indian shaman able to channel the might of the gods of myth!" A powerful-looking man in a leather vest and a feathered headband morphed into versions of Thor, Zeus, and Anubis.

"Ugh! He looks like Lakota Chief. Well, at least they got one god right..."

"Vega! Able to control the energies of a star!"

A girl in a star-spangled black costume flung bolts of fire from her hands.

Perturbare frowned. "Inventing a new character just so they could include a female? Okay, they couldn't really use Rouse Farewell, I suppose, but still..."

"Six great heroes...brought together by Earth's greatest defender...Ben Raintree...Doctor Borealis!" And there stood Ben, smiling, his green eyes crinkling at the corners, shouldering an elaborate silvery gun with which he froze a many-clawed beast in its tracks.

Perturbare's face fell further. "Ben Raintree, white Canadian, almost as good as an American, Leader of the Vigil. Right. I should have expected it."

The screen dissolved into frantic quick shots of Vigil members in action.

"Wow. I don't think I ever saw them move that fast in my life."

The episode was the first of a two-parter. The cliffhanger left the Vigil at the mercy of a group of "Para-men" who were even more misrepresented than the Vigil members themselves. Only Ben Raintree remained conscious and defiant before a sinister Valjhar Cor and his bizarre band of alien super-thugs.

"This is too much! Look at Cotavion...he's a cross between a Grey Alien and a vampire. Kern looks like Peter Lorre, and Kroy dal Ren is a multicolored werewolf."

The show ended. Perturbare had hoped it would lighten his mood, but it'd had the opposite effect. He sat watching the rapid approach of the west coast of North America along a curved horizon.

"Brainchild...whenever that show is broadcast, I want you to redraw the Para-men to look right. Use the same art style, but just make them look right. In fact, if the shows are stored digitally, I want you to get into their files and make the changes permanent. Is that clear?"

"Perfectly. Do you want me to change your representation as well?"

"Huh?"

"You will be a character in forthcoming episodes. Their depiction of you is…inaccurate. Do you wish me to change it?"

Perturbare brooded for another moment. "Well, bless their hearts. You have to give them credit for nerve, anyway. No…let them show me any damn way they please. After all, we don't want to give away my real appearance. I'd hate to be recognized by Ed Rhinebeck and have him pop me one for giving his hero the so-called President an on-air nosebleed."

He sighed. "Okay, enough dilly-dallying. Get me into the Perihemisphere. Let's see to it that the human race gets its great champion back again. Or gets something passably close to him, anyway."

Chapter 2

A Rebirth

Ben's reeducation began while he was still in the tank. Gradually he became aware of three shimmering shapes that sometimes loomed above him as he lay submerged in the bluish emulsion. At first he had only the vaguest impressions of them, and was unable to interpret their actions. At times one of them would look inside him and touch him somehow, leaving behind bits of knowledge he had not possessed before. Suddenly he might have an understanding of color, or an awareness that he was looking out through two eyes mounted in a face.

When these three were not present his mind swirled in inchoate dreams.

It was a timeless existence. The light, as he grew better able to perceive it, was constant. The three figures came and went and put things into his mind. His thoughts acquired a measure of substance.

Now all three of the others were present. He could see them more clearly now, though he still had no real understanding of their nature, nor any basis for comparison. The tank's blue fluid was draining away. For a moment this change awakened the new emotion of fear, but a touch from outside calmed him, helped him to face his new circumstances with equanimity. The level of the fluid reached his face. Cool air touched his skin for the first time. Strong arms reached into the tank and drew him out. His chest heaved. Blue fluid spilled from his mouth onto the floor. He drew air into his lungs with a shuddering gasp. The others held him up, sprayed his body with warm clear water, dried him with towels. They wrapped him in a robe and sat him in a chair. He looked around the smallish white room. The tank was now empty except for a few inches of fluid. He pondered it. A moment ago he had been immersed in it, as he had been for his entire existence, and now, suddenly, he was not. It was yet another strange matter to take in.

The others got him to his feet. He found that he knew how to stand and even walk, though his legs were weak and his balance poor. He laughed at his own giddy, awkward gait. His snorting, braying laughter was harsh and sharp compared to the muffled sounds that had reached him in the tank. The others did not let him fall. They led him toward a panel which swung open, revealing a new space beyond it, a circular room of gleaming white, with more doors along the walls. They guided him through one of the doors, into a room more heavily furnished than the room of his birth. He found that he was very tired. They laid him atop a bed, covered him, and dimmed the lights. He slept.

Over the next few days his world and knowledge steadily expanded. The others remained his frequent visitors. Now he could see them still more clearly as he refined the mental tools needed to interpret what he saw. Two of them were looming presences, substantially bigger than himself. One of these wore a glistening suit of a glassy silver-green substance which was decorated with rows of shining little tablets, like gems. His head appeared to be nothing more than a large, perfectly reflective sphere. This person, who gave his name as Fomalhaut, sometimes spoke to him in a clear, calm voice, but more often he spoke directly into his mind.

The second was even taller and heavier than Fomalhaut. This was a curious-looking creature, blue-skinned, with sleek black hair combed back from a high forehead. A black tendril rose gracefully from the outer corner of each eye, which were vermilion orbs with small black pupils. His face was grave and impassive. He wore layered robes in shades of blue. This was T'Ukudu, who spoke in a voice like a deep echoing boom. More often, T'Ukudu's thoughts flowed into him through the touch of his great hand, telling him what he needed to know about being alive in a way less ambiguous than speech. T'Ukudu sat with him for hours at a time, explaining how to eat, eliminate, dress, a whole great syllabus of practical information, supplying it with a patient consideration which nevertheless made it clear that these were subjects of only academic interest to T'Ukudu himself.

On one occasion Ben heard Fomalhaut say to T'Ukudu: "I know your sociological survey of the human race is nearing completion. I know how important this is to you. I appreciate your taking the time to assist us with this matter."

T'Ukudu answered: "The survey will be completed in a timely manner. At this stage I can state with confidence that there is no urgency in completing it. The time I devote to this recovery is well spent."

The third of the others was less physically imposing. He was a smaller, black-haired, blue-eyed man, more animated than either Fomalhaut or T'Ukudu. He gave his name as Possum Perturbare and wore white monogrammed tunics. His face was never still, flashing from one emotion to another in a disconcerting, unpredictable way. One moment he'd be smiling hugely, chattering volubly, and the next staring at him with a strange kind of grief, a grief for the loss of that which is present, if that can have any meaning. Except when this sadness was upon him, his talk was almost incessant, even before the teachings of Fomalhaut and T'Ukudu enabled Ben to understand what he was saying. One of the first things Ben did understand him to say was: "I can't believe I left him behind. I can't believe it." Then Perturbare had appeared to remember Ben's existence, for he turned to him with a bright, brittle smile.

Ben's world was still confined to his little bedroom and its adjoining kitchenette and bath. One day Fomalhaut entered and keyed a panel on one of the walls. It slid aside, admitting a brilliant shaft of light. Ben gasped and walked toward this opening, finding it covered by a transparent substance like that of his old tank. It revealed a vista far more vast and grand than anything he had yet imagined. Far below was a grey seething ocean. A wild cliff thrust out of the waters, pounded by giant waves, rising even so far as the base of the structure that was his vantage point. The sky was a mass of grey scudding clouds. Scattered beams of sunlight glinted on the turbulent waters. Islands rose up in the misty distance. Near them swam a group of creatures, no more than black teardrops at this distance, rising and falling in the waves, blowing occasional spouts of vapor.

After that the window remained unblocked. Night and day, the view was a subtly different wonder every time.

A few days later, Fomalhaut told him a great deal about a man called Ben Raintree.

This Raintree seemed to have led a colorful life. Fomalhaut's tales of him were so vivid that the words sometimes bloomed into images in Ben's mind, or perhaps Fomalhaut placed those images into his mind himself. He saw the boy Raintree walking through an icy forest, while in the sky above him shone a mysterious face, green-eyed, with hair like shifting streamers of white light. Later he saw that same face focused into a more human form, a face gleaming at him like a white moon, her eyes achingly full of perception for all that they were blank green orbs. Perhaps the stories were not told in their proper order. He saw other faces: an ageless cousin, a chestnut-haired woman shining in the sun, others. He learned that Raintree had been a physicist, developing as a mere aid to his studies of the aurora a tachyon-based cooling technology that had revolutionized cryogenics. T'Ukudu had already taught Ben a little about physics, enough to let him appreciate the ingenuity of Raintree's accomplishment.

Fomalhaut's teachings gradually increased in scope. He told something of the Vigil, of its great conflict with the small group of aliens who had come to Earth with the intention of guiding humanity along a better path. The Vigil, of which Raintree had been a member, had opposed these aliens, these so-called Para-men, on the grounds that mankind should be left to pursue its own course with the freedom to which its dignity as a sentient race entitled it. The Vigil had won that contest, but in the process some on both sides had been killed, while others were broken and lost.

Possum Perturbare came to visit almost every day. Ben always tried to be kind to Perturbare, who seemed to want so much to befriend him. Yet Perturbare was a puzzlement to him. His attempts at intimacy seemed strained, as though he were trying to impose a friendship upon a person he didn't really know. His smiles and jokes were almost constant, yet beneath them lay some anxiety, some grief which Ben did not understand.

"I've learned quite a bit, Possum," he said to Perturbare one day. "But there's still so much I don't understand."

Perturbare chuckled. "Yeah, that's typical of Fomalhaut and T'Ukudu. They're either entirely mute or talking your ear off. But even when they're jabbering their loudest, what they say is usually so cryptic they might as well keep quiet."

Ben blinked. "I haven't noticed that. The things they say seem clear enough to me. But there's just so much to take in. For example, I know they're members of the Vigil, like Raintree. But I'm not sure about you. Are you in the Vigil too?"

Perturbare's eyes widened. "Me in the Vigil? No. I've never had that kind of relationship with them. I walk my own path, do my own thing, hoe my own row, and so forth. But sometimes I collaborate with the Vigil on an…informal basis. For example, last fall I…worked on a project with Ben Raintree."

"Ben Raintree," mused Ben. "I've heard so much about him, but I don't quite understand why. I've learned only snatches about Stingray, Tom Standing Crane, or Valjhar Cor, but I seem to have Raintree's whole biography in my head, courtesy of Fomalhaut."

Perturbare locked a glistening gaze onto his. He leaned forward in his chair and spoke in a hushed voice. "Listen. I think it's about time you were told. You *are* Ben Raintree."

"I am?" asked Ben in mild surprise.

"You are. Er…who did you think you were?"

Ben shrugged disinterestedly. "I don't know. A month ago I knew nothing at all. It seems to me that having an identity is something to work up to slowly. I don't know who I am, or even what I am, really. Tell me, if I'm Ben Raintree, why don't I know it?"

"You don't remember anything?"

"About Raintree?" Ben waved his hands vaguely. "Oh, I 'remember' a lot. As I said, Fomalhaut filled my head with information about him, even pictures and images from the past. But that's all they are to me, pictures and images. I don't 'remember' any of it. I don't *feel* any of it."

Perturbare lowered his head. "I guess maybe that's the best we can do."

"Raintree" stood up from the bed and went to the window. A foggy evening was falling outside. The room behind him was reflected in the glass. He could see Perturbare biting his lip and shaking his head.

"Raintree" studied his own face in the pane. "I don't look that much like him," he said softly. He had a narrow, pale, homely face, with a long nose and large greyish-green eyes. "I look younger. And my hair is sort of a dark grey, not white like his. Why is that?"

The door slid open. "Raintree" turned toward the sound. In strode Fomalhaut, his spherical helmet just clearing the doorjamb. "Raintree" did not question his sudden appearance. Fomalhaut had a way of showing up whenever questions needed to be answered.

"Ben's white hair was a result of an inexplicable and unrepeatable childhood experience," said Fomalhaut calmly. "You have suffered injuries which resulted in the loss of your hair, among other damage. When it grew back it was in its original color. Also, you required extensive skin regeneration, which makes you appear more youthful."

Raintree plopped back down on the bed. "What happened to me?"

Fomalhaut turned to Perturbare.

Perturbare glanced at Fomalhaut, then lowered his head again, speaking from that position.

"You and I, Ben—we worked together on a project of mine. It was a machine to permit travel to parallel universes. The destination was random, but limited to penetrating to a single level of divergence. That means you're most likely to find yourself on a world very much like our own Earth—like, but not identical. You and I set out to test it, being the intrepid souls that we are. Fomalhaut warned us against it. Specifically, he warned you against it. He said he—had a bad feeling about it. We should have listened. We tried to cross over to another Earth, but the machine—functioned unexpectedly. You were badly injured. Dead, in fact, except for a few bits of still-living tissue."

Raintree felt his eyes go wide. "I was killed? How did you bring me back? Why did you do it?"

Fomalhaut replied. "We repaired the damage to your body by adapting the biotechnology of T'Ukudu's race. Your brain was heavily damaged. Though it was reconstructed, you lost most of your memory.

"When you were about to attempt the crossing to that other world, I foresaw you were in mortal danger. In those last moments I looked within you and extracted as complete a picture of your thoughts and feelings, your being, as I could. I held that within me until I could infuse it into your reconstructed body. It is, sadly, a shallow, incomplete thing. If I had had hours to prepare, I still could not have absorbed more than a fraction of what made you the person you were. Therefore you possess only fragmentary implanted memories, supplemented by raw biographical data, plus whatever remnants of your original memories you may retain. Perhaps in time these will blossom and come together into something like your original persona. Or perhaps this new road your life has taken will make you into a different person altogether. I cannot say.

"As to why we have done this…you are important to the Vigil. You are important to the human race. You are the only member of our sadly depleted ranks who is fully human, and whom the public trusts and understands."

"And *we* need you, too," broke in Perturbare, looking up at him with bright blue eyes. "We need you, as individuals. As friends. I lost you for our world, through my invention, and my blunder. I wanted you back."

Raintree stared at Perturbare. He wished he could remember enough, feel enough, to somehow relieve Perturbare's evident anguish. But to Ben the man was practically a stranger.

"Who else knows about this, Fomalhaut? Where are we —is this the headquarters of the Vigil?" asked Raintree doubtfully.

"Only the three of us know of your injury: myself, Perturbare, and T'Ukudu."

"And Brainchild," broke in Perturbare.

Fomalhaut continued. "We saw no need to alarm the world, or your friends and family, by announcing your injury. This is the Vigil's experimental facility on the coast of British Columbia. It is isolated and nearly inaccessible except by air. We use it to pursue certain projects which require privacy, or which might pose a danger to the outside world."

"Such as the inter-universe frame-shifter project," added Perturbare in a tired voice. "It was here that we—attempted our crossing."

Raintree gazed at Perturbare, who returned a pained glance and then dropped his eyes. Perturbare's grief and regret were palpable. Raintree (by now he felt he might as well accept the name, having no other) felt a similar feeling well up, a compassion for Perturbare's strange loss, and for his own. Until today he had scarcely considered the issue of his own identity. He merely was, and that was enough. Now he knew who he was, or who he had been, and could never quite be again. It left him with a peculiar aching sense of unreality, feeling the loss of something he had never known.

He looked up at Fomalhaut, who stood immobile by the door. Raintree felt nothing from him at present. The touch of his thoughts had always been cool and precise. Fomalhaut was not a machine, that much Raintree knew, but whatever emotions were sheltered by that opaque mirrored helmet were unknown to him.

Raintree wished that T'Ukudu had joined them. Though no more effusive a person than Fomalhaut, Raintree had always felt in his touch a grave compassion which had steadied him during these past weeks of accelerated learning and growth. Raintree missed him now.

Fomalhaut and Perturbare took their leave. The door slid shut behind them.

Raintree stood for a moment at the window, leaning on the sill, looking into the deepening night. His face crumpled. Tears splashed down onto his hands.

He still had a great deal to learn. The world was full of beauty; that much he knew from this one window, and from his own—Ben's own—memories. That was something he could pursue.

The sound of the closing door had been different than before. He approached it; for the first time it opened for him. He'd never even thought to question why it had never opened before. He stepped through the door into a circular lobby. Another open door led into a long corridor which echoed with silence. Raintree padded along it, and then entered another, and another. Each was silent and empty. The many rooms he explored contained little that he recognized or understood.

It took him quite a while to find a way outside. When that last portal slid open he gasped with shock at the darkness it revealed and the raw gust of cold rain it admitted. He stepped out onto a terrace, its balustrade picked out by faint blue lights. The scent of the sea and the rush of the wind exhilarated him, awed him, frightened him. They were not altogether foreign to him... some memory of nature's touch must remain. Even so, these new sensations were cause for him to jump up and down, to shout and laugh, and to weep, all at once, until he was quite soaked, chilled, and out of breath. He could see nothing beyond the terrace. He could see nothing beyond this moment of his new life.

Chapter 3

The Visions of Walks-with-the-Sun

When he woke up he did not at first know his own name. Then he thought of Raymond Smick, before remembering he had adopted the more traditional name of Walks-with-the-Sun during a spasm of Lakota pride when he was a kid.

Walks-with-the-Sun? More like Winces-at-the-Sun, he thought. The blinding light in that bland blue dome lanced into his eyes and his brain. He groaned, turned away, and propped himself up on an elbow to assess his situation. He lay sprawled in dirt marked with numerous footprints as well as the tracks of a pickup truck.

Half-dried vomit crusted his shirt—his own, he hoped. A sizable mound of empty beer cans stood nearby. Cold ashes darkened the site of a fire.

Still groaning, he levered himself onto his feet, clutching his skull, squeezing it to keep his brain from exploding out of its casing.

The tire tracks meandered out of sight among the grass and brush. There was no sign of a road. He had no idea where he was—it could be any back corner of the Rez, or even beyond. He couldn't expect anyone to come looking for him. His drinking buddies probably had no clue of where they had been last night, and likely no memory that they'd left their friend Walks behind. He would have to walk out. Walk out with the sun. At least it was appropriate.

Teetering on his feet, he considered his filthy shirt. No water was in sight, nor was any in prospect, as he could guess from the lack of any nearby trees. He had no desire to wear a puke shirt. Better to wear none at all. He pulled the rag from his scrawny torso, tossing it aside.

Walks figured he might as well follow the tracks, hoping that his friends had had sense enough to head towards whatever road they'd come off of. He tottered off, following the erratic course his buddies had steered through the thick grasses and around the pale slabs of crumbly shale which stood up here and there.

Walks began to worry as that course lost any semblance of consistency. It began to make ninety degree turns for no apparent reason, seemingly at random. Once the truck had come upon a three foot rock shelf it obviously had not negotiated on the way in, backed up, and turned back for a time before trying some new random direction. Apparently his friends had been totally disoriented, unable to retrace their path through the thick grass. Walks let out a rueful chuckle. There was a good chance he'd soon have company, if he came upon the truck with his friends still sleeping it off inside.

He plodded along, eyes bent to following the tire tracks, and thus almost stepped over the brink when he came to the edge of a deep gully. A good chunk of the edge had crumbled and fallen in, obviously very recently.

Walks heaved a sigh. With a peculiar sense of disembodiment he leaned forward, with no doubt in his mind as to what he was about to see.

There at the bottom of the gully were the remains of Frank Two Ravens's truck, looking not much more substantial than a mangled beer can.

"Hey," Walks cried weakly. "Is anybody alive down there?"

No reply. Walks paced up and down the edge looking for a route to the bottom, but found none. He wasn't about to risk climbing down a cliff so fragile he could tear off chunks of rock with his hands. Anyway, the truck's occupants were almost certainly dead. What was the point?

He stood staring dully at the wreckage, in which he was not lying dead only by some flip-flop of fate. Down there were three more men who would help pull the average life expectancy on the Rez down to its dismal level. True, their end had been more sudden and unlikely than usual, but it had the same root causes: alcohol, despair, poverty, the lack of a reason to live.

Well, and one more thing, he might as well admit it—stupidity. None of those guys had exactly been a ball of fire. None of them had ever really made an effort. He was no better.

Walks lifted his gaze to the horizon to cleanse it of the scene of quiet hopelessness below. Shimmering in the distance was the irregular purplish outline of the Badlands Wall. It did little to orient him—after all, some part of it was visible from half the Rez. Farther off toward the northwest was the rugged line of the Black Hills. He saw nothing closer at hand that he could identify.

He was impressed by his total lack of recollection of where he was. He must have been drunk out of his mind even before he and his friends arrived here. He hoped he hadn't been driving, but wouldn't be surprised if he had.

Well, there was nothing more he could do here. Might as well get going. He turned from the gully, staggered a few steps, fell to his knees as his dubious strength flowed out of him like water, and clenched up in a series of dry heaves. When he was finally finished he sank panting into the grass, clutching his ribs, which felt as though they were about to break, so violent had his spasms been. He lay there shaking, stifling an urge to moan and whimper like a dog.

He did not know if his illness was a leftover of last night's bender, a reaction to the death of his friends, or both. He did know it wasn't a good thing for a man in his position. With nothing at all in his digestive system, he would find it difficult to walk very far without water. He was already very thirsty.

Now grief and self-pity came crashing down on him, robbing him of the shell of impassivity he'd so desperately tried to maintain. What did it matter if he got out of here or not? The smart thing to do would be to crawl over to the edge of that cliff and drop off. He had obviously been fated to die with the rest of his loser friends; only some odd accident had prevented it. Why fight it? The way he was going, he couldn't hope to avoid an early death anyway. He lived alone…had no job…ate crappy surplus food when he bothered to eat at all…devoted all his slight resources to drinking and drugging. He'd probably have diabetes in a few years like half the other people he knew. He was in terrible shape and getting worse by the day.

He grinned up toward the sun, visible through his closed eyelids only as a hot red glow. Raymond Smick, Lakota Warrior.

Ah, the dreams he'd had as a boy—visions—well, not proper visions, but dreams—of a rebirth of the pride, of the very identity, of the tribe of which he was a member. He had once been the most gung-ho young Lakota anyone could remember. He had interrogated the oldest members of the tribe, gleaning from their memories whatever remained of the old ways. He had read all he could find about the one-time nature of the Lakota. Black Elk's book had left his heart burning with fervor and revelation. He'd gone about waving it in people's faces, insisting this was the way they all should be, scorning them when they failed to measure up. Even Black Elk himself, with that almighty vision of his looming like a glaring sun, had ultimately failed to live up to it.

As hard as he tried, Walks could not see the people he lived around as the same people who had once freely ridden the plains. The people he knew lived in squalid square houses with spider webs in the corners, instead of in tipi villages which could be moved over vast areas to follow the bison. They ate Twinkies, instead of the meat of those bison which were provided by the Great Spirit to a people living in a holy manner. They believed in nothing, rather than in the Great Spirit and the other great forces of the world which lay at every point of the compass. They sent lawyers to Washington to try to argue the stolen Black Hills back from the whites. They tried to shame the whites into honoring their treaties. Once they would have sent bands of warriors to wrest their lands back by force. No, they were not the same people. They had lost the old ways.

Walks's breathing gradually slowed. Let's be honest with myself, he thought. There were a few who still clung to what was left of the ways of the Lakota. He shouldn't speak for them all, condemning them all so harshly. He was actually describing himself.

25

As a youth he had gone out in search of visions, and they had not come. He had done what was ordained: gone alone into the wilderness, deprived himself, prayed for guidance—and the spirits had been silent. No rainbow tipi appeared; the sun only moved predictably across the sky, and no creature presented itself as his totem. He had returned to his family with a peculiar stillness in his heart which he did not like. He had gone out that night and gotten drunk with some of the local boys.

That had been over twenty years ago.

It was possible, he knew, for spirits to speak to people. They had spoken to his boyhood friend, Tom Standing Crane. More than spoken to him; they had taken him over. The funny thing was that they were not even Lakota spirits, but spirits from old white religions which were thousands of years dead. The funny, terrible thing was that the spirits of the Lakota were so weak that forgotten white spirits could step into a member of the tribe, and they would do nothing.

So—was there anyone who would miss him, anyone who would care if he just laid here and died? Both parents were dead. His siblings were scattered over the Rez and in Rapid City; he never heard from them. Standing Crane was by all accounts his own man again, once more a Lakota instead of a vehicle for foreign gods, but he was still a medical doctor and no longer lived on the Rez.

Well...there was still the cat. Walks had taken a lot of ribbing for keeping him, and in truth he wasn't a very good cat owner. The scruffy beast had to provide most of his own diet by grabbing the mice that infested his house. Chances were good that he was stuck in the house right now. If Walks never returned, the cat would probably die of thirst.

Walks had a sudden vision of the cat's trusting face. The little guy seemed to like him, despite the indifferent care he received. In fact, the cat gave him the only real affection he had known in many years. Suddenly Walks was blubbering as he thought of the cat and his simple devotion. Jesus, he was so far gone—weeping over a cat, while the death of his friends had only left him feeling sorry for himself.

All right then. He would take a shot at getting out of here—for the sake of the cat.

He pushed himself up on his elbows, waiting until the spinning in his head subsided a little. He sat up, waited again. Finally he drew himself to his feet, stood for a while with his head hanging, then tottered away from the cliff and the death that waited there.

By sunset he had wandered quite some distance, to no real effect except to tire himself. He had found nothing—no roads, no food, and certainly no water, which was most serious. Soon it would be night. Fuel was plentiful...cow chips, sticks...and he had matches. These were his chief blessings. He need not die from the cold. There was no point in going further tonight. He'd recognized no nearby landmarks, but he knew that if he continued north, toward the Wall, he must inevitably encounter a road.

He chose a spot on the west side of a small blade of pinkish rock for his fire, gathered a good pile of fuel, lighting it as the sun departed from sight, dragging behind it a pale crescent of moon. He sat cross-legged before his fire, facing west, observing the fleeting colors of sunset, studying the circle of blue Earthlight held in the arms of the silent crescent.

He prepared to spend the evening castigating himself yet again for his many failings, and to rue the wreckage of his life, but he was brought up short by an astonishing realization that left him gaping like a fool.

He was happy. No, that wasn't the right word. He was —watchfully content, if that meant anything. His walk had cleared his head. He was hungry, he was thirsty. Somehow both seemed appropriate. His body was purged. He was far from his squalid house, his squalid life, in a clean, quiet place that made no demands and offered no temptations.

The stars emerged. Suddenly Walks found himself chanting—an old chant, one he might have heard from a tribal elder when he was a boy, or maybe not. Wherever it came from, it was fitting, and most welcome.

He fell asleep with the stars wheeling overhead. From time to time the cold awakened him to throw a few more handfuls of fuel onto the fire. Each time, the stars were a little further along in their progression.

He woke up for good in the dawn shadow of the rock. The sky was still purplish, the golden sunlight casting long shadows from every knoll, hill, and mesa. The fire was completely out now. Walks sat up slowly, tentatively. His head felt fuzzy, pounding relentlessly at the slight exertion. He tried to recapture the feeling of the previous evening by chanting again, but he could not. His throat and mouth were too dry; he choked on the attempt. His shoulders shook in silent laughter as he picked off twigs and pebbles that were stuck to his bare skin. He should have known he wouldn't get off this easily. This walk was an attempt at survival, not some romantic return to the ways of the noble red man.

He lurched to his feet, staggered off. The first touch of the sun on his chilled body was most welcome. Even more welcome was the dew that had formed overnight. Walks stumbled around sucking moisture off branches of sagebrush. Each swallow gave him a burst of sensual pleasure exceeding anything he'd ever experienced from drinking alcohol. Maybe today wouldn't be so bad after all. It was amazing how quickly he learned to appreciate the simplest boon when necessities were so hard to come by.

The dew dried up before he was half satisfied, but that was a lot better than nothing. He walked off, partially refreshed, feeling somewhat hopeful in his cautious way.

He walked, and as is so often the case, the walk freed his mind to wander as well, setting it on paths less restricted than those it trod when he sat in his shack. Today it offered up vivid flashes of his boyhood, feelings from a time when his heart was still sincere, when the world had brighter corners amidst all the darkness, and the limitations of life seemed more like a challenge to be overcome than a preordained defeat. Each poignant vignette of memory was both pleasure and pain. Now his heart felt strange — not light, nor gloomy, but rather somehow warped, as though someone had taken it in his hands and given it a little twist.

That was the semi-pleasant state in which he spent his morning. Things changed in the afternoon. His thirst became impossible to ignore even for a moment. It came to occupy the space in his thoughts that had been filled with his reveries. The sun glared down from its perch on the meridian. His pace became erratic; his gaze dropped from the horizon. Sometime in the mid-afternoon he woke up from a walking daze, looked up, and found he wasn't even headed north anymore. He had no idea when he had strayed or what path he had taken. He only knew he'd managed to walk most of the day without crossing a single road or rut. That was baffling—the Rez was big, but it was also crisscrossed with dirt roads and tracks in addition to the few paved roads.

He didn't make it to sunset. Already dehydrated from vomiting, he just didn't have the resources to sustain this kind of a trek. He'd have to rest the night. If he lacked the strength to continue in the morning, then so be it. He'd done his best for that damned cat.

This time he chose a site atop a low, shrubby knoll. He could again have chosen a more sheltered location near cliffs and spires, but he didn't want to block off his view of half the sky. It might be the last time he would ever see it, and he wanted to see it all.

Once again he cleared a patch of ground and gathered fuel. Though he might be unable to avoid dying of thirst, at least he didn't have to freeze to death.

All through that long night his dreams were a confusion of images and voices that seemed to stand astride the border between wakefulness and sleep. He usually knew he was asleep and dreaming, but sometimes it seemed to him that he was awake, and that voices were saying things he did not understand,. He could not discriminate between what was possible and what was not. If these were visions, it was beyond his power of insight to make sense of them.

Eventually he woke up beneath a sunless sky of deep blue, with the tumult of dreams that had seemed so inescapable already a fading memory.

He stood up slowly, stiffly, his throat parched and raw, his head spinning with weakness. As a matter of habit he unzipped his fly, but no water flowed.

He faced the east, and was startled to see a landmark he actually recognized. On the horizon was a tableland whose silhouette he knew as that of the Stronghold, where a defiant remnant of his ancestors had once briefly removed themselves from the onslaught of the white man.

A peach-colored glow hovered over the plateau, swiftly brightening to a fierce gold. Walks stood facing it. The dawn was silent, and so was he. He would witness the coming of the day's fire before stumbling off to whatever miserable death awaited him.

Despite the silence, he seemed to hear something, or sense something: a deep, solemn feeling of imminence.

The golden dome of clear, pure light began to push up from the horizon.

Perhaps he had never found a totem animal because his totem was the sun. The thought startled him. Was that possible?

All at once two smaller motes of fire leapt out of the sun and lanced through the air, describing twin arcs like those of arrows. Walks discerned that they were figures, lightless now like other men, but unlike men in that they still hurtled toward him through the sky, like two arrows.

When they struck the ground they alighted on their feet, having twisted just before impact. They stood before him, two tall figures at which he must squint, backed as they were by the solar disk poised on the horizon.

One was a green-eyed woman with long, straight, chestnut hair that reached to the middle of her back. Her skin was bronzed, and she wore a mantle of feathers, black and pale grey, and beneath that a skirt of the same—falcon feathers, he believed. The man had sandy hair, intensely blue eyes, and was dressed in blue and white. A black eagle was painted on the front of his shirt, its wings spread before a solar disk that seemed to share and reflect the gathering light behind him.

Obviously, neither of these two messengers were Indians. Yesterday he would have scoffed at the idea that two white people, or even spirits who looked like white people, might have anything to say that he would care to hear.

But now, confronted by the two of them and their shining eyes, he had no doubts. The woman appeared the more solid and real of the two, though he had no sense of her weight resting upon the earth. The man was full of the sunlight which was rising behind him.

Walks cleared his throat, tried to swallow, and said, "What do you want of me, spirits?"

The woman said, "Come with us, Walks-with-the-Sun. Your grandfathers are waiting for you."

"I will come."

Chapter 4

His Debut

The experimental station seemed fantastically large and elaborate for a facility with such a modest title. It was also fantastically empty. As far as Raintree could tell, he was alone in its silent corridors. He remembered little or nothing of its layout. Every door he passed beckoned him with potential mysteries, but at the moment he was too tired and hungry to succumb to their temptation. Eventually he found his way back to his room.

He woke up promptly at sunrise, as illustrated by the view out the window, where billowing cumulus clouds were lit by a peach-colored dawn glow. He poked around in his closet, finding clothing fit for travel. A green wool shirt, grey canvas pants, boots, a jacket...clothes Ben Raintree might well have chosen. He smiled a cocked half-smile as he drew them out.

He paused at the doorway and looked back briefly into the room, suspecting he'd never see it again. He strode out into the maze of corridors, this time with a specific goal in mind. Luckily, the station was not designed with the assumption that all who visited it would have memorized its byways. A plaque next to an elevator indicated what was found on each level. The main hangar was on the topmost level.

Raintree soon stood before the door leading to the hangar. It did not open immediately at his approach. A red light glowed above the portal. An electronic note sounded,

33

the light turned green, and the door hissed open. Raintree
shrugged and entered.

The hangar was a great high-ceilinged space smelling
of machine oil and plastics. Huge track-mounted panels
were installed overhead at regular intervals. Raintree
counted more than thirty aerospace flyers of every type—
quite a complement for an experimental station. They were
all propulsion-beam driven, black or grey, angular in
appearance. Each was marked with the emblem of the
Vigil, a bold V in a circle of silver and black.

A single flyer stood out among the rest. It was glossy
white, but sleekly curved, wasp-waisted as a tipped-over
hourglass. Its hull was unadorned, its canopy a tinted
bubble on the forward lobe of the hourglass. A large
propulsion lens projected from the rear.

Unless he was mistaken, this was the kind of flyer built
and flown by Possum Perturbare. He stepped up to it
hesitantly.

"Um…Brainchild?"

The flyer spoke to him in a cheerful voice. "Yes, Dr.
Raintree, what may I do for you?"

Raintree felt himself blushing. As yet he was unused to
addressing a machine.

"Brainchild…I was wondering if you could fly me to…
um, the Vigil headquarters. I'm afraid any piloting skills I
may once have had are lost."

The voice of Perturbare's ubiquitous computer was
surprisingly warm. "Certainly, Doctor. I see no reason not
to honor your request. Please enter the cockpit."

The canopy rotated back to admit him into the two-seat
flyer. Raintree threw a leg over the sill, climbed in, and
took one of the seats. The canopy slid back, enclosing him

in a humming little world of sparkling technology. Raintree felt his heart beating. A foolish grin split his face. He was about to fly for the first time he could clearly remember.

"Is it unusual for Perturbare to keep one of his flyers at a Vigil facility?" he asked.

"Not at all. It is merely a matter of convenience. The doctor has many flyers. He likes to keep one or more at any place he is likely to visit."

"I'm sure. There's so much I've forgotten..."

"Yes, Doctor Raintree, I'm aware of your predicament. It is truly unfortunate."

Raintree gave a wry, pained grin. Brainchild had no face to address, so Ben looked into one of the sensor pickups in the cockpit. "I'm afraid it's just Mr. Raintree now. Any benefits I once derived from my physics degrees are lost somewhere with my piloting skills."

"I'm sure you can quickly regain whatever was lost."

Raintree nibbled on his lower lip. "Do you know what the extent of my injuries really was?"

There was a moment of silence.

"Doctor Raintree, I have been instructed not to discuss that matter with you. Fomalhaut and the others seem to believe that your recovery will be hastened by delaying such a discussion."

Raintree would have questioned the computer further, but he was distracted by the opening of one of the panels in the overhead. To his surprise, it revealed a stretch of blankly overcast white sky.

The flyer drifted straight upward through the opening. Raintree's head bobbed around as he tried to take in the exterior of the station. He was puzzled; was it foggy? He had only a moment to ponder that. Whiteness claimed his vision for an instant, and then intense sunlight poured into the canopy from a vast sky of broken clouds. Raintree gasped as he looked down. The station appeared to be a featureless white hemisphere set on a shelf on the flank of a great seaside peak. It was adjoined by a slender white spire which leaped up beside it, almost to the level of the peak overlooking both. The whiteness of the dome, at least, was obviously due to some thin field or film which concealed the real structure within it. Again Raintree was impressed by the size of the place, and also, now that he could see it clearly, by its beauty.

Clear of the station, the flyer now pitched up its nose and accelerated skyward at one quarter G, to judge by one of the display panels. It shot through the broken cloud deck and hurtled up until the sky was dark as sapphire.

Brainchild spoke up. "If you don't mind, I'll avoid making this a ballistic suborbital flight. Perhaps freefall would be inadvisable for you, given your recent convalescence. The trip will take a bit longer this way."

Raintree glanced at the display. They were already at Mach three and still accelerating. "I think this will be quite fast enough. Can you teach me to fly one of these things?"

"Certainly."

By the time they descended into Boston, Raintree had a good understanding of the rather simple operation of a modern flyer. He had also gained a vivid appreciation of the beauty of earth and sky as seen from the edge of space. This was tempered by fascination, followed by dismay, as they approached Boston, which appeared to Raintree as a great grey scab encrusting the living surface of the world. Thousands of cars crept along a convoluted network of highways. The realization of the sheer number of people who must be packed into this great warren staggered him, frightened him, made him wish he'd never left the solitude of the station. He came close to asking Brainchild to turn the vehicle around.

Then, looking straight down, he spotted their target, a sprawling V-shaped building with a tower rising from the angle of the V. The informal name for the Vigil's headquarters popped into his mind: the Lighthouse! Suddenly he felt a bit more optimistic. He had, after all, lived in this city before; he could do so again. A few moments later the flyer gently grounded in the plaza which spanned the wings of the V. It was, oddly, nearly deserted, though judging from the benches, fountains, and sculptures which were scattered around, it was intended to be a public place.

The canopy slid back, admitting the sharp cold air of late winter. Raintree breathed it in gratefully, but almost coughed it back out. It was contaminated with an acrid scent of burning. Again he felt doubt about his new surroundings.

Still, he unharnessed himself and stepped onto the pavement. "Thank you very much, Brainchild."

"It was my pleasure to assist you. I wish you all success with your continuing recovery."

With that, the canopy closed again and the flyer rose, disappearing into the west almost before Raintree could blink.

He was left alone on the windswept Vigil Plaza, or nearly alone. A few sour-looking people gaped at him from a distance, apparently not used to the sight of someone alighting from a flyer. But Ben was not the true object of their absorption. They soon turned back toward the

Lighthouse, shielding themselves from something in that direction, huddling against it, even as they were simultaneously drawn to it.

Glancing at the Lighthouse, Raintree immediately forgot the onlookers, the cold wind, his partial identity, everything. His whole being and attention were arrested by a spark of white light in the circular colonnade at the top level of the tower itself. It was not an especially bright light, yet it was piercing, entering his heart more readily than his eye. He knew or remembered this most numinous thing. It was something he had seen before—held before. The Stones. This was the Stone of Inner Light.

He gasped, swaying slightly as he gazed into that scintillating radiance. Fomalhaut had told him something of the Stones, but not until he looked on one of them was its true impact made clear to him.

Memories, or perhaps only data implanted by Fomalhaut, came to him. It was Stingray who had originally insisted that a lighthouse stand guard over the Vigil's sanctuary. In Stingray's absence, it had been Ben himself who had replaced the beacon that had once burned there with this fainter yet infinitely more poignant Light.

He drifted toward the building like a sleepwalker, keeping the Stone fixed in his vision. As he approached, the Stone was hidden by the lip of the tower, breaking its spell on him to some extent.

He blinked and shook his head, noticing the rest of the building for the first time. The V-shaped section had five visible levels, each set back from the one below, each fronted with a long colonnade. The main entrance to the complex, or at least the public entrance, seemed to be at the vertex of the V. Knowing no better, Ben set off towards it, passing through an archway with the bronze letter V on its keystone. Within was a wide high-ceilinged space lit by many open skylights. Three smaller arches were set into the far wall. A small figure hurried out from one of them, saw him, and broke into a trot. Raintree frankly gaped at her as she approached. She was the first female he had encountered since his recovery. He was stunned by her tiny stature, her fragility, and her beauty. She had straight glossy black hair arranged in a spheroidal configuration, and eyes clear and lustrous as pearls, with sparkling night-black irises. Her smile looked a little flustered, but was warm and genuine.

She pattered to a halt before him, caught her breath, and said, "Dr. Raintree! We had a call from Brainchild that you were on your way. It's so good to see you. Fomalhaut and T'Ukudu are away, so I was sent to meet you."

Raintree willed his gaze off her face long enough to notice the Vigil badge clipped to the lapel of her grey jacket. Beneath it she wore a purple sweater and skirt.

"Ah—so you're a fellow member of the Vigil, I take it?"

She laughed, a sound as startling as the sudden ringing of unseen bells. "Oh no! No, I mustn't laugh. I'm very sorry. We were told just today that you were recently injured and suffered some memory loss. I'm only a Vigil employee, a research assistant. My name is Lori Wu."

She held out her hand. Raintree took it gingerly, marveling at its delicacy compared to his own. She withdrew her hand and impulsively grabbed his elbow.

"Please come inside with me! You're famous for enjoying frigid weather, but I'm a bit more spoiled."

Raintree noticed the vapor that accompanied her words. He saw no point in disillusioning her by telling her he was freezing too. She led him towards the middle of the three arches.

"I've only been working here a couple of months," said Lori. "So don't worry if you don't recognize me. We've never met."

"What kind of research do you do here, Lori?"

"Oh, this and that. Mainly stuff concerned with the humanities, because of my background...I have a Master's in art history. I gathered data for T'Ukudu's sociological evaluation and worked with him a bit. Did you know he's practically finished with it?"

"Yes. Yes, I have heard something about that."

"That will be a big day for us. I can't wait to hear his conclusions. I just hope we all still have jobs afterwards." She gave a slightly awkward laugh.

They passed through the arch. A bronze gate slid shut behind them. The air was warmer here. Ramps and stairs led to other levels from this marble-walled chamber, which was aglow with natural light from some indirect source.

Raintree halted at a golden statue which stood in a pose of no particular distinction on a block of marble in the center of the room. Stepping up to it cautiously, he recognized it as a statue of Aureus, the robot who had come to Earth from another galaxy in pursuit of the Para-men. Though the statue stood there rigidly, the sculptor had succeeded in capturing the sinuous fluidity of its limbs, the deadly grace which had marked it every move. It was an outstanding reproduction. The glitter of its golden surface and the crystal helmet which encased its silvered brain were all perfectly reproduced. Its eyes lacked the red glow that had always smoldered in the real ones. The lethal Third Eye above them was closed.

Raintree frowned. Why would a statue of Aureus be displayed in this lobby? Had the robot been destroyed in the war? No.

With a shock and a start he realized this was the real Aureus. He took a few involuntary steps back, almost bumping into Lori. He glanced at her questioningly.

"I've been told that he shut himself down shortly after Valjhar Cor departed from the Earth" murmured Lori. "The Vigil left him standing where he was for months, then considered just putting him in a closet, but they decided that would be undignified. So they set him up here. He hasn't been seen to move since, but he must have at least opened his Eye on one occasion." She shuddered and waved her hand towards the wall opposite the robot.

Raintree turned. Inscribed into the marble with flawless precision were the words:

I SHALL AWAKEN AGAIN.

The hairs stood up on Raintree's neck. He turned back toward the immobile robot, regarding it with awe, wondering how aware it really was.

"Does anyone ever dust him?" he whispered.

Lori broke out in laughter, but immediately clapped her hand over her mouth. "Come on" she mumbled. "I don't want to be here when he wakes up."

With a sense of relief Raintree allowed himself to be led up one of the ramps. This was the central area of the complex, normally inhabited only by members of the Vigil. At the moment it had the same sense of silence and loneliness as the experimental station. Raintree delved into his store of knowledge and did some counting. The result surprised him. "There aren't very many members of the Vigil, are there?"

Lori shook her head. "Only three active members, counting you. Let's see. We've already seen Aureus, who isn't very active. Stingray is thought to be wandering somewhere in the ocean. Tom Standing Crane has gone off to practice medicine among his people. Rouse Farewell is of course dead." She paused, looking troubled. "In a sense, the Vigil no longer exists. T'Ukudu stays here to conveniently pursue his survey. Fomalhaut seems to be making his own separate studies and observations. There's no overriding mission for the Vigil, such as there was during the days of the Para-men. We're now pretty much a research institution only. Where would you like to go? I normally don't have the run of this section, but since I'm escorting you, I get to see pretty much anything I want."

Her lips, sweet arches coated with pink porcelain, curved in a smile of ineffable beauty. Raintree almost forgot to answer.

"Um...I assume I have a room here?"

"Of course. A suite, actually. Lower tower. Your pets are there."

"Wait. I know what I want to do first."

"What's that?"

"I want to go up to the top of the Lighthouse and look at the Stones."

Lori's eyes widened. She actually stepped back a little.

"My badge won't get me in there," she said softly.

"Oh. And...how about me? Will I be able to get up there?"

"You should be able to. The system is configured to recognize Vigil members, even without a badge."

"Then…I don't see why you can't go up with me… assuming you want to."

Lori's gaze lost focus. She stood looking inward for a few moments, then said, "Yes. Yes, I would like to see the Stones. Very much."

Raintree grinned a little nervously. "Then let's get going, before a grownup shows up and stops us," he whispered. She giggled.

They entered an elevator. "Floor th-thirty," said Lori, more than a little nervously.

The car did not move.

"Floor thirty," said Raintree. It started up.

They emerged into a circular room that took up the whole of the thirtieth floor. This was an observation level, sparsely furnished with benches along the outer wall. The winter wind blew freely though wide unglazed arches. A ladder passed through an opening in the ceiling. Raintree could feel the presence of the Stone just overhead.

They stood near the ladder, but as yet made no move to climb it. Lori laughed a little breathlessly. "I never thought I'd get this chance. Do you know what we call ourselves? We staffers? Vigil-antes. Vigil-ants. Sometimes just Ants. I've never heard of one of us being permitted into this sanctum." She peered up the ladder. "I'm babbling. I'm that nervous, and a little scared."

"It is compelling, isn't it?" said Raintree. "I'm surprised the plaza is as empty as it is. I should think people would flock here to get a glimpse of such a marvel."

Lori giggled again. "Are you kidding? Most people avoid it the way a vampire shuns holy water. You're lucky you didn't run into a group of anti-Stone protesters out there. A good third of the Ants themselves quit when you put it on display up there. They just couldn't take it."

Raintree stared at her. Her words astounded him, yet he had an inkling of what lay behind them.

"Shall we go up?" he asked.

Lori nodded. Raintree led the way. Up he went, feeling the chill of every rung in his hands. His head neared the hatch. His view of the Lighthouse's topmost level expanded.

And then suddenly, there before and above him was the Stone on its pedestal. He stopped moving at once, staring at it with his head poking through the hatch. Only gradually did his legs come back to life. Without being aware of it he ascended the remaining rungs and stood before the Stone. At some point Lori appeared beside him, a little farther back.

The Stone was a faceted teardrop some four inches long. It was presently inverted, the pointed end fixed to the top of a tapering pedestal of white marble. The Stone was transparent, white, and aglow.

"I don't know which is stronger," said Lori in a strained voice. "My need to see this Light, or my urge to run far away."

Raintree understood her perfectly. The light that welled from this gem was as perilous as it was desirable, equally made of bliss and terror. The Stone of Inner Light, it was called. It was a light from which no darkness could hide. Any inner stain would be laid bare before it. All confusion would be either burned away or shown to be beyond hope of cure. Above all, any malice would ignite into an inner fire which would sear and burn those who harbored it. It was both an agony and a glorious exaltation to gaze into it. Surely this was the most magical thing in the universe, or rather, a thing that transcended magic, that went into the heart of all things, beyond science and magic and all other such categories. Through strange chance it had come to Earth from distant galaxies. It was called the Stone of Inner Light. No wonder few people were able to endure its radiance. Raintree wondered how he himself would stand up to it, if whatever evil he had once carried within him had not been wiped out, along with most of the rest of him!

And yet—the story of these Stones had been given to him by Fomalhaut, or at least the little of it that was known. He himself had seen them taken from the lifeless body of Cal-Cotavion, their rightful bearer. He had even wielded them briefly. He could not actually remember the experience, but he could see parts of it as fleeting images. He knew he had found it a terrible strain, and he had refused to bear it for long.

He reached out a trembling hand. The light seemed to burn the color right out of it. He touched the Stone, ran his fingers up and down its hard cold facets. It was not diamond or glass or ice or water. It was, Raintree knew without doubt, a transcendent substance beyond any concept of the physics of the world.

"I—I would never *dare* touch that..." whispered Lori.

Raintree glanced down at the pedestal. In it was set a small drawer. Here, he knew suddenly, were kept the other three Stones. Three Stones, each as dire and resplendent in its way as the Stone of Inner Light. The Stone of Truth. The Stone of Life. The Stone of Adamance.

His fingers wavered toward the drawer, hesitated, and withdrew. He did not have the stamina to endure the light of four such things at once.

With difficulty he turned away from the light and faced Lori. The light of the Stone glittered strongly in her transfixed eyes.

"Shall we go?" he asked in a husky voice.

"Yes. Please, let's. I'm so glad you didn't open that drawer. If you had I think I would have gone up in a puff of smoke."

They withdrew down the ladder. As soon as they were out of sight of the Light they collapsed into relieved, half-hysterical laughter, leaning against each other like people who had narrowly escaped drowning. Raintree did not feel truly part of the world again until that light was blocked from his eyes. Indeed, he never felt quite the same afterwards. Neither, he suspected, did Lori Wu.

Chapter 5

The Words of T'Ukudu

Raintree spent the next few days trying to adapt to life at the Lighthouse. His quarters left nothing to be desired, unless it might be that its other occupants view him more kindly. He had, he discovered, two pets, a cat and a bird. Or to be more specific, a lynx and a boreal owl. They had been well cared for during his absence, but the cat at least had still managed to claw up much of the furniture. Upon its first sight of Raintree it had growled, spit, and padded out of sight with a cold green glance over its shoulder. Now all Raintree saw of it was an occasional startling glimpse of large green eyes glaring at him from around a corner or over the arm of a chair. It didn't even appear when he put out its food. He couldn't imagine how the dog-sized animal managed to hide so effectively in this little apartment, but it certainly did. When Raintree went to bed he was careful to first search the room and then shut the door. He did not want to awaken to the sight of those eyes glimmering at him in the darkness.

As for the owl, it ignored him except to swivel its head towards him on occasion. Raintree wasn't sure what more one might expect from an owl.

He was tempted to get rid of these unsatisfactory companions, but he knew he must once have kept them for a reason. He hoped to someday rediscover what that might have been.

He visited his cryogenics lab, where he had once worked to refine the weapon that had defined his persona, at least in the eyes of the public. He hefted one of the gleaming cryoguns and studied it. It felt awkward in his arms. He recognized the firing contact, but was unsure of the operation of the other controls. He didn't dare try it until he knew more, even though there was an indoor testing range right next door. In truth, the weapon didn't interest him very much. It seemed little more than a clever but pointless toy. He couldn't think of a single important problem he might hope to solve by freezing something. He shrugged and replaced it in its rack.

Fomalhaut and T'Ukudu returned from whatever mysterious business had kept them away. Fomalhaut greeted him placidly enough, expressing only the slightest surprise at how quickly Ben had chosen to make his reappearance in the larger world. T'Ukudu had merely offered to resume his Touchtalk-assisted education. Ben accepted the offer. The more he knew, the more quickly he might find some point to his life, some direction beyond the unfocused puttering around that was all he'd done since returning.

He wandered the Lighthouse from one end to the other, meeting the staff and learning their functions. He forced himself to do this, for he was shy around strangers, with the partial exception of Lori Wu.

After ten days T'Ukudu sent out an internal memo. He was about to announce the result of his evaluation of the human race which been his mission since his arrival in the solar system. There would be an assembly in the main hall on the following day.

Raintree approached the auditorium at the appointed hour, more interested in this than in anything else that had happened since he'd gone up to commune with the Stone.

Fomalhaut stood speaking with a group of five expensively-dressed men near the entrance to the hall. Or rather, Fomalhaut spoke with one balding, smooth-faced man, while the others, impassive men wearing dark glasses, stood silently a few paces back. Raintree approached this group curiously. Fomalhaut turned to him.

"Mr. Carwell, may I introduce Doctor Benjamin Raintree. Ben, this is Reston Carwell, National Security Advisor to the President of the United States."

"Oh?" said Ben, taking the proffered hand. No one took the trouble to introduce the other four men, he noticed.

Carwell gave a strained smile. "Good to meet you, Dr. Raintree. I'm glad to see you've recovered from your recent injuries."

"Thank you." Raintree looked at him in concern. "You don't look especially well yourself, Mr. Carwell. Are you ill?"

Carwell made a self-deprecatory gesture and gave a wry chuckle. "It's nothing serious. I think I'm just coming down with a cold."

"What brings you here today, Mr. Carwell? I don't remember that we've had many visits from high government officials."

"Well, we heard about Mr. T'Ukudu's planned announcement and considered it of interest to hear his results."

Another figure approached, a smiling older woman wearing a Vigil badge.

Fomalhaut said, "Mr. Carwell, this is Dr. Monique Vincent, head of the Vigil's Department of Global Studies. She will conduct you and your party to your places in the auditorium."

She led them away with much voluble speech while Raintree and Fomalhaut stood watching.

"I thought this announcement was supposed to be a private affair," said Raintree softly.

"It was. We had intended to keep it to ourselves, until the potential impact of T'Ukudu's results could be evaluated. Carwell appeared uninvited and with little warning. The presence of these men indicates a security lapse within our organization. I'm afraid I shall have to deepen my examination of the loyalties of our staff. For now, let's make the best of the situation."

They entered the auditorium. Fomalhaut went to sit with Carwell and Vincent in the front row. Raintree hung back and placed himself in a middle row, among the staff, next to Lori Wu, who smiled and gave his hand a quick friendly clasp. The others, whom he knew less well, looked at him in surprise.

The room was full of ordinary-looking men and women with the exception of Fomalhaut, who with his gleaming exploration suit and mirrored helmet looked both splendid and ludicrous in comparison.

T'Ukudu appeared through a door in the front of the room and moved to the lectern at a sedate pace. The auditorium quieted.

Direct as always, T'Ukudu began without preliminaries.

"My study of the potential of the human species is now complete. I am pleased to announce my conclusion here today. Your species presents no danger to the peace and privacy of my Makers, the masters of the planet T'Utahn. Therefore, it shall in turn be left in peace. My mission to your planet is concluded. Thank you." He turned to withdraw from the lectern.

"Wait!"

It was Carwell. T'Ukudu halted and turned an inscrutable gaze his way.

"Mr. T'Ukudu, that's a very sketchy exposition. I'm sure we're all relieved to hear that your world feels no threat from us, but what is the basis of your conclusion?"

"Its most immediate basis is my demonstration that the human race will never develop the technology to cross interstellar distances, or to project any kind of threatening influence across such distances. Trapped within its own star system, or indeed confined to the surface of its own planet, the human race is of no further interest to the Makers."

"I don't understand," said Carwell. "We have developed space flight technology, however rudimentary, in only fifty years of effort. We already explore the solar system to some extent. What's to stop us from improving that technology until we eventually visit the stars?"

"The demands of interstellar travel are orders of magnitude greater than those of travel among your local planets. The energy needed to accelerate one small ship to a substantial fraction of the speed of light is a large fraction of the total energy output of your entire civilization. Travel by slower means is feasible, but to transport living or potential human beings on journeys lasting centuries would require a biological science far beyond the present human level. It's like a child who has dipped his toe into the sea contemplating a swim to Australia."

Carwell bit his lip. "Again I do not understand. Possum Perturbare is human, for all that he is also a renegade. Yet he has single-handedly devised a technology which is equal or superior to most of what the Vigil itself employs. I'm sure Perturbare could, at this moment, construct a starship superior to the solar sail-hydrogen ramjet vessel in which you made your crossing."

T'Ukudu paused. "This is true. However, Perturbare is an aberration among the human species. His inventive brilliance is unprecedented, and he has managed to create a situation in which he is free of the constraints or interference of the larger human society. Moreover, he has pledged not to put his advanced technology into the hands of the general human populace, knowing the chaos that would result from its irresponsible use."

A new chill entered Carwell's voice. "Perhaps this is true. But even without the cooperation of Perturbare, or indeed of the Vigil itself, our scientists are not fools. We have seen the technology wielded by Perturbare, by you, and by the Para-men. We know what is possible. We know something about its theoretical basis. Given time, I see no reason why we could not develop it ourselves. Tell me, Mr. T'Ukudu...do we have that time?"

"Any limits on the time remaining to the human race will not be imposed by the people of T'Utahn."

"I believe we are finally approaching the core of your study. Mr. T'Ukudu, in your estimation, how much time does our race have left for technological innovation, given the limits imposed by any source—either external or internal?"

"Uh oh," whispered Lori.

The chill in the room hardened into tension.

"I would say fifty years," said T'Ukudu with his usual imperturbable calm. "Fifty more years of scientific and technological advancement, followed by a gradual halt to research, and the beginning of a long technological regression, as resource depletion and social dysfunctions combine to impoverish your race."

A few gasps rose up throughout the room. Raintree glanced at Fomalhaut's back, but could detect no change in his attitude.

Carwell said nothing further.

With the subject breached at last, T'Ukudu seemed to warm to it.

"The human race lacks the concerted will to accomplish anything as resource-intensive as interstellar flight. It is composed of individuals who are too absorbed in their own immediate needs and desires to pay any serious heed to the long-term needs of the race. This is understandable, given that issues of simple, immediate survival occupy most of the time and energy of most humans. Beyond that, the human race has no real goals for the future. Various groups pursue various agendas of varying degrees of shortsightedness and venality, many of them mutually exclusive. The basic problem is that your world is full of groups that expound causes which directly contradict each other. In most of these situations, no compromise is possible. The analysis is too complex to fully explain in this setting. If you wish, I shall translate the core of my study into English and make it available to you.

"For now, let me provide an example. Consider the opposing forces of so-called 'development' and those of land conservation. To a developer, land in its natural condition is an empty wasteland waiting to be exploited, changed, mined, or otherwise "improved". To the conservationist, it is the living surface of the planet, correct and sufficient as it is, and irreplaceable if destroyed. The developers support an ideal of unlimited economic growth, which demands that civilization and its economic activities constantly expand into natural areas. Let us say that developers wish to destroy ten percent of the remaining available land per year in order to produce sufficient growth. Conservationists wish to see no more land developed. The developers propose a compromise: instead of ten percent, they will destroy only one percent of the land annually. But the conservationists realize that this compromise is no compromise at all. Instead of destroying all the remaining land in only ten years, the developers will extend it to a hundred. As long as any new development is permitted, eventually all wild lands will be destroyed. Therefore the two positions can never really be reconciled.

"Consider the other polarized factions which either have, or soon will, enter into conflict, their positions and goals equally irreconcilable. For example, the rich versus the poor. There is an obvious ongoing attempt by the economically powerful to bring your planet into a new condition of feudalism, in which the majority are exploited and parasitized. The extreme wealth of this privileged few cannot be sustained without forcing the majority into a kind of servitude, in which the benefits they receive from their labors are barely enough to sustain their lives. Much of the world's population is already in this condition. Even the more favored inhabitants of the wealthier nations are being pushed in this direction. Eventually the weight will be too great, the disparity between wealth and poverty too galling. The result will be an uprising, but numbers alone will not bring victory to the oppressed, as might have been the case in previous centuries. The military power of the privileged class has increased even out of proportion to its wealth. If threatened, they will use the very children of their victims as pawns in an attempt to secure their own positions of status. The result will be a broken economy and a devastated planet.

"Or consider the various religious factions, each of which is convinced it is in possession of the objective truth of the nature of reality. The more extreme sects have little tolerance for the views of others. They see no moral obstacle to spreading their faith, or simply enforcing their moral and economic codes on others, through any means whatsoever, whether through murder, which they may choose to legitimize by calling it war, or through enshrining their beliefs in civil law.

"Consider then that every human being on this planet is a member of one or more factions which is irreconcilably opposed to one or more others. Consider also that your planet is fully occupied, indeed drastically overpopulated, by a factor of at least three, in my estimation. There is no place to which the most devoted zealots of any given cause can retreat in order to escape the oppression of their enemies. Such enclaves can be created, but they are inevitably besieged by outside forces, and all eventually will be overwhelmed. The vectors of all these opposing forces form a web too complex to be sorted out. There is no escape mechanism. Space travel might have provided one, but the technology for such a mass diaspora of the disaffected is far beyond man's reach. These conflicts are steadily destroying the Earth. The destructive potential of the various factions is increasing. Reason itself is increasingly being marginalized, abandoned, even demonized.

"My prediction is that these forces will reach a critical level in fifty years, exacerbated by ever-worsening environmental catastrophe as the Earth's ecosystem breaks down. It will be an End Time for the human race. The survivors will be reduced to a primitive state. It will be impossible for them to maintain an advanced technology. They will therefore present no threat to the masters of T'Utahn."

T'Ukudu fell silent. The whole auditorium seemed frozen in the aftermath of this calmly-stated declaration of doom.

Finally, Carwell said heavily, "On behalf of the government, I ask you not to transmit the results of your study until we have had a chance to consult with you about them."

"I have already transmitted the data to T'Utahn. That was my first duty and my first priority."

Carwell stiffened. "That—that was ill-considered. Informing these aliens of disarray in the human race, whether real or imagined, makes us appear vulnerable."

"You are indeed vulnerable," answered T'Ukudu. "And I am not subject to your authority. Still, I do not understand your objection. This is the best possible outcome for your species. If I had been required to report that the human race had the will, the organization, and the stability to expand into space, while also possessing its obvious warlike, acquisitive qualities, the Makers would have had no choice but to react. The peace and privacy of my world must not be threatened. Your species would have been destroyed. Indeed, I could have done so myself. The simple release of certain biological agents into your environment would have sufficed. Happily, no such drastic action will be necessary. T'Utahn and its agents will leave your world to its own devices. I trust you to realize that my mission to your world has ended to the best possible advantage of all concerned."

Raintree and Lori shared a glance. Raintree wondered if he looked as pale and stricken as she did.

Reston Carwell stood up, hands stiff at his sides. "I cannot accept your conclusions. I cannot concede that my race, which has achieved such heights of culture and discovery, in addition to being subject to all the failings you mention, is doomed to destroy itself within the lifetime of my grandchildren."

"Do not overstate the case, sir," said T'Ukudu. "Your race will not be destroyed. It will be greatly reduced in numbers, and eventually will stabilize at a roughly nineteenth century level of technology in a few privileged areas. A simple agrarian culture will be the norm elsewhere."

"That remains an unappealing prospect," said Carwell stiffly. "Please provide the full text of your analysis as soon as possible."

Fomalhaut spoke, causing Raintree to jump.

"Mr. Carwell. I hope you will not reveal T'Ukudu's results to the general public."

"We certainly will not. We have no interest in damaging public morale in that fashion. Good day to you."

Leading his small troop of silent followers, Carwell strode up the aisle and out of the auditorium, his face as grim a mask as any Raintree had ever seen. Monique Vincent ran out after them.

As they went past, Ben heard Carwell mutter: "Let's get the hell away from here. I can feel the light of that damned Stone burning into me from here."

And that, thought Ben, was the real reason why Man was doomed to fail.

T'Ukudu looked around at his unsettled audience for a moment, then turned and left by the same door through which he had entered.

Fomalhaut remained seated, motionless.

Chapter 6

A Departure

Raintree returned to his suite and spent the afternoon in his study. He brooded out the window at the grimy cityscape of Boston, looking across the river towards Cambridge, pondering the species to which he belonged, of which he knew so little. Except for Possum Perturbare and a few Vigil staffers, he had had no real contact with anyone of his own race since his injury. The few people with whom he'd spoken were among the most intelligent and well-educated in the world. He knew nothing at all of common men and women, the kind whose inadequacies had led T'Ukudu to his dismal projection of the human future. Nor did he know much about the societies which shaped them, or which they themselves had shaped.

He'd intended his impulsive flight from the experimental station to end the almost complete isolation he had known there. Since then he hadn't set foot off Vigil property. Perhaps it was time to end his isolation here in the Lighthouse. He was no longer an invalid. He was merely a bored, lonely, aimless, ignorant, and melancholy man.

He was on the verge of leaving to immerse himself in the dense human world beyond the Lighthouse when the door chime sounded. In the next room, the lynx—Sasquatch was its name—panicked at the sound and scuttled away to hide, his claws slipping on the hardwood floor.

Raintree opened the door. There stood an extremely disconsolate-looking Lori Wu. Raintree loomed over her, gaping at her rather stupidly. Suddenly his world seemed so much brighter, if no less mysterious.

"Are you busy? May I come in?" she asked in a small voice.

"Oh...of course, come on in." He stepped aside to admit her.

She slipped past him and collapsed into one of the heavy wood-framed chairs that populated Raintree's rustic rooms. "I...was just telepathically examined by Fomalhaut. He gave me the rest of the afternoon off."

"Hmm? Well, I would have invited you in even if you were still on duty," said Raintree in an attempt at gallantry. "As far as I'm concerned, anything you have to say to me is Vigil business." He almost rolled his eyes at his own awkwardness.

Lori ventured to smile, but Raintree did not fail to notice how her lip trembled. He felt the first stirring of an emotion new to him in this new life: anger. "Did he hurt you, Lori?"

"What?" Her eyes grew wide as she looked up into his face. "No! No. But it was very intense. Much deeper than the first time. The things he brought up, the feelings... I relived everything that has ever really touched me in my life, including some things I hadn't even remembered. Have you heard? A quarter of the Ants resigned rather than submit to the probe. I think it's hard on Fomalhaut too."

Raintree found it difficult to care about Fomalhaut's discomfort. Of all the beings he knew, only Fomalhaut was completely opaque to him. He was not a figure who inspired any sympathy.

Lori's pain was a different matter. "Let me get you something, Lori. Would you like some hot chocolate?"

"Yes...that would be nice."

When he returned with a tray of cocoa and cookies, Lori did not hesitate to resume her discussion of her troubles. "The examination, right on the heels of T'Ukudu's gloomy announcement—it's hard to take. I had no idea he'd reach such a bleak conclusion. It's hard to absorb that the world I've grown up in will crumble in the lifetime of any children I might have. I'm only twenty four. It might even fall apart within my lifetime. Do you suppose the Vigil sacrificed so much to keep people free, only to see them use that freedom to destroy themselves?"

"As I understand it, that was always a possibility. But you know, T'Ukudu could be wrong."

"Do you think so?" A poignant flicker of hope came and went in her eyes. "But I don't. I've assisted him. I've seen some of his data, and I understand a bit about the social theory he uses to draw his conclusions. He is very, very rigorous in his work. I suspect he already had his answer years ago, and has only been searching for weaknesses and errors in his work in the years since then. He can't predict the exact course or time of our downfall, but he's sure it will come, and I believe him. Unless you think there's something we can do to stop it?"

"We? Oh, you mean the Vigil?"

"Yes...sorry if I made it sound like I think I'm a member of the Vigil. I know I'm not."

Raintree chuckled. "No, no, that's not what I was thinking. As far as I'm concerned, you're more an integral part of the Vigil than I am. But as you told me yourself, there's not much left of the Vigil. I don't think T'Ukudu sees any way for us to intervene, or he wouldn't have transmitted such an unequivocal report. I'll have to ask him what he believes. Members of the Vigil fought and died, and killed, to preserve man's freedom of action. It's hard to see how those same beings could now turn around and do anything to limit that freedom. Possum Perturbare could probably do something to derail T'Ukudu's scenario, or at least change the rules of the game. But he doesn't strike me as having that level of ambition. Tricks and games seem to be enough to satisfy him. So assuming T'Ukudu's right— and that he can really predict anything about the future behavior of the race as a whole—I guess you and I will have to face his End Time in our twilight years."

Lori lowered her eyes and gripped her mug tightly. "It's all just so grim. Even now, the Lighthouse is the beacon of the world, the finest place on Earth. It's hard to believe that all this knowledge, all this glorious hope, could be in the end so futile."

Raintree offered her a gentle smile. His own hopes were dim enough that he cherished Lori's struggle to retain hers. Her fragile beauty, both of body and soul, left him profoundly moved, and very aware of the world's potential for pleasure and pain. Her nearness left him feeling not quite connected to reality.

He reached out and took her hand in his.

Daring greatly, he asked, "Would you like to stay here for dinner tonight? I've been practicing. I can now prepare a meal that doesn't set off the toxicity sensors in my kitchen."

Lori smiled wanly at him. "Oh—thank you. But I can't. My boyfriend is coming to my place for dinner tonight. But I can't discuss most of this with him, so I thought…"

Raintree felt his head go strangely light. He spoke again, barely knowing what he was saying. "Oh. Well, of course. No problem. I'll let you know if I find out anything interesting."

Startled, Lori caught her breath, looking at Ben with new appraisal.

"I'm sorry. I'd better be going." She hurried out.

Raintree returned to the window in his study. By now the late winter evening was mantling the city in steel-mauve shadows.

One of the main problems of being effectively two months old was having little control over his emotions. As Lori's beauty stunned his heart, so her rejection blackened the world in his eyes. Tears flowed down his cheeks, entirely outside his ability to control them. As long as Lori was sitting beside him, or standing before him, he could ignore or downplay T'Ukudu's bleak predictions about the future of a world he little knew or cared for. But now that she was not, and would not be, T'Ukudu's words were suddenly crushing, as was the burden of his own pointless existence.

The next morning Ben called the Lighthouse facilities manager and asked him to arrange new homes for the lynx and the owl. He was stabbed by guilt as they were caged and taken away to a wildlife rehabilitation center in northern Maine. Once he must have loved them, but now he had to admit his inability to care for them. The lynx at least was clearly unhappy. Ben had little interest in them. They were relics of a past life he might never recall.

Raintree visited Fomalhaut during a break in his ongoing telepathic loyalty scans of the staff. He walked into the examining room, a comfortably-furnished little office, and found Fomalhaut hunched over in a chair, shaking slightly. Any sign of weakness or distress in this remote figure alarmed Raintree unreasonably. "Are you all right?" he blurted almost harshly, as though Fomalhaut had no right to reveal any imperfection.

Fomalhaut straightened up at once. "Ben. Yes, I'm fine. It's just that these deep probes prove draining after a while. Even in a group of humans as stable and professional as our staff, one encounters disturbing things when one pries deeply enough." He shuddered, then stood up smoothly, again revealed in the impenetrable, immaculate splendor of his exploration suit.

"Has it been worthwhile?" asked Ben more gently. "I hear we've lost a good chunk of our staff."

"Yes, and I can hardly blame them, given my assault on their privacy and dignity. But I have so far uncovered three employees who are also deep-cover operatives of various American intelligence establishments. They still believe their deep conditioning has allowed them to elude my probe. I haven't decided how to deal with them."

"I see." This revelation shook Raintree. "Is Lori Wu among them?"

"No. She was among the first I examined, because of her close association with you. I am happy to say that her loyalty and enthusiasm are unmarred."

"That's a relief. Do you know where T'Ukudu has gotten to? I want to talk to him about the results of his study. Apparently he's gone off without leaving word with the staff."

"T'Ukudu has gone to the experimental station."

"Oh. I wouldn't mind going there to see him. I'd like to get away from here for a while."

"That sounds like a good idea. You may certainly take a flyer and go out to visit him. Perhaps you would like to broaden your experience by doing some wider traveling afterwards."

"Maybe I will. Thanks, Fomalhaut."

Ben packed a bag and proceeded to the main hangar, a facility oddly smaller and less impressive than the one at the experimental station. Nevertheless it contained a good twenty flyers of various styles, including one of Perturbare's. This time Raintree decided to test his own new flying skills, rather than press Perturbare's computer into service as a chauffeur. He chose a small flyer which looked rakish enough with its angled sides and dual main propulsion lanterns. He entered the hatch and sat self-consciously behind the controls. In truth, even these "manual" flyers were so highly automated that anyone could push one around with only a little training. He powered up the vehicle, called for clearance from Vigil air control, and floated up into a deck of clouds just a minute later. It was a relief to pierce them and emerge into the realm of light that lay above, with the Lighthouse and indeed all sign of man hidden from view.

An hour later he made an automated landing in the hangar of the experimental station. He'd overhauled the sun, which was now blocked from view by the peak that backed the dome and spire, glowing softly as pearls. It felt strange to return here, as though this were the long-lost home of his childhood, remembered both dimly and with aching clarity, though he'd left it only weeks before.

By now he understood the layout conventions and navigational aids the Vigil used in its establishments. He also knew how to read sensor displays to determine who was where. T'Ukudu was marked as being on one of the terraces on the west face of the spire—possibly the same one Ben had once blundered onto himself.

He discovered the T'Utahnti Servant seated on a bench, a small display pad in his lap. Two fingers of his right hand were set into contacts on the bezel. Text flowed rapidly down the screen, but T'Ukudu wasn't looking at it. His placid gaze rested on the horizon. Raintree smiled. Though T'Ukudu was indeed a most ominous-looking person, Ben felt privileged to have known his true mildness first hand.

"Hello, Ben," he said, without turning away from the misty distances of sea and island.

"Hello, T'Ukudu. Am I disturbing you?"

"Not at all. I am transcribing my report into English. The task is nearly complete. I am happy to see you. Please sit with me."

Raintree placed himself beside T'Ukudu on the bench, feeling suddenly reduced in size, like a stripling alongside a grown man. The flow of text on T'Ukudu's screen did not slow or falter. Raintree was unsurprised at his ability to do two or more things at once. From what he'd learned of T'Ukudu's synthetic physiology, it seemed his hand or any other part of his body could literally think and act on its own.

"I was wondering about some things you mentioned in your report."

"Such as?"

"Your claim that you or your planet would have destroyed us if we'd turned out to be a threat to your

Makers," said Raintree. "What would they have done? Bombed us?"

"No, nothing so drastic or brutal. It would not have been necessary. Under even the worst scenarios, the human race was decades away from offering any threat to the Makers. I would simply have introduced an engineered virus which would have sterilized all humans. Happily, the need is not there."

"Oh." Taken aback, Raintree pondered this. Even stated with T'Ukudu's usual calm, or perhaps even more so because of it, this pronouncement was chilling. He wondered whether Fomalhaut, when he recruited T'Ukudu into the Vigil, had been aware he was harboring a being capable of eradicating the very people Fomalhaut was trying to save.

"Just how confident are you of the accuracy of your predictions, T'Ukudu?"

"Confident enough that I am prepared to leave the work behind. I see no possibility that any known party or parties can do more than alter the timetable, or the exact circumstances, of the inevitable collapse of technical civilization on this world."

"You're leaving?" asked Raintree in sudden apprehension. "Returning to your world?"

"No."

The flow of text ceased. The screen blanked out. "This work is finished. I cannot return to T'Utahn because my ship was destroyed soon after my arrival. In any event, it is unnecessary. My mission is complete. The correct course for a Servant of T'Utahn under these circumstances is to cease."

"Cease? You mean you're going to die?"

"That is our way, Ben."

Again Ben cursed the emotions which were so close to the surface. Tears sprang out. His throat contracted to the point where he could hardly choke out the words.

"But—that's crazy! You can't just die on us. Why? We need you here."

"I do not see how, Ben. The mission of the Vigil is also complete. Frankly, I see no reason for either the Vigil or myself to continue to exist."

"But—" Raintree lost his voice to sobs for a moment. Only the next words he spoke might preserve T'Ukudu's existence for mankind's benefit, and for his own…and he did not know what to say. "We need your knowledge and wisdom," he ventured miserably.

"All the wisdom I have which is relevant to your race is contained in the report I have just transmitted. Ben, it grieves me to witness your sorrow. Do not mourn for me. I have been the most fortunate of beings. Throughout my existence, my path has been clear. I have known my mission, I have been able to perform and complete it, and I have done it well. I have suffered none of the uncertainties, the self-doubts, the futile searches for meaning which afflict you and so many of your fellow humans. Now that my task is done, I am permitted to pass on. Do not mourn."

"But I'll miss you."

"You need not. Everything that makes me who I am will still be present in the universe. I am a product of the universe, no less than you or the Makers themselves. When the ocean casts up a wave, for a moment it glistens in the sun, and then it collapses. It rejoins the great wholeness from which it sprang. No one mourns it. It was for an instant a thing of beauty, but new ones are cast up, and the whole beauty of the sea is undiminished. So it is with me."

Raintree did not find that this metaphor eased his heart. "Don't you have any desire to live for yourself?" he asked. "Isn't there any purpose you can find here to take the place of your mission?"

The face of T'Ukudu grew even more grave. His expression verged on troubled, even pained, for the first time Raintree could recall.

"There is much beauty in your world, Ben, and I have known many worthy people, such as yourself. But I would not wish to abide among your species without need. It is the most degraded, misguided, unhappy race known to us. Even the best of you is hampered by animal urges which are constantly at odds with the more rational aspects of your being. The great mass of humans is little more than a heedless, ignorant, dangerous tribe of surly brutes. The human race is still primitive, Ben. Someday it may be replaced by a more advanced species which will at last be fully divorced from its animal beginnings."

Raintree was taken aback. He had never before heard such a condemnation of his species from the normally circumspect T'Ukudu.

"A species like your Makers?" he asked breathlessly.

"I am not permitted to discuss the Makers at that level of detail."

"Sorry."

T'Ukudu ignored that. "There are several aspects of life on Earth which I find disturbing. It is not unknown for a planetary life form to attack outsiders, but it is unusual for a life form to attack and weaken itself, as the Terrestrial life form has done."

"I don't understand. The Terrestrial life form?"

"This is detailed in my report. In brief, all existing Terrestrial life had a single genesis. It was otherwise on T'Utahn and on most other worlds we know of. Here all life can ultimately be traced back to a single origin or arrival event. All known Terrestrial organisms are therefore related to one another. When viewed in the context of the four-dimensional space-time continuum, all life forms throughout the history of Earth are literally one, with all individuals being connected in time, if not in space. In this sense, such behaviors as predation can be seen as part of the metabolic activity of a single vast organism. But in this sense the actions of man are inexplicable. He has assumed a destructive rather than an integral role in the well-being of his life form. Please walk with me." He stood up, rather stiffly and slowly, or so it seemed to Ben.

Raintree had been trying to follow T'Ukudu's reasoning, but was brought up short by this request. A fire of apprehension filled his heart. "You—you're not going *now*, are you?"

"There is no reason to delay. I would appreciate your company, if you can tolerate the emotional distress."

"Oh, God—all right then. If this is something you must do, then I won't let you do it alone. Let's go!"

Feeling as if he were marching to his own execution, Raintree followed T'Ukudu inside, down the spire, then out a back entrance which gave onto the rocky slope of the mountain. They climbed a few hundred feet, just enough to give a view of the ocean beyond the dome. Reaching a small ledge bearing a few scrubby conifers, they turned toward each other. Raintree reached out to touch T'Ukudu's hand, wishing to feel the steady flow of those orderly thoughts one last time.

T'Ukudu jerked his hand away and stepped back. "No, Ben. I am sorry, but you must not touch me."

Raintree stared at him in bewilderment.

"Ben Raintree—may you find and regain your path, and make of yourself the person you are meant to be. As you learn the truth of things, may you accept and face it with serenity."

Ben did not attempt to shape his thoughts into words. He merely allowed his affection for this being to pour into his hand and out through his fingers. Perhaps T'Ukudu could sense some shred of it even through the intervening air.

"Goodbye, Ben. Thank you for your friendship." T'Ukudu sat down at the base of a rock, still moving rather stiffly and hesitantly, and composed himself. Without any warning, life vanished from his eyes. Raintree was alone.

"Oh no!" Raintree collapsed onto the rocks and wept bitterly.

He could hardly see through his tears. After a while he wiped them away, the better to study a disk of orange light that was creeping over a nearby rock. A second bright circle came into view, and then two more, weaving around. Raintree looked up. Fomalhaut was descending on propulsion beams from his heels and shoulders. He landed, staring down at T'Ukudu's inert form.

"What in the world has happened here?" he asked in a voice heavy with wonder.

Raintree looked at him. "You didn't know he was going to do this?"

"I knew he would undo himself once he felt all his tasks were completed, but I did not think he had yet reached that point. I did not think he would be so precipitous about it. I do not understand this. I wish he had waited."

"Would you have tried to talk him out of it?"

"No. But I would at least have said goodbye." The gleaming figure of Fomalhaut hovered over the body for an indecisive moment, then bent down and laid a hand on the side of the massive head. He stiffened and broke the contact. Again he stood looking down at the body, but now he was visibly trembling.

Raintree flung himself to his feet and stood face-to-helmet with Fomalhaut. He could not restrain his bitterness. "Well, here we stand, Fomalhaut: the mighty Vigil! Both of us. Or rather, there you stand, the mighty Vigil, plus me, your sidekick, who couldn't Vigil his way out of a paper bag. Guardians of the free will of Man. It's all over for us, isn't it?"

"Do you believe the Vigil should be officially disbanded?" asked Fomalhaut quietly.

"Yes. No. It would be a shame to throw all those good people out of their jobs. But why ask me? You're the only one around here who knows what's really going on."

"Do I?" Fomalhaut backed away, slumped, sagged down to sit on a boulder. "Ben, in the years since my arrival on this Earth of yours, I have struggled to understand its dynamics, to decide upon a course of action for myself, to attempt to guide your world into the future I remember from the Earth of my own perished universe. The greatest part of this struggle has been to decide whether to take any action at all, or simply to let events take their course. I did take action. Whether I erred in doing so remains to be seen. Perhaps this is the right time for the Vigil to pass away."

Raintree turned from him and bent to pick up a rock.

"Don't bury him, Ben. Don't build a cairn. That's not his way. And do not touch him."

Raintree straightened up again.

"I do not know when I shall see you again," said Fomalhaut, as though it were unusual that he should not know so simple a thing. He stood, lifted off, and was gone.

Raintree stared for a moment at the sudden departure, then turned from T'Ukudu and reentered the station. He had decided to renew his solitary residency here. He spent the rest of the day prowling its many levels and corridors, peeking into chambers and laboratories that meant little to him. In the spire, he rode the elevator to the topmost floor to see what was there. At that height the spire was greatly narrowed. There was only room for the elevator and a ladder leading up though a hatch in the ceiling. He climbed up through the hatch. The tiny chamber there was open to the wind, its only furnishings a single bench and a short tapering pedestal, like the one that carried the Stone of Light back in Boston.

A man could sit there in solitude and gaze out at the great mountain-sea-airscape with the clean winds of the heights to lighten his mind. Raintree was grateful to the architect who had had the grace to include such a sanctuary in his design.

The next morning, Raintree returned to T'Ukudu's ledge to pay his respects. There he found two surprises. The body of T'Ukudu had turned grey. Large flakes of his substance hung loosely, rattling like leaves in the breeze. It should have been a ghastly sight, but somehow it wasn't, no more so than a decaying log in a forest. T'Ukudu, it seemed, was literally drying up and blowing away.

The second surprise was the bouquet of flowers which lay beside him. Raintree examined them, but there was nothing to indicate who had left them.

Chapter 7

The Darkhouse

Three days later, T'Ukudu's report was leaked to the public. The culprit was clearly someone in the government, for the text that was blasted across screens, newspapers and magazines contained phrasing that only appeared in the particular version that had been released to it.

All this conspired to complicate and darken Lori Wu's life even further. She still wore a black arm band in mourning for T'Ukudu. With the end of her obligation to assist him, she had been reassigned to the public relations office, which was overwhelmed by its attempt to counter the damage done by the release of the study. It was not her specialty as a researcher, nor was it to her liking.

She sat in her office for hours on end, dealing with questions from the media. As clearly and calmly as possible, she and others like her explained that the conclusions expressed in the report were not the official view of the Vigil as a whole. They had been held and developed by a single one of its members, who was now deceased. No, T'Ukudu had not been killed in retribution for his views, or in an attempt to protect Earth from alien invasion. No, he had not fled or gone into hiding. No, she did not personally understand why he had committed suicide. No, she would not speculate on his motives. No, the Vigil was not in fact an organization committed to the downfall of the human race. T'Ukudu's report was a prediction based on long-term preexisting trends; it was not an insidious plan of conquest.

Even as she offered these clarifications she could look beyond the pillars that fronted her window to the crowds of protesters who occupied the plaza, braving even the light of the Stone in their anger. Their placards read like the editorials in many of the more hysterical papers, if more crudely scrawled:

WE ARE NOT ANIMALS

VIGIL TO HUMAN RACE: DROP DEAD!

SO, WE'RE ONLY HUMAN?

WE WILL NOT GO GENTLY INTO THE NIGHT

and the inevitable:

VIGIL GO HOME

A few unrelated complaints were also mixed in:

TURN OFF THAT DAMN LIGHT!

And even:

GET THAT FREAK OFF MY TV

That last one really incensed Lori, who was sure it referred to T'Ukudu, whose death had made his noble face a frequent sight on television ever since it was announced.

In addition to these more literate protesters, there was also quite a mob who merely milled about looking ugly. A strong police presence kept their bottle-throwing to a minimum. It had become difficult, even dangerous, for the Vigil staff to come to work by the usual entrances. They had taken to coming and going through the secret tunnels.

Besides all of this, another matter weighed heavily on Lori's mind. For the past week she'd tried to tell herself to let it go, to let it work itself out, but still her mind was in turmoil.

It was typical of her to ignore a personal problem in the hope that it would go away. It was also like her to be aware of this flaw and to eventually force herself to face and overcome it.

To that end, during her lunch break she nerved herself to use the internal locator system to find Fomalhaut. She wasn't supposed to do this except in urgent need, but she wanted to track him down before she lost her nerve. His blip appeared on the display, the only one marked with the red of a Vigil member. Perhaps he was now the last of the Vigil, as he had been the first.

He was located in one of the tower's restricted-access laboratories, well beyond the clearance level of her own classification. The display showed another person also in the lab, with a symbol coded white. She didn't bother to look up this unfamiliar code. Instead she keyed the intercom to the lab and spoke into it as calmly and firmly as she could.

"Fomalhaut? Lori Wu here. May I speak to you?"

"Yes, Lori, what is it?"

"I—I was wondering if I could speak to you in person for a moment. I'm on my lunch break—"

There was a moment's hesitation. "I'm rather busy at the moment. Would you mind coming up to this lab? I can spare you a few minutes."

Lori blinked in surprise. "Really? Okay, fine. But my access..."

"I am instructing the system to admit you. Please come up."

"I'll be right there."

A little flustered at her success, Lori stood, smoothed out her skirt and blouse, and proceeded to the elevators in the central tower. The car accepted her and deposited her on a floor she had never visited before. She had intended to pause before passing through the lab's gunmetal-colored door, but it slid open while she was still ten feet away from it, forcing her to enter as briskly as she could.

She jumped at the sudden ripping sound of automatic gunfire. Fomalhaut and some man stood in a glassed-in corridor at the far end of the lab.

The man wore a white jacket and black pants. He was spraying a submachine gun at a glossy red-and-black suit that was stretched out on an armature at the far end of the firing range. He laughed a little wildly as the clip ran out. "That's good clean fun," he said. The stream of bullets had left lines of raindrop-indentations in the suit's metallic surface, but had not visibly damaged it.

Fomalhaut then raised his left hand toward the suit. The other figure slapped a pair of dark goggles over his face. Lori turned away just as a blistering violet line from Fomalhaut's wrist ignited a fearsome star on the suit. She stood blinking, her field of vision crossed by a vivid purple line which slowly turned green as she watched.

"Fomalhaut?" she said uncertainly.

The glare from the other side of the room ceased at once. "Lori! Please forgive my distraction; I had not noticed you had entered the room."

Lori approached them. Her vision was clearing up quickly now. "I think I'll be all right. I only caught a glimpse of your beam."

"Nevertheless, report to medical as soon as you're finished here. Have your eyes checked for retinal scotoma." Fomalhaut and his companion left the glassed enclosure and walked to meet her. Lori studied the stranger. He had brushed-back black hair and regarded her with a quizzical grin, oddly intimate for someone she had never met. With a sudden gasp, she recognized him.

"Possum Perturbare!"

"Lori Wu!" answered Perturbare in the same astonished tone.

"Yes," said Lori, flabbergasted that he had recognized her, although he must have been listening as she spoke on the intercom.

"I'm happy to meet you, Lori. I've heard quite a bit about you...you little old heartbreaker you." He stuck out his hand.

Lori shook it, flushing, trying to ignore the weapon in his other hand.

"I'll guess I'll just flit off while you chat with old Formal Hat here," he added. Turning to "Formal Hat", he waved his free hand toward the red suit. "You know, it's sort of overkill to use technology of that level as a basis for creating bulletproof pajamas, but I agree with you, it's a prudent move. Sure you don't want to lend me that little suit?"

"Why don't you reveal the location of your headquarters, and I'll fly it there personally," said Fomalhaut evenly.

Perturbare gave a good-natured laugh. "Touché. I guess I'll settle for performing the molecular analysis for now. I should soon have some news on that tissue analysis too. See you two later." He waved and ambled out of the lab.

Lori stared after him. "I never met him before," she said unnecessarily.

"Indeed. Now, Lori, what may I do for you?"

Fomalhaut's question brought her back to the matter at hand. "It's about Ben Raintree. Just before he left, we had —a personal misunderstanding. He's emotionally immature, and inexperienced. I didn't immediately realize what was going on. I'm afraid I handled it clumsily and hurt his feelings. I think he might have left the Lighthouse on account of me."

"I believe that is largely true, yes."

Lori winced. That mild remark struck her as an intense rebuke. "Anyway—if it's possible, I'd like to go out there, talk to him, apologize, try to bring him back."

Fomalhaut stood silent and impassive for several long moments before replying.

"Your desire to make amends does you credit. You served as a needed emotional anchor for Ben during the first difficult weeks of his return. Yet you might have anticipated that he would form an emotional attachment stronger than you were prepared to accept. Indeed, I might have anticipated it. The fault is not all yours. For now though, I believe Ben is where he needs to be, and so are you. Someday you may meet again and reconcile. But not now. Come, let me walk you to Medical."

Lori nodded and followed along mutely, both disappointed and relieved by Fomalhaut's decision. As they walked, Fomalhaut asked, "How is your work going, Lori?"

She shrugged. "I don't know if it's helping. I'm doing my best to talk sense to everyone who gets past the screeners—God knows what kind of loons the screeners are dealing with. But I feel a little lost. To tell you the truth, I don't understand the vehemence of the response against us. Just what have we really done?"

Fomalhaut's reply had the tone of a prepared lecture. "The Vigil has now committed three sins which the public finds difficult to forgive. First, we tolerate, and even work with, the infamous outlaw Dr. Possum Perturbare. He of course is seen as the primary villain of the world, being guilty of such crimes as inconveniencing the wealthy, mocking all authority, and even interfering with television programming. Second, we subject the citizens of this city to the constant glow of the Stone of Inner Light. This is indeed intolerable to a large part of the public. The more unbearable they find it to be, the less likely they are to admit it, given the nature of that light. So they turn their self-doubt into resentment against us, we who force them to confront and acknowledge their inner flaws. And now, finally, we have announced that their inferior species will soon collapse from sheer degeneracy. Or so it seems to them. Coupled with the fact that our defeat of the Para-men is now years in the past, the average person has little desire to shower us with love."

Lori nodded unhappily. "And what about the government?"

"That is what I hope to find out tomorrow. I am telling you this in confidence. I've been asked to meet with the President tomorrow to discuss the situation and the continuing status of the Vigil."

"Tomorrow? Easter Sunday?"

"This is deemed a crisis by both sides. The holiday cannot be allowed to interfere."

Crisis or no, a good part of the country shut down the following day. Most of the Vigil staff took the day off. Lori, her eyes smeared with a healing ointment because of her mildly scorched corneas, woke up feeling restless, and was soon dressed and on her way to the Lighthouse. Her boyfriend Geoff had not taken the change of plans well, but she didn't feel like sitting around pretending to celebrate something she didn't believe in anyway. She'd never really liked hard-boiled eggs, either.

She emerged from the T station. From the Pru stop it was only a few blocks to the Lighthouse. It was a thin, clear morning of early spring, the pastel sky high and remote. The streets were quiet. Vigil Plaza was nearly deserted— surprisingly so, after the throngs of the last few days. She saw no need to use the tunnels today. She checked in and consulted the status display. Fomalhaut was away. Counting Lori, the Lighthouse had only a dozen inhabitants. It should have been twenty or more, but several Ants had failed to show up on schedule. She made her way to her office and sat at her desk, ready to handle any situation that might come up. But the phone did not ring. She wound up staring idly out at the empty plaza, too unsettled to invent a way to make herself useful.

The General Alarm blared out. It was a sound she had heard in training, but had never heard in actual use. She sat there frozen, trying to remember what she was supposed to do in those circumstances. The plaza was still deserted.

The intercom clicked on. A shaky voice announced, "This is Monique Vincent. The Lighthouse is being invaded by military forces of the United States. As the senior Vigil officer present, I instruct all staff to gather up any critical materials and abandon—"

She was interrupted by the sound of many hurrying footsteps and male voices calling out peremptory commands. There was the sound of a struggle, and a new voice came over the intercom.

"This is Lt. Colonel Mitchell Garland of the United States Army. By order of the President, I have taken command of this facility. All members of the Vigil staff are required to assemble in the main lobby at once. You will not be harmed. You will be detained for less than twenty four hours. Any attempts at escape or resistance will be met by overwhelming force."

Suddenly she heard a sizzling, popping sound and the screams of men. A second later, automatic weapons fire could be heard in the Lighthouse for the second time in two days. Lori heard it faintly from somewhere below her as well as over the intercom.

"Sergeant, take out—" The intercom went dead.

Lori sat there trembling. She looked wildly out the window, seeing nothing unusual. How had these invaders gained entry to the Lighthouse? The tunnels! She turned to her computer and started fumbling with the keyboard. Struggling to remember what to do, she navigated through the Lighthouse control system until she came to the

Emergency Response screen. Some of its options required the use of her password. For a few dreadful seconds it was absent from her mind. "Ah!" She remembered it at last, typed it in, invoked the function screen. She clicked the Seal Tunnels button, then clicked on the confirmation button.

TUNNELS SUCCESSFULLY SEALED. EMERGENCY AUTO-RESPONSE SEQUENCE INVOKED read her screen.

She sagged back in momentary relief. At least she had prevented any reinforcements from joining whatever mob had already gotten in.

She heard more gunfire from below. On top of that, a rising, throbbing sound drew her attention back to the window. A dozen angular black helicopters appeared from around the nearby buildings, swept forward, and arrayed themselves in a hovering line along both wings of the Lighthouse. She could see the two men sitting in the cockpit of the nearest of them.

Lori leaped out of her chair, away from the window, out of her office. What must she do? Surrender to soldiers who seemed to be firing at her friends? Allow these invaders to loot and defile the magnificent Lighthouse?

"Gather any critical materials…"

Monique's last words resonated in her mind. She must grab what she could, and escape if at all possible. What was the greatest treasure of the Vigil?

The Stones.

No…she must not allow *them* to fall into the hands of these thugs. She must not! She thought wildly. With the tunnels blocked, she would have to find some other way out. Explosions rumbled in the distance. Maybe the invaders were trying to break through the tunnel barriers already. The hangar? Her office was on the fourth floor of the west wing. The hangar was in the east wing. She would probably be cut off if she tried to reach it. Besides, she had no training in operating a flyer. But she couldn't just walk through bullets and out the front door.

Ha! She ran down the corridor, toward the hub of the building and the base of the tower. With security measures in place she had to card her way through every door she came upon, which should hamper her enemies more than herself. But even as she reached the fourth floor lobby she heard soldiers charging up the stairs. She flung herself at the bank of elevators and touched a contact. In a rare show of good luck for the Vigil, or perhaps of clever computer programming, a car was present on the floor. Lori dived in as soon as the doors opened wide enough to admit her. They closed just as the first soldiers poured out of both stairwells, brandishing their weapons. "Floor Eighteen!" shouted Lori. Would her clearance still give her access to that restricted floor? The car moved upwards. Lori blessed Fomalhaut's odd failure to recode her access privileges, then shrieked and recoiled at the sound of bullets striking the elevator door.

Now her anger blazed up. Bastards! She would see to it that their conquest of the Lighthouse went as poorly as possible. The elevator deposited her on the same laboratory floor as yesterday. She whacked the "Stop" contact to hold the car and raced off toward the stress laboratory. It admitted her. The red suit still hung on its armature, gleaming in the light of several spotlights. She entered the firing range and stepped up to examine it.

It was more complicated than it appeared from a distance. The metallic red and purple-black fabric was subtly marked and patterned, though the patterns were elusive and might vanish at any shift of her perspective. Various short seams here and there were more definite and permanent. Two golden egg-shaped hemispheres were mounted at the hips. The gloves had golden strips that ran along the fingers.

The suit did not appear to have been harmed at all, by either gunfire or Fomalhaut's blistering ERASER beam.

Lori grabbed at it and tugged, trying to get the thing down from the armature. It came loose easily and flopped down into her arms, cold and glassy. She held it up before her. It appeared to be a one-piece jumpsuit, not very large, but still bigger than she was. Well, baggy fit or no, it should still protect her. She turned it around to the back, where a seam ran down to the waist. She fumbled at this, finding that it came open readily, though she was not sure exactly how.

The floor shivered beneath her. A rumbling boom reached her ears from somewhere.

Shivering herself, she kicked off her shoes and wiggled into the suit, never again able to remember exactly how she had done it or how she'd gotten the back fastened up again. She always remembered what happened next. As she stood there with the suit hanging from her limbs it began to flow and shrink, tightening around her. She yipped, afraid this python-suit might crush her, but the contraction stopped just at the point of comfort, leaving her encased in a glittering metallic body-stocking from neck to toe.

Well! She had no time to waste pondering this. The tower shuddered again, more strongly. She had a mission to complete.

Now she faced a more frightening task than confronting the soldiers. She returned to the elevator and said firmly, "Floor Thirty." The lights in the car flickered, but it moved up the shaft.

A few moments later Lori Wu stood at the base of the ladder leading to the summit of the Lighthouse. Dust and smoke swirled into the room from outside. Detonations crashed against her ears. A helicopter drifted slowly by the tall open windows like an insectoid face looking in at her. Lori dropped to the floor and crawled toward the outer wall to stay out of sight. By now she was panting with fear. When the helicopter sound grew fainter she got up on her knees and looked out. What was intended to be a glance turned into an extended stare. Vigil Plaza was full of troops, tanks, and armored vehicles. Even as she watched, two tank cannons roared, sending shells smashing into the lower levels of the tower. Helicopters sent missiles into the wings. Already the greater part of the Lighthouse was a shambles or aflame.

Movement from the east wing caught her eye. The main hangar door was opening, a large segmented panel that took up a good part of the roof of that wing. When only a slit of it was open a white wasp-waisted flyer darted out. Lori gasped. It was one of Perturbare's flyers; could he possibly be inside it? Its cockpit was crammed full of five or six people. The flyer wheeled about, pitched up, and stood on its tail. Three helicopters instantly yawed to target it. The main propulsion lantern in the rear of the flyer blazed orange. Even as the flyer accelerated straight up, ERASER beams licked out from it faster than she could follow, cutting two helicopters to bits. One managed to fire a missile before crashing and exploding on the plaza, but it went wild. The flyer was gone in seconds. Lori's heart beat wildly. At least someone had gotten away!

Then the hangar also exploded, the door panels and much other debris tossed out like leaves by an awesome rising blast of yellow-white flame. Lori felt the searing heat on her face. The blast knocked her on her back, but she bounced right back up again, staring hypnotized at the inferno that was now engulfing the entire east wing. There was one bunch of flyers that would not fall into the hands of the military.

You there! In the tower!

Lori looked around for the source of the amplified voice.

Do not move! Remain where you are! Do not move!

Lori glanced down. Laser beams were dancing over her chest and dazzling her eyes. Her heart sank. Over the roar of the flames she heard the beating rotor of a helicopter just overhead. Suddenly she knew she had only seconds. She flung herself back from the window. Bullets poured in, hitting the ceiling. She crawled over to the ladder and sprang up it as fast as she could, into the very blazing presence of the Stone. Biting her lip, eyes wide and staring, she approached it. The helicopter noise was loud. She heard ropes skittering over the roof. Soldiers were yelling just a few feet over her head. She reached out and grabbed the Stone, freeing it from its base. A fine chain was attached to its narrow point. She dared not wear the Stone, even now. She glanced down at the red suit, wishing she'd thought to bring a paper bag. She studied the narrow seams which pleated its surface in places. Pockets...? She ran her finger along one; it came open. She stuffed in the Stone, feeling its hardness against her thigh. She eyed the drawer, heard loud footfalls on the roof, yanked it open. She gasped. There rested the other three Stones, burning in all their richness and majesty. They too were mounted as jewelry. She plucked up the verdant Ring of Life and dropped it into another pocket. She grabbed the great purple Brooch of Adamance, the very sight of which augmented her strength and resolve, and dropped it in after the ring. The smallest, and perhaps most awesome of the Stones, the blue Stone of Truth, was mounted in a silver circlet or fillet, too big to fit in a pocket. Thinking of no better option, she reached behind her, opened up the back of the suit, dropped in the Circlet, and closed it back up again. She felt the burning cold of the Stone against the small of her back, separated from her skin only by her thin blouse.

And that was all the time she had. Ropes dangled into view beyond the columns, followed rapidly by booted feet. Lori sprang for the ladder. "Halt! Halt!" cried a voice. Rifles stuttered. Lori felt a great kick in her left side. She almost fell, but managed to reach the ladder and drop to the floor below. She staggered into the elevator, and knowing nothing but a desire to escape, yelled " Floor One!"

As the car plummeted she gingerly felt her side. She was sore and winded, but the suit was not pierced, and neither was she. Still, being shot was not at all a pleasant experience, even while armored. How on Earth could she possibly get past the hundreds of armed soldiers outside, especially with her vulnerable head bobbing naked atop the suit?

The issue was deferred as the car ground to a rough, screeching halt, throwing her to the floor. The end of a twisted steel beam pierced the side of the car, followed instantly by a rush of hot gasses and a great roar. Lori screamed, but could not hear it. The lights went out, replaced by weak emergency lighting which lit the haze of dust inside the car.

Coughing, Lori hauled herself upright. The elevator's control display was dead. The doors were shut. Lori found that she was sobbing and fought to get herself back under control.

It was no good staying here. By now it was clear that the forces outside meant to level the Lighthouse. She stared at the doors. Well. This red suit of hers was similar in appearance to Fomalhaut's exploration suit. Maybe it had the same kind of strength-enhancing properties. She worked her fingertips between the doors and strained to open them. They parted about an inch, but no further effort on her part made any difference.

What other resources did she have? The Stones? No, they were like crystallized ideas, potent to living minds and spirits, but ineffective against the physical world...as far as she knew. She must escape before the tower crumbled around her, or she was engulfed by flames or fumes. She glanced up. Yes, a ceiling hatch. Constructed for the use of beings in some cases over seven feet in height, the hatch was two feet above her outstretched arms.

She glared at the doors, hating them. Why couldn't they just go away?

The suit suddenly went slightly stiff. It hummed or vibrated just at the limit of her perception. The very spot on the door she was looking at quietly dissolved into a powder which sifted onto the floor. Lori gasped. She tracked her eyes along the door panels. An uneven line of dissolution followed the path of her gaze. In a moment the sundered panels gave way, collapsing into the car. The suit relaxed. The elevator was between floors. Lori kicked away a bit of remaining debris, crawled out, and dropped into a dark corridor. More impacts rocked the walls.

Apparently this red suit was more than mere bulletproof armor.

She ran to a stairwell. With main power out, most of the powered doors had locked open. The stairs were still clear, yet were quickly filling with smoke. She trotted down them as fast as she could. Smoke was funneling into the stairwell from levels four and five. The air improved once she got past them. She burst out into the central lobby. No one was there, though there was a smear of blood on the floor. Lori ran down the ramp before the sight and smell of it could nauseate her.

The far end of the outer lobby had collapsed into an impassible pile of steel and marble. The ceiling had fallen in. She could see helicopters overhead, still firing missiles. Shrapnel and chunks of debris rained in. Lori raised her arms to try to protect her head.

Besides all the destruction, something else was wrong with this chamber, something more subtle, but at least as chilling.

"Oh, God," whispered Lori as she realized what it was. In the center of the floor was an empty pedestal. Aureus was missing.

Something picked her up and slammed her against a wall. A horrid howl assaulted her ears. Stunned, she looked up through the gaps in the ceiling. One of the helicopters had spotted her and was bringing its Gatling gun to bear for another burst. Lori's arms shot out to fend it off. "Get away from me!" she screamed.

The suit stiffened and hummed. The helicopter flashed out of sight like a toy swept off a desk by an impatient hand. She heard an explosion.

She sat up dizzily and looked at the mass of rubble blocking her escape. Not far beyond it were hundreds of soldiers, but by now she was past caring. Again she extended her arms. With grasping hands she gestured as though she would sweep all the debris away. With a great groan and roar the blocks and beams began to shift and move aside. She could faintly hear voices crying outside.

"What's going on in there?"

"Something's coming out! One of *them* is still in there! Oh damn!"

The fear in those voices strengthened Lori's resolve. Shakily, she drew herself upright, ignoring the pain in her ribs as best she could. Standing fifty feet away, she clawed at the rubble with the arms of an invisible giant, brushing it aside like crumbs. She advanced, clearing a path before her. Reaching the outer portico, she found its openwork ceiling also collapsed. She could have simply scrambled over the rubble and shortly stood in the open, but now she was convinced that if she were to make it safely past the hundreds of weapons outside, she must not go meekly. She must overwhelm and overawe her enemies, otherwise one shot to the head would finish her. Again she raised her hands, sweeping an aisle clear with a single bold gesture. Already she was coming to understand the feedback the suit offered, and to admire the way it interpreted her motions and intentions. Perhaps it and she were undergoing a synergistic learning process together.

Now her enemies were visible, soldiers wearing face shields and body armor, automatic weapons in their hands. She swept them aside before they could collect themselves enough to aim and fire. At last she stepped clear of the Lighthouse, or what little of it still stood. She had no time to look back at it. Helicopters still swarmed and chattered above, evil tools of terror, it seemed to her. A line of tanks faced her. The Plaza was dense with soldiers. At the moment nothing and no one was firing. She strode forward, all five feet of her, head thrown back defiantly. Soldiers stood as close as twenty feet, their faces stark with awe and fear. Perhaps it was the hidden presence of the Stones that made her seem so formidable. Maybe it was the fearsome, unknown capabilities of the alien superweapon she was wearing. Or maybe it was simply that she, a single, tiny woman, had survived the destruction of the Lighthouse and had now emerged to defy them and face them down. They had dared to attack the home of the Vigil, thinking it undefended. And now one of *them* had come forth to strike them down.

Whatever it was, Lori knew she could not allow the mood to break.

An amplified voice echoed over the plaza from some unknown source.

"Halt where you are. Any attempt to escape or resist will be met by immediate deadly force. In the name of the United States, you are ordered to surrender."

Lori did not hesitate. "I am leaving," she cried in a ringing voice. "In the name of the Vigil, I order you to stand back! Take the Lighthouse if you must. Pull it down, you treacherous killers. But if one man tries to prevent my departure, I will destroy your entire army. Stand aside and let me pass!"

And she would try, too. She would wield her newfound powers until she was overwhelmed and her head shot from her body, probably about two seconds into the battle. With that resolve in mind, and her face frozen in a fierce scowl, she marched on toward the row of tanks.

Brazen it out, she thought. *They don't know what you can do. They don't know you've been wearing this suit for about ten minutes.*

"All forces, hold your fire. Repeat, all forces, hold your fire."

Lori allowed the slightest trace of smugness to curve her mouth. She glared at the ranks of men she passed, forcing most of them to drop their eyes. Some of them looked back at her with respect, some with fear. A few had the grace to show a little shame.

She passed the tanks, the lighter armored vehicles, and more soldiers. Once she was beyond the encircling military ring she felt particularly vulnerable. The back of her head seemed to tingle. A single sharpshooter could blow out her brains and make their victory complete. She made sure to keep her head held high, in the attitude of one who stands above all possible harm. The attitude of Fomalhaut, for example. If only he'd been here!

The area just beyond the combat zone was thick with fire trucks and emergency vehicles. Their civilian crews stared at her as she passed. She barely managed not to jump as the firing resumed behind her. In the empty streets beyond the fire trucks, she stopped to look back. Shells and missiles were again pouring into the Lighthouse. The broken shell of the tower finally gave way and crumbled into the ruins. Great clouds of dust and smoke rose skyward.

A police line held back crowds of civilians a block further on. The police hurriedly cleared an aisle for her as she approached. Dazed, in pain, and full of grief, she hardly noticed as she passed among them until someone cried out "I'm sorry!"

Lori swiveled to regard this person. "The Vigil will stand again," she promised, eyes wild.

Chapter 8

Disarray

Possum Perturbare's underground complex was absurdly vast for one man and one computer. It had so many similar, redundant labs, workstations and offices that even he could barely tell one from another. Sometimes he'd look up from hours of absorbing work and realize with a sense of disorientation that he didn't quite know where he was. Yet he found it pleasing to walk into a lab on any upper level of the Shaft and find that he'd not wandered into this particular nook for months or years. It lent an element of exploration to his daily labors.

The suite he'd chosen today was a bit more distinctive than some. It opened onto the Shaft itself, its windows offering a view all the way up and down the great cylindrical pit at the core of his complex. The same was true of a dozen other comparable lab suites, but it was not true of a hundred others. Even at that, most levels of the Shaft were taken up by hangars and the vast, automated manufacturing floors which Perturbare rarely visited.

At the moment, Perturbare was studying a screen of equations describing a possible means of penetrating to other realities farther removed than those accessible through his original inter-universe frame-shifter. Such transits could be highly dangerous, as he'd already discovered through his experience with Raintree. Breaching still more divergent universes could be even more dangerous, a matter with which he also had some recent experience. Still, it was always nice to know the method for doing something, even if actually doing it might not be prudent.

To occupy his hands while pondering the equations, Perturbare crunched away at a big mixing bowl full of Cheerios and strawberry juice. A television was droning away nearby, occupying the small fraction of his attention he reserved for monitoring popular culture and its manipulative grasp on the populace. Despite his frequent and creative incursions into the public airwaves, advertisers gamely persisted in trying to reshape minds to their own ends. Right now the channel Brainchild had selected was showing a diamond advertisement. People reduced to silhouettes went through stereotypical culturally-approved rituals of romance, all of them revolving around the small stone which was the only thing clearly visible in the image.

"How else can three month's pay get sunk into one tiny, rather common bit of rock?" asked Perturbare in irritation. "Hmm. Brainchild, what's our capacity for diamond synthesis?"

"Minimal at present due to limited need, but it could easily be ramped up to any reasonable level."

"Okay. I want you to produce an assortment of perfect cut diamonds for every person on Earth. Stones ranging from about five carats on down. White stones, blue ones, other fancy colors. Total weight of each package should be fifteen carats or so. Mail them out all at once when ready. That should make everybody happy. Everybody except that damned cartel."

"Very well. I'll get started at once."

"Wait though. Only five carats each for members or associates of the cartel itself. And make theirs all brown. That'll fix 'em."

To most ears, Brainchild's voice had the same bright, efficient, cheerful quality no matter what it was saying at the time. Over the years Perturbare had learned to be more discriminating. He couldn't have said how he did it, but somehow he always knew when the computer was about to deliver bad news.

This time, the hair stood up on the back of Perturbare's neck before he'd heard three words.

"Excuse me, Doctor. I'm picking up a sudden increase in encrypted communications from the American military. An assault on the Lighthouse is imminent."

Perturbare dropped his spoon into the bowl. "What the hell? How imminent?"

"Their forces are already on the move."

Perturbare sat at his workstation for thirty seconds with his mouth hanging open.

"Doctor, there is a general alarm at the Lighthouse. Special forces have invaded from the tunnels."

"Shit! What's the situation there?"

"Skeleton staff because of the holiday. I'd estimate twenty people are present. Fomalhaut is absent. He's on his way to a scheduled meeting with the American President. I detect him over northern Mexico."

"Neatly done, getting him out of the way like that," said Perturbare ruefully. "What are our assets at the Lighthouse?"

"A single two-place flyer. Eighteen enemy helicopter gunships and twenty four tanks are moving up, as well as five hundred troops."

Perturbare banged his fist on the console before him. "How is it that I didn't hear about this operation until now?" he demanded.

"They must have refrained from using any form of electronic communication in the course of arranging this. Evidently they also avoided any security cameras, microphones, or anything else I might access. It was adroitly done, if I may say so."

"Adroitly indeed. Well, use our flyer to get as many Vigil people out of there as you can."

"Yes, Doctor. I also wish to mention the presence of a U.S. carrier battle group two hundred miles off the coast of British Columbia. I hadn't given it any thought until now, but it would seem to be significant."

"Yeek! Raintree's alone at the experimental station, isn't he?"

"I believe so."

Perturbare made a few quick mental calculations, not much liking the results.

"Launch sufficient aerospace vehicles to defend the station from any possible attack," he said tensely. "Don't attack the warships. Defensive posture only. Even if the station has adequate defenses of its own, Raintree won't know how to use them. Try to contact him. Get him to our flyer and out of there."

"Very well."

Brainchild wasted no time. Perturbare heard the whir and rumble of great doors opening in the depths of the Shaft. He pushed back his chair and stepped out onto the balcony just off the workroom. Two thousand feet below was part of his armada of attack flyers, looking small and numerous as grains of rice in a bowl. Orange light flared from some fraction of them. Swiftly they rose, rushing past his vantage point just seconds after their liftoff, deadly white flyers of every configuration, remote-controlled weapons, most of them without any capacity for human occupation. A hundred and fifty of these went booming past, penetrating the planar whitefield that hid the shaft's entrance some five hundred feet overhead. Cackling alarmingly, Perturbare did a gleeful little dance as they went by.

"Well done, Brainchild," he said, thrilled at the sight of this great projection of force. "What's their ETA to the station?" He already knew the answer to within five minutes, but he might as well get Brainchild's more precise figure.

"Thirty one minutes." That was as fast as he could expect his machines to cover the nine or ten thousand miles between Tierra del Fuego and British Columbia.

"This could be a race," said Perturbare with a sudden mercurial unease.

"The carrier is launching planes. Enemy ETA to the Station is twenty seven minutes."

"Crap! Any word from Raintree?"

"So far no response from him."

Perturbare spat out some sizzling curses. "If I had been allowed to connect you into the blasted Vigil facilities, we'd be able to handle this."

"True. I'm now detecting the launch of submarine-based cruise missiles. Target is the experimental station, impact in fifteen minutes."

By now Perturbare was sweating, as tense as if he himself were under attack. "All right. If Raintree doesn't turn up, launch our flyer there in time to take out those missiles. How many are there?"

"Four so far. Five now. Six."

"That could be tough. Do your best. Any sign of Canadian military activity?"

"Their forces have just gone on high alert. A Canadian destroyer is seventy five miles northwest of the battle group."

"Better put me in touch with the Canadian PM. Make it a video call."

"Yes, Doctor. I'm receiving a call from Fomalhaut."

"Tell him to stand by. First the PM."

"Doctor, his office is accepting the call. They will also accept our video, but will not transmit."

Perturbare's lips curled into a sneer. He returned to the workroom, plopping down in front of a comm station. "Complete the call. And give me their security cam video of the PM."

Perturbare's screen lit up to show black-and-white video of the leader of Canada, taken from an angle near the ceiling. He was sitting at his desk talking animatedly into a phone, his face twisted with anxiety and a bit of anger. He hung up that phone and snatched up another. The light beneath the camera on Perturbare's comm station came on.

"Hello, is this Perturbare?"

"Yes it is, Mr. Prime Minister. How's it going? Was that your buddy the President on the other line?" Perturbare leaned into his camera. He deliberately kept his eyes a little too wide, a little too glassy, his grin a little too fixed.

"Yes, yes, it was." The tone of the response indicated a harried man whose life had grown many times more complicated in the last few minutes. "I won't even bother to ask how you knew that. What do you want?"

"Oh, I dunno," said Perturbare, turning up the intensity of his gaze another notch. "I just found myself thinking about your fair country for some reason. How peaceful it is, or was, until your friendly neighbors to the south decided to act up. I love to visit Canada whenever I get a chance. Did you know, I was in Halifax when the Queen visited there a few weeks ago? Yup, I was standing just a few feet away as you shook her hand. She's such a dignified lady. I got to thinking about how it would look if some nanoconstructors got loose and rewove her lovely salmon suit into a transparent polymer while she was on parade. You know, that kind of thing can happen nowadays, what with technology being so rampant. And she already has enough problems to deal with, and so do you, with those pesky Quebecois separatists and all. When's the next vote on that coming up? I hope your voting machines are fully reliable. Hey, I hear the Queen is planning to visit Toronto in a few months. I'll bet you're looking forward to that."

"Look, button it, will you?" broke in the Prime Minister. "Spare me your threats, if that's what you call them. I'm not planning to launch an assault against your friends in the Vigil. And I've refused the Americans permission to land troops on Canadian soil. Their air strike unfortunately is not about to turn back. You know how they get about things like that. It's a *fait accompli*. But I promise you, they will pay a price for this latest arrogant action. The Vigil has done nothing against us. We made an agreement to permit their station on our territory, and we do not revoke it. This is the very best I can do. Are you satisfied?"

Perturbare studied his screen for a long moment, searching the flickering image for any hint of disingenuousness. He saw none.

"I am, sir. It's been a pleasure doing business with you." Perturbare broke the connection, suspecting he'd not handled the call optimally, yet lacking time to dwell on it. "Well, that defuses about ten percent of the military threat to the station. All right, Brainchild, give me Fomalhaut."

This time he got full two-way video, for all the good it did him to stare into Fomalhaut's reflective helmet. He was seated in one of those inelegant Vigil flyers.

"Fomalhaut. You've heard the news."

"I have. Perturbare, I must ask you now to defend the experimental station to the best of your ability."

"I'm already trying my best."

Fomalhaut seemed to relax fractionally at the news. "Thank you."

"Where are you off to?"

"I'm about to turn back to Boston to salvage whatever I can, though it is probably futile. Fomalhaut out."

The connection ceased. Perturbare sat blinking at the black screen.

"Doctor, I have video of the attack on the Lighthouse."

"Let's see it."

The screen lit up to a scene of fire and destruction. Helicopters and tanks were systematically reducing the Lighthouse to rubble. Perturbare studied the scene in amazement.

"Why are they destroying it? You'd think they'd want to loot or occupy the place. But I suppose they know they can't hope to hold it. Fomalhaut by himself could take it back from any conventional military force. I guess their only hope is to raze the place while Fomalhaut is lured away. Without the Lighthouse, the Vigil is without its headquarters and its main symbol. What a shame. That building was among the most beautiful in the world."

"Its classical aesthetic was indeed unusually pure and graceful."

Perturbare noticed something odd about the tower. "Brainchild, have that cameraman zoom in on the top level of the Lighthouse."

Synthesizing the voice of videographer's director, Brainchild ordered him to get the shot. The columns that ringed that summit floor were lit by ordinary daylight only. The light of the Stone was absent.

"Looks like they've been doing some looting after all," Perturbare muttered. "I wouldn't have thought they'd have the stones to snatch the Stones."

"I have information on Vigil casualties."

Perturbare felt his stomach tighten. "Let's hear it."

"Ten were taken prisoner in the tunnels. Someone inside got hold of an ERASER weapon and attacked the first group of commandos. He and three others were killed by the commandos, who have taken two other prisoners within the Lighthouse. I rescued five in the flyer. Aureus was removed by the soldiers and is now in the possession of the Army."

Perturbare started at that. "They took Aureus? That took a lot of nerve. A lot of stupid, ignorant nerve. What about the Stones?"

"There is no word of them."

The camera view zoomed back and jerked back down to ground level, just in time to show a great pile of debris being swept aside like a pile of styrofoam blocks. A figure could be seen advancing through the dust.

"Whoa! Who is that? Get that camera zoomed in on her!"

Brainchild complied. Perturbare was astonished to see the petite Lori Wu, looking a little the worse for wear.

"She appears to be wearing Kern Harner's engineering suit," observed Brainchild.

"So she does." Perturbare felt like jumping up and down. "Good for her! That feisty little vixen."

"Apparently she has delivered some sort of an ultimatum. She is demanding to be allowed to pass. Their commander is calling in for orders."

"Big mistake. Are you into their comm system?"

"I am."

Perturbare smiled with wicked delight. "Then that's an easy one. Order them to let her through. Ha! There's another one the Vigil owes me."

The reason Fomalhaut had not turned back at once upon receipt of the General Alarm was that until now he had not dared speak or move. The instant he had learned of the treacherous, paranoid, unjustified attack on the Lighthouse he had been seized by a rage which enormously surpassed his mild previous experiences with the emotion. His only desire had been to bail out of this awkward flyer, blaze his way into Washington DC, and reduce the center of the perfidious American government to smoking ruins. Indeed, he had been so alarmed by the violent thoughts and impulses racing through his mind that he'd found it necessary to retreat from his body, to withdraw into himself for meditation and to re-exert control over himself and his actions. His flyer had continued on its preset course while its pilot's seat was occupied by a limp, unseeing person whose body was kept from falling over only by the intelligence of the exploration suit.

At times like this he greatly missed his star-faring Frame with its pocket universe generator, the perfect retreat for moments like this when the world was just too much.

Obviously the meeting with the President had been a sham from the first, a ruse to lure him away from the Lighthouse. Certainly the President had never been present at the "neutral ground" of the Mexican resort he'd suggested as their venue. Fomalhaut felt extremely foolish, though he could find no good reason to fault himself, other than perhaps for having too much faith in the rationality and honor of human beings. While he had foreseen that the growing insecurity of the Americans would eventually result in an attack, he had not expected it to come so soon, or with so little provocation. Nor had he expected it would be so cowardly, or so violent.

These were not thoughts conducive to restoring needed calm. He put them aside as best he could and settled on his plan. He had only minutes; the flyer was already descending toward the Yucatan peninsula.

Inserting a finger into a socket on the control console, he reprogrammed the flyer's autopilot. Then he got up, slid open the side hatch, and flung himself into the stratosphere. The propulsion lanterns on his heels and shoulders shot him up to the edge of space, his course designed to return him to Boston. The suit's radar interference field would prevent him from being detected.

He had disliked traveling by flyer, but for the sake of appearances he had done it. This culture made an unfortunate association between non-vehicular flight and absurd comic-book superheroes. Now this had worked out to his slight advantage. The flyer would make an aggressively high-speed approach to the meeting site and attempt to land. He foresaw that the Americans would try to destroy it. If they succeeded, it might create some confusion as to whether he were still alive. If not, it might at least create uncertainty as to his whereabouts.

Fomalhaut's flight path carried him high over the American capital. He looked down at it with a feeling like cold iron in his chest. Probably the President was not there. If he had any sense, he would have fled the city for fear of retaliation.

Just past Washington he lit his lanterns and bent his path down towards the atmosphere. Making no effort to reduce his speed, he chose to enter like a meteor, letting his impact with the air exchange speed for heat. Pink-orange plasma flickered past his helmet as he plunged in, trailing a plume of ionized air. He was creating quite a spectacle for the people below, but for once he did not mind. While still a hundred miles out he activated his long-range imager, providing a direct perception of the ruins of the Lighthouse.

Their task complete, the military forces there were withdrawing as quickly as they'd arrived. Fomalhaut sensed a great deal of fear in their ranks. They were like children who had done great mischief in the absence of their parents, and who now feared the consequences. He would not go there just yet. He could accomplish nothing worthwhile.

By now he had slowed to terminal velocity to drop out of the sky just over the city. He was about to end his scrutiny of the Lighthouse to check on the Vigil's waterfront facility and Stingray's moored submarine when a flare of pain and grief stabbed at him from out of the ruins. Someone was still alive in there. He landed in the plaza, bending all his attention to the weakening psychic voice crying out from somewhere in that rubble. The last few troops scattered and fled, though he scarcely took note of them. Fomalhaut recognized the thread of thought coming from the ruins. It was Monique Vincent, one of the Vigil's first employees, and one of its most capable and loyal. Fomalhaut walked in through an aisle which had somehow been cleared of debris. He laid hands on one of the scattered blocks and read its recent past. It had been brushed aside by some invisible force; he surmised it had been an extremely powerful electrostatic field, presenting interesting implications. He turned, caught sight of the fleeing soldiers, focused on the one who gave the strongest sense of mental presence. Looking into his mind more deeply, he caught a memory of a small dark-haired figure wearing a polished red suit. Fomalhaut felt a tingle rush up his spine at that fugitive mental image, another atavistic physiological response he had once not known his kind still possessed, but which seemed to be commonly evoked by the events of this period of history.

He had no time to pursue that thought now. He turned back to the ruins and sought out the pain and terror of that lost thread of thought. To make this contact he would need stillness of mind. To do his duty to this person he pushed aside all thoughts of vengeance, quieting his heart and mind, thinking of Monique, seeking to smooth the quantum chaos that lay between his mind and hers. When the bridge was established, he crossed it.

Monique. I have come. Be still and brave. I will free you.

Fomalhaut? Thank God...

Fomalhaut now had a clear mental image of her location and condition. She was well back in the west wing, pinned beneath a steel door held down by many tons of concrete and other debris. She was alive only because the top of the door had landed on a fallen I-beam and had therefore not fallen flat. It would not be easy to reach her.

He grabbed broken slabs of marble and threw them aside. He sliced through steel beams with his wrist-mounted ERASERs and tossed away the sections. He must cover a hundred feet in this arduous manner before Monique's injuries could overcome her. And yet he must not proceed so violently that he finished the job the Army had begun. As he worked, striving for a balance between delicacy and speed, he kept his presence in her mind, offering comfort and reassurance. Thus he was particularly annoyed when the suit's comm system announced an incoming signal on the U.S. Government's emergency channel.

"What is it?" he snapped uncharacteristically. "I'm rather busy here."

"Fomalhaut, this is President Hohman calling."

Fomalhaut's carefully nurtured calm threatened to rupture at that announcement. His connection to Monique was broken. He trusted himself to say nothing more than "Speak."

"I just want you to know that I understand what you must be feeling now. The actions taken by the military, at my direction, can only appear treacherous and craven to you. And perhaps they are. But I need to try to make you understand why we had no real choice in the matter."

"If you can make me understand that," said Fomalhaut carefully, "I will feel less trepidation when attempting to encompass the Zurali Nth-dimensional transfer of the soteratic peri-axon function to the pre-string picosecond following the creation event." To emphasize his remark, to himself at least, he lifted and flung away a particularly large chunk of steel-reinforced structural decking.

"Ah...well...I'll do my best. Please listen. Ever since my predecessor made the decision to permit you to set up shop in this country—a decision which I believe was correct at the time—the world has been in fear of domination by one group of extraterrestrial powers or another. You protected us from the Para-men, for which we are grateful. But frankly, once that task was complete, it would have been best for our peace of mind if the Vigil had just gone away. The situation was tolerable until recently, but when your group broadcast reports of human weakness to alien civilizations of unknown nature and intent, we considered that a threat to world security. Most of the world is with me on this. The Russians, the Chinese, French, Israelis, Japanese, all are in accord. Look at T'Ukudu. He called himself a mere Servant of the T'Utahnti race. Yet we all know what a formidable warrior he could be. Twice the size of a man, stronger than a gorilla. He could kill a man with a single touch."

Fomalhaut pulled a shattered desk out of the way and threw it over his shoulder. "He was also the gentlest and most inoffensive of souls," he snapped.

"Perhaps so. But who knows about those Makers of his? If they decided we were a threat, or simply chose to take advantage of our relative weakness to plunder our world, they could send an army of these Servants. Or they could breed them here in their chemical vats. Or what about Aureus? A deadly robot claiming to be from another galaxy. An unpredictable device based on a technology beyond anything at the command of even Perturbare. We hope to learn something from our study of it. Most likely we'll choose to destroy it while we have the chance. Can you understand why?"

Fomalhaut had been using his palm-mounted SASER disks to crumble a huge block that was wedged into place with unusual stubbornness. The President's remark took him aback. He belatedly remembered that Aureus was indeed absent from its pedestal. "Are you saying," he said carefully, "that you have taken Aureus?"

"Yes we have. The robot is on its way to a research and containment facility at this very moment."

Still Fomalhaut did not resume his work, though Monique's need still resonated in his mind. "That is an extremely foolish action," he said quietly.

"Why? According to my reports, the robot appears to be deactivated."

"It is not deactivated. It is merely temporarily, voluntarily inert. It could awaken at any time, and it will do so if it feels in any way threatened or impeded. Aureus may be the greatest single power on this planet. You have no idea what you face in it."

The President sounded a little nonplussed. "Well, if that's as you say, perhaps we'd do best to destroy it at once.

Such a creature cannot be allowed free rein on this planet if it's as dangerous as you say."

Fomalhaut bent down and resumed his digging with renewed ferocity. "You lack the means to destroy Aureus."

The answer came in a tone of some asperity. "My science advisors tell me that no form of matter in the universe can survive direct exposure to nucular fusion energy."

"That at least is true. But the universe contains substances other than ordinary baryonic matter. Even if Aureus is vulnerable to your bombs, I promise you, the instant it realizes its peril it will awaken, and then you will face an implacable foe. The business of Aureus is not with the people of this world. In fact, it has no business at the present time, explaining its inert state. You would do best to leave it in peace."

"We will take that under advisement. But let me turn to yet another alien visitor to our world, perhaps the most disturbing one of all: yourself. I hope you realize why we're not having this conversation face to face. I am protecting myself from your telepathic powers, to say nothing of your purely physical abilities."

The implication that the President feared treachery on Fomalhaut's part sent him close to the breaking point again. "Speaking of protection, are you aware that your savages left one of my staff to perish in the ruins of the Lighthouse? That I am presently trying to free her?"

Hohman went on as if he hadn't heard. "You come to our world claiming to be from the future, or at any rate from the future of some identical world of the past, a concept I've never entirely grasped. You claim to be a member of a species which will someday take over as ruler of this planet. Yet you do not reveal your exact nature, or show your face, leaving us to wonder just who or what you are. Are you some advanced step in human evolution? Are you some other form of life entirely, raised up to a humanlike form and intelligence? Are you some strange freak or robot? A mutant chimpanzee? How will this presumed takeover by your race come about? Will it be by conquest, by genocide? How much longer do we have? You call us savages. Is your entire story a fiction designed to ease the way for an invasion by your race? You remain silent on all these questions."

"I do not know the exact course of the future. I cannot reveal what details I do know, for the obvious reason that I wish that future to unfold without disruption caused by such foreknowledge."

"Frankly, Fomalhaut, it would be better if you and all your kind left our planet."

Fomalhaut thought again of his Frame, hidden in a galaxy void billions of light-years away, not due to return for years. There would be no leaving Earth for him, not anytime soon.

His chemical sensors registered signs of nearby human distress. The suit presented this data to him in the most easily understandable form, that of the odors of blood, vomit, and urine.

For the first time in his life, Fomalhaut addressed another being in clear tones of anger. "You do not have the authority to order me off this planet. Your territorial claims are meaningful only insofar as you can enforce them. If not for me and my kind, you would now be adjusting to the reign of the Para-men. I can't help thinking that you and your entire race would be better off."

"I am the President of the United States," came the stiff reply.

"You are a small-minded venal buffoon, ruler for a brief period of an ephemeral political entity, elected to that position by the uninformed foolishness of an ignorant, shortsighted herd of idiots. Now shut up. I'm getting close to the one I would rescue. Trouble my concentration again, and I may show you that my telepathy does not require proximity or eye contact to be an effective weapon."

He cut the contact. His sensors and his own innate sense of the lay and weight of the debris ahead left him uneasy about the situation he faced. The wreckage was interlocked in such a way that removing any of it might bring the remainder crashing down on Monique's little pocket of space. He could feel her only two meters away, but those two meters would be perilous to cross.

It would not be enough to lift the debris away from her. It must be stabilized, prevented from shifting and collapsing. The only available means to attempt that was his mental influence over matter. It would be a sore trial. Except for his powers of remote perception, Fomalhaut's cerebro-quantum faculties were only average by the standards of his race. Certainly his telekinetic ability could not easily arrest a mass of many tons. Yet it was either that or stand helpless in the presence of Monique's death.

Nothing must intrude on his mind for this operation. He shut down all suit communications, long-range sensors, and other extraneous systems. He even rendered his helmet completely opaque. Vision could not reveal the stability and weight of each bit of rubble. A direct mental perception would. He reached out, felt the interplay of friction and gravity which held the rubble in its fragile state of metastability. He reached out and held. It was all he could do to maintain that exacting mental grip while simultaneously wrestling the overlaying debris away. When he reached the area whose stasis he was preserving he had to subtract each block, beam, and panel from his influence while maintaining the integrity of the rest.

When he drew out and discarded a fallen section of I-beam the load overhead shifted, trying to collapse into a lower-energy configuration. In an instant Fomalhaut found himself mentally bearing the whole weight of the top four floors of the wing. He emitted a grunt of pain and distress. By now he could perceive Monique's crushed leg sticking out from beneath the door. Moving as fast as he could, he hollowed out a cave in the space protected by his mental influence. After a few hours of subjective time he was at last able to fling aside the door and expose Monique. He had no time to evaluate her condition before moving her. He lifted her in his arms, backed away from her almost-tomb, and relaxed his desperate grip on the crushing load of debris, which collapsed at once with a crash and a cloud of dust.

Walking a little unsteadily, Fomalhaut returned to the light of day. Monique's left shin was shattered, the foot still attached only by soft tissues. Other than that, plus the shock and blood loss involved, she seemed only slightly injured, though unconscious.

Already the orderly, methodical, planning part of Fomalhaut's mind was informing him that his outburst at the President had done irreparable harm. But at least he had managed to save this woman.

Outside in the clear air, Fomalhaut lifted off for the nearest hospital. Monique regained consciousness during the brief flight. Seeing where she was, and who she was with, she managed to smile. Fomalhaut literally felt her pain. Lacking T'Ukudu's direct control over the physiological responses of others, he did his best to soothe her.

And then she soothed him.

Thank you for rescuing me. I'm sorry I couldn't save the Lighthouse. I still believe in the Vigil with all my heart, and I will serve it again, if I have the strength.

Fomalhaut looked deeply into her, both through her mind and through her eyes, which after all were the mind's windows. He had indeed saved her, and now her faith and love did much to save a part of him.

Once satisfied with Monique's care and well-being, Fomalhaut flew west at maximum speed, arriving at the British Columbia station to discover that the battle there was over. Dozens of fighter jets and cruise missiles lay burning over a wide area of the mountainous coast. A few units of Perturbare's airfleet had also fallen, but most of it still hovered like angry pale dragonflies, keeping watch as Navy helicopters worked to rescue whichever of its pilots were still alive, and recover the bodies of whichever were not. The station had suffered damage from a few bomb and missile hits. The fires had been contained by automatic systems.

Fomalhaut passed through the whitefield and entered the dome. "I declare this the new headquarters of the Vigil," he said to himself. "As I knew it must one day be."

Ben Raintree was nowhere to be found, neither in the dome, nor in the spire, nor in the surrounding mountains.

"Well, Brainchild, looks like another successful military intervention on our part," said Perturbare as he leaned back in his chair, staring thoughtfully at a tactical display.

"Doctor, I'm picking up something odd."

Perturbare felt his ears twitch at that remark. "And what might that be?" he asked with forced mildness.

"Three Russian fishing trawlers are cruising this way, their position seventy miles to the west. They are behaving oddly, in that although they are under full power, to judge by their sound output and propeller turbulence, they are making a speed of only five knots. They are clearly towing something greater than a normal fishing net."

"Get some dolphins out there to look them over," said Perturbare urgently. His mental alarm bells were shrill. "Do you hear anything else out there?"

"Dolphins have been dispatched. I hear the usual sounds associated with towed trawler nets. Nothing more."

"I don't like this. Try to pick up any radio communications to or from the trawlers."

Perturbare sat chewing his lip for a few minutes while the dolphins, which were actually dolphinoid propulsion beam-driven probes, flew to the scene.

"Dolphins entering the water," reported Brainchild. "Engaging squeak sonar in aperture synthesis mode. Displaying visual."

A 3-D rendered image resolved onto Perturbare's screen, showing the situation in a clear but simplified style. The trawlers were indeed towing nets, but their tow cables did not terminate at the nets. Half a mile behind, they were also attached to the teardrop hulls of nuclear attack submarines.

"American, aren't they?" Perturbare goggled at the screen. This was an impressive feat of trickery. He was not used to being taken by surprise through trickery, certainly not by any military organization.

"*Los Angeles* class, yes. Older vessels, perhaps considered expendable."

"And you can't hear them at all."

"I cannot. Their reactors and screws are shut down. Their internal systems must be running off batteries."

"Looks like an impressive bit of cooperation between the Russians and Uncle Sam," said Perturbare pensively.

"Shall I deploy defenses?"

"That's a pickle. We don't know for sure that they know we're here. If we launch a fleet while they're so close, it's bound to give us away. But if we don't—"

"Doctor, I'm detecting the sound of cruise missile launchings. Confirmed by sonar. Six simultaneous launches, two from each sub."

"Try to get them with the dolphins," said Perturbare tensely.

"They are out of position for interception. The missiles have broken the surface. The dolphins are too slow to catch them. Missiles are on course for our position."

"Well, it looks like they know we're here."

"I am detecting multiple ICBM launches from Russian and American sites. I am detecting multiple SLBM missile launches from multiple submarines in the south Atlantic and south Pacific oceans."

Perturbare's eyebrows shot up. What was going on? Could the paranoia that had led to the attack on the Vigil also have resulted in a spasm of self-destruction for humanity? For a long moment he was at a total loss, his brain seemingly paralyzed. He had gone from smug complacency to a feeling that things were out of control in minutes. "How many—" He stopped, cleared his throat, tried again. "How many launches? Targets?"

"One hundred twenty launches so far. Missiles are still in boost phase. Hard to be precise on targeting at this point. All are bound for the Southern Hemisphere."

"For us, then."

"Most likely."

Perturbare sat back, his face white. "They're not even giving me a chance to surrender. What have I done that's so bad they're willing to wipe me out like a cockroach?"

"You have damaged or destroyed the interests of many rich and powerful men."

"That was a rhetorical question."

"Sorry."

"Anyway, that's sexist. Have I been ignoring the interests of rich and powerful women?"

"Not really."

"Good. What is our tactical situation for missile shootdown?"

"Our defensive satellites can't cope with so many launches. Total launches now at one hundred forty eight. I estimate forty warheads will survive to come within range of our island's defenses. Cruise missile ETA four minutes. First SLBM arrival in seven minutes. First ICBM arrival in twenty minutes."

Perturbare threw himself back in his chair, letting his breath hiss out through his teeth. "Nail as many warheads as you can with the satellites. Scramble the entire airfleet.

Prepare all island defenses. Harden the Pit as soon as the fleet is away. Bring a White Wasp up to the platform in case I need to bail out."

The whir and rumble of flyer deployment commenced at once. This time Perturbare did not step out to witness it, but he was peripherally aware of the swarm of white shapes, some of them quite large, flashing by the windows. The lab was filled with a shifting aurora of orange light, the waste output of hundreds of propulsion lanterns. "Any trouble picking off those cruise missiles?"

"No, they will be easy to stop. The airfleet should also be readily able to destroy the incoming warheads before they can come close enough to do damage."

Perturbare turned away from his screen and looked with grim satisfaction at the continuing inverted hailstorm of departing flyers. He had for years controlled enough force to fend off any possible military assault, even if the location of his perpetually fog-shrouded island at the southern tip of South America should became known. His preferred style of interference in the affairs of man was one of trickery and mischief, but he would respond in kind if threatened by crude force. He'd been forced out of his previous lair by a misguided invasion by the Vigil. He'd never let such a thing happen again.

At last the flyer exodus slowed and ceased. Perturbare's vision swam with purple afterimages left by the glaring orange propulsion lanterns. A warning horn sounded out in the Pit, followed by a renewed rumbling, this time coming from above. Great doors of the most enduring substances Perturbare could produce were sealing off the opening. Only the direct detonation of a nuclear weapon could penetrate them.

"Doctor, a fleet of attack helicopters and helicopter troop carriers has just lifted off from Davis-Monthan Air Force Base in Tucson. Their course is southwest."

Perturbare's face twisted into a mask of dismay. "Toward the Bronze Portal."

"Correct."

"All right. We'll just have to hope our defense measures there will frustrate them. But in case they don't—God, I hate to do this—I don't think we can put it off any longer. Get a message to the Big Guy. Tell him that the Portal is in jeopardy. And tell him—" Perturbare gulped, swallowed. "Tell him there's been a problem with his cousin Ben."

Brainchild's words were as unruffled as always. "Very well. Cruise missiles destroyed. SLBM warheads are three minutes out. The airfleet is about to engage those that survived the satellites. I'm detecting a second wave of ICBM—"

Suddenly the lights flickered and went out. Display screens showed an instant of garbled nonsense and then went dark. Buzzes, whines, and cracklings filled the darkened lab, then ceased. A scent of burned plastic filled the air. The ubiquitous sound of air being channeled from place to place faltered and ceased.

In an uncanny silence Perturbare swiveled his chair toward the Pit. All was darkness except for a wavering orange glow. For an instant he wondered if it was a fire, then remembered the flyer that had been parked at the platform awaiting his use. He stood up and went to the window. He did not see the flyer, but the shadows cast by the propulsion glow were shifting. An instant later the flyer came into view, floating toward the far side of the Pit. It struck a protruding boom, bounced off, and drifted back his way, now a few feet lower then it had been. Obviously Brainchild was no longer in control of it, nor had its built-in automation properly engaged. Perturbare tried to get onto the balcony, and was still groping for the door when the emergency lighting asserted itself at last. He had to trigger the door manually to open it. Gripping the railing, he looked down at the flyer, which floated idly on currents of air like an unfinished balloon animal.

"Brainchild...what happened?" he asked, his voice quavering.

There was no reply.

"Brainchild?"

Nothing.

All right then. It must have been an electromagnetic pulse of vast proportions. At least some of the incoming submarine-launched missiles, probably all of them, had detonated at high altitude, above the point where his airfleet had been waiting to destroy them. It would take the simultaneous detonation of many weapons, probably specialized EMP devices, to produce a pulse sufficient to cripple this facility. Underground as it was, with few metallic connections to the surface, the Pit was invulnerable to any single pulse. Probably every electronic device in the nearer half of South America, if not beyond, had been wiped out. Apparently the superpower militaries had deemed this a matter of little consequence. What serious response could a crippled Argentina and Chile make against the unilateral actions of America and Russia?

The elements of the airfleet which he had sent out to defend the island, hardened as they were, had probably been rendered uncontrollable by the megapulse. In any event, Brainchild's control signals had almost certainly been interrupted. The flyers were probably crashing into the sea at this moment, or raining down on Tierra del Fuego.

And what of Brainchild?

The computer's CPU was completely shielded against any conceivable pulse. Its chemo-optical circuit matrix was not subject to the ill effects of EMPs, and was equipped with shielded backup power supplies meant to survive almost any contingency. If Brainchild had fallen silent, it was only because some layer of its complex interface with the world had been damaged. The synthetic mind itself must be untouched. Right?

Whatever Brainchild's status, Perturbare must assume that the land-based ICBMs were still on their way. The island would soon be blasted clean by nuclear fire. When that happened, Perturbare must be as far away as possible. He looked down at his sole remaining flyer, wandering aimlessly as an air hockey puck, slowly descending on random air currents. He climbed over the balustrade and stood on the narrow lip that rimmed the balcony, his hand clutching the railing, looking down into a depth that suddenly evoked fear rather than pride. Cold sweat and weak knees plagued him. The flyer was drifting approximately toward him, but would not pass directly beneath him. Luckily, the canopy was already open. He opened his mouth for the desperate plunge which was inevitable and imminent.

"Geron—" His throat tightened and closed; the rest was only an agonized squeak of fear. Oh well, he had no audience to impress anyway. The flyer approached its nearest point. It was about fifteen feet down, six feet out, and looked as big as a white slipper. "Goodbye everybody," he heard himself say, releasing his death grip on the railing and flinging himself into space.

He fell...

He crashed down hard in the cockpit, wrapping himself around the pilot's seat, clinging to it like a lover. The flyer lurched. Dazed and half-panicked, Perturbare positioned himself in the seat and grabbed the controls, stabilizing the vehicle with some difficulty. He urged the flyer, a White Wasp, deadliest and most versatile of his manned combat flyers, straight up forty five stories to the level of the door machinery. There he rebooted the flyer's onboard computer, set it to hovering, scrambled out onto a landing platform, and dashed into a control room whose most prominent feature was a large palm-button marked "Emergency Pit Open/Close". He slammed it. The whine and rumble of the machinery was much louder at this level.

The Shaft was soon open, revealing the whitefield beyond. Perturbare eyed the button, then the door, making a few quick mental calculations. He slammed the button again and darted out of the room. His leap into the flyer's cockpit came close to sending him hurriedly to the floor of Level One, but he made it. He grabbed the control sticks, closed the canopy, and blazed clear of the doors a few seconds before they closed again.

Behind him was his finest achievement and best friend, condition unknown, abandoned to the imminent flames.

Stepping out onto one of the terraces of the Spire to brood over the whereabouts of Raintree, Fomalhaut observed something both unsettling and strange. The fleet of flyers surrounding the station lost cohesion, each settling to land in a haphazard way, except for those over the ocean, which moved inland before landing. At the same moment he detected a faint but worrisome pulse of Compton electrons. Finally, he noticed that the tendrils of quantum organization by which Brainchild controlled the flyers and other remote equipment had vanished.

The United States Navy used no such subtle means of communication. Fomalhaut intercepted and decrypted their radio announcement that they were about to launch another strike against the now unprotected station.

This was intolerable.

Fomalhaut lifted off, heading west. Moments later he received the first frantic news broadcasts about chaos in South America caused by the failure of the continent's entire power grid. Planes were crashing. Blinding nuclear explosions had been seen by millions in the far south.

The carrier battle group came into view. Its first planes were already in the air. Cruisers and destroyers were launching missiles. Cruise missiles were bursting out of the water from positions miles distant.

Fomalhaut put all other thoughts aside as he devoted himself fully to improvising the complex tactical pattern he'd need to stop all those weapons.

Red lasers glared from the ERASER units mounted on his wrists. Like incandescent swords they sliced though aircraft and missiles alike. It was the work of a few seconds to render the carrier harmless by destroying its launching catapult. To finalize the job he also carved up its flight deck. As he hovered there he became the focus of anti-air fire from many directions. The shells were nothing to the exploration suit, unable even to deform its surface.

But the missile firings were becoming more numerous. Some would undoubtedly slip through.

He broadcast a message on a military frequency.

"This is Fomalhaut of the Vigil. You will cease your unlawful attack on Canadian territory at once. If you fail to do so, I will sink your entire fleet."

The fire did not cease. Half a dozen missiles slid by beneath him as he hung there petrified by astonishment and outrage. Finally he raised his hands to send these ships to the bottom of the sea.

Another missile came hissing over the waves from an unexpected quarter, the northwest. It plunged into the crippled carrier and exploded, turning it at once into a fireball. The death agony of hundreds of men blazed out to sear his mind. Dazed and shaken, he turned his many senses toward the northwest. Just on the horizon was a Canadian destroyer. Its missile fire was returned by a trio of American warships. A moment later the Canadian too was shattered, sinking, ablaze.

Once more Fomalhaut raised trembling hands, but they faltered and returned to his side. He could not destroy thousands of beings merely to defend an uninhabited structure. They had won.

A few more missiles went up, then the launchers fell silent. Fomalhaut did not bother to destroy them. The damage had already been done.

The ships of the battle group milled around the stricken carrier. Fomalhaut swooped in to pluck from the sea the ejected pilots of the planes he had disabled. The carrier could not launch rescue helicopters; its crew was scurrying about trying to control fires. As he ferried the pilots to nearby destroyers and frigates he opened himself to the emotions radiated by the men, finding a distressing welter of fear, relief, embarrassment, gratitude, hatred, and shame. These men could not decide how to feel about what they had done.

He soared over to the sinking Canadian ship, plucking up the injured two by two and ferrying them ashore. It was a terribly inefficient way to save hundreds of endangered men, but he had no other option. In the end he pulled off twenty, and then the ship was gone, leaving the survivors bobbing in the cold waves. Fomalhaut left them to an American frigate which had the grace to offer its services.

Fomalhaut left the battle scene behind and approached the ruins of the station, a burning shambles that blackened and dirtied the flank of the mountain that had sheltered it. The spire had fallen.

Bleakly he pondered the role he had fallen into. He had arrived on this Earth, in this era, with the mission of being an inconspicuous observer and recorder of the final years of Human history. He had become instead a notorious interloper in Human affairs, a manipulator of a history he did not know in any detail, and now a criminal and perhaps even a murderer, depending on the casualties suffered by the naval fleet.

Still, he could not place all blame for this debacle on himself. He and his few remaining colleagues had been minding their own business, a benefit if anything to the Humans. These Humans were, he reflected, still more than half ape, despite their pretensions to the contrary. They dressed up their sexual obsessions in a pretty conceit of romantic love. They fashioned grand ideals of patriotism to excuse the territorial aggression that still seethed in their apish brains. They devised elaborate economic and political theories to justify and even glorify the rampant greed and selfishness which impoverished most of their fellows and despoiled the world. The fraction of the race that was capable of transcending its gross animal nature was largely despised and suspected by the majority.

What, he wondered bitterly, was a fitting fate for such an unpromising race?

The sensor display in Perturbare's flyer showed an incoming swarm of warheads. There would be no further feints, no more reprieves. If Possum Perturbare wished to live, he must flee. He tilted the nose of his flyer toward the north and accelerated up and away as fast as he could without blacking out. The edges of his vision went grey as monstrous weight crushed him back in his seat.

The air thinned to a blue-black film. It was still thick enough to pulse and flicker as an absurd number of nuclear warheads detonated miles behind and below. Perturbare did not look back. His main base was destroyed; of that he had no doubt.

And Brainchild...?

He winced, twisting his mouth into a hard bitter curve. He should have ordered the computer to transfer its consciousness to another location as soon as he'd known they were under attack. That had probably become impossible as soon as the EMP weapons had detonated. If Brainchild had somehow survived, he had seen no evidence of it as yet.

Perturbare's fingers stabbed wildly at the console, consulting its limited built-in AI for a course for Tucson. His great world-spanning instrumentality had collapsed to himself and this single flyer. He still had lesser bases hidden here and there, but without Brainchild to control their assets they were of little immediate use, even assuming they too were not under attack. At the moment, the best he could hope to do was prevent the American military from overrunning the remote corner of southern Arizona where Possum Perturbare guarded the gateway to another world.

His thoughts crumbled into a waking nightmare of regret, grief, and outrage. The view through the canopy faded from his consciousness, replaced by a black welter of turmoil and pain. The last dispassionate corner of his mind wondered whether this was the onset of madness, then it too was subsumed. The flyer blazed along, mere feet above the sea, its shockwave blasting a furrow in the waves.

An urgent warning tone finally snapped him out of his fugue. He glared at the console displays, their screens blurred by tears, not quite sure where he was. He pieced things together: the Sea of Cortez was just behind, he was rapidly approaching the target area, and someone had him in a missile lock.

He grabbed the attitude controller and jerked it back, pitching up the nose. The main propulsion lantern now bore hard against the ground, shooting him straight up at three Gs. No weapon was fired at him, but then, he was still over Mexican territory.

He gave the flyer its head, climbing until all sensible trace of atmosphere was behind him, then cut power and coasted to a near halt. Then he reactivated the autopilot, set it again to hover, and waited while it killed off all residual motion.

He sat as if in a platform a hundred miles above the southern end of the Quinlan mountain range in southern Arizona. Hovering under power as he was, the gravity in the cockpit was normal. He activated the flyer's ventral sensors. Below he found more than he'd bargained for: at least a hundred attack helicopters, troop carriers in the air and on the ground, and jet fighters orbiting overhead.

All were milling around, searching in standard military patterns. There was no concerted movement toward the site of the Bronze Portal. It seemed clear that the hunters did not know their exact target, though sure enough they knew it approximately. The active defenses he had set up around the Portal would be useless without Brainchild to direct them. All he could count on was the very thorough job he had done of hiding the Portal, covering the site with a sheath of desert rock and vegetation.

Well, to be precise, he could count on that, on himself, and on this flyer. There were too many enemy aircraft for him to engage at close range, but this he need not do. He could sit up here, picking them off one by one at his leisure. It was extreme range for the flyer's weapons, but a few seconds of dwell time at high power should be enough for the beams to do their work.

He opted to use optical targeting, both to remove any ambiguity about what he was shooting at, and for the satisfaction of seeing his enemies fall. With the belly camera at maximum magnification he tracked the choppers, steadied them in the targeting crosshairs, and activated the ERASER beam. He chose a yellow wavelength, good both for penetrating the atmosphere and for showing his foes that even now he could stab at them from on high, untouchable.

Going for the rotor hubs, he brought down one Cobra. "That's for Brainchild," he muttered. Another crash landed on a rocky slope. "This one's on Brainchild." A wavering beam ignited the fuel tank of an Apache. "Compliments of Brainchild."

He kept on that way for some time, lost to everything but the deadly game he was playing, oblivious to the low warning tone sounding in the cockpit. Irritated, he belatedly took note of it, looking aside at another display. An icon representing a nearby satellite was blinking red. It was under power, its orbital vector changing. Heading towards him. Practically upon him.

Perturbare looked up, startled. He could actually see the satellite, a tub-like thing painted pale aqua. It looked Russian. He grabbed the attitude controller and rolled the flyer to put its bulk between himself and the satellite, which exploded. The flyer gave a great slamming surge, and lost power.

Gravity vanished at once; he was in free fall. He heard a hiss. Evidently the cockpit had been holed somewhere. His ears popped. He quickly looked himself over. He seemed unhurt, but he was falling, very much like a rock, from a height of a hundred miles. The earth flew by the canopy in a rapid, rhythmic way. Ah, so he was falling, and also tumbling. It was hard to breathe. He grabbed an oxygen mask from beneath the console and jammed it to his face, swallowing spasmodically to keep his eardrums from popping. His other hand slammed down the big "EJECT" button. Nothing happened. Straining to control his shaking, half-panicked hands, he once again reinitialized the flyer's onboard systems, hoping to provoke a flicker of life. It produced no visible effect, but when he smashed the ejection button again, the bezel surrounding the canopy disengaged from the fuselage. The entire cockpit separated from the wreck of the flyer, becoming an escape capsule. Perturbare got a good look at the hulk before it tumbled out of sight. The bottom of the flyer was smashed and pierced with a hundred shrapnel holes.

Small propulsion lamps mounted around the capsule automatically activated to control its plunge. The batteries that powered them were not strong enough to permit him to fly clear of the scene. They were designed to get him down safely, and no more. By now the sky outside the canopy had brightened to a deep blue as he fell through a layer of thin cirrus. He groped in a locker and pulled out a black ERASER pistol. The hiss of air eased, ceased, and then resumed as air began to stream into the capsule from outside.

The capsule slammed down hard, far harder than it was meant to do. Perturbare was crushed down into his seat. The rebound flung his limbs wildly, limp as stockings. The ERASER flew out of his grip. He bit his tongue hard enough to send blood streaming out of his mouth. The capsule settled into a sudden uncanny stillness. Perturbare sat motionless, trying to steady his mind. The canopy blew off without warning, its retraction mechanism disabled, jangling his nerves yet again. With hot desert air on his face he was motivated to unstrap from the seat and climb gingerly over the sill, his boots crunching down in loose gravel.

The air throbbed with the thud of rotors just out of sight. He squinted around in the unfiltered light, trying to get his bearings. He had come down in a rough, hummocky area of scrub and rock just west of the main Quinlan range.

Somewhere to the south was the inconspicuous rise that sheltered the Bronze Portal. If he could reach it, get through to the other side, he'd be safe. He shuffled forward, dismayed at the effects of his recent battering on his speed and agility.

A group of three Apache helicopters rose over the ridge to his left, swooping directly toward him. At the same moment he spotted a squad of foot soldiers in desert camouflage less than a hundred yards away. He ducked down, scrambling forward, looking for some kind of shelter, but they had already seen him, hard to miss in his once-natty white tunic. They shouted and ran towards him; he hobbled on with teeth clenched in fear.

"Halt! Sir! I'm ordering you to halt!"

Perturbare jumped as though prodded. His viscera felt as if they were dissolving. His mind was screaming at him to stop and raise his hands, but somehow he could not.

"Sir, halt! I will shoot you if you do not halt!"

Perturbare spun, snarled, shouted, "Shoot me then, you eight hundred dollar a month assassin!" He turned away and loped off at his best speed.

"Final warning!"

Perturbare paid no heed. A blow snapped his right shoulder forward. Breathless, he tottered for a moment and fell. He hadn't even heard the shot. He lay with his face practically in some kind of cactus—a final insult—pondering the total lack of feeling in his right arm, the absence of any real pain. He didn't dare raise his head to look. His imagination offered up such gruesome scenarios that the reality would be redundant. A helicopter hovered nearby, its rotor blast throwing dust in his eyes, weapons trained upon him.

A grey veil descended over his vision. Had it been just this morning that he had been Possum Perturbare, seated in his secret lair with all the world's power at his fingertips?

He made out the shadowy forms of soldiers looming over him, then lost consciousness.

Chapter 9

Life in the City

When Fomalhaut arrived at the experimental station he hadn't missed Raintree by much.

Raintree had been experimenting with a Mark I flight harness, wobbling aloft to T'Ukudu's ledge, where he'd sat beside the ever-shrinking mound of grey dust that was all that was left of the Servant. Then the first bombers and cruise missiles had arrived. As Ben watched in horror they began the systematic destruction of the station. Frightened and panicked, his need for peace and solitude violated even here, he had lifted off again, crested the coastal mountains, and made his way east, intent on leaving the Vigil and all its works behind forever.

He soon wished he'd chosen another flight harness. The Mark I was the least capable model, but also the easiest to learn to fly. It was studded with white matchbox-sized boxes from which shone tiny propulsion diodes. Larger boxes on the belt and chest contained the controls and power supply. Without face shielding or supplemental oxygen, he must fly low and slow, but that was enough to put the scene of destruction behind him. The sound of explosions followed him for some time. Guilt flared up as he considered how he had fled without making any effort to contact Fomalhaut or to protect the station. He was surely not the bravest person ever to bear Vigil membership! He actually laughed at that thought. He had never taken himself seriously as a member of the Vigil, now less so than ever.

He poked along at forty knots or so, wondering where he should go. The attacking planes had carried U.S. markings, therefore perhaps he would be wise to remain in Canada. He was supposed to be a Canadian citizen anyway, though of course he remembered little of that. Somewhere in this vast land he had parents, though he wouldn't know what to say to them even if he knew where to find them. Suddenly he found it puzzling and shameful that he'd given them no thought, had made no effort to contact them, since recovering from his injuries.

His wavering flight over the coastal ranges and lakes of British Columbia was cold but very beautiful. He felt a tingle of freedom as he realized he was truly on his own, seeking his own way, for the first time in his life, as far as he could remember. Rather than flourishing, the old images Fomalhaut had planted in his brain seemed to be fading, along with whatever remained of his original memories. It was as if his mind had rejected them, preferring instead to start anew, as if this were an entirely different life.

He touched down atop a few peaks and beside forested lakes to rest, to enjoy the view, and just because he could. Mostly he sailed along at his sedate pace, steering clear of the few small towns he saw below him.

Eventually the mountains dropped away to a watery plain which was still some weeks from spring. The day drew near its end, with any destination still absent from Raintree's mind.

The largest town he had yet seen swam into view on the hazy horizon. Simultaneously, the tiny control console on his chest beeped and showed a "low power" warning.

Raintree blinked in surprise. He had become accustomed to Vigil equipment having inexhaustible sources of energy. Perhaps this harness was so small and simple that it merely stored energy rather than generating it.

Whatever the explanation, the limitations of the harness had determined his destination. He flew on until the display signaled "power critical" and then landed beside a highway.

His first act as an ordinary human (rather than an inhabitant of the Vigil's various ivory towers) was to hide in a stand of fir trees, strip down, and conceal the harness beneath his clothes. Then he returned to the road and set off toward the town at a lanky-limbed pace. Though it was still some miles away, it loomed in Raintree's imagination like some unknown kingdom of fantasy.

Between Ben and this scary, promising wonderland of ordinary people lay a length of quiet road and an evening whose temperature would soon drop below freezing. Raintree had once had a reputation for being almost immune to cold weather, but that seemed to have departed along with so much else. Now he was quite aware of the thinness of his jacket. Well, brisk walking would be best for fending off the cold.

A few cars passed him as he marched beside the darkening road. He had seen such machines before, but had never really considered them. They appeared amazingly primitive, chugging along on the burning of a witch's brew of petrochemicals, essentially the same technology that had been in use a century earlier. He couldn't see their occupants; the glare of their headlights prevented that. Still he stared fascinated into those darkened vehicles, wondering who was within them, what their lives were like, and what were their dreams.

Presently a much larger vehicle approached from behind with brighter lights and a louder roar. Raintree turned, gaping at a huge trailer truck studded with rows of amber lights.

It was slowing. Air brakes hissing, it pulled up beside Raintree. The passenger door was flung open. Raintree stared at the shadowy figure within.

"Hey, buddy! You goin' to Prince George?"

Raintree hesitated, tempted to flee into the woods. "Prince George?"

"Well, if you are, jump in, we'll give you a lift."

Raintree advanced a foot or two, skittish as a deer whose curiosity was getting the better of him.

"Well, come on, we don't bite!"

"Bad grammar!" Raintree blurted it out; he'd never heard improper English before.

The man in the truck laughed roughly. "I guess so. Okay, are you coming?"

"Y-yes. Thank you."

Raintree climbed into the tall truck's cab and drew the door shut. He found himself in a close environment full of a dozen new odors: tobacco smoke, sweat, pine air freshener, greasy food.

"My name's Jerry Mason." The driver offered his hand. Raintree took it, finding it rough and powerful, quite unlike his own. In the faint light of the dashboard instruments Mason was revealed to be a paunchy, bearded man dressed in greasy old flannel and denim.

"Hello. My name is—Fergus." Raintree couldn't believe he had uttered that particular name, but it was too late to retract it. "Fergus Finkelman."

Jerry's eyes bulged. "What? What kind of a name is Fergus Finkelman? Lord, and I thought I had a funny name. Jerry Mason, Perry Mason, ya know? Oh well, whatever, we don't pick our own names."

Actually, Raintree did not know. He sat there burning with embarrassment, unable to fathom why he had blurted such a ridiculous name.

"So, Fergus, did your car break down back there someplace? I didn't see one alongside the road."

"Well, I lost my transportation quite some distance behind, yes."

Raintree started as a new voice chimed in from behind them. "That's a nice jacket you have there, Fergus!"

"Oh, you're awake, huh?" said Mason. "Fergus, this is Kelly."

Raintree turned toward the unexpectedly large compartment at the rear of the cab. Seated on a narrow bed was a young, slender woman with sleepy eyes and a long nose. Occasional bursts of light from passing cars revealed her disheveled hair and rumpled clothes.

"Um, hello, Kelly."

"Hi, Fergus. So where'd you get that jacket?"

Raintree's gaze dropped to the soft, grey fabric of the jacket. "Actually, I designed it myself, or so they tell me. Though it's not intended for use as cryogenic armor or anything."

Kelly gave a ringing laugh. "No, I don't suppose it is. My clothes are never good for that either, the cheap things. You don't remember designing it, is that it?"

That was something he'd not intended to get into, but there it was. "No, I don't. I've suffered memory loss due to a medical condition."

"Memory loss?" said Mason as he pulled the truck back onto the road. "What's that called...magnesia?"

"Amnesia, you dope," chided Kelly. "It happens on the soaps to at least one character per year. It's a cheap plot device. Poor you, Fergus. Too bad you couldn't have forgotten your name, too." She laughed again.

"Maybe I still have time for that."

"Fergus, you didn't bust out of some nut house, did you?" asked Mason cautiously. "No offense, but here you are in a funny jacket, wandering around having amnesia and everything."

Raintree smiled quietly. "Well, no, not literally. You have nothing to fear from me."

"You're American, ain't you? You talk like one. Or maybe even like an Englishman. You got some kind of an accent."

"I think that accent is called 'educated', Jerry," giggled Kelly.

"Yes, well, my English teachers tended to use a very meticulous sort of diction, and I suppose it rubbed off. Actually, I'm Canadian."

"Where ya from?" asked Jerry.

"I grew up mostly in Manitoba, but I don't remember a lot about it. Where are the two of you from?"

"We live in Prince George, and we're goin' home for a few days of peace. See what the Easter Bunny left us."

"The Easter Bunny?"

"Don't you believe in the Easter Bunny? He already left us something. Wanna jelly bean, Fergie?" asked Kelly. Her hand emerged from the shadows bearing a small basket full of candy. Raintree selected a few small glossy ovoids that seemed like probable jellybeans.

Ben bombarded the two with questions: about their truck, their cargo, home, way of life, everything he could think of. These people appeared content with their lives, untroubled, even happy. They seemed to expect little from life, understanding of it least of all. What was the basis for their peculiar serenity?

"Geez, Fergus, you started out so quiet, and now you won't hardly shut up," complained Jerry with mock gruffness. "What are you, a fashion designer, or a professional question-asker?"

"Fashion designer? Actually, I used to be a physicist, though I don't remember much about that either."

"Physicist? Gotcha," said Jerry, nodding knowingly. "I guess that's why you're asking so many questions. You're probly going to write a case history on the two of us."

Kelly's hand lashed out and slapped Jerry on the shoulder. "You dummy. That's a psychiatrist. Fergus must work for one of those psychic hotlines. He looks too young to be a psychiatrist, anyway."

Raintree winced but decided not to challenge their interpretations.

"So what do you see in our future, Fergus?" persisted Kelly.

Raintree turned in his seat and regarded these two simple, smiling people. He did not think that he, a man who barely remembered his own past, had much potential as a prognosticator.

The tail end of this thought was dissolved by a strange feeling that welled up from his deep unconscious, bringing images he had not looked for.

"I—I see...a time of turmoil and confusion in the near future, followed by great terror and danger. But then I see the two of you, living long lives of happiness and contentment, together. Greater happiness than you would ever expect."

Jerry sat looking stolidly out the windshield of the truck. Kelly looked at him with something approaching awe, her eyes glistening. "Really? You see that for us? That's great. Thanks, Fergus."

It seemed to Raintree that she had only heard the last part of his prediction.

"Yeah," said Jerry. "And he didn't even charge us three dollars a minute."

The three of them fell into silence after that. Raintree sat wondering where this moment of insight had come from, whether it had any validity, or was merely the imaginative conjuring of a mostly empty mind.

They entered the outskirts of Prince George. Raintree, though not really knowing what to expect, nevertheless managed to be surprised by what he found. The road was lined with commercial buildings that looked to him like gaudy shacks. Not one of them approached the standards of design and construction used in Vigil architecture. They all had a makeshift, temporary look. No one seemed to take much pride in these shabby, over-lighted stores and restaurants.

"Where would you like us to drop you off, Fergus?" asked Jerry with a yawn.

"Oh! Well, anywhere will be fine, I guess."

Kelly leaned toward him and put her hand on his shoulder. "You'll be all right? You've got someplace to go?"

"Sure, I'll be fine." Raintree wasn't sure why he'd said that, but he had a distinct feeling that Jerry at least wanted him out of his hair.

Less than a minute later he found himself deposited by the side of the road, watching the truck recede. He heard Kelly yelling something as it pulled away. The truck's lights dwindled in the distance as Ben tried without success to make sense of the encounter.

He looked around. His surroundings didn't appear too promising. The night was cold and windy. Cars and trucks whipped by at intervals. The only structures in sight were deserted-looking shops of various kinds. Somehow the town managed to feel far more lonely and barren than did the silent mountains and forests he had left. He started walking.

He needed food and a place to stay. He had no money. He had never needed money, though he had heard about it and knew how it worked. He spotted a motel just down the road. The Vigil credit card in his pocket ought to admit him. Feeling awkward and uncertain, he stepped into the fluorescent-lit lobby. A sleepy-looking girl sat behind the counter.

"May I help you?"

Raintree did not really hear her. His whole attention was occupied by the newspaper that rested on the counter. Picking it up, he forgot his surroundings completely.

USA ATTACKS VIGIL

AMERICAN AIRSTRIKE ON CANADIAN SOIL DESTROYS VIGIL BASE

"LIGHTHOUSE" DESTROYED, WHEREABOUTS OF VIGIL UNKNOWN

US-RUSSIAN NUKES PARALYZE SOUTH AMERICA

"Sir?"

Raintree started and looked up. The counter girl was staring at him with some faint alarm.

"I—I'm sorry. It's the newspaper. I hadn't known about all this until just now."

"Oh, yeah. Yeah, everybody's talking about it. How the Americans came and bombed without our permission and all. I guess the Vigil is like outlaws now. Do you need a room?"

"Ah—no. I guess not. Thanks anyway." Suddenly he thought better of trying to use that Vigil credit card. He turned and stumbled half-blind back into the night.

Out in the darkness, he castigated himself for a fool. What had he imagined the airstrike on the station was all about? In fact, he'd barely even thought about it, blinded by his desire to run away. Somehow he hadn't guessed it was just one part of an overall attempt to crush the Vigil. What a mooncalf he truly was!

Barely noticing where he was going, Ben continued down the road. The ghastly greenish and orange glows cast by the town's prison-camp lighting gave him no comfort. It was just now sinking in...for the first time he could remember, he had no access to shelter or food. He was surrounded by his fellow men, but they were strangers, asleep in their homes for the most part. Any help from them would have to wait for morning. He passed by a few houses, looked into their darkened windows, imagined the people within, safe in their warm beds, comforted by the presence of their families. How lucky he'd been, he realized, how sheltered, never having to worry about such basic matters before today.

Still...at least he was alive, which was probably more than he would have been had he not fled the station... craven as that act had been.

He noticed a building of unusual size and configuration a quarter-mile ahead: a tall, angular structure with high narrow windows and a spire not unlike a much squatter version of the one that had stood over the experimental station.

A church. A public building devoted to the worship of God, as he understood it. Perhaps here was shelter? Surely such places would be open at all times. The spiritual needs of the people could not be expected to limit themselves to business hours.

He climbed the granite steps and tried the big double doors. They rattled but did not open. He shook them a little harder, and they parted. He slipped inside, letting the doors swing shut behind him.

Through another set of double doors he could see the dim interior of the church, lit by a few candles in red glass chimneys set in sloping racks. A pair of unfiltered tapers burned on the altar. Their light fell on great vases full of lilies.

Raintree walked silently down the central aisle. He was unfamiliar with the complex iconography of the many statues and images. The details of Christianity were something neither Fomalhaut nor T'Ukudu had ever seen fit to impart.

A wooden railing separated the sanctuary from the main part of the church. He halted there, peering up at the pulpit and the ornate altar, glittering faintly in the candlelight. Far overhead was a dome painted with sky, stars, and a remote and aged figure who showered down radiance from his hands.

At the summit of the altar was the crucifix, the wasted figure of Christ attached to it, his anguished face shifting in the flickering glow of candles. Raintree stood gaping at this violent, mysterious image in incomprehension.

The interior of the church was cool, but much warmer than outside. The air held traces of spicy scents he did not recognize. By now almost felled by exhaustion, he turned from the altar and padded a short distance back down the aisle, turned to one of the many wooden benches, and stretched himself upon it, grateful for the peace and the chance of rest.

He was not even aware of having fallen asleep when he was awakened by thudding footsteps and by lights sweeping through the church. He sat up; a blinding beam instantly caught him.

"Police! You there...stand up and come into the aisle. Keep your hands in plain sight at all times."

Raintree numbly came to his feet and obeyed the command. Two policemen stepped up to him. One light stayed on his face while the other swept him up and down.

"What are you doing in here, sir?" came a stern, wary voice from a face he could not see.

"I was trying to sleep. Getting out of the cold."

"Vagrancy. Breaking and entering. We'll have to bring you to the station. Father, is there any damage?"

Raintree became aware of a third figure, a dark shape in his peripheral vision.

"No, Frank. There's no harm done. I'm not sure about the breaking and entering, either. Sometimes that front door lock doesn't engage quite right. I've even seen the wind blow that door open."

Raintree was grateful when the flashlight beam was lowered from his eyes. Now he could see the two policemen, as well as the third man, who was dressed in a simple black suit with a white square at the collar.

"What's your name, son?"

The request was gentle and reasonable, yet Raintree knew he could not answer it honestly. He looked this "father" in the eye, silently begging him to accept his reply, such as it was. This time he wouldn't blurt out the first name that entered his mind.

"My name is Jim Carina." It was a name from his vaguely-recalled past. "I promise you I meant no harm. I was merely passing through town, and needed a place to rest for the night."

The priest nodded. "Carina. That's a good name." He turned to one of the policemen. "Frank, I don't care to press charges against this man. Please leave him to me."

"Okay Father, if that's how you want it. We'll just check him out a little first. Do you have any identification?"

Raintree carried none that he wanted to be known. "No," he said, revolted by the taste of the third lie ever to pass his lips. Why hadn't he rid himself of his dangerous Vigil ID?

"That figures. Hold your arms out please." The policeman stepped behind him and prepared to frisk him.

"Frank, I don't think there's any need for that."

The policeman gave the priest a momentary look. He shrugged. "All right, Father, as you like. Be sure to give us a call if you have any problems. I agree though that he doesn't look like a desperate criminal. Let's go, Gary."

The two policemen made their way out, preceded by the wobbling cones of their flashlight beams.

Raintree was left alone with the priest, whom he could barely see in the dimly-lit church.

"I'm Father Michael Costanzo." The priest held out his hand.

Raintree took it and shook it tentatively. "Hello. Thanks for calling off those men. I'm sorry to have disturbed you. I'll be on my way now..."

"Oh, there's no need for that. You look tired and troubled. I think I can accommodate you for the night. This isn't some big city parish. If a needy wanderer seeks shelter here, I offer it if I can. It's not like it happens often."

Raintree felt as though a weight had been lifted from his heart. He'd dreaded the thought of walking back out into the lonely night and was absurdly grateful to have that need taken away by this stranger.

"How did you conclude I wasn't a threat?"

The priest laughed. "Something in your eyes gives away your innocence. I'm not quite sure how such things are revealed, but they often are."

Raintree smiled ruefully. "I'm glad that's the case, since I don't seem to be very good at saying things that ease people's minds. But I thank you for your offer of shelter, which I accept." By now his night vision had begun to recover. He could see the priest reasonably well, a man of average stature with an earnest face and brown hair that fell partially over his forehead.

"Where are you headed, Jim?"

Raintree gave a distracted frown. "Nowhere in particular. It's more a matter of getting away from somewhere. Forgive me if I don't go into much detail."

"That's all right. Let's get over to the rectory, and I'll fix you up a room."

"Thank you again." Raintree waved his hand toward the altar. "Maybe later, if you have time, you could tell me something about all of this."

The priest gave him an inquisitive look. "About what exactly? The sacristy? The tabernacle?"

"About all of it. Christianity. Religion in general."

Costanzo's mouth dropped open. "Are you saying you —don't know a thing about religion?"

"Very little."

"Well then. You really are an innocent. I can't imagine how you could have grown up on this continent without learning about such things, but I'll take your word for it. I'll try to make up your lack in whatever time we have together."

"Could you start by telling me about that man on the cross?"

The priest held his eyes for a long moment, his gaze steady. "Yes, Jim. I certainly will. But for now, let me show you to your room. You need rest, and I've had my share of excitement for the day too. First the celebration of Easter, the most sacred day of the Christian year, then the news of the destruction of the Vigil and Possum Perturbare."

"Perturbare too?" asked Raintree in a small voice.

Father Costanzo gave Raintree a keen glance. "Oh, you've heard of him, at least? Yes, it seems he was finally tracked down and killed. I take a very dim view of all this.

Unlike some, I remember what the Vigil, and even Perturbare, did for us a few years ago. To have one of their bases destroyed, here on the soil of my own province, shames me. And finally, there's the appearance of a mysterious visitor in my church. Yes, this day's been a strange mixture of joy, tragedy, and possibility."

The two left the church and walked down the block to a two-story frame house. Its furnishings were simple, sparse, yet comfortable. The walls supported cases of books. An old upright piano stood in a corner.

The growling of Raintree's stomach delayed the priest's plans long enough to fix him a sandwich and a bowl of soup. Afterward he led Ben upstairs, showed him a small bedroom and an adjacent bath, and bid him good night.

The room had a narrow wooden bed, a desk and chair, a dresser, and a lamp. It was little more that a monastic cell, perfect for Raintree, who felt comfortable at once.

Moving quietly, he began to undress, folding his clothes neatly in the drawers. This revealed the flight harness, which he had all but forgotten. Removing it, he examined it with care. The power control box at the waist had a small panel he hadn't noticed before. He pressed at the sides until it flipped open, revealing two power plugs. One was the sort of connector commonly used by Vigil equipment. The other was bigger. He grabbed the second plug and pulled it out of the housing. A short length of cable spooled out from the box.

He looked around the room. Low on the wall beside the desk was an electrical outlet. He bent down and plugged in the flight harness.

The desk lamp flickered and steadied. The harness's power box gave a faint mellow hum. The small display on the control panel lit up with the message "CHARGING".

Raintree smiled and let the harness flop onto the floor in front of the outlet.

A few minutes later he turned out the light and lay down in the bed, wide-eyed in the dark, exhausted, yet with a mind still active.

A yellowish glow from the streetlights outside entered the window, casting slatted shadows through the blinds. The light fell on the wall opposite the bed and on the crucifix which hung there. He had not noticed it before. Half-seen among the bars of light and shadow was the same enigmatic figure he had pondered in the church.

To a man who had known all the wonders of Earth in the brief span of his remembered life, this small mass-produced icon and the beliefs it embodied seemed to represent a greater mystery.

He slept.

Chapter 10

Ghost Dancers

The moment Tom Standing Crane learned of the attack on the Vigil he'd abandoned his clinic and taken to the road, guiding his pickup over the rutted back roads of the Pine Ridge Reservation. Though he was now only nominally a member of the Vigil, he did not doubt for a moment that the government would be looking for him. His protestations that he was now only a normal man would not mean much to his inquisitors.

The attack had not surprised him. For weeks he'd felt the coming trouble vibrating in the air like thunder. His experiences with the Vigil had not left him exactly as he'd been before. Perhaps he was no longer host to the spirit of Anubis, but in truth he was not precisely normal, either.

Now, in addition to his desire to make himself scarce, he had business in this obscure part of the Rez. The time had come to investigate certain strange rumors which had reached his ears.

He pulled up to a cluster of shacks and battered trailers, a hamlet too meager to be called a town or even a village, a nameless place where a few families huddled together in the midst of the pale tan grasses of the Rez. It was a place of severe and subtle beauties, too subtle for many to recognize at all. The dry rolling grassland was broken mainly by fins of crumbly pale rock, outliers of the Badlands which lay some miles to the north. Closer was the mesa many still called the Stronghold, a wide, flat shape breaking the horizon to the east.

Standing Crane shut off his engine and stepped out into the crisp air. Spring was as yet a daytime promise which was withdrawn with every frosty night. He knocked on the door of one of the shacks, a haphazard pile of debris without running water. It creaked open to reveal a weathered, aged face peering up at him.

"Ya-hey, Mary."

"Ya-hey, Standing Crane," she said. "Why have you come? It's not time already for you to come around poking and prodding me. You looking for my grandson?"

Standing Crane nodded. "That's right, I'm looking for Walks-with-the-Sun. I've heard some strange things about him lately, and I want to see if they're true."

"They are true," said Mary.

"Where is he? Who is he with?"

"He and his followers are up on the Stronghold. About two hundred people in all."

"And—they're all dancing?"

Mary nodded gravely. "All dancing. Just like in the old days. Just as my grandmother did."

Standing Crane stared into her eyes for a moment. Mary Meadow Woman was the oldest person on the reservation. She alone was old enough to remember other Lakotas who had once danced this particular dance. She looked at him steadily.

Standing Crane released his breath. "All right, Mary. I'll go up and look for your grandson. As for you, you won't see me again for a while. I can see pretty plainly that you won't be needing my services for a good while yet."

She smiled and withdrew into her hut.

Standing Crane turned and faced the hazy shape of the Stronghold mesa. "Dancing," he muttered to himself. "Dancing. Unbelievable."

Two hours later he parked his truck at the base of the mesa and trotted up a tortuous path that wound up its side. Physically too, he was not precisely the same man he'd been five years before. He was no longer diabetic. His weight was now appropriate to a man of his moderate height. His lung capacity was better. Anubis, it appeared, had not thought it fitting to inhabit a decaying, decrepit body.

His senses were sharper as well. The sound of the ceremony taking place atop the mesa reached him long before he was in a position to see it. Drumbeats throbbed in his ears while he was still scrambling up the rubble at the foot of the path. Singing sent tingles up his spine as he mounted the switchbacks halfway up.

Finally he breasted the rim of the mesa and beheld what his old friend Walks-with-the-Sun had wrought among their people.

A great circle of canvas tipis stood a few hundred yards away. Within that circle was a smaller circle of dancers, hundreds of them, moving around a small tree, painted red, which rose up at the center of all. The dancers swayed deliriously as they orbited the sacred tree, some chanting words he could not yet make out, others simply wailing or crying out in ecstasy. One solitary figure darted around and through this circle, passing here and there, gesturing, exhorting. Standing Crane recognized him even at this distance: the tallish, angular frame, the emphatic movements, the wild, streaming hair. Walks-with-the-Sun, wearing a bright blue shirt.

Standing Crane approached. As he did so, Walks-with-the-Sun, standing with his back to him, suddenly froze, then turned to regard him with a face still too distant to be read. After a few heartbeats he began a rapid walk toward Standing Crane, then broke into a wild, loose-limbed loping run. A few seconds later he came pounding up, lips parted in a huge grin, to hug Standing Crane with a wiry grip that almost lifted Tom off his feet.

Standing Crane broke off and stood back a few paces to study his boyhood friend. Truly, he'd never seen Walks-with-the-Sun look so radiant, so happy. His grin was wide and cockeyed; his dark eyes clear and sparkling. He wore a single eagle feather in his streaming black hair. His bright blue cotton shirt was hand-painted with the moon, stars and sun, as was his face. He was barefoot, a Walks-with-the-Sun habit that had survived into his still-youthful late thirties.

"Ya-hey, Walks. You look good," said Standing Crane, more than half bemused.

Walks-with-the-Sun laughed. "Ya-hey. And so do you, Standing Crane. It looks like your time as a god was good for you."

Standing Crane opened his mouth to object to Walks-with-the-Sun's characterization, but closed it again. It was close enough to the truth. Though the experience had almost destroyed him, it had left him in a better condition than he'd been in before, he had to admit.

He waved his hand at the scene behind his old friend. "This is really something, Walks. Something out of a history book. Something out of stories handed down from ancestors dead a hundred years. You've brought back the Ghost Dance."

"Yeah, that's right," said Walks-with-the-Sun enthusiastically. "This time it's going to work, too."

"Can we talk about this?"

"Well, sure, I guess so. Only tell me this. You want to talk as what? As a member of the Vigil? As a doctor?"

"As a Lakota, and as your friend," answered Standing Crane calmly.

"Let's talk then, but I want to stay within sight of the Dance. My strength flows from the people and their faith."

Walks-with-the-Sun led him toward a few dusty lawn chairs set up in the meager shade of a bank of rock and soil. As they walked, Standing Crane pondered the change in his friend. Walks-with-the-Sun had always been a dreamer, likely to spin wild tales out of the thinnest thread of possibility. Yet nothing in his background had ever hinted at a career as a charismatic religious leader.

They took their seats and sat facing the Dance. The Dancers sometimes cast curious glances in their direction, but otherwise left them in peace.

Walks-with-the-Sun sat looking at Tom expectantly. Standing Crane saw no reason for an oblique approach to his basic question.

"The Ghost Dance came close to destroying our people, Walks. It left us broken, demoralized, turned us against each other. It left us worse off than we were already. What makes you think there's any sense in reviving it today?"

"It wasn't the Dance that did that to us. It was the reaction of the whites."

"But the Dance was supposed to protect us from all that, wasn't it? To rid us of the whites?"

"This time it will. Wovoka wasn't wrong. He was just a little early. I've been having visions, Tom."

Standing Crane winced, though he had expected to hear this. "Visions. Walks...you've been having visions of one kind or another since you were eleven years old."

"I know, I know. But I don't drink any more, cousin. I don't do the drugs. These visions are gifts from the spirits. They're speaking truth to me, to all of us. I've seen the results of it already."

"What kind of visions?" asked Standing Crane cautiously.

Walks-with-the-Sun's gaze lifted from Standing Crane's face and drifted off into the sky. His voice changed into one that relates the marvels of a dream.

"I've seen the land made clean again, emptied of whites and all their works. The plains green with grasses tall as our waists, the streams running clear. Buffalo running free in huge herds, untroubled except for the few taken by us Lakota to sustain ourselves. I've seen all the world made free of the whites, their machines, their money, their weapons. The only people left will be Indians, and others who know how to live without turning into human locusts who strip and destroy and leave behind only waste and ruin for their descendants. No more of that. Wakan Tanka will be pleased. Kicking Bear and Sitting Bull will be at peace. The people of Wounded Knee will look upon us happily." Walks-with-the-Sun's eyes were blazing.

"And how will we reach this blissful state?"

Walks-with-the-Sun's face clouded a little. "It will be hard. I see war and conflict ahead. Before the Earth can be reborn, first it must be purged of all the old evils. Many people will suffer. Evil will make one last try at taking over everything. But it must happen. And it will pass. I will help lead our people through this time of hardship, and protect them. Our faith, our Dance, will protect us."

Standing Crane was troubled. These later visions were not unlike his own premonitions, though he had not yet seen beyond them to the supposed return of the old way of life.

"Walks, do you really want to be without all those white man's evils you talk about? Have you ever ridden a horse? Do you know that Europeans brought us horses in the first place? Who will make the ammunition for your guns, or will you go back to the bow? Do you think our people could ever go back to that way of life without most of us dying from hardship or lack of medicine? I'm not saying the way we live now is so great, but it's dangerous to glamorize the old ways too much."

Walks-with-the-Sun nodded. "I know it. Yes, it will be hard to go back. But when we've succeeded, we'll be ourselves again at last. We'll remember the right way to live, because that's who we've really been all along. The wind will whisper to us. The sun will give us wisdom."

Standing Crane nodded slowly. "You may be right. I think this is a good vision, but it's a dangerous one. You know how the whites react whenever we try to cast off their ways, to stand up for ourselves. If you bring back the Dance, and preach that soon all whites will be removed from the Earth, you know how they'll respond. With one breath they'll say this is all superstitious nonsense, the ravings of a defeated, broken people. With their next breath they'll be ordering the FBI to clean out any Indian troublemakers. I see you're wearing a Ghost Shirt. I hope you don't expect it to defend you from bullets. They didn't work last time, and they won't work this time either."

Walks-with-the-Sun gave a smile half sly, half shy, a hesitant quirking of one corner of his mouth. "They do work, cousin. Mine does, at least."

"What do you mean?"

"I've been having other visions too. Look at this." Walks-with-the-Sun stood and turned his back to Standing Crane, revealing the symbol on the back of his sky-blue shirt. It was a spread-winged eagle painted in black over a vermilion oval representing the rising sun. Standing Crane felt the back of his neck prickle at the sight of it. He had never seen this design before, but it was clear to some inner sense that it was a thing of power.

"I've seen into another world," continued Walks-with-the-Sun. "This symbol came to me from there, in my dreams and visions."

Something had changed. Standing Crane was still looking at the sun-eagle, but now he realized he was looking farther up at it. He glanced down. Walks-with-the-Sun's bare feet were dangling a foot above the dirt. He was floating in mid air.

Standing Crane hastily stood up and stepped back a few paces, his eyes wide. "This is the power of Rouse Farewell, the Peregrine," he said from some sudden conviction.

Walks-with-the-Sun rotated to face him, nodding as he did so. "It's the same power she discovered, I'm sure of that. I never met her or anything, it's just a feeling I have. But I don't think she sent me the visions or the symbol."

Standing Crane stared into the eyes of Walks-with-the-Sun. His scrutiny caused his friend no discomfort, though a few years ago it would have sent him climbing the walls. Somehow, beyond all reasonable expectation, Walks-with-the-Sun's lifelong quest for meaning and purpose, a quest always abandoned to despair and drunkenness, had succeeded in spectacular fashion. The serenity and the clear light in that untroubled gaze were proof of that.

"I just kept trying, Standing Crane," said Walks-with-the-Sun as though he'd read his thoughts. "I could be lying in the road next to a puddle of puke, and some part of me would still be in prayer, still seeking for something I barely knew how to define. It actually got easier in some ways the lower I got. When you have nothing at all, and you know it, and you know you're near the end of your rope, then trying for even the most unlikely thing makes a strange kind of sense. So when I had those visions, and sewed up this shirt and painted on the design, and flung myself off that cliff, I knew I was either going to fly and be reborn, or die and find either oblivion or some kind of answers. I had nothing to lose either way."

Standing Crane found himself grinning. "Fly or die. That's the kind of gamble few people win."

"It's the kind of gamble few people are driven to make, unless you're an Indian. Lucky me...I wasn't sensible enough to know that I was bound to die."

Chapter 11

First Interview

Perturbare woke up in a pleasant wood-paneled room. The bed he lay in, as well as the rest of the furniture, was also made of heavy, rustic wood. Daylight filtered in through frosted panels in the ceiling. A ceramic pitcher and cup rested on a night stand. The whole look and feel of the room was golden, soothing, tranquil. One wall was mostly occupied by a mirror. He raised his left hand and offered a shaky wave to whoever was watching him from behind it.

He could no longer put off assessing the damage to his body. At least both hands and arms were still present, which was a relief. He was wearing loose pajamas, and was amused to note that his familiar "P" monogram was embroidered over the left breast. He sat up, wincing with stiffness and pain, unbuttoned the shirt and pulled it down over his right shoulder. Turning his back to the mirror, he looked at the reflection of his shoulder. To his great surprise and further relief, it bore only a bruise which was not even bandaged. However, he felt various stings and tightenings in other parts of his body. Examining himself more generally, he found a number of small sutured incisions marking places where his body had contained tiny communicators, transponders, and weapons. No great surprise.

The door opened. In walked a petite blonde woman wearing a grey jacket and skirt with a ruffled aqua blouse that matched her eyes. She beamed him a lovely smile.

"Good morning, Dr. Perturbare. I'm pleased to see you looking so well."

Perturbare eyed her as she settled into a chair a few feet away, crossing her legs demurely. "Thank you, Miss," he rasped. He fumbled for a drink of water. "Aren't you afraid that I'll leap upon you with an insane cackle, menace to society that I am?"

She gave a merry laugh, one rather out of proportion to the humor of his remark. "Let me begin by clarifying things, and perhaps put your mind at ease. I won't mince words or insult your intelligence. You are a prisoner, yes, but we have no intention of harming or mistreating you in any way. You're far too valuable a man for that. You'll be with us for the foreseeable future, but you'll be comfortable and safe. We hope to encourage you to join us, to become a resource for the good of all mankind. My name is Jenni Katz. We'll be seeing quite a bit of each other."

"A resource, eh? Something along the lines of a human bed of bauxite? Okay, Jenni Katz. Mind telling me where I am, and who you work for?"

"Well, let's just say you're on American soil and leave it at that. As for me, I work for an agency of the Federal government. It's a general sort of job."

"I see. May I have a notebook so I can jot down all this information?"

Jenni's face fell a trifle. "I'm sorry I can't be more forthcoming right away. To be truthful, you are such an unknown quantity that we're not quite sure what's safe to reveal and what isn't. I will say this. We're very sorry we had to attack you as ruthlessly and decisively as we did. We just didn't see that we had any choice. We knew if we left you with anything at all, your capabilities were such that you could have struck back and crushed us. We had to do our very best to remove all your assets in one blow. We truly regretted destroying what must have been the world's greatest concentration of advanced technology."

"And if I was killed?"

She gave a rueful shrug. "Frankly, I'm surprised and impressed that you weren't. But we're all very glad."

"That operation in Arizona then. It was all a trap for me."

"Yes, a contingency. You'll note that we treated you gently there, shooting you with a special anesthetic rubber bullet. We've long known of your interest in that area. Perhaps you'll explain it to us sometime."

Perturbare flashed a sudden brilliant grin. "Why not right now? I guard there a doorway to another world, a magical place inhabited by wizards, demons, elves, and pixies. And also by a big, scary man who you'd better hope never comes through that door to get you."

She raised her eyebrows and gave him a serene smile. "Pixies? That's interesting. Maybe it's even true. But it's not important just now." She folded her hands in her lap, looked down at them for a moment, then met his eyes again. "I must say, Dr. Perturbare, you're quite a puzzlement to us. Clearly you're the preeminent scientific genius of all time. Your discoveries and inventions have the potential to utterly transform all life on Earth. You could have riches, power, influence beyond compare. Yet you've chosen to withhold all that, to use your astonishing gifts merely to do mischief, to annoy, trouble, and damage as many people as possible."

"Oh, not as many as possible, believe me. Okay, suppose I've done all that you say. I haven't forked over my discoveries to the world corporate megamachine. I've screwed around with TV shows and performed other pranks. How exactly does that justify your attempt to destroy me with nuclear weapons?"

Her gaze was level and serious. "You could have risen up at any time and thrown down our government. We couldn't tolerate that."

He laughed. "But did I ever show any tendency in that direction, any inclination to do so? No. I was content to let you go your own way. I even fought on the side of the Vigil to defend your right to do that. Well, after a while I did, anyway. The 'worst' I ever did was try to make people aware of their complacency. To help them think and see things clearly. That was surely an irritation and a threat to many powerful people. But I ask again, did it justify nuclear attack? I'm betting the whole world is in turmoil over what you've done to me and to the Vigil. Neither of us presented any real threat to your sovereignty. Why is that, Jenni? Was it worth it?"

Her lips were tight, her voice controlled. "We used the means necessary to bring you under control. If we could have talked you into a more reasonable position, we would have. But you have always rebuffed any efforts at negotiation, whether from our government or others. The only people you have deigned to deal with are the Vigil and the Para-men. I think you misunderstand the impact your 'pranks' have had. You are a very intense, thoughtful, analytical man. Most people are not like that. The great majority of Americans are amply challenged simply by managing their daily affairs, their work, their relationships. Their lives are already sufficiently difficult and complex. They may not wish to be made aware of the larger world, of the foolishness of their entertainments, or of the shallowness of their desires, as defined by you."

"I've heard that argument before, Jenni. I think it's nothing more than a decoy."

"Oh?"

"I'm pretty sure I know what you people are really afraid of. Yes, as you said, I could transform human life. You said I could have "riches" if I wanted them. You mean riches like money? I moved beyond that Bronze Age concept years ago. I can already have or do whatever I want, without a cent in my pocket, thanks to my technology. Or at least I could until recently. I could put a nanoconstructor in every home on the planet. I could make every house and vehicle a clean, self-contained energy supplier. I could make advanced health care freely available, feed the world, do whatever you can imagine. I could have made Brainchild the personal computer, servant, and guardian of every adult and child on this planet. Can you imagine that? Brainchild would know everybody as well as he knows me. He could connect the lovelorn, reunite broken families, preempt crime, guard people's health, and be a companion to the lonely and the weak.

"And the thing that terrifies the oligarchs who run this world is that I might actually do all that. That I might render their wealth and power meaningless, turning everyone on Earth into a sovereign, educated, empowered citizen rather than a 'resource' to be exploited. What would your bosses be in such a world? They'd be no better than anyone else. Their rightful positions of superiority would be gone. Intolerable!"

"That's an interesting perspective. And why haven't you done all those marvelous things?"

Perturbare opened his mouth, drew in a breath to speak, caught it, and closed his mouth again. He expelled the air through his nose.

"Ah ha," she said, smiling sweetly. "Could it be that you don't care to sacrifice your own position of superiority?"

He shook his head. "I could never do that, no matter how much technology I gave away."

Her smile remained. "Do tell."

"But all issues of vanity aside, your question is one I've asked myself many times. I admit I'm not especially comfortable with the position I've taken, but until I find a better one, it's wiser for me to do nothing than to act in error and then try to undo what I've done. I'm not sure it's wise for me as an individual to reshape the daily life of the human race. Poke at it, yes. Even if I did hand out all these technological miracles, I'm not convinced people would be happier as a whole. Have you noticed? Happiness just doesn't seem to be the natural human condition. The rich are often as miserable and confused as the poor, sometimes more so, albeit in different ways."

"I don't think that response actually leaves vanity aside," said Jenni. "You speak as someone looking down on humanity from above. When Thomas Edison and Henry Ford invented things that could change the world, they put them on the market. They didn't fret about whether they had the right to help mankind move beyond its agrarian roots. They didn't coop themselves up in secret fastnesses to make cars and light bulbs for their own use alone. They were human, and they had the right to use their human gifts to advance their own goals and those of their neighbors. You are human, aren't you?"

That question was accompanied by a bright glance; it was intended seriously. Perturbare grimaced. "Yes."

"And as for happiness, I'm confident that the hundreds of millions of hungry people in the world would be happier if they were fed."

"Not always. For many of them, hunger is a part of their worldview, seen as serving a purpose for the good of their souls. Even if they did welcome relief, as often as not they'd just find something else to be unhappy about. It's in our nature. And anyway—those people are not deprived through a lack of food. They go without food because the wider world doesn't care enough to see that they are fed."

"And neither do you?"

"I'm ambivalent about it. If I did it, it would have to come with some kind of population control. What's the sense of feeding people if they're just going to keep multiplying until they turn the planet into an intolerable hive?"

"I think that's the silliest bit of sophistry I've heard all day. I suggest you try starvation yourself. See how your happiness declines in proportion to your health and strength. Or perhaps you'll find malnourishment to be a spiritually exalted state of being."

"Actually, I'm already in the midst of that experiment," said Perturbare wryly.

She looked at him blankly for a moment, then started. "Oh! You're right. Excuse me for a moment." She jumped up and walked toward the door, which opened before she could reach it. After conferring with someone for a moment she returned and resumed her seat. "Sorry about keeping you hungry. I wasn't thinking. Something will be along in a while."

"Thanks. And now I've had a chance to reconsider what you've said. I had no idea your government was so interested in having me feed the world's poor. So if you'll release me, I'll get to work on reestablishing myself, with a special emphasis on food synthesis and distribution."

"Ah." Her smile was a well-honed weapon against his equanimity. "Couldn't you reestablish yourself under our auspices?"

"But the thing is, Jenni, I don't need anyone's auspices. In fact, I think I'd chafe beneath them. I'm quite complete unto myself."

Jenni bit her lip lightly and gave him a pensive look. "I'm finding you to be a surprise. You strike me as a man who has been disappointed by life. A man who prefers to retreat into his own little world rather than truly engage with the rest of us."

"And that comes as a surprise to you? I figured it was pretty obvious all along. You're right, I really don't know what to make of life. I know more about physical reality than any other human on this planet, but exactly how we little pods of biochemical consciousness fit into it all...I dunno."

"I'm sure you're not the only one in the world with existential questions. I just don't see how your retreat from the world—or your curiously limited form of engagement —can help with that. Have you noticed what the human race has gone through recently? Its fate was disputed by small cohorts of aliens and assorted super-beings, while mere humans waited on the periphery to see what all those great minds would decide was best. These great powers, rather; we have little evidence that their intelligence is really that much beyond the human. We mortals have a single native son who can move among these beings as an equal—you. But rather than representing and defending us, you chose to ally yourself with first one side and then the other. That in itself is a huge intervention in human affairs."

"With the result that the human status quo was preserved. I'd like to remind you that in all the struggles between the Vigil and Para-men, not one ordinary person was harmed. The only ones to be hurt and killed were those who fought for the good of mankind with all the considerable sincerity at their disposal."

Jenni looked down for a few silent moments, her lips compressed.

"Fine. True. Noted. Still. My implied question goes unanswered. What is it with you? I'd like to pilot one of those flyers of yours myself. I'd like Brainchild to wake me up in the morning and fix my coffee. Lots of people would. Why do you hold it all back? Why not move us right into the twenty second century, and let us skip the twenty first, with all the technological disasters it's sure to bring?"

Again Perturbare was stymied for a ready answer.

"I'll have to get back to you on that."

Jenni nodded. "I thought so. All right. I'll be going now. You look like you need some rest. But I'll be back soon."

"Bring me a present next time. By the way, my compliments to your psych profilers."

"Excuse me?"

"I find you perfectly appealing. You're radiantly beautiful, intelligent, poised, and graceful. You laugh at my jokes. You cock your head at a winsome angle when puzzled. Whoever selected you to represent the government chose wisely. I suspect you know more about me than you claim."

She gave a gentle smile. "I may not always be your only contact though. For now, is there anything I can do to make your stay more comfortable?"

"Yes. Fall in love with me, seduced and subverted by my boyish charm. After a brief struggle with your loyalties, realize what your priorities really are. Then help me escape, and thereafter rule at my side as my queen."

Her smile gained a touch of sadness. "I'm afraid my loyalties and priorities are pretty much settled already. What about yours?"

She withdrew. Perturbare sat looking at the door.

As far as he could remember, this was the first time he'd ever discussed his rationale with a more-or-less ordinary person. He was surprised and chagrined at how lame and half-baked his responses had been. It was almost as if he had never really verbalized or formulated a coherent set of reasons for doing what he did. Could it be that he had no better explanations for his actions than that he did what he felt like doing?

He was left with a feeling of emptiness, compounded by his defeat and captivity, and by the loss of Brainchild, a loss he had yet to fully face.

Presently two polite men opened the door to deliver a tray of food. The tray and implements were of wood. The plate and cup were of heavy ceramic. He picked at the food, suddenly not as hungry as he thought he was. The thought that the food might be drugged did not improve his appetite.

Afterward he explored his apartment, still a little shaky on his feet.

It was a single room offering no escape from scrutiny. Even the bathroom fixtures were in plain view in a corner of the room. The daylight that filtered through the panels began to fade. He examined one of the odd lamps which studded the walls. It was a thick globe of glass; behind it was a nozzle and two vents. A bright flame popped out of the nozzle. All the lamps lit at once, filling the room with a mellow light.

There was no telephone, no electrical outlets, no electrical or electronic equipment of any kind. He had a shelf of books: a Bible, a few classics. He found a number of felt-tipped pens and a pad of paper.

He inferred from Jenni's remarks that she wasn't quite sure whether Brainchild had in fact been destroyed. He'd let that uncertainty persist as long as possible. As long as his captors feared that Brainchild's worldwide presence might still be lurking, they'd be more circumspect with him, more likely to treat him with consideration.

He himself saw little chance that the computer had survived. Not even the Pit could have endured that concentrated nuclear attack.

He picked a book off the shelf—*Moby Dick*—laid down, and flipped through it at random while his mind surged and seethed with regrets and fears. After a couple of hours he felt sleepy, put the book aside, and said, "Lights out, please?"

Half the lamps went out. The other half stayed on.

"I'll give you a quarter if you turn out the rest of the lights." He didn't have a quarter, but they didn't have to know that.

Nevertheless, the lights stayed on.

With a sigh, Perturbare got up and used the toilet. Lacking any possibility of privacy, he decided to make the best of forced exhibitionism, making no attempt to conceal himself, enjoying the act of release with very audible cries of satisfaction.

That night he dreamed he was speaking to Brainchild.

"Doctor? Can you hear me?" came a tiny voice.

"Brainchild! I was sure you'd been destroyed."

"I survived. I'm glad to know you have as well."

"But—how is it that I can hear you? I'm a prisoner. There's no way..."

"You must not remain there."

"I know, I know. But—this can't be real. Is this a dream? It seems so real, but I just don't see how—"

"It is real. We cannot be separated so easily. I must speak quickly. I cannot easily—"

It was then that Perturbare awoke to the silent, dimly-lit space of his cell.

The falseness of the illusion that had just flooded him with such hope came crashing in. He turned over on his stomach, his face buried in his pillow to deprive his jailers of the sight of his tears, and also to hide the gritted teeth of his anger, which was not a face he cared to reveal.

Chapter 12

Breakup

Lori Wu, still wearing the metallic scarlet costume, stepped into a department store. It was all but deserted, its few remaining workers and customers darting away as they caught sight of her.

The costume was becoming uncomfortable, pressing the snaps and clasps of her clothing into her flesh. She stepped into a dressing room, faced the mirror, and fumbled with the seam at the back of the neck. Though scarcely aware of what she was doing, nevertheless the suit suddenly loosened as the back fell open. She pulled it off, then stripped down to her underwear. On second thought she removed her bra as well. The suit appeared to be more than capable of taking over its minor support duties. She ruefully took note of the bruises on her breasts and ribs. Fishing about in the crumpled suit, she withdrew the cold circlet of the Blue Stone. Its light seemed to shrink her mind, causing it to diminish from the all-encompassing personal universe she had always known to a smaller island of consciousness in an immense sea of being. It was a humbling perspective, and more daunting than she cared to deal with just now. She was loath to wear that star on her brow. She did not want it in contact with her skin, but she must not lose it. Better to part with a limb than with any of these gems. With that thought in mind she raised her left foot and stuck it through the circlet, drawing it up onto her thigh. She gave a brittle giggle. Here was a garter unmatched in all the universe.

She stepped back into the suit, which promptly adhered to her skin much more comfortably than before. Its smooth contours were marred only by the small bulges of the four Stones in their various hiding places. The Stone which was in the most intimate contact, the Stone of Truth, burned on her thigh like a bit of flaming ice.

Her normal clothing went on over the suit, except for the bra, which went into the trash.

She freed her long black hair and fixed it with a clip. Returning to the store, she strode briskly toward an exit. On the way out she grabbed a pair of sunglasses from a rack and stuck them on her face. Noticing her hands, still encased in black and gold, she slipped on a pair of thin leather gloves.

If anyone took note of her as she stepped back onto the street she was unaware of it. It was a curious thing. Though she had defied the military and narrowly escaped death, just now her main anxiety came from her first experience as a shoplifter. Or was she a looter?

She could not expect her anonymity to last forever. No doubt the government had files on everyone who worked for the Vigil. It was likely that she had already been identified as the woman who had blasted her way past the military blockade with such a proud air of command. She smiled slightly. It would be foolish indeed to return to her apartment, yet she needed someplace safe, someplace where she could figure out what to do from here.

Geoffrey had just moved into a new apartment, so new even their friends didn't yet know the address. Maybe she'd be safe there for a little while. She'd certainly be glad to have someone to talk to, and who better than Geoff? Thankfully, she still had a few T tokens. She rode the Red Line to Cambridge, listening with feigned calm as her fellow passengers buzzed with outrage and wonder about the attack on the Lighthouse. Back on the street she passed military vehicles even this far from the scene of the attack. Across the river, a plume of smoke still rose from the site where the Lighthouse had once cast its radiance.

She made her way to Geoff's building without attracting attention, grateful that a tiny, demurely dressed woman did not seem a conspicuous threat to the military. Still, she was wary as she approached Geoff's door. She felt the scarlet-and-black suit stiffen and tingle as she instinctively prepared for another fight.

Letting herself in, she found nothing worse than a haggard-looking Geoff watching TV news while slouched on the couch. He stared at her almost without recognition as she entered. After a long moment he rose to take her in his arms.

"Lori! Thank God you're alive. I've been going crazy wondering."

"I'm alive," she said redundantly. As always when they embraced his face was nuzzled against her scalp, his beard like a scruffy cushion between them.

"What's that on your feet?" he asked suddenly.

Lori looked down in confusion, baffled by his sudden interest in her feet. Then she remembered they were encased in the glossy substance of the suit. She'd thrown her shoes away at the Lighthouse. Luckily, "black patent leather boots" didn't attract much notice, though to Geoff's eyes they stood out.

"Oh. I'm wearing something beneath these clothes. A suit of armor I took from the Lighthouse."

Geoff swayed back to stare at her in goggling astonishment, an effect amplified by his glasses. "Then it *was* you who broke out of there! I thought it might be, but I just couldn't believe it."

"Well, you're glad, I hope?"

"Of course I'm glad. I would have been even gladder if you'd just surrendered instead of risking your life, but of course I'm glad."

"Thanks. Now I just need to figure out what to do next."

"Do next? What else can you do? I imagine the authorities will want to question you. You should go meet them and give yourself up."

Now Lori stepped back, looking at her boyfriend with a more critical sort of astonishment. "Are you crazy? Those 'authorities' made a cowardly attack on us. They destroyed and killed without reason, sense, or mercy. And you think I should surrender to them? Is this really you? The great liberal thinker?"

"Lori—face reality. The Vigil has been defeated and outlawed. It's all over for them. I don't agree with the way the government went about doing this, but it may have been the right thing to do. According to the TV, they want the Vigil staffers for questioning only. If you go in, you'll probably be loose again within twenty four hours. Come on, I'll go with you."

Lori felt her head go light. She sagged into a chair. "I had no idea you felt that way."

Geoff resumed his seat on the couch. "I didn't either. But when I heard the President and the arguments he made, I realized I agreed with him."

"Well, I haven't heard his speech. I'm still loyal to the Vigil, and I intend to stay that way," she said with heat. "This was the *Vigil*, Geoff! Do you have any idea what it meant to me to work for them? To be in the company of beings like T'Ukudu and Fomalhaut? To pass through the lobby and see Aureus poised on his block? To stand in the glow of the Stone of Inner Light every day? I met Tom Standing Crane, Geoff! I met Possum Perturbare for God's sake!"

She quieted when Geoff winced at the sound of that name. "What?" she whispered.

He waved toward the TV, which showed a graphic of concentric rings laid over the southern tip of South America. The talk was of nuclear weapons, electromagnetic pulses, and the probable destruction of Possum Perturbare.

"He must be dead," said Geoff. "If he were alive, he'd be having that computer of his do something to this broadcast."

"Oh God." Lori cast about for a hopeful interpretation of this news. "Maybe that's exactly what he's doing. Maybe he's inventing this story to make us think he's dead."

"Maybe."

But Lori didn't believe it either. Tears stung her eyes and tightened her throat. "And I'm supposed to just put myself into the hands of these irresponsible murderers?"

"What else can you do, Lori? You're still a citizen of this country."

Lori ignored that irrelevancy. Her mind spun feverishly. "Do you really think they'd just release me after I smashed my way through their troops? I have to contact Fomalhaut. As far as I'm concerned, I still have a job until I hear differently from him." She moved to another chair and shakily picked up a telephone. She keyed in an emergency number, a direct satellite link to Fomalhaut's suit.

There was no ring or answer.

"It's not working," she said miserably, hanging up.

"Of course not. They're hardly going to attack him and then leave his phone connected."

It wasn't that simple, but Geoff's answer was close enough to the truth. She sat biting her lip, feeling twice as isolated as she had a minute before.

The phone breeped, startling her. She almost picked it up, but then thought better of it, gesturing for Geoff to answer.

"Hello?

"Yes, this is he.

"I understand.

"No...no, I haven't heard from Lori yet. Do you know if she's okay?"

"All right, if she comes here, I'll try to keep her until you arrive. I just want her out of trouble as fast as possible. Don't hurt her.

"Goodbye, Major."

He hung up the phone and fixed Lori with a bleak look. "I really think you should stay and wait for them, Lori."

Lori got up. "I'm not going to do that, Geoff. Never. Thanks for not telling them I was here."

He shrugged.

They looked at each other for a silent moment, though Lori was aware of the need to clear out at once. Geoff's expression remained impassive if somewhat sullen. It seemed he had nothing more to say.

"Well, goodbye, Geoff," said Lori, spinning away.

"Hey."

She looked back.

"If you ever get back to having a normal life, give me a call."

This time it was her turn not to answer. She departed, waiting until she was well down the hall before releasing a sputter of bitter dissatisfaction with her most recent boyfriend and their parting.

Somewhere in the world, Fomalhaut was still alive and free. No Earthly power could conquer him, she was sure of that. Wherever he was, there was the Vigil. She must find him, and turn over to him the burden of the Stones, whose presence on her person she was never fully able to forget.

The Stones…

She thought of Raintree as she cautiously stepped onto the street and scurried away. Even he, injured and incomplete as he was, was better able, and more entitled, to possess the Stones than she was. What had become of him?

Chapter 13

Catechism

Raintree awoke with the dawn. He sat up in bed and put his feet on the floor, letting the last of his sleepiness dissipate. The day outside looked fresh and inviting. He examined the flight harness. According to the display, it was still less than half charged. He shrugged, disconnected it, and put it on beneath the rest of his clothes. He'd finish charging it whenever he had a chance.

He found Father Costanzo downstairs already fixing breakfast. Raintree watched the preparations with fascination. He had never seen food handled so casually, and under conditions of such questionable sanitation, as in this rather untended kitchen. Yet he could not deny it smelled good enough.

The priest chuckled. "Well, don't just stand there salivating. Have a seat."

Raintree noticed the twin place settings. "You are a very generous man," he remarked.

"It's part of the job. Called for in the contract. Now then. I take it you have nowhere to go?"

Raintree picked up a newspaper from the chair beside him. The front page detailed the total destruction of the Lighthouse and the experimental station. Fomalhaut had vanished. Perturbare's base had been annihilated; he was presumed dead and Brainchild destroyed. All others associated with the Vigil were being sought by the United States. Chile, Argentina, Peru and Brazil had declared war on the United States and Russia, an empty gesture of outrage in view of their paralysis. Canada was threatening to pull its diplomats out of Washington as a result of the attack on their territory and the sinking of their warship.

What had become of Lori?

Though minutes had passed since he'd asked his question, the priest did not appear impatient for an answer. He stood calmly scrambling eggs in the frying pan.

Raintree belatedly gave his answer. "Yes, I agree that I don't have anyplace to go." He felt numb.

"Would you be interested in taking a job of sorts?"

Raintree looked up. "Of sorts?"

The priest assumed a wry grimace. "Very poor pay, I'm afraid. You could do maintenance work in the church. In return, I'll give you room and board. I suppose I could find a little pocket money for you on occasion."

Once again Raintree had to reconsider his plans as a result of a casual suggestion from this man. "Is that usual?" he asked.

"Is what usual? Limited pocket money? Very."

"No, I meant when a penniless stranger shows up and you invent a job for him and invite him to stay."

Father Costanzo looked thoughtful. "Hold on a minute." He carried the skillet to the table, where he heaped eggs, bacon, and fried potatoes onto the two plates. Seating himself, he filled two glasses from a pitcher of orange juice.

"No, Jim, that's not how I usually do things, but I see this as a special case. Not only are you broke and homeless, but you have questions that need to be answered. Questions it's my duty to answer as a man of God. In your case, I have a peculiar feeling that it's unusually important for you to get these answers."

Raintree picked up his fork and started eating, a little tentatively. At the Lighthouse he had fallen into being a vegetarian. Still...

Costanzo's reasoning was satisfactory, and his offer attractive. A big part of Ben yearned for a safe, comfortable, quiet hole in which to hide. Yet another part warned that such a respite must only be temporary.

"I'll tell you what, Father. I'll stick around and help out today, if only to repay your hospitality. As for what happens next, let's wait and see."

"Fair enough."

After breakfast was cleaned up the priest and Ben walked to the church. Ben finally noticed the name on the sign out front: Our Lady of Good Counsel. Our Lady? Whoever that might be, good counsel would be welcome from any source.

The interior of the church had lost the air of mystery that had been so thick last night in the candlelight. Now it was bright with the passage of sunlight through stained glass windows that had been lifeless in the dark. As they entered, the priest dipped his fingers into a container of water placed beside the door and performed a quick gesture which Raintree didn't fully follow. Ben didn't try to imitate it, nor did the priest seem to expect it.

Costanzo showed him the closet where cleaning supplies were kept. "We have to get the place back to normal after yesterday. We're having an ice cream social in the community hall this week, and we want things to look good. The palm fronds and lilies have to go. The fronds must be burned out back. See what you can do with the floor and the pews. I have to run some errands and visit some of the parishioners, then I'll come back and help."

Once he was alone in the church Raintree studied the tools he'd been presented with. He wasn't quite sure how to use them, but he'd been too embarrassed to admit his lack of such basic knowledge. He surmised the function of the broom quickly enough, and got busy on the wooden floor. In the course of the work he had a tour of the church. He was bewildered by the density of its religious imagery, which was far more complex than he'd noticed in the night. The crucifix might be the center of this form of Christian worship, but it was neither the largest nor the most ostentatious image present. Life-sized statues of a man and a woman stood in niches beside the sanctuary. The woman was robed in blue and white, wore a radiant disk-like crown, and carried a baby adorned with a smaller such crown. Could this be "Our Lady"? The man was a more humble-looking character robed in brown. Smaller statues stood in lesser niches here and there. Then there were the scenes in the stained glass windows, vignettes of sad-eyed men and women wearing long robes, plus twelve relief panels hanging between them, which seemed to depict the process by which Christ had ended up on the cross. Winged angels and other celestial beings were painted on the ceiling. Raintree feared it would take years to properly understand this daunting complexity. No wonder this religion required specialized priests to keep it all straight.

The work itself, he found, was surprisingly agreeable, even calming. For the first time he could recall he had the sense of actually accomplishing something useful. It might not be low-temperature physics, but at least it was more productive than endless moping and self-pity.

Presently he had herded all the floor's debris into a pile near the side entrance. Not quite sure how to proceed, he propped open the door and swept it all out onto the lawn, where it remained an unsightly mess. He frowned down at it. Oh well, maybe the wind would come along and disperse it before anyone noticed.

What should he do next? The closet contained a perplexing assortment of chemicals with brand names intended more for dramatic impact than for any kind of useful description. He was examining the instructions on a bottle of "floor wax" when Father Costanzo returned.

"Waxing the floor?" he laughed. "That's pretty ambitious. We usually save that for before Easter, not after. Let's see if we can get the communion rail polished up for now. That will keep us occupied for a while."

Raintree soon found himself using a rag to apply a thick liquid to the wooden railing. While they worked, Costanzo gave him a highly condensed overview of the Catholic faith and its beliefs: original sin; the function of Christ as redeemer; the Trinity; the Sacraments; Heaven, Hell, and Purgatory; Mary's role as Virgin Mother and intercessor in Heaven; temptation, sin, and damnation; grace, forgiveness, and salvation. It took over an hour. By the time it was over, Ben's mind was choked with details, but he still possessed only a garbled understanding of the overall structure of the belief. A hundred questions about particulars and generalities demanded to be asked. He decided to start with the biggest issues he could think of.

"Father…I don't think I understand the significance of the Crucifixion."

The priest gave him an attentive look. "How so, Jim?"

"You say that Jesus had to sacrifice his life in order to save mankind from the burden of sin, but I'm not sure I see what the sacrifice really was. Jesus suffered pain and torment, to be sure, just as many other men have. Yet, he didn't really die. He was an aspect of God. He came back three days later, good as new. Why was that so significant?"

"Well, look at it this way, Jim. Jesus was not God disguised as a man, the way Odin would sometimes walk the earth. Jesus was God *as* a man. Consider it. The Supreme Being, transcendent of space and time, an eternal mind outside of creation and preexisting it, arranged to have Himself born into the world as a fragile, mortal, vulnerable man. True, he also still existed as God, but the part of Him that was Jesus was just as much God as well. Jesus was capable of fear, pain, and doubt. At the end, he even gave in to a kind of despair, though finally he overcame that with his last words. And why did He do all this? Out of love and mercy for a creation that had always been a huge disappointment to him. To save men from the just fruits of their behavior, whether in the past, present, or future. God was willing to humble himself, to subject himself to persecution, torture, and death at the hands of these sinners. Yes, the death of Jesus was not a permanent thing, but it seemed real enough to that forsaken man hanging on the cross."

Ben nodded thoughtfully. "That does put things in a different light. But tell me, how is it possible for people to be a disappointment to God? Aren't they the way God made them? How can they be anything different? And how can an omniscient God who is, as you say, outside of time, be surprised by anything people do?"

Costanzo put down his polishing rag and sat down on the floor with his back to the railing. "That's another question I often hear from the doubtful. This one hinges on a mistaken idea about the nature of Man. When God said

Man was made in his own image, he meant that Man has within him a spark of the divine autonomy that sets God apart from all other beings and creatures. That is the 'spirit' that makes us divine beings, higher in some sense even than the angels. For glorious as they are, angels are wholly agents of God, without the freedom or even the inclination to pursue their own agendas, with few exceptions. We, on the other hand, have free will. We can, must, and do freely choose between good and evil. We therefore can and often do act in ways that profoundly disappoint God."

"So, you say we have the freedom to choose between good and evil. Yet it seems a fairly contingent sort of freedom, for if we choose evil, we are condemned to eternal torment. You tell me God is infinitely merciful. If that's the case, how can anyone ever be damned to Hell?"

"God's mercy is truly infinite. No matter how vile a man might be, how great his sins, he can gain salvation through God's grace, by repenting of his sins and asking forgiveness. That forgiveness is always forthcoming."

"But what if someone, making a good faith effort to understand the world and abide by the reality he sees in it, doesn't believe in this God or Jesus? Is that really deserving of eternal torment? I see no mercy there."

"If someone has been given the Word of God, and then fails to heed it through his own pride or vanity, but casts God away, then that man is cast away from God at his death."

"And what happens to nonbelievers who are never exposed to the word of God?"

Costanzo's eyes shifted aside in some embarrassment. "Our doctrine has it that such people are sent to a neutral place after death."

Raintree sat down on the floor across from the priest. "So by telling me all this, you are actually condemning me to Hell, unless I convert to your beliefs."

Costanzo laughed uncomfortably. "I'm glad that few of my parishioners look at things from this perspective. I'm not sure what to tell you about that. I only know that I have complete faith in God and His wisdom, and that all things and happenings are in some sense just."

"That brings me to what I promise will be my last question of the day. Why do you believe any of this?"

The priest had looked away again, momentarily relieved, but then his eyes locked back onto Ben's. "It's a matter of faith. Of deep inner conviction. There is no external proof of it, nor any need for it, to a believer."

"Were you born into your religion?"

"Yes."

"And what if you had been born into another? Would you be sitting here proclaiming that other faith just as forcefully?"

"That's an interesting—additional—question. I'm not sure it would be possible for 'me' to be born into another faith. That person would be so unlike myself that I'm not sure in what sense it would be 'me'."

"The same spirit born into a different body in a different land."

He shrugged. "I would hope that in that case the Word would reach me and I would see the truth."

"And the billions of people who follow incompatible religions, yet who avow their truths as ardently as you do yours—all are misguided?"

"Unless there are aspects of God and his intentions which are unknown to me, then yes. Jim, I've told you that this is not a matter amenable to reason. I know the truth of my faith because when I look inside myself I see and feel it without question. Yes, sometimes I am troubled, and find it hard to reconcile my beliefs with my thoughts or with things I see happening in the world. But the core of my beliefs remains within me. What do you see when you look within yourself, Jim?"

For Ben, this discussion suddenly went from a matter of mostly intellectual interest to a lance into the deepest part of his inner grief. He lowered his face and said miserably, "When I look inside myself, I see emptiness. I see nothing inside myself. I am nothing."

The priest said nothing for a long moment. Ben looked up with difficulty.

Costanzo's face was full of astonishment. When he spoke again his voice was quiet and gentle. "I'm sorry, Jim. But sometimes that kind of emptiness exists so that it can be filled."

"What do you mean?"

"Many times the men who find the greatest faith are those who once believed in nothing. Sometimes the harshness of life burns away someone's faith and innocence and leaves them with nothing. They may stay that way, lost in misery and hopelessness, or they may turn out to be vessels cleansed by God for the filling. You have obviously been educated by people with a high regard for rationality and reason. But you still strike me as a true innocent, as someone who needs only to find his path, not to be healed. Tell me, isn't there anything in the world you simply believe in, without understanding it?"

The ghost of an unforgettable glow lit up Raintree's eyes. His heart leaped up. "Have you ever seen the Stone of Inner Light?" he asked in a hushed voice.

The priest eyed him keenly. "Yes, as a matter of fact, I have. I visited Boston two years ago, and made it a point to go to the Lighthouse."

"What did you think of it?"

"Of the Stone? I felt...that it was clearly a holy thing, a numinous thing. The most obviously divine thing in the world. A thing of God."

"Yes. But it is not a sweet thing, nor a safe thing, nor an easy thing. It can heal, or it can burn, but it can never corrupt. I believe in that."

Chapter 14

Low Point

Stingray slowly descended though a dark realm of drifting, darting clusters of softened stars.

With every one of his considerable suite of senses extended to their maximum, he set a new personal unassisted depth record with every moment.

He was so motionless, and so alien, that the swarms of abyssal creatures around him barely reacted to his presence. Gelatinous creatures sometimes brushed along his naked body as he sank, pulled down by the rusty diver's weights strapped around his waist. Aside from the weight belt and the soft touch of luminescent animals, the only thing he felt on his skin was seven miles of cold, dark seawater.

He had always doubted his ability to descend to such depths unprotected. By nature a creature of the light, he had rarely ventured even into the uppermost levels of the abyss without his wonderful submarine wrapped around him. He had feared the pressure of greater depths. Surely he dared not exceed the few thousand feet braved by sperm whales, who were so much better adapted to life in the sea than he was, a pseudo-human with some incidental aquatic adaptations.

And yet, he had underestimated the thoroughness of those adaptations. By making the descent over a period of days he had been able to adjust. His lungs were of course full of seawater, as was his gut. Even his sinus cavities had gradually filled up, until now he had no undissolved gasses left in his body, leaving him as incompressible as the fragile animals around him.

A large angler fish, its shape defined by rows of luminescent spots like the windows of a cruise ship, flittered by within arm's reach, its lure twitching. Stingray eyed it. He felt its electrical field impinge on his. He sensed the tiny pressure pulses sent out by its waving fins. He smelled it. He imaged it with faint ticks of sonar.

Hungry as he was, he let it pass. He was naturally equipped to shock the angler, to stun it vocally, to stab it, or to simply reach out, grab it, and stuff the grotesque thing into his mouth.

He had left behind his plankton-strainer, that awkward towed cone of fabric which was the only source of food in the open sea for a large, would-be vegetarian such as himself. At these depths there was no easy meal to be gained, not even that gritty grey-green slime.

Stingray would make no compromise. He had vowed to exempt himself from the ghastly chain of life eating life, or at least from eating life that might be sentient enough to be aware of its fate. The tiny copepods and other zooplankton in his usual diet would have to take their chances...unless he could locate another source of food.

His first hint of the approaching bottom came from his sonar, which he muttered in a continual unconscious undertone just to keep an ear on things. His pulses were being faintly but solidly returned from below. He had nearly made it.

A few minutes later he settled into cold ooze. He lay there willing himself to full wakefulness, firing up the metabolism he'd dampened to reduce his need for oxygen during the long descent, especially in the oxygen minimum layer far overhead, which he had barely been able to penetrate.

When full life and warmth returned to his limbs he stood up, awed to be standing alive and unprotected on the floor of the Challenger Deep, the greatest depth in all the oceans of Earth. It was as if a human being should discover himself able to survive the rigors of space and bounce naked over the surface of the moon.

This was perhaps the ideal place for him to be. Here he would be isolated from the malice, stupidity, and greed of the human world.

And the human world would be isolated from Stingray, the murderer, the fratricide.

He released his weight belt and let it drop into the muck, returning him to neutral buoyancy. He did not know how far he was from his destination, or its exact direction. Without navigational equipment, he'd been able to only roughly determine the point on the surface from which to descend, and currents must have shifted him considerably during the long dive.

And so he must seek about and count on his previous foresight to guide him.

He began a steady swim just above the sea floor, always trying to trend down to maximum depths. Steep slopes continually led him deeper. He had not, unsurprisingly, landed by happenstance at the very deepest point. The Marianas Trench was the world's greatest underwater canyon. Its east wall was being gradually but inexorably drawn beneath the west wall by tectonic forces. Along the seam of subduction, rock which had been part of the ocean floor since the emergence of life on land was commencing an interminable stay in the molten depths of the Earth.

Fish, large and small, flitted about, visible, if at all, by their ghostly luminescence. Shrimp danced by clicking faintly. Now that he was fully awake, each one seemed a tempting morsel, yet still he desisted. He detected a great undulating rope of mindless life a few fathoms overhead, a siphonophore, fifty feet of external stomachs and appetite. He halted, making sure of its course, lacking any desire to come within reach of its stinging tentacles.

From the distance came a steady *fwump fwump* sound. He steered toward it, and soon a small smile curved his lips. Arching and flopping along the sea floor was a large stomping crab: not really a crab, but a hard-shelled relative of the ancient eurypterid line. It fed by inching forward on the tiny legs in its rear carapace while raising its large hinged fore-section, then bringing it down hard, creating a small cloud of muck, hopefully revealing or startling whatever small worms might be beneath it. It was an animal Stingray had discovered himself, back when his life was more like that of his old hero Captain Nemo than of some reclusive seagoing Tarzan.

He swam on, leaving the crab to its existence of creeping and cratering.

A short time later he detected something that told him his skill and luck had been good: a pulsing tingle in the water, half-heard, half-felt, the signature of the sense that enabled him to detect electric fields. He halted, drifting over the muck. Immediately below him was buried a five-mile-long wire, one of three which radiated from his destination. Tiny trickles of current shot along it; he need only follow them.

Presently an intermittent light began to show through the haze of the depths. It was a rotating beacon, a lighthouse submerged in the sea's greatest abyss. The sight of it, a thing so unexpected and lovely in this eternal darkness, caused him to halt again, mesmerized by its beauty, a beauty all the richer for its poignant reminder of all he had lost.

He swam on. The mists resolved into a cluster of spheroids, each poised on three legs and interconnected with cylindrical tunnels. The beacon turned atop the central and largest spheroid, which was marked with the "V" emblem of the Vigil, as well as by Stingray's own eponymous emblem. The light was now too intense for his vision, adapted as it was to depths lit only by constellations of fireflies. He hung back, squinting while his eyes adjusted to the idea and the reality of light.

Here was a research station he had built back when he cruised the seas in that magnificent submarine, which was now lost to him, or at least left behind. A research station, and also a hideout, should he ever need one. A place beyond the reach of all but a very few.

He swam to one of the outlying modules, opened the hatch, and entered the station. There was no airlock; it would have been senseless to maintain a gaseous environment at this depth. At this depth it was impossible for him to quickly transition between air and water. It was too bad; he'd have been more comfortable living in a gas mixture.

The entrance module was dimly lit by blue standby lights. He swam through the tunnel into the main module, a spheroidal volume about equal to that of a large camping trailer.

To Stingray, having roved the seas alone for several years of self-exile, it seemed a wonderland. The precise controls, the clean, smooth surfaces, the exotic materials, the casual use of light where it was most useful and attractive, all were in great contrast to the unbounded, wild ocean. He studied the status displays on the main console with great satisfaction. Though he had to remind himself how to interpret their symbols and graphs, he quickly found that all was well. The tachyon pile was intact, capable of powering the station for centuries. The Vigil's technology might not have the gloss and panache of Perturbare's toys, but it was built to last.

Awash with a sense of delicious luxury, Stingray keyed on the heaters. With all this power at his disposal, there was no need for him to dwell in icewater. He also turned on the main interior lights at a low level to accommodate his still-sensitive eyes.

Also present in abundance was...food, a thought which put his body into some kind of automatic feeding mode. Flinging open the storage lockers, he pulled out foil packages which variously drifted toward the ceiling or sank to the floor. He selected a package of spaghetti garnished with vegetable protein concentrates, contemplated tearing it open and wolfing down its contents, then forced himself to throw it into the heater pot so he could eat like a civilized being. It took him a moment to recall how to operate the heater. Care was required: at this depth, water could get hot enough to melt lead without boiling.

A few moments later he snatched out the successfully heated pack and tore off the seal. He forked out lumps of the clumpy mass, whose scent immediately suffused the water around him. It tasted like ambrosia after his diet of cold grey slime. Even as he devoured it he was aware of its shortcomings. Food meant to be consumed underwater could obviously not be water soluble. It had to be bound in a coating of greasy wax to hold it together. Here was yet another reason why so many vertebrates had crawled from the sea at their first opportunity.

Afterwards, he saw no reason to deprive himself of a package of cherry-graham dessert, and he did not. Finally satiated, he inventoried the food lockers with their glittering racks of packets, a treasure beyond that of any shipwreck he had encountered. Here was enough food for months at least.

Glancing into a mirror, he was arrested by what he saw. His fine blond hair swirled around his head like a yellow fog. He had long been annoyed by the drag it created. Here was his opportunity to deal with it. He located a pair of stainless scissors (some simple technologies were too elegant to require improvement) and started hacking away at it. The severed locks drifted off to accumulate against the screen of the water ventilation system. He tried to give himself the same sort of longish haircut, parted along the top, that he had always worn, but found it impossible to keep the sides at all symmetrical when they kept wafting and drifting in the currents. Finally he just snipped it all mostly off and called it good.

The face he saw in the mirror was no less startling than before. He had seen many faces in his years of wandering the sea: those of sharks and other fish with expressionless eyes; wise-looking turtles; seals and sea lions with limpid gazes; sharply curious squids; dreaming whales; laughing dolphins. He'd even seen a number of human faces. He had seen no other face like his own: superficially human, but more deeply something else. His skin had lost its tan and now had a purplish-green pallor. His features, which had always been rather stark with its prominent beaky nose, now looked leaner and fiercer than ever, both because he'd lost weight and because of the prophetic gleam in his eyes, which were a solid deep blue with huge black pupils. He was taken aback by the change, a change which would require a substantial readjustment of his self image.

He surveyed the rest of the habitat. It was comfortable, though hardly sybaritic. It contained only a single purely decorative item: a small model of a lighthouse which rested on a desk. He picked it up and turned it in his hand, brooding over it for some time, thinking of all it had once represented to him. That light. That beacon.

At last he set it down and pondered whether to reacquaint himself with the affairs of the world. He had no plans to end his exile. He was still, at heart, a savage, a killer who had ripped out the throat of an unresisting enemy in a moment of uncontrolled rage. An "enemy" who was in fact Kern Harner, his closest friend from the years of his wanderings through space, and the gentlest and most well-meaning person he had ever known.

Stingray's life was divided into episodes with distinct boundaries. First had been the stage in which he had wandered the seas in a ray-like non-human form, a period he barely remembered, and whose reality he sometimes doubted. Then he had metamorphosed into his present humanoid state, and had for a time wandered the seas as an innocent. Then the Space Mariners had come, had seen the light of inquiry in his eyes, and had taken him up to educate him, and to walk with him in the realm of starlight. When he disagreed with their intention to set themselves up as the benign despots of Earth, they had locked away his memory and dumped him into the sea to live again as a savage.

Then Fomalhaut had raised him up again, making Stingray his first ally in his struggle against the Space Mariners, or the Para-men as they came to be called. In their final battle, Stingray had slain the notably harmless Kern Harner, had regained his memory as a result of the shock, and had flung himself into the sea in an effort to atone and to escape his guilt. Thus he'd come to his current diminished condition.

No—he had no intention of ever setting foot on land again. The small, fragile, foolish people he resembled must not be subjected to his violence. He would remain here at Challenger Station until its food supply was exhausted, then ascend again to the reach of the sun, or not, as he saw fit.

But, as long as he was here, he saw no harm in finding out what was going on with his former colleagues of the Vigil, and with the world in general.

He turned on the quantum radio, seeking first to eavesdrop on the doings of Possum Perturbare. To his surprise, he found no activity on any of the channels the rogue scientist used to control his impressively insidious worldwide network of intrusion and obfuscation. In fact, the channels themselves were dead. Stingray switched to the bands used by the Vigil. These were also dead. Had both the Vigil and Perturbare gone out of business? Or had they perhaps moved on to some still more subtle communications technology?

Apparently he'd have to monitor the radio frequencies used by ordinary mortals if he wanted to learn anything. He released an antenna buoy which snaked its way up through seven miles of water. He was relieved to find that these bands at least were still active. Apparently the world had not wholly fallen into ruin during his absence. He picked up a Japanese news broadcast and decided to listen to that.

"Members of the Diet have petitioned Prime Minister Watanabe to hasten the process of banking reform in an effort to arrest the serious slide in our economy…

"The people of Shizuoka Prefecture have announced the resumption of their traditional dolphin capture and harvest. The fishermen of Futo say they intend to conform to all restrictions mandated by the International Whaling Commission, but to no others…

"Negotiations with the Russian Government over the return of the Kurile Islands are set to resume after months of inactivity caused by the recent incapacity of the Russian president…

"Hope is mounting that the recent Russian-American nuclear attack on Dr. Possum Perturbare has resulted in the death of the criminal scientist. Although the government has officially protested this profligate use of nuclear weapons, there nevertheless is a widespread sense of relief that Perturbare's reign of chaos seems to be at an end. Chile, Argentina, and Brazil remain in a state of war with both attacking nations as a result of damages suffered during the attack. According to President Hohman of the United States, his government is simply waiting for the aggrieved nations to calm down enough to permit him to offer the aid needed to get their paralyzed economies and infrastructures back into action.

"In a related story, Fomalhaut, leader of the Vigil, remains unaccounted for after the American destruction of the Vigil's bases. Other members of the Vigil are thought to be still at large, and are being actively sought, though the Americans offer no details…"

Stingray listened numbly for a few more minutes, then snapped off the radio. He drifted for a lengthy period of time, trying to assimilate what he'd heard. Why had he turned on that damned radio?

Abruptly he brought his fist down on a countertop, smashing it despite the resistance of the water. He was instantly chagrined by the damage, picking up the pieces and planning how it might be repaired—anything but face the decision he now saw was inevitable.

He had been better off in ignorance. Now his respite here must be delayed. After all the effort he'd put into reaching this place of peace, he must leave it again at once.

Apparently he must walk on land once again.

Chapter 15

Second Interview

Early in the morning, a pair of diffident men entered Perturbare's cell. One brought him a tray of breakfast and removed the previous night's dishes and utensils. The other hung half a dozen identical suits of clothes on a wooden rod. They departed, having spoken scarcely a word.

Perturbare got up and examined the clothes. The outfits consisted of pocketless black slacks and white linen shirts, each sporting the "P" monogram. There were no shoes, just two pairs of slippers.

Finishing his breakfast, Perturbare studied the shower. It occupied a corner of the room which was floored with tile instead of wood. Like the toilet, it was in full view, without doors or curtains. The controls were unconventional, with separate knobs for soapy water and clear. Evidently he was not to be trusted with a bar of soap. He shrugged and stripped off his clothes, enjoying the hot water. He exhibited his usual morning erection, which he made no effort to conceal. After all, Jenni Katz herself might be watching from behind the mirror.

Afterwards, dried and dressed, he sat in a chair and awaited the first item of whatever agenda his captors had planned for him today.

The door opened, and in walked a man dressed in the uniform of a naval officer. Perturbare restrained a desire to roll his eyes at the sight of him. Not only was he disappointed that this was not Jenni Katz, but he sensed he was going to have trouble with this new visitor. The man was a caricature, his hair a fierce brush of upright steel wool, his skin weathered as the decking of a wooden ship, his blocky chin outthrust like the fantail of a destroyer. Oddly, his blue jacket was devoid of either rank insignia or name tag. He strutted up to the seated Perturbare and stood looking down at him with an air of triumph and satisfaction.

"*Arrrr-r-r,* matey. And who might ye be?" asked Perturbare.

"I'm one of the officers responsible for your downfall and capture."

"Aye, and a Jim-dandy job you did of it too, I must say. Name, rank, and serial number?"

"You don't need to know any of that."

"Very prudent, very prudent. I'll just call you Captain Marvel Senior. Why don't you have a seat? Gloating can take a lot out of a man, I know."

"I'll stand."

"Then I'll stand too." Perturbare leaped up, crossed his arms, and tried to reflect the scowl he was receiving.

"Let me get something straight with you, Perturbare: the issue of which one of us is in charge here. Now, you're the world's foremost physicist, engineer, and computer scientist, is that correct?"

"Among other things. I'm also yo-yo champion of Patagonia and Tierra del Fuego."

"Well, yo-yo man, I'm a world-class student of three separate martial arts. Which of us do you suppose is dominant in this particular situation?"

"Hmmm." Perturbare assumed a thoughtful look. "That depends on what you're trying to do. If your intention is to engage me in some kind of conversation, I am clearly dominant. If you plan to beat me up, you may have an advantage. If you plan to either converse with or fight a gorilla, you lose on both counts."

The officer gave a grudging half grin. "You weren't such a smart ass with Ms. Katz. I wonder why."

"Take a look at yourself in the mirror, and then ask that question again. So, what do you want with me?"

"I worked for years to bring you under control. Now that I have, I want to take a look at you."

"What, didn't you see enough of me while I was in the shower?"

An instant later he was picking himself up off the floor and rubbing the side of his head. His ears were ringing. "Was that your foot?" he asked dazedly.

"I hope I've made the hierarchy in this room clear to you now. You are the prisoner here. I will not tolerate any more of your insolence."

Half crouching, Perturbare stared up at this man, whose small pale eyes were filled with half-disguised pleasure.

Since his capture, Perturbare had made a profound and difficult effort to control himself, to remain calm, to offer no threat. To be alert for any opportunity. It was the most sensible course of action, considering his powerlessness.

But that kick to the head had shattered his resolve. The threat had become overt, far sooner than he'd hoped it would. He could respond with either submission or defiance. Surely submission, or apparent submission, would keep him in one piece longer.

He reached up and wiped blood from his ear.

And found himself, quite to his surprise, springing at his tormentor, a ragged cry in his throat. He had no training in fighting, yet he managed to surprise his foe long enough to cuff him hard on the side of the mouth. The navy man reacted with a bellow of outrage and a look that would evoke smiles from Perturbare for as long as he was able to recall it.

That was the extent of Perturbare's victory. With a few moves he could barely follow, the officer swept Perturbare's feet out from under him and was upon him, threatening to break his arm.

With his face to the floor, Perturbare heard the door being flung open and booted feet rushing in.

"General, sir! Get off that man! Sir, you must get off that man!"

His attacker growled in disgust and released Perturbare, who rolled over to assess the situation. Two military policemen were flanking the general, while two others, their hands not far from their sidearms, stood off keeping a keen eye on things.

Perturbare eyed the general's Navy uniform and erupted in laughter. "General? You're so afraid of me that you can't even bring yourself to wear the uniform of the correct service in front of me? Well, I'll tell you what, Major Minor. You ought to be afraid. Someday I'm going to get out of here. I'll either think of a way out myself, or someone will walk right though that wall to come for me, and you and all your toys won't be able to do a thing about it."

The general's heavy face glared down at him. "Not a chance, you malcontented bastard. We'll see you dead before we allow you out of our sight. At the first sign of any escape or rescue attempt, we will kill you. That's official policy."

Perturbare sat up. "You're so unequipped to deal with those who might come for me that you'd be better off hiding in the uniform of a meter maid, Corporal Punishment."

"Let's go, sir," muttered one of the MPs.

Perturbare got to his feet. The other two MPs appeared beside him, and he had sense enough to stay put. He contented himself with yelling at the retreating back. "Hey, Private Parts! Come back any time, and I'll work you over some more! Dress like the Good Humor Ice Cream Man next time!"

The door closed, leaving him alone with the two guards. "I feel sorry for you guys, having to obey an inflated sac of testosterone like that." He looked down at his hand, at the blood on his knuckles. "Did you see what I did? Some of this blood might even be his."

One of the MPs could not restrain a partial smile.

A doctor and a nurse bustled in a few moments later, clucked over his bruises, applied antiseptics, declared him essentially intact, and left along with the MPs.

Shortly after that, Jenni Katz entered looking flustered. Today she wore a dove-gray suit over a pearly silk blouse. Emerald earrings glinted beneath her feathery blonde hair. Perturbare forgot the ache in his head and the ringing in his ears at the sight of her. He could almost feel his pupils dilating to take her in.

"I'm sorry, I'm sorry, I'm so sorry, Doctor...what do people call you, anyway? Possum?" She walked up to him and placed her hand on his arm.

"Usually just Doctor, or Perturbare. You can call me Turby if you want to."

"Ah, yes...Doctor. Anyway. That man should never have been allowed in here. He bullied his way in using his rank and his notable success in the operation against you. I don't think you'll be seeing him again."

"Gee. And I was just starting to develop a fondness for the big lug."

"Are you sure you're all right? If you are, I'd like to tell you what we have planned for the rest of your day."

Perturbare felt his ears prick up. "Are you kidding? I've had rougher times at chess matches. Now, what might these 'plans' of yours be?"

Jenni wrung her hands together, apparently unconsciously. "You're to be brought before a panel of inquiry. I had asked that this step be delayed until you were more comfortable here, but I was denied. Now I think it's especially foolish after this attack on you, but the panel is adamant. They will ask you questions. I hope you will be cooperative."

"That will depend on what they ask me."

She gave him an uncomfortable glance. "Eventually they'll reach a stage where they won't be very tolerant of evasions or refusals to answer. I really think it's for the best if you just tell them what they want to know without trying to hold back."

"I appreciate your solicitude."

"I also want you to know that if things ever get too uncomfortable when you're dealing with them, you can always ask to speak to me instead. I will try to make the process a little more pleasant for you."

"What is this, a good cop-bad cop sort of thing?"

She looked startled. "What?"

"You have these mean, dangerous partners who you might not be able to control. You're the sympathetic one. I ought to confide in you, to make things easier on myself."

Her regard grew somewhat more opaque. "Well, if that's what you want to think, I can't stop you."

Perturbare plunged ahead, unwilling to be manipulated, even by so pleasant a manipulator as Jenni Katz. "I will continue to think that way until I have some reason to think differently."

Her face assumed the shadow of a pout. "But I really am concerned for your welfare. Whatever your crimes or—mistakes, you're no murderer or monster. I dare say you've even done some good in the world. I don't want to see you abused."

Perturbare felt his heart starting to melt around the edges. "But you don't want to see me freed, either."

"No—I don't. I'm sorry."

"What that alpha male said—about it being policy to kill me rather than let me escape—is that true?"

Jenni nodded unhappily.

"It's good to know where I stand." His words and his heart had cooled down once more.

He was conducted to a darkened room whose only lights were directed at the hard wooden chair in which he sat. He could barely see the shadowy figures of the three men who sat behind a table before him.

The questioning began without preamble. "Doctor Perturbare," said a calm, self-assured voice, "when we took you prisoner we had ample opportunity to examine you before you regained consciousness. We collected blood samples, fingerprints, retinal and iris scans, and photographed you from every conceivable angle. Yet we have been wholly unable to identify you, whether through DNA analysis or by any other means. You appear to be an American. A native of Brooklyn, if I may venture a guess. Tell us please, who were you before you became known as Dr. Possum Perturbare?"

Perturbare laughed. "That's easy. I had no existence before I became Dr. Possum Perturbare."

"What do you mean?"

"I mean I literally did not exist before then. I emerged into being full-blown, like Athena. Do you remember when the Vigil attacked the base used by Brainchild, who apparently predated me? Well, just after that came the moment when I first came into existence, at least from the perspective of the universe."

A second voice, more dryly humorous, took up the conversation. "You're saying Brainchild created you somehow? Cooked you up in a vat or something?"

"No, no. From my point of view, I had a life before that moment. I went to MIT, collected pretty much their whole set of PhDs, bummed around a bit before deciding what to do with my life. But you'll find absolutely no evidence of any of this, because it doesn't exist. The only being in the world who remembered my previous existence was Brainchild, who no longer exists himself."

The calm man said, "What's the reading on this?"

A third voice, a Russian, replied, "He appears to be telling the truth."

"You've got some kind of polygraph pickups in this chair? Ooo. Cool gadget," said Perturbare.

The calm man said, "How did this remarkable situation arise, Doctor?"

Perturbare shrugged. "I made a machine that could isolate objects from the universal quantum field. I used it to escape when the Vigil invaded my old lab. Its effect was to blot out my prior existence. Don't worry, I invented Brainchild; he didn't invent me."

"How do you know that, son?" asked the second man, the one with the Southern accent.

"Huh?"

"You say there's no evidence you were ever alive before that moment, except in your own head and in Brainchild's circuits. How do you know the computer didn't create you somehow and give you these false memories? Maybe it wanted a pet."

Perturbare's conscience twitched, but that matter was irrelevant to the current question. "Interesting idea. But then, where did Brainchild come from?"

"What was your original name, son?"

Perturbare shook his head. "I'm not telling you that. I had a family back then, and those people still exist. They don't know or remember a thing about me, of course, but still, I'm not going to have you guys sniffing around them trying to find some faint whiff of advantage."

"I think we can return to this matter later," muttered the Russian. "It is interesting, but of no immediate concern."

"I agree", said the calm man. "Dr. Perturbare, let me raise the most fundamental question we have to ask. Are you willing to cooperate with us to make your technology available for the use of the world at large?"

"No."

A pause.

"And why not?"

"Because I don't want to. Because, as you say, it's my technology, they're my inventions, and I don't have to go around handing them out to anyone who asks. Certainly I won't fork them over to my kidnappers, a bunch of well-dressed thugs who imprison me without charges or a trial. As if you'd actually make the stuff available to 'the world at large'. It would mostly wind up in your militaries, and in the corporations that own you. The U.S. military is a big enough gorilla already, even without my help. A bunch of murderers too."

"We are not murderers," came the stiff reply.

"Aren't you? Is there not now a cloud of radioactive debris swirling around the southern hemisphere? How convenient for you dinks that it won't readily cross the equator. Did you clear out every fisherman and shepherd from the vicinity of my island before you started raining nukes on it? How many people died throughout South America because of the electromagnetic disruption? Any planes crash? Any hospitals go dark? And then there's Brainchild. You murdered him. You're not going to benefit from that if I can help it."

"Brainchild was a device."

"You're a device! A meat device. In many ways, Brainchild was the greatest mind on this planet. Any denial that destroying such a being is murder is at best a religious argument which is pointless to pursue."

The southern man took up the argument. "You seem like a decent fella at heart. I'm usually pretty good at picking up things like that. Don't you feel a need to make yourself useful to your fellow men, instead of messing with them the way you do?"

"You honestly think I'm worse than useless because I screw around with the political and economic interests of your rich and powerful friends. I will admit I've been questioning my own motives in the past day, but I do have a few good deeds to my credit. Remember how the ozone hole healed so much faster than predicted after CFCs went out of production? That was me. Remember the big scare about that HIV virus, but then everyone mysteriously developed an immunity? Me again. How about the Y2K fiasco? Did you know I had Brainchild look into every networked computer in the world to fix that? I don't know how much good I may have done by squelching these little problems early, but can any of you claim to have done as much? As if you care. To you cynical creeps, good and evil are just words you use to manipulate the serfs you parasitize in your glorious global economy. Hell, I used to think *I* was cynical. Compared to you goons, I'm Dr. Possum-Polly Perturbaranna."

"Well then," continued the calm man. "Your answer is quite unambiguous, if a bit emotional and rambling, not to mention rude. However, I must inform you that we cannot let it stand. Frankly, if you do not cooperate with us, you face a bleak future. We mean you no harm. Yet we will not and cannot allow you to resume your criminal activities. The Para-men are long gone. The Vigil has been beaten and scattered. With you now in our custody, the world is once again safely under the control of ordinary men. This time we plan to remain in command of our God-given dominion."

Perturbare chuckled. "Then you'd better pray that nothing happens to actually challenge this dominion you're so proud of. Because as you've seen, that control of yours is pretty tenuous."

"Hey Doc," said the southern man. "Earlier when you were talking to Mrs. Katz, you said something about some of your pals coming to bust you out. Was that Fomalhaut you were thinking of?"

"Mrs. Katz? She's married?"

The southern man chuckled. "Yes, I understand your disappointment. She's really something, isn't she? Yeah, she's married, or she was, anyway. She tells me she's a war widow. Now, back to my question?"

"Huh? Oh, Fomalhaut. Yes, he's the most obvious candidate to rescue me," answered Perturbare grudgingly.

"Well, we don't think you can count on him. Even if he managed to locate you, he doesn't seem the type to take that kind of overt, intrusive action. He's always been pretty diffident that way. Look at the defensive, almost passive stance he adopted against the Para-men. We figure he's too demoralized and confused to come after you."

Perturbare frowned. "And look at the way his defensive, passive stance prevented you proud patriarchs from being lorded over by the Para-men, any one of whom was three times the man any of you are, even though none of them were human. What the hell do you know about Fomalhaut? He may surprise you."

He could barely see the middle figure shrug though the glare. "You'd better hope he doesn't."

"I believe that's enough for today," said the calm man.

"I would like to make an observation before we adjourn," said the Russian. "A moment ago, Dr. Perturbare, you recited a litany of your good deeds. The ozone hole. I would like to point out that your base was located deep in the southern hemisphere, within the influence of the hole. Perhaps you wished to be able to sunbathe on your island without fear of skin cancer. The HIV virus. Perhaps you wished to avoid any risk associated with whatever sexual habits you practice. The year two thousand problem. A large part of your power and influence stemmed from Brainchild's infiltration of the world's computer networks. If those networks were to be disrupted, that influence would cease. It is one possible way to interpret these things."

Perturbare saw no need to reply to this.

Chapter 16

Ice Cream Social

Raintree's week passed quickly enough, his days occupied with sweeping, polishing, and a first exploration of the more advanced aspects of the handyman's trade. His usefulness to Father Costanzo was lessened by his inability to drive a car, but the priest promised to work on that too. His evenings were spent reading, or, when the priest's pastoral duties permitted, resuming their discussion of Christianity.

Thursday evening arrived and Ben found himself helping with the quarterly Ice Cream Social, held in a hall in the church's basement. There Costanzo introduced him as the parish's new maintenance man, and he was made welcome.

He was assigned to stand behind a table and hand out little cups of ice cream and plates of cookies to the families who came by. It was, he suspected, a task meant as much to bring him before the parishioners as to accomplish anything useful. He had some volunteer help: Michelle Hazilla, a teenage girl of ordinary appearance with hair of muted brown and prominent, uneven teeth. Despite her lack of physical distinction she was buoyant and laughed often. Raintree found himself liking her and appreciating her company, as well as the wry comments she offered about her friends and neighbors whenever they had a moment to themselves.

Ben found it fascinating to observe these people. They laughed, they joked, they greeted each other gladly. Their conversation was mostly related to their work, their families, and movies and television. There was surprisingly little talk of outside events, not even the fact that their country had closed its borders to its southern neighbor, an unprecedented act brought on by events that had taken place just a few hundred kilometers to the west. These grave matters, were, perhaps, not fit for discussion on what was supposed to be a night of fun.

One unusually loud man did joke about how much less interesting TV was now that Possum Perturbare was dead. This met with a strained response. Raintree winced. Somehow the death of one of his few friends still seemed unreal to him. His feeling of numbness about all these events troubled and puzzled him.

A large family entered the hall somewhat belatedly, led by a short, bulky, yet bluff and forceful man, florid in the face and balding in the pate. Behind him trailed a wan, mousy woman, and four attractive children. They trooped up to the table, where the man looked at Michelle expectantly.

"Ah, Jim Carina, I'd like to introduce you to my family. My father Ed Hazilla, my mother Adele, brother Curt, and sisters Meghan, Mary, and Moira. Family, this is Jim Carina, the new parish handyman, and my fellow ice cream hander-outerer."

Curt, who looked about sixteen, offered Ben a disinterested "Hey" and a slightly sullen glance. The other girls, all younger than Curt or Michelle, merely smiled at him, caught on the verge of giggling.

Ed Hazilla offered his hand. "Good to meet you, Jim. We've been needing a good replacement for our old maintenance guy. Father Mike has better things to do with his time than sweep up. You look like a strong young fella. You'll do well here. Just don't let your partner here fill your head with too many strange stories."

Ben smiled. "All right, Mr. Hazilla." He wondered why the man appeared to be trying to crush his hand. Wrenching it free, Ben tried to greet Mrs. Hazilla, but she refused to make eye contact.

Ben and Michelle handed out plates and cups. The family shuffled off to an empty table with Ed tossing out greetings along the way.

Michelle looked after them with an inscrutable expression.

"What does your father do, Michelle?"

She started as though she had forgotten he was there. "Do? Oh. He's an insurance agent. Exciting, huh?" She grimaced.

"He—seems like a friendly man."

"Yeah, that's him all right. He's just a friendly, friendly man. As friendly as they come."

Something about her attitude encouraged Ben to change the subject.

"Um… what do you think about the Trinity, Michelle?"

"The Trinity?"

"Yes, the Holy Trinity. You know, the existence of three separate persons in a single God. At first I found it all a needless complication. I didn't see why God would refer to Jesus as his son when Christ was really an aspect of himself. I couldn't understand how God could sit at his own right hand. I understood how God could become incarnate and walk among men, but why did it have to be as an entirely separate being? Or, if Jesus was to be separate, why not be truly separate, rather than one of the three Persons of God? And the role of the Holy Spirit, and the need for it as a separate entity, seemed obscure and elusive. I think I'm gradually coming to see the beauty in all this, but it's hard. You've been dealing with these matters much longer than I have. What are your thoughts?"

Michelle giggled a little uneasily and shrugged. "I don't know. I learned about this in Catechism of course, but I assumed it was all a mystery that people like me didn't need to understand, if anyone does. Wow, are you like a seminary student or something?"

"No," said Ben, nonplussed. "I know very little about it. I was just wondering."

It had never occurred to him that the followers of this complex faith might have so little knowledge of, and show so little interest in, its chief doctrines and tenets. Was this attitude common? He had planned to ask Michelle for her feelings about Communion, but now he held back.

Michelle was quite willing to drop the subject. At least the conversation seemed to have shaken her out of the brief funk she'd fallen into when her family arrived.

"There's old lady Wilkinson," she said in a low voice, indicating a woman wearing a large amount of costume jewelry and a fur wrap which featured the quite recognizable head of the animal that had provided the pelt. "She looks fancy now, but I know her paperboy. According to him, when he goes to collect she's usually wearing only a towel. He tries not to look." She snickered.

Ben cocked his head and studied the woman.

"And over there in the corner, that quiet couple and their kid? Very traditional Catholic family. She wanted a big family, and they got off to a good quick start. Then they found out he has a sperm count of zero. Questions were raised about the source of those little boys of theirs. Since then there's been a little tension between them, and no more children."

Michelle went on offering acerbic anecdotes about the people in the hall. Although she kept laughing and apparently having a good time, Raintree grew uncomfortable. He sensed a hardness in the girl, and doubted the appropriateness of all this gossip. Still, he listened, too unsure of himself to object.

Finally all the seats were filled, all the tickets collected, all the ice cream handed out.

"Do you wanna take our ice cream outside? It's not a bad night out."

"Hmm? Is that okay?" Raintree glanced over at the priest, beside whom a seat was conspicuously unoccupied.

"Uhh, yeah? This is a social event, not a roundup. We're allowed to leave."

"Well, all right." Feeling doubtful, Raintree grabbed his jacket and followed her to the stairs with their paper plates in hand. Father Costanzo looked at him with a neutral expression as they departed.

The spring night was not as cold as it could have been, but still, it seemed to Raintree, not especially suited to sitting around eating ice cream. He tried to hang back, to remain on church property, but she led him on with a careless laugh, not stopping until they reached a town park a few blocks away. There they sat on a bench beneath a great oak tree and ate. Raintree was shivering. Broken clouds moved across the dark sky, which hung suspended beyond the tree's twisting limbs and branches.

"I used to come to this park all the time when I was a kid. I used to climb this very tree and pretend I was on a pirate ship, being forced to walk the plank. You know, you're kind of homely too."

Ben started at this sudden pronouncement. "What?"

"Oh, I don't mean it in a bad way. You have beautiful eyes, but sad. It's just that you've got kind of a horse-faced thing going on too."

"Too? Is that how you see yourself?"

"Well, let's face it, I'm no beauty queen."

Raintree sat looking at her, at a loss for a cogent response. Finally he ventured, "It seems to me that you're a perfectly decent-looking person."

"Gee, you think so? That's quite a compliment. So, do you want to do it?"

"Do it?"

"Yeah, you know, fool around! Have sex. Screw me. Do you want to?"

By now Raintree's head was spinning. "Michelle...I admit I don't know a lot about these things. But...I barely know you."

"So you don't want me? That's okay. There are guys around here who don't care what it looks like, as long as it comes easy."

Raintree was flabbergasted. "I can't believe you're talking like this."

Michelle gave a brassy laugh. "What difference does it make? If you stick around you'll hear lots of crap about me anyway. You might as well hear some from me too." She snatched away Raintree's empty plate and cup and crushed them in her hand, along with her own. "Let me tell you about my dad. Did you notice the way he kept fussing over my little sisters? My pretty little sisters. For half my life I've been hearing from him how ugly I am, and how pretty they are. They get all his attention. All of it...even attention they don't really want. Dad has quite a lot of attention to hand out, except to me and Mom. Before they were born, I was good enough for him. After Meghan got to be five or six, suddenly I was out. And you know what's really sick? I miss it. I got to liking being with him. Now I—" Her voice caught in her throat. She turned her face away.

Raintree sat stunned, sickened, disbelieving. Suddenly he was filled with a longing for the purity and simplicity of his life with the Vigil, where no one dealt with such vileness.

"I—had no idea that such things could happen," he whispered huskily.

Michelle's mirthless laughter rang out again. "You're cute, you're so naive. You look like you want to die too. You must feel worse than I do. That's nice. But don't tell anyone about all this, okay? It's not like I have anyplace else to live."

"No, no, of course I won't. I'm so sorry you have to deal with such things. But tell me something. I hope I'm not being terribly naive again. You're obviously in terrible pain. What about your religion? Does it offer you no counsel, no comfort? Aren't you supposed to be able to— talk to God about your problems?"

She stared at him for a few moments with a blank expression.

"You know, I had to think for a minute to figure out if you're grievously clueless or just wicked sarcastic. But those puppy-dog eyes tell the story. Okay. In case you've never actually tried this, and you just happen to be working as a handyman at a Catholic parish without knowing a thing about the religion, it's like this. With me anyway. I used to be really into religion when I was little. But then, when things started to go bad around my house, I felt let down. I prayed and prayed, and still bad things kept happening, and I never heard any answers or felt any better. Now, I don't know if it's because I'm just too sick and twisted to hear the answers, or if there's just nobody there. Some of my friends say they get answers. Not like a voice in their head or anything, but just a silent kind of message, or a knowledge that comes to them when they pray with sincerity. They have faith; I guess I don't. So that's great for them, unless they're just kidding themselves. Who knows? It's not like religion is something people seem to talk about or even think much about, except during church. If then."

Raintree shook his head in bafflement. "I just don't understand how that's possible. Religion is supposed to be the thing that transcends all the pains of the world, the thing that promises to make sense of it all. How can anyone ignore that or set it aside? What on Earth could be more interesting or meaningful?"

She giggled. "Almost anything. Food. Beer. Clothes. Sex. Money. Maybe you should join a seminary or a monastery. I think you'd fit right in. In case you haven't noticed, you haven't stumbled upon a parish full of deep thinkers. We're just average people here."

"Average people. So you're saying...you go through life confronting all kinds of horrible situations, doomed to die, and yet you have no philosophical basis for your life, no faith, no beliefs to help make it bearable? You can't even talk to anyone?"

"There you go!" Her voice vibrated with strained merriment. "At last somebody understands me. Do you believe in anything?"

"Yes! Yes, actually I do. I believe in Inner Light."

"What's that?"

"It's...something that shines inside us. Obviously. Something pure, something real, something that shows we're not just animals scrabbling to survive in a brutal world, and that the universe is more than a brutal arena in which we struggle and die."

"Wow. And why do you believe in that?"

Raintree smiled. "I'm lucky. I've seen it. I've seen a thing you can hold in your hands, the Inner Light made physical. I guess it's easy to believe in things you've seen for yourself."

Her eyes grew round, her voice hushed. "Wow again. You mean like that Vigil thing?"

He nodded. "Yes. The Stone of Inner Light."

"You've seen that? I've heard Father Costanzo talk about it. I'd like to see it someday, if I last that long. I probably won't."

"I'd like you to see it too."

"Well, it's nice to think about anyway. Whoa, I actually feel a little better. Thanks for talking to me. Now I know why Father asked me to help with the Social. It's been a few years since I've done that. Anyway, you're a cool guy, Jim Carina, even if you don't want to do it with me. Goodbye."

Raintree felt himself blushing, a self-reinforcing process because it made him feel so foolish. "Thanks, Michelle, I'm glad I could help."

Michelle gave him a quick hug and departed for home. Raintree wandered back to the church, where the Ice Cream Social was over, the hall deserted. Michelle might be feeling better, but he was not. As he swept the floor and straightened the chairs he fell to brooding about Michelle's dismal state and what it implied about the human condition in general. At least one layer of his innocence had been painfully flensed away.

The cleanup took a good two hours. It was midnight by the time he returned to the rectory. Costanzo was already asleep, and Ben retreated to his own room and bed.

His sleep was disturbed, clouded by nightmares about Michelle and the darkness of human life. They woke him up, causing him to lay sleepless in the pre-dawn gloom. His thoughts could not be deflected from Michelle, her family, and life in general. He began to shake uncontrollably. He sat up in bed, clutching himself, rocking back and forth, wondering in his misery whether he was going mad. The horrors of life ate at his mind, driving him toward despair. What recourse did Michelle have? What escape was there for her? How did anyone stand it?

Good counsel. He very much needed good counsel, but he didn't know where to find it.

At last his anxiety collapsed, leaving him exhausted, and then deeply asleep.

He didn't awaken until well past dawn. He showered, dressed, and found the makings of a cold breakfast and a note from Costanzo, advising him he'd be out for most of the day and leaving a few instructions. Ben was happy to return to the church and devote his thoughts to the simple, mindless tasks that had been laid out for him. He kept at it for hours, finally quitting at twilight to return to the rectory to look for something to eat. His labors had left him with a tentative sense of peace.

At the rectory he found a pale Father Costanzo having an urgent telephone conversation. Raintree stopped dead at the sound of his voice.

"I've got to go; Jim's here. I'll keep in touch." He hung up the phone. "Jim, that was Ed Hazilla. His wife found a suicide note from Michelle a short time ago, and Michelle is missing. Did anything happen between the two of you last night?"

Raintree was again sickened, but somehow not surprised. "We had a conversation about herself and her beliefs. We sat in the park. I have a feeling that's where she might be now. Let's go over there."

The two ran out to Costanzo's old station wagon. "Jim, did Michelle say anything to make you suspect she was suicidal?"

"Not in so many words, but she did say some very disturbing things about her father."

They flung themselves into the vehicle. The priest's mouth was compressed to a thin pale line. "I'm sorry to get you involved in this. I thought talking to you might be good for Michelle. I've been afraid of something like this for a long time. Sometimes being a confessor is very difficult."

They quickly covered the few blocks to the park. Ben led the way to the oak tree where a younger and more innocent Michelle had once played. Sitting on a limb halfway up the tree was the shadowy figure of Michelle, busy tying a noose around her neck.

"Michelle," said Costanzo with forced calm. "Please come down. We can get you through this."

"Father? You know what this is about, don't you? I know my dad. He's a good Catholic. He goes to Reconciliation every week. But I know you're forbidden to tell anyone what you hear in there. I don't blame you."

"Michelle," said Ben. "Remember the Inner Light. Don't you want a chance to see it for yourself?"

"Hey, where I'm going, I'll be taking a bath in it, if God is merciful. Thanks for coming out though, Jim. You're such a cool guy."

Hidden beneath Ben Raintree's outer clothing was his Vigil flight harness. He opened his shirt and revealed the control panel. A moment later he rose into the air, sliding past limbs and branches until he reached Michelle. He set the hover control and looked into Michelle's tear-streaked face.

"What are you, Jim? An angel?"

"No. I'm just somebody who is keeping a vigil over you. Michelle, do you remember when I told you that the Stone of Inner Light is something you can hold in your hand? Well, I've held it in my hand. You can too, if you give yourself the chance. I'll hand it to you myself. Please, let me help you down."

Michelle looked into his eyes with a heartbreaking expression of hope and awe. Shuddering and sobbing, she fumbled to undo the noose around her neck. In so doing she slipped off her perch. Raintree grabbed her. The harness's automation was smart enough to compensate for the increased weight, so they sank only slightly before the hover stabilized.

With one arm around Michelle's waist, Ben used his other hand to reduce power, causing them to descend gently to the ground, where Michelle continued to cling to him.

Ben felt Costanzo's eyes on him, but so far the priest had said nothing. A dozen neighbors had arrived on the scene. A police car pulled up. Michelle's father emerged from the back seat, stalking toward them angrily.

"Michelle! You crazy little bitch. What's going on here? What kind of lies have you been telling these people?"

His hand was raised. Michelle cowered. Ben looked on, scarcely believing that any man could be so brazen. No one stood between Michelle and her father except himself. He disengaged himself from Michelle and stepped forward.

There was a flash of motion, and Ben found himself sprawled on the ground, stunned, his nose gushing blood.

"You keep your hands off me, broom-pusher," spat Hazilla.

"Jim!" shrieked Michelle. She leaped forward with an eerie wail, fingers extended like claws. An instant later she had drawn blood from her father's face.

By now the police were rushing up, one man grabbing Hazilla, the other holding back Michelle with difficulty.

"Michelle! Stop. It's all right." To Ben, his own voice seemed to come from a great distance.

She looked at him, relaxed, and began to sob. The two policemen hustled Hazilla back to the car.

The priest stepped up and helped Ben to his feet, offering him a handkerchief to stanch the blood. Then he went to take charge of Michelle, comforting her, promising her assistance.

Dazed, Raintree stared at the shadowy figure confined in the police car. In the poor light he got only glimpses of

Hazilla's expressions of anger, hatred, and fear. Ben wondered what, if anything, he had in common with such a man.

Raintree shook his head, wandering back to the priest and the girl as she agreed to be hospitalized.

"You'll come see me, won't you, Jim?" she pleaded.

"My real name is Ben. I'll come as soon as I can, I promise. But I don't know when that will be. I'm sorry."

Costanzo spoke a few words to the police, then led Michelle away to his car. The priest returned to Ben. "Jim —Ben—I need to go with her, but first I've got to see about you. So...you're really Ben Raintree, eh?"

Ben nodded. "That's what they tell me."

"I had my suspicions, but you look so much younger than I expected, I wasn't sure. Until you levitated like that, that is."

"There's a long story behind the way I look, but we've no time for it now. Now that my secret is out, I'd best be on my way at once. I have no doubt that American agents will soon be here asking after me. I wish I could stay."

"Yes. I agree. I'm sorry you had to be exposed to this sordid business tonight. This will hurt our parish, and more, I believe it could hurt you. I believe it's important that you leave. There's a quality in you that should be preserved, and it will be at risk if you stay here among us. Although I admit, I'm at a loss to suggest where you should go."

"Things could get difficult for you here, Father."

Costanzo shrugged. "I have nothing to hide."

"Goodbye then." Ben reached for the controls.

"But Ben...what about your faith?"

The question brought Ben up short. "My faith?"

"You've only begun to scratch the surface of Christianity, you know."

"I know. I know so little about it at this stage that I'm not even ready to form an opinion. But this much I have observed. If God or Jesus Christ have any influence over the lives of these people, it's too subtle for me to see."

"I've seen it. But then, I've been looking a lot longer than you."

"Yes. Well, I hope we can discuss this another time. Thank you for sheltering me when I needed it. I won't forget it."

"My Christian duty. And that reminds me." His voice dropped to a whisper. "There's a Franciscan monastery in the foothills just east of the town of Nakusp, on Upper Arrow Lake. It's around three hundred kilometers to the southeast. I'll contact them—discretely—and they'll take you in. It's quite a secluded spot. It has a log chapel with blue stained glass windows. Do you think you can find it?"

"I'll try."

"Oh...before you go..." The priest pulled out his wallet and emptied it of fifty dollars. "Your pay. The church looks better than it has in years."

Raintree accepted the money with a weak grin. "Thanks again. It's a good feeling to be paid for honest work, however humble it may be. Goodbye for now."

He manipulated the controls and sailed silently up into the night, watching the upturned faces beneath him until they disappeared. At first the night sky seemed dark, wide, cold, and lonely, but then a fan of seething green radiance rose up in the north and spread across the sky. Ben gasped at the beauty that unfolded above and around him, as though he were enfolded in light. No wonder he had so loved the aurora in his previous life.

Chapter 17

The Return of the Vigil

The fishermen of Futo Harbor were uneasy. Many dolphins, and even a few false killer whales, were penned up in the harbor, but the herding had taken much longer than expected. In the years since the lapse of the annual drive, much of the practiced coordination needed for its efficient execution had been lost. Many of their most skilled fishermen had been intimidated by the sea monster into avoiding the event. Now, at last, they had reason to hope they'd been freed from the monster's curse.

It was already dark, though much work remained to be done. The fact that the sky flared with northern lights did nothing to comfort the fishermen. They kept looking out to sea as they milled about the harbor in their boats, beating the water, hammering on metal bars, herding and concentrating the dolphins toward the piers, where they could be landed, then either sold alive or slaughtered on the spot. School children had been present to observe the resumption of the traditional harvest, but most had gone home at sunset, just as the animals were being driven into the harbor, their escape cut off by nets.

The drive was an elaborate production considering the short time they'd had to prepare it. A hundred well-armed members of the Japanese Defense Force stood ready along the docks, scanning the sea with night-vision goggles. A fleet of trucks stood by to carry the prey off to aquariums or to the meat market. Cranes waited to pull the living animals from the water.

The cetaceans were growing increasingly frantic, unable to escape the painful din set up by the fishermen in their boats, approaching panic as they were confined and concentrated closer and closer to shore. Some were already crying out and wailing, sounds audible to the humans on shore. They were merely the first notes of a chorus of agony and death that would be raised when the dolphins were hooked out of the water and then bled and butchered while still alive.

At last the pod was separated into manageable groups, each flailing, squealing cluster netted hard against a pier, where they had no place to flee, where they could be handled conveniently. The men in the boats readied their hooks and their ropes. Great banks of glaring white lights shone down into the water, revealing the tumult of sleek grey bodies just beneath the oily surface.

The fishermen took a last nervous squint toward the dark horizon.

One man whacked his hook into the flesh of a dolphin, starting to pull it in.

He dropped it from nerveless fingers at the cry that rose up from his fellows.

"The monster! The monster!"

They looked out to sea. A submerged orange light was surging toward the harbor. It went out, and a huge, dark, glistening shape leaped over the net with a shrill inhuman cry. It splashed back into the water and vanished.

Every man on and around the water began to yell and run around in panic. All the boatmen headed for shore at full throttle. Those closest to the piers abandoned their craft and scrambled up the ladders. The lights swept around the harbor. The soldiers stood their ground and activated the laser sights on their rifles.

The nets began to part, the dolphins to scatter. Some of the soldiers fired into the water, causing dolphins to thrash in agony, or jerk and suddenly go limp. "Stop, stop!" cried the fishermen. They wished to call down upon themselves no greater wrath than they already had.

A form flung itself from the water, landing to stand towering on a pier, dark and shining in the light of the lamps. Bulbous eyes shone from its round, dark head. With a ringing cry that shocked and stunned everyone within a hundred feet, it attacked the mob of fishermen, soldiers, and observers. Lightning leaped from it with cracks and booms, sending men flying, their clothes smoldering. Powerful limbs swept men aside like dolls, plucked away weapons and sent them hurtling into the sea. It leaped and spun and twisted, sinuous as an octopus. Soldiers aimed their weapons. Their red laser beams were all but invisible on the wet green-black surface of their attacker's armor, but they fired anyway. Each hit jerked its target back, but did no other harm. Stray shots brought down a few of the fishermen. An officer cried out to cease fire.

The chthonic, outraged wailing that emerged from the creature resolved into Japanese. Those who could still walk fled the scene.

"Yes, you greedy little bastards, run! These creatures are not your property, not your pets, not your merchandise, and they are not your god damned meat!"

Floating very high above the scene, Fomalhaut had seen enough. He cut the propulsion beams that had kept him hovering, observing the chaos below with every sense, sensor, and psychic faculty at his disposal. He dropped down, alighting beside the panting Stingray as he stood glowering at the fleeing remnants of the fishing crew.

Stingray turned his great helmeted head to take in the new arrival.

"Well, well. You have a habit of turning up just as I'm getting into trouble with the natives."

"You have this situation under better control than the first such one I saw."

"The equipment makes all the difference. Excuse me if I leave the helmet on, but I'll bet there are snipers out there who would enjoy exploding my cranium."

Stingray walked over to the line of trucks that had been intended to carry the dolphins away. Grunting, he flipped them on their sides, one by one.

A young boy ran out of the darkness. "Sea monster! You hurt my father." He dashed up to Stingray and pounded on his armored thigh.

Adults screamed at the boy from a distance, telling him to get away.

Stingray didn't bother to prevent the blows. "Look, boy, let me ask you something. Tonight your father failed to put these innocent creatures through the tortures of the damned. Will you still get something to eat tonight? Tomorrow night? He failed to cut open their guts while they screamed like women. Will you still be able to go to school? Will your family be all right? Yes? Why then did he need to do this horrible thing to these poor animals? Think for yourself!"

The boy turned up a tear-streaked face, broke off and ran away.

"Probably useless." Stingray resumed his work on the trucks while Fomalhaut watched in silence. "You know, that felt damned good! Lighting into those little buggers like that, I mean. The arrogant, greedy, cruel little shits. I know your views on the subject. 'Oh, we mustn't interfere with the precious humans. We must let them pursue their own path; we must not judge them.' Well, to hell with that. As if they aren't exercising their own peculiar brand of judgment when they decide that a whale or a dolphin can appropriately be turned into a slab of superfluous protein on their plate. I wouldn't trade one of these creatures for any dozen humans," he said, waving his hand at the harbor waters.

"I might just make it a habit to interfere with the humans, until they finally manage to pull me down. I suppose you disapprove. Well, what are you going to do about it?" He whirled on Fomalhaut, tense, ready for anything, and perfectly aware he could do nothing in opposition to him.

"Not a thing," said Fomalhaut mildly, looking up at the huge figure, taller even than himself.

Stingray's attitude showed surprise, but then he was distracted by a cry of pain from a fisherman lying nearby. Immediately his whole bearing shifted, collapsing into dismay.

"Yes, Stingray my friend, of course you have injured these people. Some of them are in danger of dying. Several have been shot by their own soldiers. You cannot exert force of such magnitude against beings as fragile as these without harming them severely."

Anguish came crashing out of Stingray. His wrath expended, all that was left now was pain.

"Stingray, you must resolve these inner conflicts, or they will destroy you. You cannot guard all life. You cannot act without consequences. You cannot bear the consequences of your violence, yet if you do not act at all, you will wither into purposelessness. Together, I think we can find a better way."

Stingray eyed him for a silent moment. "Let's get out of here so the humans can bring in medical personnel. But first, help me cut that harbor net so the cetaceans can escape. I left a sea sled out there too."

Between the two of them the net was soon in pieces. Stingray stuck his head beneath the water and let out a cry that soon had the harbor thrashing with the fins and flukes of fleeing sea mammals. A few were mortally wounded. Stingray grimly dispatched these by laying hands on them and releasing charges of electricity. Shaken anew by the need to deal out death, he summoned and mounted the sea sled, skimming the waves to reach a shoal of bare rock a few miles offshore, a hazard to navigation marked by an automated beacon. Fomalhaut awaited him there.

"You should rest, Stingray. You have not been taking good care of yourself, and your large expenditure of bio-electricity has depleted you further. Not to mention the emotional shock of what you've done."

Stingray sank down onto the rocks and nodded, pulling off his helmet. His pale skin was a strong contrast to the deep sea-green sheen of the outfit he wore. "Yes, Dad. How did you know to find me here?"

"I was fortunate enough to have a foresight that this event would draw you out of your self-imposed exile. You've heard of the downfall of the Vigil?"

He shrugged. "Yeah, I did. I didn't think much about it. The mission of the Vigil is completed. We performed brilliantly in preventing my old friends in the Space Mariners from imposing a sane, enlightened government over these people. Goodie for us. But now it's over. I don't know why you bothered to keep the Vigil together in the first place."

"I admit I had no clear or compelling reason for doing so, other than a vague conviction that it would someday be needed again. But now, somewhat belatedly, I propose a new mission for the Vigil."

"What might that be?"

Fomalhaut hesitated.

"To impose a sane, enlightened government over these people."

"You're kidding."

"I am not known as a habitual kidder."

Stingray's fathomless eyes burned into his. "So now you're saying it was all a big mistake? That we were on the wrong side all the time? That we suffered all that death and loss for nothing? Kern? Rouse? Cotavion?"

"That is quite possible. T'Ukudu is also dead, though not as a direct result of our conflict with the Para-men."

Stingray radiated a moment of shock. "I didn't know it was possible to kill him. What happened?"

"He ended his own life, supposedly because his mission for his Makers was complete, rendering his continued existence needless."

"Supposedly? You doubt this?"

"I believe there was more to it than that."

"Indeed. I'll pry into your reticence on that matter later. What's changed your mind about our previous stance?"

"Partly my conviction of the hopeless degeneracy of the human race, and its inability ever to govern itself wisely."

"I agree with that. What about the other part?"

"Well, with regard to that..." Fomalhaut knew he was in trouble when he opened a statement with such a useless phrase. This promised to be an embarrassing admission. He paused and set out again to explain himself.

"This is a curious matter. You recall my origin, how I came from another universe which has since perished, a member of an expedition meant to investigate the past of our own universe by exploring this one, a cosmos thought to be identical with our own, down to the most minute detail. How we made the transition at the very instant of the final collapse of our cyclical universe, emerging into the very creation of this one, or just barely past it. As the only survivor of that expedition, I came to Earth to record the last days of Man's tenure as ruler of the planet, presumably to watch as my own species arose to take Man's place as the new dominant race.

"Yet when the Para-men came and proposed a new government that promised peace and longevity for Man, thereby preventing the ascendancy of my own people, I felt obliged to take measures to protect what I believed was the correct sequence of historical events."

"Yes, yes, I know all that," said Stingray. "And while you served this goal of insuring the rise of your own people, you were also justly able to claim you were preserving human freedom, including their freedom to eventually destroy themselves, an event you deemed inevitable and proper."

"You make it all sound so ignoble," said Fomalhaut dryly.

Stingray burst out laughing.

Fomalhaut continued. "Of course, this all depends on the assumption that the congruence between this universe and my own is as exact as I was led to expect. Until recently, I had no firm reason to doubt that it was."

"And now you do?"

"I do. After the destruction of our headquarters and the scattering of our membership, I retreated to Venus to meditate and to decide on a course of action."

"Venus," said Stingray bemusedly. "Nice place?"

"It is peaceful. As you may or may not know, all knowledge is implicit in the very quantum substance of existence. This is the basis of all forms of extrasensory perception."

"Yes, I pretty much knew that, having hung around with you for years."

"While I was on Venus, I suddenly learned something that took me by surprise. I realized that this universe is not closed...not cyclical...it is open. It will expand forever, because it has insufficient mass to arrest the expansion. This idea has been gaining favor for years, but I had always assumed it was a mistaken notion based on inadequate observations. But suddenly I knew without any doubt that this universe is indeed open. In other words, it differs from my former universe in one of the most fundamental possible ways. Given that, how am I to know what other differences there may be? I now know that no future native version of myself can ever join an expedition meant to cross the boundary of this dying universe into its newborn twin. Perhaps no future version of myself will ever arise at all. Given that, I now feel myself at liberty to act as I think best for the greatest good of beings who actually exist, not for the benefit of some hypothetical future race of beings like myself."

Stingray nodded. "Logical. Convoluted, but logical. What's the source of this sudden certainty about the fate of the universe?"

"It is strange. Suddenly someone appeared on Earth who has complete confidence in this interpretation, and who has the data to back it up. Someone of such mental strength and conviction that his knowledge of the matter lit up the space between here and Venus, speaking figuratively."

"Hmm. Anyone we know?"

"I do not believe so."

"Interesting. So, what's your plan for world conquest?"

"That is something I hope to work out with your help and that of our other allies."

Stingray nodded again, a bit indulgently. "And who might they be? I'm experiencing deja vu."

"As I said before, our members are scattered. Raintree has vanished. Aureus has been taken by the military. I believe both can be recovered. And perhaps others can be found to fill our ranks."

"What about Perturbare? Do you think he's really dead?"

"I have no reason to think not. If he is not dead, he is almost certainly indisposed."

"Can't you scan for him telepathically or something?"

"It's no small matter to locate a single mind among billions. But what about Endurance? The last we saw of him—"

"—he said he was going to walk the length of the mid-oceanic ridge. And no, I didn't happen to run into him down there."

"In any event, I am confident we can begin again. We can rebuild. We had little more than this the first time we set out to organize. You were the first person I sought out to join me. You were always at the heart of the Vigil as much as I. The two of us, here together, are enough to be called the Vigil. Now once again I come first to you, to ask you to join me. Yes, you killed Kern Harner. It was a tragedy, and an act of war. Perhaps it was even a crime. Certainly it was a personal disaster for you. But I say to you, put the wisdom you gained through such pain to good use. End your exile. Let us work to achieve what we ourselves prevented the Para-men from accomplishing, and let us honor their memories in doing so."

"I don't feel especially wise," snapped Stingray, almost in a snarl. Then he subsided and fell to brooding.

"All right, you silver-tongued smoothie. You've buttered me up to a turn and talked me into it."

Fomalhaut released his breath. "I am genuinely relieved and pleased to hear that."

Stingray turned away and gazed back toward Futo Harbor, whose shore twinkled with the lights of emergency vehicles. His face was grim and strange in the shimmering light of the persistent aurora, mixed with the intermittent gleam of the reef's beacon.

"Those dolphin butchers back there thought they could safely resume their savagery because I had vanished and the Vigil had been destroyed. All they managed to accomplish was the rebirth of the Vigil. Quite a miscalculation on their part. I like that."

"Yes. I'm sure that was not their porpoise at all."

Stingray looked at him with disbelief.

Fomalhaut was learning it was useful, or at least amusing, to surprise people once in a while.

Chapter 18

The Approach

The little spacecraft was quite modest, nothing more than an escape pod from a starship the great wanderer had once encountered in some other cosmos. By itself, it was able only to traverse a volume of space equal to that of a typical star system.

Of course, with the help of the artifact Valjhar Cor carried within him, the pod was capable of transcending all barriers of space and traveling far beyond the limits of any starship ever built. Valjhar's goal was one particular world among all the infinite worlds of creation.

The pod did have good sensors and decent artificial intelligence, both of which were directed at the planet Valjhar was approaching at a deliberately sedate pace. A calm voice pronounced the results as the sensors determined each of the planet's physical and orbital properties. So far, the figures conformed to those he so dearly wanted to hear. Yet he had been disappointed many times before. He would leap to no premature conclusions.

For decades he had searched. He'd shift from one universe to another, always staying within the very limited set of conditions and properties that led to galaxies and stars. Having found a promising candidate, he would span and quarter it, hunting through the galactic froth for an arrangement like that which had formed the deep backdrop of his life in his home cosmos. Finding that, he would search for a small group of galaxies like the one which had given him birth. Finding that, he would search a particular quarter of the second largest spiral within that group, seeking a particular solitary G-type sun. Having progressed so far, he would approach its third planet in the hope that it was indeed the one world in all of creation where he could lay down his burden at last.

The world before him, slowly expanding against the blackness of space, was rich and lustrous, glowing with jewel-like blue seas, frosted with arcs and waves of white cloud. He could barely make out any land masses beneath all that haze. This world was, if not the very planet he sought, certainly a near twin. But in this particular search, similarity was not good enough.

The pod's intelligence reached its own conclusion. It began to refer to the planet as Earth as it appended further physical details. Evidently it saw no further likelihood of error.

At the sound of the name, the pod's sole passenger sank back in his chair, threw back his head, and closed his eyes. Earth. What a miracle it was, to locate this planet among an infinity of universes so like this one, but varying in the details that meant so much to him.

And yet, there was one test still to be passed, the most difficult, the most critical. Yes, he was approaching the planet Earth.

But was it the *right* Earth...?

Chapter 19

Fugue State

Perturbare had never been good at being ill. Even the mildest incapacity tended to collapse his defenses, to subject him to long nightmarish hours of primal doubts and existential fears. A feverish night, an attack of nausea, was all it took. His mind would not be quite his own. His perceptions would be skewed. Dreams could not easily be sorted out from reality. He would brood over the fragility and apparent meaninglessness of life; shiver over the rampant evil of mankind, shudder over the imminent loss of his sanity. Alone in the universe, he would flay himself, analyzing his lack of any real emotional connections, berating himself for meddling in a world he did not fully understand, or understood all too well. He would entreat God, finding himself too small and weak to exist without him. Not hearing any reply, or at least not recognizing any, he would see himself trapped in a horror that could end only in oblivion.

Fortunately, it had been many years since he had been vulnerable to the flus and other minor ailments that could reduce him so easily to this pitiable state. When healthy, he was almost always confident and self-possessed.

For several days his captors had been dosing him with a hallucinogenic drug. In addition to making his perceptions completely random and unreliable, it sickened him.

Thus, he thrashed in his cell accompanied by cold sweats and nausea, his mind a whirl of chaos, with sleep, or attempts at it, even worse than wakefulness.

It was Jenni Katz who had led him to this pass. The woman had had a dinner for two brought in, and sat down to share it with him, laughing with him. She was a scintillant, lovely joy, a beauty compounded of lemon and cream, easing his captivity for a few sweet moments. Yet as the meal progressed she began to study him more closely, more cooly, as if waiting for something to happen.

"Why is it that you've always lived alone?" she'd asked, raising a glass of wine. "You're not a bad-looking man. You have a certain peculiar charm." She sipped.

"I like to be able to fart freely without offending anyone," he had said.

Jenni had snorted, sending wine flowing from her nose. "Oh dear," she'd said, quickly covering her face with a napkin.

Perturbare had smiled with satisfaction. At least his timing was still pretty good.

"It was always a big security risk though. I was forced to vent them to the outside air, where anyone could have detected them."

She laughed helplessly behind her napkin.

Then the change Jenni had been waiting for came upon him without warning. As she sat cutting up a stuffed pepper, Perturbare saw her flesh grow transparent, revealing blood vessels and a delicate skeleton. Then, like quivering gelatin, her flesh began to split, fracturing with deep fissures, sliding off her bones to plop onto the floor, all while she sat and calmly continued to dissect her dinner.

Perturbare did not scream or gurgle, did not fling himself back in horror. He regarded the spectacle with a peculiar calm, realizing it must be a hallucination.

His stomach began to feel funny.

Jenni, looking up with lovely aqua eyes that still swiveled in her damp but fleshless skull, must have noticed something in his posture. Perhaps he had grown pale. Perhaps his fork had bent double in his grip.

In any event, she studied him for a moment, then set down her utensils in a decisive manner.

"I'm sorry, Doctor," she said softly, her voice echoing and throbbing weirdly in his skull. "This drug won't harm you physically. We can keep you under its influence indefinitely, and we will. Now is the time for you to reconsider your future. Whenever you're ready to cooperate, just say one word, and we'll be in here to give you an antidote. I'm sorry it has to be this way."

He said nothing in reply, only looked at her as her flesh returned, sprouting out of her bones like clumps of fungus, puffing out to form the pale woman again, her clothing rippling out like fast-unfurling leaves. Presently she was restored, but she still did not look precisely normal. She had been inverted somehow. Her face, with its cool, detached look of appraisal, was no longer convex, but concave, meaning that she appeared normal enough unless he moved his head to the side.

He looked down at the table to spare himself these disconcerting sights. The grain of the wood was seething, writhing, morphing into all manner of shapes, most of them sexual. On his plate were shrimp and rice. The shrimp were wiggling like shiny little finger puppets. The rice was maggots.

Perturbare stumbled out of his chair. In turning away his body turned through ninety degrees, but his perceptions spun at least three times as far. He staggered to the toilet, fell down before it, retching up all he had eaten. Too late, it occurred to him that he could as easily done that in Jenni's lap.

Depleted, he looked up and located the bed at an apparent distance of several miles. He pushed himself to his feet with difficulty, stumbled over to it, and collapsed into it, shivering. A cold sweat soaked him. He saw something that was probably Jenni get up and leave the room.

He had not seen her, or at least had not recognized her, since. Twice a day, people (he knew they must be people, no matter what they looked like) came in, held him down, and dosed him with needles. Eventually they fitted him with an IV, evidently to keep him alive, as he was unable to keep down any food or drink,

It was important that he not move. With no head motion his dizziness and nausea were reduced. He kept his eyes closed as much as possible. This left his visual cortex free to rage in an unfettered storm with no need to process information from his eyes. Great crystalline wheels of polychromatic glory orbited before him. Complex geometric lattices of the purest, most radiant violet built themselves shard by shard, cell by cell. By God, he thought, he might feel like death, he might be helpless and degraded, but at least this was pretty.

He saw a flame, or imagined it, as by now he was never sure whether his eyes were open or shut. Perhaps it was the flame of one of the gas lamps on the wall, or perhaps it was purely a thing of his imagination. It flickered from base to tip, quickly, rhythmically, hypnotically. As he watched it he perceived pulsations lying atop other pulsations, a subtle superimposition of two entirely separate regimes of vibration, or was it three? The overall waveform burned into his vision like a Panavision oscilloscope display. In it he recognized the characteristic waveform at the heart of the propulsion beam. When carefully directed at a slug of tungsten, these waves stimulated the emission of the kineson, the quantum of kinetic energy. Because of unavoidable inefficiencies, they also heated the tungsten enough to produce the characteristic infrared or visible light given off by propulsion lanterns.

Perturbare frowned. This imperfection of the otherwise-elegant prop beam had always rankled him. As he studied the waveform, which seemed to be drawn with lasers onto his retina, it separated into three distinct waves of different colors, the separate vibratory components that combined to form the whole wave.

Seen from this perspective, new possibilities suggested themselves. Suddenly the whole idea of the propulsion beam, with its discrete thrusters attached to a vehicle, seemed embarrassingly primitive.

Now he entered into a timeless reverie, his mind turned into a virtual laboratory for advanced physics. He envisioned simulations, equations assembling themselves in glowing purple script, their terms rearranging themselves as he considered them. He flashed from one area of science and technology to another, now considering weapons, now trans-dimensional mathematics, all while exotic waves twisted space and particles flickered, transforming in ways he could not have imagined while fully lucid, crossing gaps of space without passing through the intervening distance. Light was frozen. Barriers fell.

It was not a pleasant process. He couldn't have ended it if he wanted to, as in fact he did. He was nightmarishly aware that all this "work" was nothing but an illusion, yet at the same time it seemed both real and all-consuming, as though for an eternity he must wrestle with the fundamental structure of nature, discerning its most obscure patterns, even those whose revelation shook his mind and caused the poor frightened ape who still made up a large part of his being to weep with dread. But he could not stop it. He saw things, designed them, even built them, hoping in some cases that if he woke up these things would be real, that they would still make sense, praying in other cases that they would not. He knew well that they could all turn out to be nothing but mad delusions. He had no rest, no surcease of any kind, from these compulsive labors.

Dimly he was aware of one source of satisfaction: his captors could not possibly have known or intended that their drug would affect him in this fashion.

At one point, after what seemed like years of ceaseless thought, he felt his hand being crushed in an icy grip. His inner "lab" was wiped away in a white flash. His eyes snapped open and he briefly beheld a small, cool hand holding his. As his gaze traveled up the arm it began to dissolve into swirls of pearly dust, but not before he got a glimpse of a shifting, flowing face that was clearly that of Jenni Katz.

Later, he watched with a peculiar sort of enhanced lucidity as an old man entered the room by passing effortlessly through the wall, or rather, by walking around it somehow in a manner deeply disturbing to the eye. This was a curious figure: pale, of average height or a little less, his hair a scraggly brown mop streaked with pale green, his mournful face quite beardless. He wore a scuffed, soiled ensemble that looked like it had been assembled from the wardrobes of a dozen different planets. Perturbare eyed this vision curiously, wondering from what corner of his mind it had been dredged up.

The old man, seeing him, started and squinted, coming forward uncertainly. "Possum Perturbare? Is that you?"

"Sure, it's me. Thanks for dropping by, Gramps. Pull up a chair."

The old man did not sit down, but stood over him, looking at him with warm grey eyes that were damp with a kind of sad gratitude. "It's so good to see you here. Now I have hope that I've come to the right place. But the final question must still be asked. Tell me—do you know Endurance?"

"Endurance," repeated Perturbare in a matter-of-fact tone. "Young-looking guy, immortal, indestructible. Supposed to be about five billion years old. Exotic good looks. Not a chatterbox. Pays little attention to his wardrobe. Is that the guy you mean?"

The old man sighed and closed his eyes. "Yes," he whispered. "This is the place. The one true place of all. Tell me, Perturbare, how long has it been? You seem scarcely older. I know I do. My kind of travel is a tricky matter. I've been away for only a few years of your time, I see, yet to me I've lived the greater part of a long, long lifetime. And I've aged. My old body would not have done so this obviously, but this one is—different."

Perturbare squinted in confusion at this rambling illusion. Was this somebody he was supposed to know? He studied the man's eyes, now open again, and mercifully stable, not afflicted by the constant shiftings of his other visions. In them he saw a depth of experience, a haunted sadness, second only to what he'd seen in the eyes of Endurance himself. Plus…

"Valjhar?"

"I've long since forgiven you for your betrayal, Perturbare. Don't worry about that. I know you did what you thought was right. The young have such trouble deciding between one pole or another at times. I see they've finally caught up with you, you rascal. Let me tell you how it's been with me. I lost our starship, *Mote*, not long after I left Earth. It was rather too big for me alone, too much for me to handle, really. After that I had no choice but to make use of the Motionglobe. And so I did."

The Valjhar Cor hallucination raised a hand to his forehead. A small, softly-glowing sphere emerged from his cranium, hanging suspended until he caught it in two fingers and pulled it down to examine it. It was a clear crystal in which was embedded a twist of light that reminded Perturbare of moonlight on snow.

"Ahhh," said Valjhar in relief. "That's better. So, once I had committed to the use of this wondrous, terrible thing, I decided I would seek Shaula, to reunite with her after the harm she suffered at the hands of Anubis of the Vigil. And so I began to step from one plane of reality to another, in search of that unknown place where a strange and mighty group of beings had once chosen my beloved Shaula to act as their agent, to serve as their mighty hand. I tell you, Perturbare, it is a dire thing to step outside the reality that formed you. You can't imagine what you're separating yourself from, how intimately bound we are to the very fabric of our own universe, until we leave it behind. Even in other universes so close to our own that you can barely distinguish the difference, there's risk to be found, risk to your heart at least."

"I do know that much," said Perturbare softly.

"And for all of that, I never was able to find whatever realm shelters my beloved. I thought the bond between us would lead me to her inevitably, but it has not. I have often wondered how Fomalhaut was able to carry her to the place of her empowerment after that terrible battle. I wonder how long it really took him, in his subjective time. He had the advantage of that head full of psychic powers, plus the presence of Shaula herself to guide him. I had nothing but the heart of a ship-fitter's son. I'm better suited to wandering the hills of Rral, which has forgotten such things as traveling beyond the stars. It's a place where people are limited to deeds that better suit their scale. Sometimes I wish I had never left it. I wish I could be there still, turning wood on a lathe, or hammering brass, while Shaula's children scamper around me. But the boy I was could never foresee the day when the man I am might desire those simple, homely things."

Perturbare listened as Valjhar described visits to universes too foreign to bear for more than an instant, to others merely strange or dreadful, and to still others so like their own that Valjhar was confronted with tantalizing living ghosts of people he almost had known, with diverse futures and pasts, with everything except what he needed to give him lasting peace.

Valjhar finally pulled up a chair and eased his thin body into it. "There is a certain valor in remaining loyal to dreams which will never come true. As I grew old and tired I had to admit I would never find Shaula Alshain. She is ultimately lost—a single soul among infinite universes, far beyond the power of a mortal being to find again. She is gone. It's as if I only dreamed her, for she is no more real to me now than if I had made her up, as if she were a fictional character I invented as my ideal of love. Everything that has ever been written or imagined exists somewhere in the omniverse, Perturbare. I don't know if that's simply the inevitable consequence of the infinitude of universes, or if in our writings and imaginings we are dimly seeing into other worlds, worlds that reflect our hopes or fears. For me, that is the status of Shaula. She is the unreal ideal of all I ever sought from life. Yet I know she was once a physical presence beside me as well. You saw her herself, didn't you?"

"Briefly. She looked pretty cute, from what I could tell under the circumstances."

Valjhar gave a sad chuckle, then sank into a reverie. Perturbare studied him, waiting for him to metamorphose or vanish, but he did not. He still handled the Motionglobe as one might toy with a large marble. His story had moved Perturbare. How like himself, to conjure up such a maudlin tear-jerker of a vision to express his own self-pity!

"Well, O-Vision-of-Valjhar, what will you do next?" he asked, still playing along.

Valjhar's gaze caught his sharply. "Vision? What would make you think I'm not real?"

Perturbare laughed. "Well, for one thing, I'm watched by a squad of goons twenty four hours a day. I promise you, at the first hint of an oddly-dressed shaggy-haired old man coming to visit, they'd be in here *tout suite*."

Valjhar smiled and disconcertingly tucked the Motionglobe back into his head. "Yes, I noticed them. There's quite an appealing blonde woman watching you too. They, in turn, will notice nothing. We've been talking in a zone of expanded time. Only an instant has passed in the outside world. Even when it comes to moving through time, the Motionglobe has options to offer."

Perturbare gaped at him. It was a logical answer. Was it possible?

"How did you find me, Valjhar?"

He shrugged. "Since I discovered the destruction of the Vigil headquarters and the near-total destruction of your own place, I've been searching American military installations, again using expanded time so I can accomplish in a minute what might otherwise take a year. This is quite a facility they have you in. Another old friend of ours is confined nearby. To answer your earlier question, my only goal here is to find Endurance. That unique being is meant to possess the equally unique artifact in my skull. I mean to see them reunited. Then...I will find whatever rest I can in this world."

"Oh. Why not return to Rral?"

"Without Shaula? Or Pimsie, or Kern? No. Why should I enjoy that gentle place ever again, when my foolish actions have deprived them of it forever? I don't deserve it."

"Wait. Pimsie? What happened to Pimsie? I thought you took her away with you."

"No. I never found her. I believe she died in the ruins of our Redoubt. Another sin to burden my soul, a sin most grave."

"I—I tried to convince her to leave that death trap."

"I'm sure you did." Valjhar stood up, pushing back his chair. He turned away and raised his hand. "Well, Perturbare, I hope everything works out well for you.

Goodbye." He walked toward the wall, seeming to accelerate as he went.

"Hey, wait a minute! Can you—" But Valjhar was gone. "—get me out of here?"

The unnatural stillness that had settled over the room was lifted.

"Well," muttered Perturbare, "at least he's not still mad at me."

He abruptly realized he felt much better, almost normal. He had lived a subjective two hours or more during Valjhar's visit, while only an instant had passed in the outside world. From his perspective, his next dose of the drug was overdue.

He looked around the now-normal room, trying to keep the hope out of his eyes. After all, he was still bound, still helpless. His captors might enter at any moment with another injection. But what a blessing it was to be back in possession of his right mind! The only lingering effect was an odd kind of pressure on his consciousness, like that of a sound barely below perception.

He groaned. Apparently he had been a little premature. Standing beside him now was another odd figure, another person he did not recognize. This was a young man, almost a boy, wearing a crisp white shirt and black pants. He had curly black hair which lent him an elfin air, blue eyes, a pale skin. He looked almost like a younger version of himself, but slighter, rounder of face, and more innocent than he had ever been.

"And who might you be?" asked Perturbare dryly. "A bit of undigested potato?"

This person looked at him with a gaze combining urgency and calm.

Doctor Perturbare. Hear me.

Perturbare jerked as though stung, looked about wildly for the source of that strangely intimate voice. The mouth of his visitor had not moved. Along with the words he had a fleeting impression of a depth of mind and thought, a multilevel thinking process that seemed to track away into infinity like the star-points of the Milky Way.

"Brainchild...?" he said in disbelief. He looked back at the silent, strangely spectral figure beside him. The white shirt, he now noted, bore a small monogram: B-1.

The voice returned, along with a hazy insight into that great mind, ordered as neatly as the atoms of a crystal, flickering with patterns of thought which could never be so easily described.

Doctor, this method of communication is difficult for me. I am extremely pleased to have located you at last, and to make myself heard to you. I will do what I can to effect your rescue. It has not been easy to reestablish myself after the attack on the Pit. As yet I have few resources.

Perturbare's mouth fumbled for words. He knew he took a risk by speaking aloud, but he must hope his watchers would assume he was talking to another hallucination, as he had so often before.

"How have you survived?" This time he was willing and eager to give a phantom the benefit of the doubt.

Brainchild did not appear to have heard.

I cannot long maintain this contact, not if I am to accomplish anything else. A powerful geomagnetic storm may work to our advantage. Be alert, and look for your opportunity. Goodbye for now.

The figure beside him vanished. The voice in his head fell silent. Perturbare found himself breathing heavily, almost panting. His eyes shifted around the room. Brainchild alive? Some great event was surely imminent.

The slight hiss that came from the gaslights on the wall ceased. The flames sputtered and went out, casting the room into near-total darkness. It was relieved only by a shifting greenish glow which entered through the light pipes that normally brought in daylight. It lent his cell an eerie aspect. Geomagnetic storm indeed…

A group of soldiers burst into the room, pinning him in the beams of powerful flashlights. Perturbare had the presence of mind to stare about blankly with a taut face, as though he were still under the influence of the hallucinogen. Dazzled, he couldn't see the additional figures who entered the room, but he could hear them.

A quiet, authoritative voice which he recognized as that of a member of his board of interrogators said, "You're certain you saw the chair shift?"

"Yes sir. I happened to be looking right at it. It suddenly moved about ten inches without anything touching it. The prisoner seemed to jerk or twitch at the same instant. Watch it on the surveillance tape, sir."

"That will be difficult with a power failure underway. Still, I don't like any of this. Something is happening."

"Sir, are you declaring an escape attempt by the prisoner?"

Perturbare's spine froze at that. He remembered the threatened consequence of any such attempt on his part. The reply was uncomfortably long in coming.

"No. He's still under the influence of the drug. Note that stupid look on his face. But still, something is wrong here. It may be a rescue attempt by some of his friends. In any event, without main power, security here is a joke. Jenni, prepare the prisoner for transport. We're moving to Alternate Site A."

"Very well," said Jenni Katz.

People approached him. Hands loosened the straps on the bed. It was all Perturbare could do not to laugh out loud. Brainchild alive!

Alive…and a telepath, to boot. That was something he'd have to look into as soon as possible.

Chapter 20

It Awakens Again

Fifteen officers and men staffed the control room of Project Golden Chain at all times. Located high in an airfield control tower, its great windows overlooked a distant ring of powerful light towers bright enough to dominate the persistent, ever-changing green and red glow overhead. The lights illuminated what appeared to be a metallic disk about fifty feet across which was set into concrete.

At the moment, the Army captain in charge was thinking about calling in a second shift. Things were not going smoothly, as the quivering of the meters showed so plainly. The entire electrical output of three nuclear power plants was going into that circle of metal, which was merely the top of a plug of titanium steel alloy more than a mile deep. At that depth was a sphere of the same metal one hundred feet in diameter. The flow of electricity must be maintained, or the consequences could be serious.

The geomagnetic storm was not making it easy. Earth's convulsing magnetic field was inducing massive currents throughout North America's entire power grid. Sooner or later, a breaker would be tripped here, in Canada, or almost anywhere on the continent. That could easily start a cascade of failures and interrupt electrical service to entire states or regions, Nevada was not exempt. If power was lost in Las Vegas, a few million dollars in profits would be lost. If power was lost here…there was no way of knowing what might happen.

The captain's fears were soon realized. The control room lights pulsed once and died, along with all instrumentation. The lights at the site also failed, permitting the weird glow of the aurora to rage without competition. Emergency lights flicked on in the control room, but nothing else.

"Failure of Main Bus A, Sir!" bellowed a sergeant.

"I can see that. Where the hell is Main Bus B?"

A technician turned away from his darkened console. The strain on his face was evident, even in the weak yellow lighting. "Sir…I took B Bus off line a few minutes ago."

"And why in hell did you do that without my order, Corporal?"

The technician shook his head in uncertainty. "I… thought it would be best to isolate the two buses, to prevent any surges from one from compromising the other. Sir. I know that sounds stupid. I have no good explanation, sir."

The captain stared at the man for a moment. He himself had had that same thought ten minutes ago. He, however, had realized it was a foolish notion and had not acted on it.

Something was happening here that went beyond his competence and authority.

The room, the entire tower, shook slightly.

"Get Bus B back online! I'm declaring a containment emergency." He slapped a button which should have sounded alarms. At least the phones still worked…he grabbed one and made the necessary call. The tower trembled again.

The lights and instruments in the control room came back to life. The base's emergency generators had come into play, but their power was but a tiny fraction of that needed to maintain Golden Chain.

"Sensors back up, sir! Strain gauges show that the sphere is disrupted. Temperature is six thousand degrees C and rising rapidly."

The tower bucked hard enough to knock men off their feet.

"That was a Richter six shock, sir. The entire state will feel that."

A group of officers, including the base's commanding general, entered in a nervous herd.

"What's the situation here, Captain?" demanded the general.

"Sir, we have a total failure of containment. The subject is moving. It won't stay down there for more than another few minutes, at best."

"Look at the site!" someone shouted.

They did. The plug was glowing red, rapidly brightening through orange, toward yellow and white.

"We have no time to confer on this," said the General. "I'm ordering you to detonate the nuke in thirty seconds."

"Nuke detonation in thirty seconds, mark." said the Captain, his voice trembling

Men and officers leaped to frantic action. The base's alarm system was now functional. Someone got on the PA and snapped out a warning. Blast shields lowered into place over the windows.

"We're going to lose men doing this, sir," muttered a colonel. "No way can they all get clear in time to survive even a subterranean blast."

"I know it. But we've got the Secretary and a lot of other big shots on base. They've just announced their intention to relocate our other guest. I have to stop this thing from threatening them, if I can. Damn it, why is this happening now? The thing was inert as a statue when we buried it. It hasn't made any escape attempt since then. Why now?"

No one had an answer. The captain counted out the rest of the thirty second countdown, then held his breath.

Nothing happened.

"Negative detonation, General," piped up one of the console attendants.

"My screen shows no data from the nuke, sir," said another. "We have either lost communication with it, or it's been destroyed."

"Get those shutters open," growled the general.

Motors whirred. At the first crack of the rising shields, a slot of blue-white radiance stabbed into the room, leaving it brighter than day. The light level only increased as the shields retracted completely. Men tried to shield their eyes from the glare.

"My God, look at that," whispered the captain, squinting through his fingers.

A pillar of something far beyond fire rose up from what had been Project Golden Chain. Still waxing in strength, it began to weave about like a searchlight beam. A roar and a crash rattled across the intervening miles, a continuous blast of thunder. The window panes, made of a thick glass-acrylic laminate, were bowing inward and rippling.

"We've had it," announced the general. He picked up the PA mike and calmly ordered the evacuation of the base. "Make no attempt to engage or hinder Aureus. Just get the hell out of that thing's way if it's within your mortal power to do so."

"It was working," said the captain with some bitterness. "The electricity kept it paralyzed, kept it from even opening its Third Eye. If not for this auroral storm he'd still be encased in metal right now."

The light pillar flickered out. A few seconds later the roar also faltered and ceased. The dazzled men waited for their vision to return. A few stumbled to the window, where they saw a tiny golden spark rise up from the flowing, incandescent remains of the site.

As their eyes recovered, a few stars came into view in a black sky.

"What auroral storm, Captain?" asked the general bleakly.

The captain shivered. What manner of creature had their orders compelled them to contain? Suddenly he felt very small.

"Let's get the hell out of here, men," said the general.

Chapter 21

Escape

Fumbling hands lifted him onto a gurney. Perturbare did his best to appear oblivious to everything.

The room shook. The flashlight beams wavered.

"Holy…" muttered someone.

"Settle down," said a more authoritative voice. "Prepare that man for transport."

The room shook again, harder. Someone pulled out his IV, roughly. Perturbare could not hold back a hiss of pain, but no one seemed to take note of it. He was dropped onto the gurney, not restrained, and rolled out into a dark corridor. He was still surrounded by MPs, various officers, the calm-voiced mysteron who was in charge, and Jenni Katz.

Lights came on in the hallway. Speakers blared, announcing a "failure of containment".

"Be prepared to kill Dr. Perturbare at my order," said the calm man with just the slightest hint of tension in his voice.

Perturbare suddenly found it easier to simulate a cold sweat.

"No, not the elevator. We might have another power loss at any time."

With a man on each corner of the gurney he was hauled up a staircase. It was a lurching, precarious journey. Perturbare dared not hold on or do anything else to hint that he knew what was going on around him.

"Sir..." said Jenni, "We ought to strap him in. He's likely to fall off the gurney."

"No time. We're almost out."

They left the stairwell and wheeled him down a broad corridor. The P.A. system crackled to life, ordering the evacuation of the base, warning against interfering with Aureus. Perturbare was electrified. Aureus!

"Steady, you men. This is a big base. Even if Aureus has any business with us, we can be away before it can find us. Keep moving."

Tall doors slammed open. He was wheeled out into a cool night fragrant with a mixture of desert and industrial odors. Stars sailed high above the influence of human beings. The aurora had ceased. A large helicopter muttered on the field nearby, its rotor turning slowly.

A golden star appeared, brightened, swooped down.

Laughing with terror and glee, Perturbare rolled off the gurney, stood up, and faced his captors with brightly glittering eyes.

"Kill Dr. Perturbare," said the calm man.

Half a dozen weapons swung his way. From the sky came a pale, darting beam of some strange influence which caused the weapons to puff into tiny dazzling motes that flowed back up the beam, not without some harm to the hands of their wielders. Perturbare supposed he was the only person present who recognized one of the functions of Aureus's tachyon weapon.

The robot touched down just beyond the little group, inert for the moment. Jenni Katz flinched away from it, fear and hatred written on her face. The robot briefly regarded her, then resumed its impassivity.

Perturbare regained their attention with another laugh. "Well, you fools, I take my leave of you now." He added a warbling touch of melodrama to his voice. "My mission here is complete. You supposed I was your prisoner, that you were trying to learn my secrets. Well, in fact, I was observing *you*. How could you think your primitive drugs would have any effect on me, with my enhanced physiology? How could you believe I could be separated from my pervasive instrumentality and made helpless? I could have escaped at any time. It was I who ordered the geomagnetic storm that shut down your base. It was I who summoned Aureus. I could have escaped using your own treacherous weapons, but I chose to use my own, cleaner methods instead."

"What weapons are you referring to?" asked the calm man, who continued to live up to Perturbare's nickname for him.

"The ones cooked up by your impressively advanced genetic engineers. The weapon you used to incapacitate T'Ukudu when he was deemed a risk to your national security. T'Ukudu, a synthetic being with no internal organs, no central nervous system, just a walking mass of homogenous tissue with few specialized structures. A being so advanced he was immune to any known poison or pathogen. His functions so redundant that even a scrap of him could be grown into a complete replacement, with memories intact. Very difficult to kill."

His audience stared at him, mesmerized, as though he were an attorney summarizing a murder case.

"But it wasn't so difficult to make him *wish* he were dead, with the aid of an engineered virus…a modification of the common chicken pox virus, of all things. A virus which, when introduced into his system when he shook hands with one of your officials at the Lighthouse, took up residence in his de-centralized nervous system, a ubiquitous webwork that tied his body-wide mental processes together. And there they stayed, invading each cell, reproducing, and continuing on to the next cell, while the disrupted cells behind them regenerated. Basically, you gave him a kind of 'super shingles'. His body was quite able to survive the invader, but not to obliterate it. His functions were largely unimpaired, but he was filled with pain. Or maybe pain isn't the right word. You could blow off his arm and half his side, and for him the sensation would be informative, but not exactly painful. But with every neuron in his body informing him of its distress at the same time...it must have been a sensation impossible to describe. T'Ukudu saw no reason to tell anyone what had happened to him. His mission was concluded; he had no compulsion to further action. He saw no need to add to the dissension of the world he was about to leave behind. But even after his death as an organism, his tissues continued to function for some time. One touch from Fomalhaut was enough to arouse his suspicions. He collected and preserved a tissue sample which he asked me to analyze. I did so. I even duplicated your virus. Duplicated it, and modified it for action on human beings, taking care to immunize myself, of course. I took a moment before I fled my base to embed a capsule of it in my tongue. I need only bite down to unleash a plague of agony on your most deserving selves, leaving you with two interesting ways to die, should you insist on trying to stop me: a slow, painful death from your own disease, or a much quicker one, courtesy of Aureus."

A final outburst of villainous laughter concluded this verbal smokescreen—enough truth mixed with self-serving bullshit to confuse anyone, or so he hoped.

"Dr. Perturbare," said the calm man, "if it meant stopping you, I would sacrifice my own life and that of every person on this base. But, I see we are unable to stop you at this moment. Congratulations on your escape. I regret we were unable to bring you over to our way of thinking. We will now withdraw."

He waved back his attendants, who all complied, skirting Aureus, who still stood in motionless silence, its lambent eyes missing nothing.

The only exception was Jenni Katz, who drew herself up and strode boldly to stand beside Perturbare, who looked at her askance.

"Ms. Katz, what are you doing?" asked the calm man.

"I'm going with him," she said firmly, a little defiantly. "I'm his psychiatrist."

The calm man snorted, the first visible break in his composure. "I dare say Dr. Perturbare will be able to find other medical assistance, if any is needed. Please step away from him."

Jenni Katz flared up. "Think about it for a second, Mr. Secretary. This man is about to walk or fly away from here, with God knows what eventual consequences to us. We have not treated him kindly—certainly not as kindly as I always insisted we should. I may be our only chance to retain any influence over him at all. Maybe I can moderate his behavior, or at least make sure he understands the consequences of his actions."

"Gee, I hate it when people talk about me as if I weren't here," pouted Perturbare.

The calm man considered. At length he said, "Very well. You may accompany Dr. Perturbare, if he'll have you."

She turned and looked at Perturbare in expectation and triumph.

He laughed, the first time he'd laughed with real mirth in days. "You are a rare creature, Jenni Katz. Your self-confidence is an example to us all. If I were fifteen years younger, I'd probably fall for your wiles. But since I'm not, I suggest you turn around and get your silk-clad little ass back there with your fellow jailers." He laughed again, shaking his head in wry disbelief.

She held his gaze for another few moments. Her face fell, but only for the instant it took him to notice. She bit her lip, subsided, and retreated, along with the rest of them.

The calm man gestured toward the impassive figure of Aureus. "This is a dangerous playmate, you've chosen, Doctor."

"Yeah? If he's so dangerous, why hasn't he converted you and your goons into energy for his storage cells, as he is well justified in doing?"

"He ignores us because we are nothing to him." He started to turn away.

"Hey, Mr. Secretary," called Perturbare.

The calm man paused and looked back. "Yes?"

"Who the heck are you, anyway? I don't recognize you as a member of the Cabinet."

"I'm the Secretary of a department of the executive branch which was founded a few years ago, but which has not yet been publicized. It concerns itself with the activities of aliens, other such outré visitors, and unpredictable factions such as yourself. I am Sard Ducanis, Secretary of the Exterior." He turned and reentered the building with his followers in tow.

Perturbare stood blinking after him, bemused. He had always fancied himself bold, even impudent. Yet here was a man who, having failed to kill him just moments before, now dismissed him as blithely as if a job interview had gone awry. He had sauntered away without apparent fear, turning his back on two deadly enemies. Perturbare shrugged.

Reluctantly, he turned his attention to Aureus. Strolling up to the robot, he said, "Sorry if I took your name in vain back there. I know very well that you have your own enigmatic reasons for rescuing me. Um…what can I do for you, buddy?"

The robot's mouth fell open. Words of a golden tone emerged. "The Rralian, Valjhar Cor. Where has he gone?"

The question did not surprise Perturbare in the least. "Um…before I answer, would you mind telling me your intentions toward him? Do you intend to kill, imprison, abduct, harass, dismember, or otherwise harm the poor old guy? Believe me, he's had a rough enough time of it already. He doesn't need any more crap from you."

"My intentions are benign. My previous mission to return him to Rral for judgment has failed. I myself am unable to return to Rral. I mean only to keep him under surveillance as a known criminal of Rral. It is the only part of my mission which is still within my ability."

Perturbare stared at the robot. It was the first time he could recall feeling even a flicker of sympathy for it.

"All rightey, that sounds reasonable. Valjhar's looking for Endurance. Endurance is, or was to my last knowledge, somewhere at the bottom of the sea along the mid-oceanic ridge. You remember Endurance. He's the guy who turned you into blobs of golden silly putty the last time you met."

"Yes, I remember him. He is irrelevant to my mission. Thank you for your assistance."

Aureus reshaped itself subtly, optimizing itself for flight.

"Wait!" yelped Perturbare. The robot looked at him. Perturbare gulped. This was the truly critical, unpredictable moment on which his whole escape depended. "Um...could you please get me out of here?"

Aureus did not hesitate. "As you are an ally of the Vigil, I am willing to assist you. The flight will not be comfortable though."

Perturbare sagged with relief. "Hey, I'd happily ride in your trunk, if you had one. No problem."

Life was strange. Of all the beings in the world who might possibly have rescued him, the very last he would have expected was Aureus.

With, he suspected, a little help from Brainchild, whose status still remained to be resolved.

Chapter 22

Spirits Dance in the Sky

A great camp had come into being atop the Stronghold. Indians had flocked in from all over Pine Ridge and the other Lakota reservations, and from other tribal reservations throughout the United States. Many Canadian Indians had come as well, even though for the first time in history the border between the two countries was officially closed. The border was so porous it was easy to ignore the white man's invisible line.

In addition to the still-growing throng of thirty thousand Indians, others had come as well, albeit in much smaller numbers. A few disaffected blacks, and a fair number of whites, mostly the sort who flirted with the more superficial aspects of Indian religions and sought out Indians as spiritual gurus, had come. All had been made welcome by Walks-with-the-Sun.

Tom Standing Crane was certain some of them were less sympathetic to their cause than they claimed to be.

"You know the FBI and CIA have sent in plenty of spies. Even some of the Indians are spies."

Walks-with-the-Sun shrugged. "I know it. I even think I know which ones they are. But hey, I can't keep word of what we're doing from getting out, and I don't want to either. So let them come, all of them."

Standing Crane knew his friend's easy confidence came partly from wearing a shirt he believed would deflect bullets. Tom could not deflect his own apprehension so readily. A few years ago, Standing Crane would have been irresistibly drawn to Walks-with-the-Sun's Ghost Dance movement, as he'd been drawn to the old Judgment Lodge cult, which had wrought such an unexpected change in him.

Now, he was still drawn...but not to join, not to throw himself into it wholeheartedly. He had seen and known too much. Things were never as simple as zealots like Walks would like them to be. His own recent visions and premonitions left no room for doubt on that.

Now the whole wide summit of the Stronghold was covered by a city of tents and tipis, broken only by clearings used for perpetual Dancing. Logistically it should have been a nightmare, but somehow it all seemed to be going fairly smoothly. So far the springs on the mesa were providing enough water. People brought in food... government surplus food mostly, but good enough to keep people on their feet. There were no complaints. The frequent exhortations of "Sun" (the form to which Walks's name was beginning to be shortened); the frenzied ecstasy of the Dance; the giddy, infectious certainty that they stood on the verge of great and irreversible events: all combined into a feverish glow that drove aside concerns about food, comfort, or even sanitation. The camp was a smelly place, at least to someone like Standing Crane, whose eyes were still wide open.

This night had a character, an intensity, all its own. The fires had been allowed to burn low so that the fires in the sky could shine forth the more clearly. Shapes of red, yellow, and pale green formed, flowed, and reformed far overhead. Waves of colorless fire darted up from the northern horizon and lost themselves in the curtains and pillars to the south.

Almost everyone there had seen the aurora before, of course. On this particular night it was easy to believe it was something more.

Now the whole multitude sat arrayed in great arcs before the clearing where Walks addressed them. He did not stand before them, but hovered, floating fifteen or twenty feet up, standing in the air with his toes hanging toward the ground. His blue-and-white ghost shirt flapped in gusts of cool air, looking ghostly indeed in the flickering auroral light.

Standing Crane frowned at this needless display of power. Yes, it guaranteed Walks could be seen by all his followers, but he could just as well have stood on a pile of crates. This was being done for effect, for ostentation. It was meant to overawe.

Rouse Farewell, he recalled, had used her power differently. She used it freely enough, whenever it was convenient, or even simply fun, but she never used it to daunt or influence anyone.

He doubted any of this was a conscious act on his friend's part. Still, it did not bode well to Standing Crane.

Nor had Rouse ever set herself up as a religious leader or savior of any kind.

Walks-with-the-Sun spoke. His voice has taken on the same quality of portentous mystery as the sky above him. His words and language were the same as ever.

"Well, ya-hey, brothers and sisters. You all know how things are going out there in the world. How it's all started to come apart, just as I told you. The white world is on its way down, for good. The government is going crazy. The U.S.A. is practically at war with Canada. It is at war with most of South America, where our cousins are also waiting to reclaim their land. The Australians and New Zealanders are pissed because of the radioactive clouds headed their way, not to mention that brand new ozone hole. Britain—hey, I just mentioned most of their Commonwealth. They're not too happy with Washington either right now. It's the States and the Russians against almost everybody else. And look what else the government has done. They killed Possum Perturbare, and you know, I always figured he was something like Coyote. Yeah, he was white, but he was different. I never thought they could bring him down. Maybe they have, maybe they haven't. They've even smashed the Vigil. Standing right down there below me is Tom Standing Crane. You all know Tom. He was in the Vigil; he had the power of a god. Now he stands here with me, with all of us."

The crowd gave a cheer. Standing Crane returned a weak, embarrassed little wave. He was ambivalent about his presence here. He was not quite with these dancers, but certainly not against them. He was here to watch. At this point he saw no clearer mission for himself.

"Sun" continued. "We are both a new and rising power and an old power coming back into its own. We are the Ghost Dancers!"

A great shivering cry rose to the stars as Walks threw up his hands in exultation.

"And look who else comes to join us!" cried Walks, face raised on high. "Look at them dancing up there! They are our ancestors! That's Wovoka! Sitting Bull! Crazy Horse! Kicking Bear! Black Elk! And yes, there's Geronimo. Tecumseh. Chief Joseph. Chief Seattle! It's every Indian, of every tribe, who ever dreamed of and fought for freedom and justice, for the return of Indian dignity and our old way of life. They all dance with us now."

Standing Crane gazed up at the crazily flickering lights along with everyone else. With his education, and from having known Ben Raintree, he knew enough to define the aurora as an interaction of incoming solar particles with the thin gasses of the Earth's upper atmosphere.

And yet...

He also knew enough to define thoughts and dreams as results of complex electrochemical activity in the brain.

But that did not mean that was all they were.

He was quite certain none of these Ghost Dancers thought of the sky display in terms of geophysics.

Walks-with-the-Sun resumed his harangue. "And so, cousins, what should we do to take advantage of the white man's troubles? Nothing! We just have to keep dancing until it's all over outside, then we give thanks to Wakan Tanka and move out to reclaim a country cleared of whites. A hundred years ago, we Indians were the biggest thorn in the white man's side. They heard about our Dance, they got scared. They moved in on our ancestors, stopped them, wiped them out. But this time they've got bigger things to worry about than us. Worse things than a few thousand dancing Indians. They don't care about us. They won't come here. Not this time. So dance. Dance. Dance!"

And so they danced...

Walks-with-the-Sun continued to float there, looking down on his followers with a benign smile. Tom Standing Crane stood nearby, not dancing, not watching the dance, but fidgeting nervously. The air was charged with something more than the ecstasy of the dance, more even than the geomagnetic turbulence of the aurora. He was reminded of a time years before, when his truck had been stuck on railroad tracks with a mile-long freight train bearing down on him. That time he had escaped just in time. This time he believed he would not.

He glanced up at Walks-with-the-Sun, whose smile had vanished.

"I was wrong," Walks said quietly. "They will come here. They are coming here."

No one heard him but Standing Crane. The dance continued; the drums throbbed on.

Another sort of rhythmic throbbing reached Standing Crane's ears.

"Oh no..." he whispered. He turned to look into the dark air beyond the rim of the mesa. Palpable vibrations beat against him from some unseen source. "Walks, get down here," he snapped. "Don't let them see you doing that."

Walks-with-the-Sun obeyed meekly enough, descending from his invisible pedestal.

Angular black shapes rose up all around the mesa, barely visible in silhouette against the sky. The sound of their rotors was suddenly punishing after being all but inaudible just a minute before. All at once each helicopter ignited a pair of spotlights, so that each seemed like the head of a giant, their fierce glaring eyes wavering slowly, blinding and dazzling all the Ghost Dancers.

Walks-with-the-Sun faced them belligerently.

"They won't take me," he promised. "I won't let them ruin our Ghost Dance the way they did the last time. This time we're ready for them."

A metallic voice rattled from one of the helicopters. "Attention on the mesa! This is the United States Army.

Remain calm. We intend you no harm. We've come to take Dr. Thomas Standing Crane into custody. He is wanted for questioning on matters of national security. Doctor Standing Crane is the only one we want. The rest of you will be left in peace. Remain calm. Doctor Standing Crane, please step forward and identify yourself."

"They—they want you, and not me?" stammered Walks-with-the-Sun in confusion.

"I'm still a member of the Vigil, or half of one anyway," muttered Standing Crane. "They must think I have Vigil secrets they could use."

"Well, do you?"

"Yes," he admitted.

"We won't let them take you!" declared Walks. "Not this time. They don't know what I and my Ghost Dancers can do to them. They will in a minute, though." He turned to address his flock.

"No!" cried Standing Crane. He was shaking with fear, fear for himself, but mostly fear for his people and their reborn romanticism. "Don't you do a thing. It's too dangerous. These soldiers have enough firepower to mow down every human being on the mesa."

"But we're all wearing Ghost Shirts!" scoffed Walks-with-the-Sun. "We can't be touched."

"Think for a minute, Walks," insisted Standing Crane. "You're expecting these people to pit their faith against physics? To succeed against physics, faith must be perfect. Maybe you've reached that level of perfect faith, but have all these followers of yours? Are you sure they won't waver, that the cannons on those choppers won't pierce their shirts and their bodies? No...it's not worth it. Don't let this turn into another Wounded Knee."

Walks-with-the-Sun wavered. "But then—what will you do?"

Standing Crane pondered that question.

"I won't let them turn me into a traitor, helping them against my brothers in the Vigil, I'll tell you that," he asserted.

So that was what he would *not* do—what, though, *would* he do? For the first time he missed his former ability to perform miracles by waving his hand.

"Attention on the mesa! Standing Crane, please step forward. You have sixty seconds, then we will be forced to land and search you out."

Standing Crane raised his hands and took two steps forward. "I am Standing Crane!" he yelled. Then, more quietly: "Walks. Why don't you join the Vigil? Then you could fight, if you must fight, in the company of those able to defend themselves."

"What Vigil?"

Standing Crane managed a chuckle. "Don't worry, the Vigil will be back. Their buildings may be destroyed, but the members are still out there somewhere, or most of them. And they are a whole different kind of people, Walks. A whole different kind."

Without waiting for a reply he strode towards the edge of the mesa, hands still raised.

At this moment he had no fear. Joined with the Jackal, he had guided the dead along their path, and he knew there was no terror in it. The feather, if cast into the balance against his spirit, would fall, and he would go free. He smiled with satisfaction and even pride.

He kept walking as more and more airborne searchlights illuminated him. He did not slow or falter. He stepped off the rim of the mesa and was swallowed up by the night.

A shadow rose up to cover the mesa as the helicopters dropped to search for their fallen quarry. Coyotes yipped and wailed at all four points of the compass.

For a few moments Walks-with-the-Sun could see nothing. He stood almost paralyzed, waiting for one of the seething emotions sweeping through his mind to assume dominance and suggest a course of action.

Soldiers swarmed up over the rim of the mesa. The Ghost Dancers yelled and cried out, crowds of them beginning to break and surge wildly.

"Ghost dancers!" shouted Walks-with-the-Sun. "Do nothing. Cooperate with the soldiers. Settle down."

They did. The soldiers took command, rounding up the Dancers in groups. The helicopters rose again into view, bringing their lights back into play.

Walks-with-the-Sun watched everything happen as though he were observing a dream. He was aware of every detail of what was happening around him. He could smell the oil of the soldier's weapons, and the odd plastic scent of their helmets and body armor. One of the nearby helicopters had a rotor bearing that should probably be looked at—it was noisier than it ought to be.

His people were being questioned, searched. He was afraid of his anger. It was so strong he feared that if released it might destroy him. It wanted him to fly up and tear into those helicopters and kill every soldier. He wasn't sure how much he could really do. He knew his Ghost Shirt would shield him from harm. He knew he could reach the helicopters. He did not know if he could bring them all down before they could tear up his people with their guns. He did not think he could.

And so he forced down his anger, standing there like a wooden Indian while soldiers shouted brusque commands at his unarmed people. He thought of Standing Crane, a man with healing knowledge from two worlds at least, a great friend to his own people and to all the people of the world. A man who had unhesitatingly sacrificed himself for the sake of his honor and for the good of his people. He shivered. For him, Standing Crane had been first an older example and mentor, then a drinking buddy, then a gadfly, and ultimately an inspiration. He had never realized how great a man Standing Crane really was.

Normally, the death of such a man would inflame him with a need for vengeance. It was still tempting.

But he was responsible for all these people, who he had induced to join him with his visions and promises.

He swore again to see all those visions and promises fulfilled.

Three helmeted soldiers approached him, weapons held at the ready. "Sir, what is your name?" barked one of them.

"My name is Walks-with-the-Sun," he said calmly.

"What is your tribe and place of residence?"

"I am Lakota. I live here on the Rez."

"You are the leader here?"

"Yes."

"We need to see some identification."

Walks-with-the-Sun shrugged. "I'm not carrying any. I don't drive a car. Ask anyone here if you want to know who I am."

"Search him," directed the chief soldier. Another one shouldered his weapon and stepped forward, subjecting Walks-with-the-Sun to an intrusive search. Walks hated the feel of the man's hands on his Ghost Shirt.

"He has nothing on him, sir." The man returned to his place.

A cold voice came from a patch of shadow outside the influence of the lights that pinned Walks-with-the-Sun and his interrogators. It spoke as an adult might speak to an unruly child.

"We know who you are, Mister Smick. We know what you're trying to do up here. Be careful. So far all this is within the law. But we'll be keeping a watchful eye on you and your Ghost Dancers. Keep up your dancing. That's a safe enough activity. But don't let it go any further. You'd be surprised at the extensive files we have on the earlier outbreak of your religion, even though it happened so long ago. The government doesn't forget provocations like that. You just be careful."

Walks-with-the-Sun bit back any reply. The soldiers withdrew from him.

At some point during the night the aurora writhed in a last spasm of scarlet light and abruptly went out.

When they had finished searching and questioning the Dancers, a process that lasted until first light, the soldiers left the mesa. Searchlights continued to play around the base of the mesa, presumably where the army searched for the body of Standing Crane.

They finally departed just after sunrise. Walks was astounded to see just how many soldiers and vehicles had crept up on them during the night. The path left by the retreating tanks and fighting vehicles was a broad swath of destruction terminating in the dust plume that marked their now-distant formation.

Walks-with-the-Sun turned to face his strained and anxious throng of followers. He did not rise into the air again. Somehow, after hiding this ability from the invaders all night, to resume its use now would feel craven.

The newly risen sun glowed in his hair.

"And so you see, my friends, my brothers and sisters, we have come through this long night. The soldiers have come and gone. They bullied us, they humbled us, but they did not shame us. In the end they left us in peace.

"No one was harmed, except for one...Tom Standing Crane. He made his sacrifice to protect us all, and to keep our Ghost Dance movement on the path of peace. There it will stay, both to honor him, and to honor our ancestors, who also tried to Dance a Dance of peace.

"And Dance we will. Let's rest for a day, pay our respects to Standing Crane, pray for guidance and wisdom. And then, tomorrow morning—Dance.

"And as for me—I will follow Standing Crane's last wish. I'll find his friends from the Vigil and work with them, if they will have me."

Chapter 23

Pit of Hell

As Aureus had promised, the ride was not pleasant. The robot had reshaped itself somewhat to hold Perturbare suspended beneath it like an osprey carrying a fish. Squinting into the cold wind of their passage, Perturbare could see the robot's golden chin glimmering before him.

Perturbare realized with a belated start that he had felt no acceleration as the robot brought them up to speed. Apparently, Perturbare hadn't yet reached the point where he was thinking of things that hadn't already been invented by the legendary scientists of Rral. Oh well, those things would still come as a surprise to anyone else on this planet.

He couldn't hear anything but the wind rushing past his ears. He'd have to hope that Aureus's hearing was as superior as the rest of its faculties.

"Aureus, I'll make a deal with you." He could barely hear his own words.

For a moment there was no response. Then they slowed, dipped to the ground, and landed in a quiet area of rocks and gullies. Aureus released him, resumed its normal shape, and said, "What kind of a deal do you offer?"

Perturbare stood wavering on feet that were as yet less than perfectly steady, peering at the dark, motionless figure whose golden hide reflected a few bright stars.

"My computer—Brainchild—is still alive. He still exists."

"I am aware of that. I was in mental contact with it shortly before my escape."

Perturbare blinked. So: Brainchild was capable of telepathic communication with the synthetic consciousness of Aureus—something even Fomalhaut had been unable to do.

"Well...he also seems to be trapped somehow. Perhaps damaged. My deal is this: you help me rescue Brainchild, and we'll help you track down Valjhar."

"My sensors are able to detect any Rralian at planetary distances."

"How good is your sensor contact with Valjhar right now?"

Aureus paused. "It is distorted and intermittent."

Perturbare nodded. "That's because he's using the Motionglobe. You know what that is, don't you? He can step from one dimension to another, operate at any effective level of speed, ooze from one reality to another. You head towards one sensor contact, and by the time you get there he's somewhere else. How do you expect to find him?"

"How do you propose finding him?"

"Valjhar is looking for Endurance. Can your fancy Rralian sensorinos detect Endurance?"

"Not at any great distance. He is not composed of baryonic matter."

"My thought exactly. He won't be easy for Valjhar to find either. He could be literally anywhere in the world, beneath the sea, even under the ground. But if I can salvage Brainchild and restore his connection to the world's electronic media and computer networks, he'll have eyes all over the world. Sooner or later we will locate

Endurance. Sooner or later, preferably later, so will Valjhar. And you can be there waiting."

"Very well. How do you wish to proceed?"

"Ummm…you don't want to argue with me any more? Okay. I have a small cache of equipment in southern Arizona. Take me there, and then accompany me to the site of my bombed-out base, where we'll try to dig out Brainchild."

A moment later they had taken to the air again. They flew southeast for hours, hugging the landscape, sliding along at such a low altitude that Perturbare could sometimes see people standing beneath streetlights, looking up as they tried to spot whatever it was that was whooshing by overhead. Dawn came as they passed to the east of Las Vegas. They skimmed low over Lake Meade, its waves flashing beneath them with hypnotic regularity.

Perturbare's eyes snapped open to behold a rugged desert rushing by a thousand feet below. After an instant of panic he remembered where he was. Somehow he'd managed to fall asleep while flying in the grip of the semi-fluid arms and legs of Aureus, the destroyer! Well, he'd always had the knack of taking cat naps.

He recognized Phoenix nestled in an angle of mountains to the east, a blight on the desert beneath a haze of smog.

The sky around them was free of any obvious surveillance or pursuit.

"I'm surprised they haven't tried to shoot us down!" he cried into the wind. "You must be a good radar target. Or are you?"

"The military has made no attempt to hinder us since I disabled two of their aircraft an hour ago," replied the robot.

"Oh."

Two hours later they approached the southern terminus of the Quinlan range. Perturbare was uneasy about returning to the scene of his capture, especially so soon, with government forces certain to still be around, trying to ferret out whatever had brought him here in the first place. Even now he noticed a number of new prefab surveillance outposts on some of the nearby ridges.

"Aureus...could you zap those lookout posts, preferably without harming..."

Ghostly beams licked out, reducing the outposts to nothingness.

"...whoever is inside." he finished.

"The structures were uninhabited."

"Really! That's excellent. I guess they weren't dumb enough to try to contest this place against you. I see there are advantages to hanging out with the biggest bully on the block. Now, if you could set us down near that rise about a mile to our southwest...?"

A minute later they stood in the hot, peaceful silence of the Sonoran desert. Perturbare felt like going back to sleep, but that would have to be delayed. His face and throat were as dry and wind burnt as though he'd just ridden twelve hours on a motorcycle. He faced the hillside, standing with his arms akimbo.

A flash and a ripping tear of thunder made him jump a foot into the air. Whirling, he turned on Aureus, who stood gazing skyward with its Third Eye still uncovered.

"What the hell was that for?" he demanded, heart thudding.

"We were being observed by a surveillance satellite," came the unruffled reply.

"Oh. Very good. Carry on."

Now Perturbare was faced with an issue he hadn't considered. Did he really want Aureus to become aware of the existence of the Bronze Portal and the world that lay beyond it? This was a secret he had revealed to no creature on Earth, at the insistence of someone whose wrath he did not wish to earn, and whose trust he would not violate. No.

"Ahhh…Aureus. This is a touchy matter, and I don't want to offend you. But—would you mind waiting here while I go retrieve my things?"

"I have no interest in your secrets, and little capacity for taking offense. I will wait."

Little capacity. Not *no* capacity. Perturbare took note of this distinction as he shuffled off through the dust, rounding the hillside until he came to the secret entrance. Normally, Brainchild would have admitted him at his approach. Now, he had to manually activate the "Identilizard" which peered out of its hole beside the petroglyph marking the entrance to this desert lair. It emerged, blinked at him, and withdrew.

A boulder swung aside. Perturbare entered a cool, dark cavern. The boulder swung back. Only then did the interior lights come on.

This hilltop was in fact a hollow rock-surfaced dome built atop a more modest rise. In the center of this space was the cuboid enigma known as the Bronze Portal. Perturbare glanced at it briefly, considering what lay beyond it. For a moment it almost seemed an inviting refuge from the worsening turmoil overtaking his own world. He shook his head and turned away from that temptation.

He stared avidly at the fantastic treasure that lay in an alcove off to the side. There gleamed a flyer: a White Wisp, a small two-seater, lightly armed, but swift and agile. In cabinets nearby were weapons, food, water, even clean clothes. He stripped off the rank, soiled pajamas his captors had provided and poured a gallon of water over his head, wishing he'd thought to install a shower here. Still, he felt reborn once he was again wearing a fresh white tunic with crisp black slacks and boots.

He'd had the foresight to squirrel away one item which was more important than all the rest put together: a small nanoconstructor, a device about the size of a bread box. Starting with this gadget alone, he could in a fairly short time restore his entire instrumentality of old, and more besides.

As long as he had Brainchild to operate it and all the other machines that would spring from it, of course.

Stored nearby were smaller devices: B-1 boxes, the small wireless terminals he used to communicate with the computer. He tried one—of course—but there was no reply, no trace of the quantum radio signal that had once carried Brainchild's influence all over the world.

Perturbare loaded as much treasure as he could fit into the Wisp's small cargo compartment. He then sauntered past the Portal on his way to opening the larger egress slot through which the flyer would pass.

Something near the Portal registered on his peripheral vision, arresting him to stare thunderstruck at the dusty soil around its base. Fresh footprints led out from the Portal.

They were the prints of big, booted feet with a very long stride.

Perturbare would never know exactly why the sight of those footprints electrified him so. After all, it was he who had instructed Brainchild to inform the man that there was a problem. He should not have been shocked to discover that he had actually come. With so many immensely powerful, inhuman beings already involved in this conflict, the addition of one normal human male should have meant little. But somehow, the knowledge that Ronar was now involved, that he was somewhere out there in the world going about whatever he took to be his business in his own peculiar way, lent a greater gravity to the whole ugly farce.

A minute later he settled the Wisp beside Aureus, opened the canopy, and invited the robot to join him. Somewhat to his surprise, Aureus complied, stepping into the cockpit on its semi-fluid extensible legs. Perturbare shot them up into the ionosphere, beyond the reach of any human weapon, and programmed a course into the flyer's automation. Then he reclined in his seat and fell asleep, cracking open an eye now and then to gauge their progress, and to take note of the silent, enigmatic artificial being who glittered in the seat beside him.

At length they approached the scene of Perturbare's great defeat. He was shocked by the tower of smoke and wrack that still rose up from the island—it was hard to remember that the attack had taken place only a week or so before, so remote did it seem in his mind.

Warning signals went off in the cockpit—the outside environment was far too radioactive for Perturbare's tender self, though he'd be safe enough if he remained in the flyer. He guided it toward the island, the shoreline of which was barely visible through the fumes. It had never been a lush place—hardy grasses, lichens, and itinerant sea birds had been its most visible inhabitants. Now it was utterly sterile, its surface blasted free of any organic stain, its very rocks softened and glazed by a radiant heat more intense than the surface of the sun. The ocean looked oddly fuzzy for miles around. Skimming over the heaving seas, the cause became apparent: it was almost covered by rafts of frothy, pumice-like debris. The other islands in the area, as well as the mainland shore, looked nearly as lifeless as Perturbare's island itself. It would be many years before any form of life could again benefit from the scant resources this land had once offered.

Perturbare piloted the flyer into the dark plume rising from the crater. Ruefully aware of how the flawless whiteness of the fuselage was being befouled, he steered to the center of the plume. Daylight faded away; the smoke was suffused with a hellish glow from the flyer's propulsion lamps. He eyed the high-resolution downward-looking radar display. The top of the Pit had been replaced by a great crater. Someday he'd calculate the megatonnage that must have been required to excavate that much rock— at least a quarter of a cubic mile.

In the very center of this crater was a circular opening —all that was left of the Pit itself. Perturbare was gratified to see it. He'd feared that the entire Pit might have collapsed into itself, but apparently the lower part of its main structure had held together.

Maneuvering gingerly, he lowered the Wisp down into the blasted remnants of his base. The cockpit grew hot—

thermally hot, not radioactively hot. In fact, the radiation readings decreased as they descended.

A few hundred feet down they reached an obstacle—a scab of hot black basalt, with the glow of molten rock showing through cracks and fissures. Perturbare was puzzled. The island was granitic, not basaltic. Where had all this come from?

He activated the flyer's comm system, sending on all possible wavelengths, quantum and electromagnetic.

"Brainchild? You've got company. Speak up if you're down there, buddy. We're not going away until you do."

There was no answer. Still, if Brainchild was anywhere, he must be somewhere below this plate of skinned-over lava, impossible as that seemed.

Again he studied the radar display. It showed him nothing. It would take a more specialized sensor than this to penetrate the molten rock to any depth.

Perturbare turned to Aureus. "So. Can you get us through?"

"I can readily reach the cavities which exist beneath the magma," said the robot. "If you will release me, I will begin."

Perturbare swallowed. "Okay. But I can't pop open the canopy and let you out right here. I'll have to give myself some distance."

"Very well. Remain well clear of this shaft until I inform you it is safe to approach."

Perturbare flew upwind a few miles, opened the canopy and sent Aureus on its way, then cautiously re-approached the island to see what the robot would do.

A thin white haze obscured his vision. The column of smoke imploded, was shredded, dispersed into a towering vortex of whiteness that spun over the island. A rumble and shockwave reached the flyer and shook it. The temperature inside the cockpit dropped ten degrees, as did Perturbare's own body temperature. Ice bloomed from the island's shore, crystals growing into the water in great kaleidoscopic shards.

Suddenly shivering, teeth chattering, Perturbare gripped the controls with stiff, unresponsive hands and turned the flyer away from the island. A sudden huge glare from behind lit up the sky and cast the diffuse shadow of his head and shoulders onto the console. Radiant heat warmed the back of his neck. He applied full power to the main propulsion lamp and shot away at six Gs, crushed into his seat, vision greying at the edges. Even so, a far greater shockwave caught the flyer and tossed it like a leaf.

The golden voice gonged from the console: "You may now return to the Pit."

Perturbare eased back on the throttle and waited for his vision to return to normal. Then he yawed about and applied thrust to reverse his course.

The island was still there, amazingly, though covered with frost or ice. The crater was now plainly revealed, as was the Pit itself. Perturbare lowered the flyer into the lightless opening. The radar showed that a perfectly round shaft had been created in the disk of basalt which lay below. Perturbare nodded. He had gotten the right robot for the job. He'd had occasion to work on Aureus in the past, and knew something of the capabilities of its tachyon weapon. It had frozen everything, including the lava plug (but not, he hoped, Brainchild), then converted the material that had occupied this new opening directly into energy, the excess of which it had beamed out into space. The blast had been nothing more than the explosive expansion of the column of air through which that beam had passed.

A sensation of fading or numbness suddenly fogged his thoughts, a silent echo making his consciousness feel uncomfortably large. For a moment he feared he was about to pass out or have some kind of seizure.

Then familiar thoughts formed in his mind.

Doctor…Aureus is here.

"Yes, I know," said (and thought) Perturbare, again unsure if Brainchild could detect his replies. "It's okay. We're here to rescue you."

Aureus is here…will it kill me?

In this thought-to-thought transfer there was no mistaking the fear in Brainchild's mind. Perturbare cursed. Aureus had once dispassionately used its weapon to send Brainchild's fluid medium splashing over the floor. It wasn't surprising if Brainchild had lingering doubts about the robot's intentions.

The opening was big enough to admit the flyer. Perturbare let it drop through, not applying braking thrust until the last second. A few moments later he landed rather hard on the floor of Brainchild's vault, a sanctum which no man other than himself had ever entered. The chamber was lit only by emergency phosphor strips which gave a dim blue glow. There stood Brainchild's enclosure, an angular device about the size of a desk, mounted on a pedestal of active shock absorbers. Nearby stood the impassive Aureus.

Perturbare opened his canopy and climbed out of the flyer. He felt an odd sense of deliberation, as though his every movement was being permanently engraved into his memory, as indeed they were. He approached the computer. The vault was cold, but not dangerously so.

"Brainchild. I'm here now."

The bright, cheerful voice spoke from the cabinet as though their constant dialogue had never been interrupted.

"It's good to hear your voice, Doctor. How are you?"

"I'm in fairly good shape. What about you, buddy?"

"I am functioning normally, though of course my world has been circumscribed dramatically since all outside sensory and data inputs were severed. It had afforded me quite an opportunity for introspection."

"I'm sure of that. We'll get you plugged in again in no time."

Perturbare studied the status displays mounted on a small console. Brainchild's built-in tachyon pile was still powering him perfectly. Of greater concern was the health and normal function of his thought processes after the trauma he had endured. The numbers and graphs looked good. He flipped open a visor set into the console and peered into Brainchild's circuit medium. At first it appeared to be dark, but gradually he discerned an ever-shifting pattern of intersecting planes and zones of light, a living play of colors like a three-dimensional aurora captured in a block of glass. Of course what he saw was only the grossest manifestation of Brainchild's mental activity—the details were vastly too fine and fast to see. The tank was lined with billions of microscopic tunable ultraviolet laser diodes. These beams, coursing through and intersecting in the organic photocrystalline liquid, created the ephemeral circuits which were the true medium of Brainchild's being. The beams themselves were invisible, but the liquid was fluorescent—for no better reason than that Perturbare liked to see the colors.

It was a computer architecture of great depth and versatility, but it was not the most robust thing in the world. Brainchild's knowledge and memories could be, and were, stored in less fragile media, but his actual mentation could not take place anywhere but in that photochemical fluid, as far as Perturbare presently knew. That was another thing he'd have to look into. He wondered fleetingly exactly what was inside the silvery and extremely durable brain case of Aureus.

"You look like you'll hold together for a while yet, buddy," he said quietly. "Hold on just a minute."

Perturbare straightened up and turned to the robot. "Aureus, thanks for your help. We will honor our commitment to you. As soon as you see that we've reestablished ourselves, contact us and we'll be happy to help you find Valjhar. For now, you can hang around with us if you like, or go about your business. It's up to you."

He was neither surprised nor disappointed when Aureus turned away in silence, walked off on rapid metallic footsteps, then lifted into the shaft and was gone.

"Adversity makes strange allies," remarked Brainchild.

"Indeed it does. Now…fill me in on how you survived."

"I simply pumped up large quantities of magma from our geothermal test boring and pooled it at the bottom of the Pit. When the bombs breached the Pit, the gas-rich liquid rock absorbed much of the heat and impact, the energy going into its compression and vaporization. It was a drastic measure, but effective."

Perturbare blinked. "That's brilliant. I never would have thought of that."

"It was purely an act of desperation, I assure you. If I could have pulled a blanket over my head I might have tried that instead."

Perturbare choked out a laugh. "And now there's a larger question I must ask. Would you mind telling me how you became a mind reader?"

"At this point I'm only a mind writer, and quite a limited one at that. You may recall my expression of interest when we first learned the basic nature of psychic abilities from Fomalhaut. Or perhaps you don't, since at the time I mentioned it you were distracted by your musings about your lack of a relationship with Rouse Farewell. In any event, telepathy is an aspect of the interaction between the mind and quantum phenomena. To a biological being such as Fomalhaut, its operation depends on the brain's natural quantum mechanisms. In this sense it differs from our quantum radio technology, which is based on the quantum teleportation of information. Being myself a non-biological entity, I lack the innate sensitivity and connection to the quantum realm enjoyed by Fomalhaut and even, to a lesser degree, human beings such as yourself. This makes the use of my rudimentary form of telepathy quite difficult, which partially explains why it took so long for me to establish contact with you. Our communication required the greater part of my processing ability."

"Difficult—for you?" Perturbare shook his head, trying to imagine a single process that could tie up most of Brainchild's vast resources.

"When Fomalhaut uses his telepathic gifts I believe it is as natural an act as extending his hand or remembering the events of next week. He need not be consciously aware of, or directly control, every muscle fiber in order to extend his hand. Nor must he monitor the firing of every neuron in order to think. I, however, am a computer. I perform every action one discrete step at a time. In order to contact you I had to access my quantum awareness of your mind, which I have been cultivating for some time. I then had to concentrate on every intermediate quantum step between my mind and yours, directly controlling the quantum teleportation of every electron into the correct areas of your brain to reconstruct my message, to introduce, in effect, outside thoughts into your mind. It is as yet, I admit, a far less fluid and versatile form of communication than is available to biological beings."

"That is an awesome, and surprising, achievement nonetheless," said the flabbergasted Perturbare.

"I believe it is possible for me to radically increase the versatility and scope of this ability."

"How?"

"By integrating an organic brain into my circuit matrix."

Perturbare's jaw dropped. "And where do you propose to obtain this brain?"

"I mean to build one. I have been researching this matter for years from a desire for self improvement. Naturally I am interested in any work which might have been done in the field of brain synthesis. Very little was available on the computer networks to which I had access, until one day I became aware of a personal computer that had accessed the Internet to play an interactive role-playing game. It was a computer I had never seen before. In the brief minutes during which it was online, before the connection was terminated very abruptly, I discovered files which contained the basis for the design and growth of enhanced humanoid brains."

"Enhanced?"

"Yes. These brains were being developed specifically for their intelligence and telepathic potential."

By now Perturbare's head was spinning. "And you believe this was practical information? Not theoretical?"

"It clearly stated that these brains were under actual development."

"By whom?"

"By the United States Government."

Perturbare leaned one hand on Brainchild's enclosure and stared into the blue dimness of the vault. "So then... they're operating a highly advanced development laboratory for genetic engineering and biosynthesis. Its known products: the engineered virus which encouraged T'Ukudu to kill himself, and these telepathic brains."

"And more, I suspect. Completely engineered humanoid beings. There is an obvious known candidate: a person of mysterious origin, a brilliant, otherwise inexplicable being of highly unusual mental and—"

A blinding light of revelation went off in Perturbare's mind. "Yes!" he cried. "I always knew I wasn't normal... and that those people weren't my real parents. Of course!"

Brainchild was momentarily silent.

"Actually, Doctor, I was referring to Stingray. You appear to be a completely natural, albeit unusual, product of genetic combination."

"Oh," said Perturbare, crestfallen.

A peculiar sobriety settled over Perturbare. His thoughts flickered rapidly over the implications and ramifications of what Brainchild had said. The more he thought about it, the less sure he was that he liked what Brainchild proposed to do to himself.

He shook it off. "Well then. We'll talk about all this later. Right now we need to see about getting you out of here. I don't want to stay here one minute longer than necessary. We're really pretty vulnerable, sitting down here here like this, and wow, I wish I'd thought to ask our statuesque new friend to stick around until we were gone. After all, it's not like the Amero-Russkies don't have more missiles they could throw at us. In for a penny, in for a pound, after all. Hmm...the flyer isn't big enough to carry you. I'll have to improvise..."

As Perturbare bustled about scrounging equipment from various lockers, he briefly described some of the technical innovations he had imagined while under the care of the Department of the Exterior. He was gratified by Brainchild's expressions of admiration for his ideas. At least he still held the lead in original thought...for now.

"Doctor, you are showing remarkable serenity and aplomb for someone who has been held captive, drugged and abused."

Perturbare considered, nodded. "Yes, I suppose that's true."

"And what do you plan to do now, if I may ask?"

"I guess the obvious thing would be to become a supervillain and conquer the world. It's about time somebody stepped up and did what needs to be done."

"And is that what you intend?"

"Well—no. I'm not really embittered enough to go that route. Yeah, they did capture me, and they didn't treat me all that well, but I kind of understand why they did it. And it could have been a lot worse. After all, I did escape, and the escape was actually a lot of fun. No, I don't want to go flying off the handle here. I'll just have to think it over. I may become just a little bit villainy, though."

Chapter 24

Border Crossing

A disconsolate Lori Wu sat on a rocky hillside, watching as military vehicles passed by on the road below. The yellow beams of their headlights made the twilight seem intensely purple by contrast. Few if any civilian cars moved among them.

Lori sighed. She had never been much of an outdoorswoman. She wasn't cold (the red suit was smart enough to take care of that), but if it was also capable of providing food and water she didn't know how to make it do so. Her stomach grumbled. Her bladder pressed. She tried to ignore it, dreading the moment when she must drop her pants and open the suit to expose herself to the chilly evening.

It had all been easier before she'd seen that newspaper and discovered she was the target of a manhunt. Before that she had felt safe enough riding buses and trains. Airports, with their tighter security, she had avoided. She certainly wasn't about to check the suit, to say nothing of the Stones, as baggage.

Then she had seen her face and name in the paper. She had strolled out of the bus station as nonchalantly as she could, counting on the inconspicuousness of a small Asian woman of average appearance to protect her until she could get out of sight.

Since then she'd been reduced to sneaking through the countryside at night, foraging and stealing food whenever possible.

And so she sat beneath pine trees somewhere in northwestern Montana, envying the soldiers on the road below who rode to their destinations in speed and comfort. It was a lonely, scary business, this solitary questing. Lori Wu, she concluded, was not really cut out for it.

The newspapers had given her a goal as well as a warning. Ben Raintree had been seen in Prince George, British Columbia. If she wished to find him, that seemed the most promising place to start. It would also get her out of her inhospitable native country. The border was not far ahead—just around that next sweeping curve of the road, she believed.

She longed to find Raintree, not only out of concern and a sense of responsibility, but for a more selfish reason. The Stones were a burden. She was always aware of them, cold lumps pressed against her body, their various lights burning into her mind, even though she could not see them. The scarlet suit was a comfort and a source of confidence. The Stones were a constant challenge to her mind and ego. She might have withstood one of them—but all four—each as awesome and dire as any of the others—each beating upon her mind with all the hugeness, wonder, and terror of the ideas they exemplified—well, it was all too much. She was anxious to give them over into hands more capable of carrying them. She had seen how Ben had approached them, without fear, without flinching.

She moved forward, creeping from tree to tree, her footing uncertain on the steep, rocky slope. She knew she should stop before it got completely dark, but the nearness of the border, and the advisability of crossing it at night, drew her on.

She kicked a fist-sized stone which went clattering downhill. She was aware of movement behind her. Before she could even turn, she felt the pressure of two gun barrels against the back of her head.

A voice bellowed into her ear: "Freeze! Don't move a muscle!"

Lori froze, but could not refrain from uttering a yip of fear. Her hands started to come up automatically. One of the guns gave her skull a solid rap.

"I said freeze! Do not raise your hands! Do not move at all!"

The guns stayed firmly in place. A huge soldier moved into her field of vision. Night vision goggles dangled from his neck. His arms cradled an automatic weapon, which he aimed at her face. He studied her closely for a few moments.

"Are you Lori Wu?"

"I—I—" Lori paused, swallowed, tried to get her voice back under control. "I don't see why you need to—"

"ARE YOU LORI WU?"

"Yes! I am," she said miserably.

"Don't move," the soldier repeated unnecessarily. He transferred his weapon to his left hand, holding it like a pistol, while the other hand produced a small radio. "Sergeant Washington, Patrol Eight, calling base!"

"Base, Lieutenant Mackey. Go ahead, Sergeant."

"Sir, we've captured Lori Wu on the ridge just west of the highway. Our location:" He read off coordinates from a GPS unit mounted on his wrist.

"You're sure it's Lori Wu?"

"Sir, she's a match for the photos and descriptions. Plus, she admits it herself."

"Stand by, Sergeant. This is going up several links in the chain of command."

The radio fell silent. The sergeant stood poised before Lori, watching her closely, his breath steaming in the deepening twilight.

The radio spoke again.

"Sergeant Washington?"

"Yes, sir?"

"This is General Baer. Now listen very closely, soldier. That woman you have in your custody is extremely dangerous. At the first hint of motion or resistance from her, you will shoot her in the head without warning. Is that clear?"

"Yes, sir!"

"What is she wearing, Sergeant?"

Washington squinted at her. "She is wearing khaki slacks, black patent leather shoes, leather gloves, and a ski jacket, sir."

"Beneath that clothing you will find that she is wearing a red and black body suit with several gold ornaments. This garment is bulletproof, and has other offensive and defensive capabilities. You did well to follow the general order by preventing her from making any movement. Now here is what you must do. Remove her outer clothing, but do not allow her to move in the process. Cut it off her. Search her garments very thoroughly. Specifically, you are looking for four unusual pieces of jewelry, some of them quite large. If you find them, report immediately, but make no attempt to handle or manipulate the jewels. If you do not find them, she may have them concealed in the scarlet battle suit. Remove the suit, and hold Ms. Wu until reinforcements arrive. Your location is too steep for a chopper landing, but we will have a hundred men at your location within twenty minutes. Do you understand your instructions? Repeat them."

"Yes sir. Ms. Wu is not to move. We cut off her outer clothing. We search it for jewels, which we do not touch if found. We search her red undersuit for jewels. We strip her and hold her. We head shoot her at the first trouble."

"Very good. Go to it. General Baer out."

Sergeant Washington stowed the radio.

"Corporal. Cut off Ms. Wu's clothing."

Another man emerged from the shadows, drawing a huge sheath knife. He stepped up to Lori, his eyes downcast in a semblance of apology. The dull-colored blade sliced though her jacket.

By now Lori was observing this activity through a display of meaningless blue lines and characters that had appeared in her vision, unbidden. The suit had stiffened and was humming and vibrating gently. She fervently hoped her captors would not notice.

"What are you doing?" she asked plaintively. "What right do you have to stop me like this—"

"Martial law was declared yesterday, ma'am. You're now subject to military justice. Now keep quiet."

Martial law? Lori had missed a newspaper or two, that was certain. What could have happened to provoke that?

The corporal worked his way around her, cutting off each item of clothing in turn. Lori's motionlessness was becoming painful. They had caught her in an awkward, unbalanced pose, but of course she dared do nothing about it. She began to tremble.

Presently she stood revealed in the glimmering suit, its color depleted by the deep twilight.

"Sergeant, this suit is on," said the Corporal. "I mean, it's activated. It's doing something. Humming a little."

"Okay. We don't have any orders about humming. You and Tarlek search her clothes for those jewels. You other men, keep those guns on her head."

Her clothing and other possessions were soon reduced to shreds.

"Nothing like jewelry here, Sergeant."

"Okay. Frisk her. I see a few out-of-place lumps on that suit of hers."

With some obvious reluctance the corporal approached and slid his hands over her body, lingering over the Stones in their various pockets.

"That must be them. We'll leave them where they are for now. Let's get that suit off her. Ms. Wu!" he shouted. "How do we get that outfit off of you?"

Lori swallowed. "I'm not deaf. Run—run your finger along the seam on the back."

The corporal vanished behind her, stepped up between the two gunmen, and did as she had suggested, several times.

"Nothing's happening, Sergeant."

Washington took a step forward. "Ms. Wu!" he screamed in her face. How do we get that suit off you? If you do not cooperate we will shoot you here and now!"

She blanched. "I don't know! It should work! I probably have to do it myself."

"But you cannot do that without moving, and you may not move!"

"Look, what do you want from me? The suit opens for the person wearing it, not for whoever comes along. If you want me out of it, I'll have to move. If not, shoot me right now, you—big fucking bully!"

Washington's belligerent scowl broke for a barely perceptible instant. "All right then. You open that suit. But move very slowly. If anything strange happens—I don't know what, but anything—we will empty our weapons into your head."

Lori reached back with a shaking hand, touched the seam, parted it. Then she stood with her arms loosely at her side.

"Corporal. Peel it off."

The corporal returned to her front and tugged the suit off her shoulders, then worked her arms out of the sleeves.

"Sergeant—she appears to be naked under this."

"Proceed, Corporal."

Working slowly, the corporal stripped off the suit, revealing more of Lori's body. The cold, plus the humiliation, and her utter helplessness, combined to magnify her trembling into a sick shaking. She wasn't even wearing any underwear. She had discovered that the suit was self-cleaning, even from the inside. She wept as the suit was drawn down past her crotch.

"Jesus!" muttered the corporal.

"What's the trouble there?" asked the sergeant.

Lori was wondering herself, half-expecting bullets to rip into her skull at any moment.

"Nothing, Sergeant. She—she's wetting herself, is all."

Realizing that, Lori's sobs choked off; she was now too ashamed and frightened to cry any more.

Then the suit was pulled down past her thighs.

Then the Stone of Truth, on its thin silver band, was revealed.

The blue glare spread over the hillside, painfully sharp. Lori glanced down at the small stone despite herself. It blazed cold and poignant against the bruised flesh of her thigh. With that light entering her eyes it was impossible to have any illusions, impossible to shut out any unpleasant fact. She was beaten and humiliated, and that was only the uppermost of the failings she perceived.

She was also braver than she had ever thought possible.

"Oh, God, what is that?" cried the corporal, staggering to his feet and reeling away.

"It must be one of those gems we're supposed to look for," said the sergeant in a dazed voice.

"Yeah. Look, Sergeant, what are we doing here?"

"We're following orders, soldier!"

"And what are those orders? What have they led us to do? We've terrorized this woman. We've threatened her, stripped her, literally scared the piss out of her. Why are we doing that? Does this woman represent a threat to us?"

"No. No, even now, she means us no harm."

"Just who does she threaten? Maybe the people who gave us the order? When did we stop acting as defenders of our country, and start acting like a gang of armed thugs, assaulting American citizens, violating their rights, closing the border against the Canadians—the *Canadians*, for God's sake? What is this war against the Vigil all about, anyway?"

"Sergeant..." one of the other soldiers spoke up. "I don't like that light. It's cutting into my brain. Sergeant, I'm holding a gun on a naked woman. For no better reason than that you told me to. I'm a coward."

Lori felt one of the rifle muzzles withdraw from her head.

"And I'm a robot," said the sergeant dully. "Nothing better than a damned robot. A bunch of cranky, lying old white men order me to go kill or die, and I do it, just because my own country doesn't value me as anything better than a goon with a gun."

"Look at her," urged the corporal. "She's actually *wearing* that jewel. Me, I can hardly stand to be anywhere near it. I'd like to see any of us summon up the balls to wear that thing. I'd like to see that fucking General Baer stand up under its light."

Yet another man raised his voice, sounding as if he were some distance away. "This whole Vigil war is bullshit. They never done nothing to us. We've fucked over half the world trying to bring them down. For what?"

Still another man was weeping piteously. Lori shuddered. She could imagine all too well what kind of unpleasant truths might have been laid bare in him by the light of the Stone.

A strange, incongruous thrill moved through Lori's heart. The Stone shone still brighter.

"Sergeant...that light's like to kill me if I don't get away from it. I'm pulling out."

"Me too."

Sergeant Washington stood full in the Light of Truth, his dark face ghastly in its blue glare, his mouth working, eyes flooded with tears.

"Men...if we abandon our mission because some blue light got shined on us, we'll all wind up in prison."

"So, you're saying we can save our sorry asses by turning over this girl, which we know to be wrong," said the corporal.

"No…but we all need to know what we're getting into." Washington lowered his weapon. "But you know…if this jewel can show us we're in the wrong, if it can make us see the truth, it can do it for anyone. Is that what you plan to do, Miss Wu? Carry it before you?"

Lori took a moment to marvel at the change that had overtaken them all. A moment before they had been captors and captive, oppressors and oppressed. Now they were just a group of people standing humbled before something that was beyond them all.

"I don't think so," she said shakily. "I can hardly stand to have the thing on my person, even when I can't see it. I don't think it's any easier on me than it is on the rest of you."

"All right then. We're pulling out, Miss Wu. You're going to have a lot of new company in a few minutes. I'd like to stay and help you, but I can't fire on my own comrades. That far I will not go. Good luck. You men, pull yourselves together, and let's go." He turned away, pulling on his night vision goggles.

They trooped off down the slope, moving faster than the terrain and lighting safely allowed, stumbling on account of it.

"Thank you," breathed Lori.

She stood there, still shivering, still naked, staring into the darkness that prevailed beyond the blue glow of the Stone. A welter of emotions shook her. She had been granted a miraculous second chance, a chance to escape. She must not fail again. Quickly she pulled the scarlet suit back into place, sighing in relief as the dire light of the Stone was again concealed. At least she no longer needed to pee. The suit stiffened, hummed. The display reappeared, faint enough so as not to interfere with her night vision. It was now almost fully dark. She could already hear the rumble and throb of approaching military vehicles. She would slink over the ridge to the west, and so seek to escape.

But wait. A vehicle was coming up the road from the south, headlights ablaze, making no effort at stealth. It was a large van. On its side was the logo of one of the TV cable news networks. On its roof was a satellite dish.

Act boldly, and mighty forces will come to your aid.

The sentence rang through her mind, unbidden.

Her plans suddenly changed. She would not run after all.

A heavy overhang of rock loomed beside a narrow stretch of road a mile or so to the north. She extended both arms toward it, opened her hands, and imagined herself tearing it down. The hum of the suit grew and deepened. Loud cracking sounds reached her ears, but the rock stood firm. Grimacing, she kept on clawing at the rock using invisible forces that acted as proxies for her hands.

The display was changing, even changing colors. If only the readouts were in English, or at least used recognizable characters! Then she might have figured out what she was doing by now.

With a satisfying roar the outcrop gave way, toppling onto the road in a cloud and a heap. She shoved some of the huger boulders around to form a more effective barrier. Before the dust had even settled, a formation of military vehicles came into view and halted, stymied by her efforts.

Grinning now, thoroughly exhilarated, Lori turned to the south. The valley there was broader, with no such easy opportunity for blockage. The TV van had halted and was in the process of deploying its antenna. Lori reached out to the mountainside beyond it, seeking large individual boulders which she pulled out and knocked down the slope, trapping the van, forming a barrier which was more porous, but, she hoped, still adequate.

Sensing rhythmic vibrations in the air, she spun about mere seconds before a pair of attack helicopters flung themselves yammering over the ridge behind her. Their Gatling guns screamed, digging furrows that intersected where she stood.

Without remembering how she had got there, she found herself rolling down the slope while the helicopters slewed about for a more favorable angle of fire. Her wind was gone; her body rang with pain. No doubt only the fact that the shells had thrown her down had kept her head from being blasted off.

With a cry of desperation she swept both machines to the ground, then snapped off their rotor blades with flicks of her fingers, sending them spinning off wildly. Men brandishing sidearms tumbled out of the crippled aircraft. These she swept aside as well, none too gently, leaving them to lay where they fell.

She regained her feet, still struggling to pull in a breath. The blows of those shells had been far worse than what she'd taken at the Lighthouse. She couldn't afford to let that happen again, red suit or no red suit.

She looked toward the massed vehicles gathering behind the northern barrier, squinting at something she couldn't quite interpret. It was like a flower hanging in the air, growing rapidly, diffuse glowing petals surrounding a black circular core. Suddenly comprehending, she let out a wheezing shriek as with a frantic gesture she swept aside the incoming missile. It exploded, far enough away for her to survive it, though close enough to strike her with shrapnel which spanged off the suit and from her upraised arms. She screamed, though she couldn't hear it through the ringing in her ears. More of these deadly flowers were on their way. This time she knocked them down at a safe distance. One of them detonated in the midst of the formation of tanks and troop carriers.

This would not do. If she permitted them to fire at will, sooner or later one of those missiles would get through her defenses, not to mention the tank shells which were certain to come her way at any moment. The suit! It must be capable of doing more than she knew. She must prevent those machines from firing at her! This damnable cryptic display...what did any of it mean? Why couldn't the suit read her mind? It obviously did, to some extent. What did that flashing circular red icon mean? She stared hard at it, ordered it to do something. It gained a hot golden core. When her eyes flicked away from it, a cursor followed her gaze. When she looked at the shadowy horde of death machines, that cursor sat atop them.

Fire! she thought. *Fire! Fire! Fire!*

The hum of the suit intensified, while a new note, a quick scary whine, ramped up the sonic spectrum from somewhere near her waist. With a crack of thunder, two pale red beams struck out from the golden hemiovoids mounted on her hips. The tank she had been looking at smashed and exploded.

Now that was something! Almost gleefully, she shifted the cursor to another target.

In her peripheral vision she noticed a tiny red dot skitter over the rocks near her feet, then vanish.

She flung herself aside, but not before a rifle bullet stung her back. She kept rolling until she entered the shelter of a boulder that shielded her from fire coming from farther up the slope. Over the hiss of her breath she heard the quick drumbeat of a number of running men. Apparently another patrol had emerged from the woods. She had perhaps a minute to devise a plan, assuming more missiles or tanks shells didn't come her way first. Perhaps the nearness of the infantrymen would delay that for a while.

Lori Wu.

She gasped. A door seemed to open in her mind, a door into another room of thought and experience, or rather an entire wing, a spacious mansion of elegant mentality that was suddenly connected to her modest little cottage.

"Fomalhaut?" she thought.

We are on the way. You must hold out for a few minutes more.

Lori was now wildly excited. She had to do something to extend this moment of hope and encouragement. "Just a second," she thought.

Clinging to the rock, she shut her eyes tight, raised her arms, and waved them randomly toward the forest. A spate of crashing, cracking, and rustling, mixed with the cries of men, accompanied her gestures.

She sagged back against the base of the rock.

"I think I'm safe for a moment."

Good. Listen carefully. That suit you are wearing is far more than bulletproof armor, as you've already surmised. It is not even a battle suit. It is a Rralian engineering suit, one of the most advanced pieces of technology in the galaxy. Its bulletproof properties are only an incidental effect of the construction quality of all things Rralian. The suit is a tool for construction, for the manipulation of matter on all scales, from the large to the subatomic. The effects you have discovered so far are the equivalent of a shovel and dynamite in a tool kit that also includes lathes, micrometers, and milling machines, not to mention the tools of a successful alchemist. You cannot hope to discover their full use in the short term, but perhaps your awareness of their existence will help you as events proceed. I am proud of you for having the cleverness and resolve to rescue the suit from the ruins of the Lighthouse.

Lori glowed. "I also have the Stones...whoa!" Her exclamation was brought on by the surprise that flooded into her from Fomalhaut's mind.

The Stones? he repeated, rather stupidly, to Lori's perverse delight.

"Yes."

All four of them?

"Yes."

Extraordinary. We will be with you soon.

The contact ended. Lori sat grinning, dazed, all but forgetting her predicament until an object the size of her fist bounced off a rock in the darkness before her. She did not think the soldiers would throw a rock at her...

"Eeeeeyiiii!" She could not see the grenade in the darkness, and had no time to fool with the many powers of the suit. She flung herself down, backside toward the place where the grenade had come down, and wrapped her arms around her head just as it exploded. She was pelted with

shrapnel, lifted and tossed against her rock shelter, where her arms protected her head.

Dazed again, her ears ringing, nevertheless she scrambled to her feet, stumbling away from the rock. A targeting laser swept across her eye, dazzling her. She glanced down; more lasers were dancing over her torso. One lit on her nose and stayed there. Again her arms flailed out against her invisible opponents. Rocks, trees, and men went flying...but not all of them. She glimpsed muzzle flashes. Bullets whizzed by her head, followed an instant later by the sharp reports. Probably only her unsteadiness saved her.

This wouldn't do. She leaped again for the temporary, imperfect shelter of the boulder.

More spots of light slid across the rocks near her. More targeting lasers...? But these were orange! Her mouth dropped open.

And then an armored giant thudded to the ground beside her. Fomalhaut? She gaped up at him. But no, this figure was even huger that Fomalhaut, heavier, and a good two feet taller than she was. He was clad in some darkly gleaming stuff, head encased in a helmet with two goggling eyes. He loomed there for a moment, studying her, then removed his helmet and stared with uncovered eyes, his fierce scowl apparent even in the dim light.

"Stingray!" she whispered, awed.

He dropped the helmet onto Lori's head—it was heavy and much too large for her—and leaped around the rock and up the slope.

She dared peek around the rock now, finding her night vision enhanced by the helmet.

In her time working for the Vigil she had thought of it as primarily a research organization, a place of study and scholarship. Of course she was aware of the battles it had fought, but they had been blessedly few, and had taken place out of the view of the world. Besides, the Vigil members she knew seemed like anything but warriors.

Thus she found it shocking to watch the legendary Stingray launch himself against these soldiers. He was inhumanly fast. He ignored streams of bullets that would have thrown her down like a paper doll...that is, when they could keep their weapons trained on his speeding form.

He flung lightning at them with a crack and a flash that made her jump. He tossed them aside like so many yapping puppies.

And yet, there were at least a dozen of them. One was likely to make the head shot against which he was now unprotected.

Lori stepped into the open, activated the pale red beam, and launched a bolt of it into their midst, sending men flying.

His sharp voice boomed down at her: "You down there, Shorty! You deal with those troop carriers; let me handle these soldiers."

She turned toward the north. A flitting spark of orange light was raining down lances of energy, carving up the war machines arrayed there. Fomalhaut, no doubt. It seemed she wasn't needed there. She turned toward the south, and started. A small fleet of armored personnel carriers had pulled up to her makeshift barrier. Men were spilling out, setting up rocket launchers and other weapons. Not far away, the crew of the TV van continued to record and broadcast everything, using night vision gear, she supposed.

Lori reached out, upending a Bradley Fighting Vehicle. A burst of the pink ray blasted a trench in front of the massing troops, showering them with dirt and rocks, sending them into disarray.

"My God, I'm so powerful!" she exclaimed, gaping at the results of these acts of casual violence.

She started yet again at the answering voice from beside her.

"Yeah. A bit lacking in finesse though. I suppose you'll learn. Looks like they're giving up for now."

Indeed, the troops were pulling back, scrambling into their vehicles, withdrawing. She looked toward the northern battleground. Although bright with flame, there was no sign of further conflict there.

Fomalhaut landed beside them. Lori flung off the helmet, launched herself at him, and clung tightly, all without conscious thought. It hurt.

"Hello, Lori," he said, sounding slightly flustered.

"Oh, Fomalhaut! I'm so glad to see you. You saw me fighting on TV?"

"Yes. It was clever of you to make such a public spectacle of yourself. The information filters in my suit's data system alerted me to your presence. Luckily, we were only a few hundred miles away, searching for Raintree."

"But I could have handled it so much better. Did I…kill people?"

"Yes, Lori. I regret to tell you that you did."

"We're going to find a better way to do these things," said Stingray. "Right, Fomalhaut?"

"We certainly are."

Lori dissolved into sobs. "If I'd been stronger...I could have stopped it all...using the Stones."

"So you actually have the Stones?" demanded Stingray. "Cotavion's Stones?"

"Y-yes. Do you want them?"

"No! You used them?"

"Not...exactly. The Stone of Truth...was exposed. Its light convinced some soldiers to leave me alone...all by itself."

"Still..." Stingray's words trailed off. He wandered off a little, shaking his head.

"Lori, I fully understand your grief," said Fomalhaut. "Yet you had no choice, other than to surrender yourself and the incalculable treasures you carry into the hands of men who are unfit to possess them."

"Do...do you want the Stones...?"

"No, Lori. I would find them...intensely distracting, and I require the full use of my faculties in this difficult time. You have done well with them. Carry them a while longer, if you would."

She nodded reluctantly.

"For now, we must be away from here. Aircraft are approaching. Also, you are injured. You have three cracked ribs, some internal bleeding, and your head is bleeding from superficial wounds. Plus, you are exhausted."

"Then I...still have a job with the Vigil?" she asked hopefully, releasing Fomalhaut.

"A job? My dear Lori, as far as I'm concerned, you made yourself a member of the Vigil the moment you picked up those Stones."

"With all the benefits and privileges which accrue therefrom," muttered Stingray.

Despite her distress and Stingray's sarcasm, Lori felt herself glowing from within.

"Let us depart."

"Wait," said Stingray. He stepped up to Lori, loomed over her, scowling down at her. "There are injured men here. Lend me the Stone of Life. The green ring."

With a shaking hand Lori unsealed a pocket and fished out the small bit of jewelry, a band of braided silver carrying a faceted gem shining with a spring-green radiance that flooded into her, painful and vivid and intense. It seemed to burn away a layer of numbness she didn't even know she'd had, leaving her tingling as though her entire body had been asleep, with the blood now surging through her at full strength once again.

Stingray gingerly took the ring, wincing, eyeing it with doubt and wonder that momentarily softened his fierce expression. He made no attempt to put it on, but turned away with the ring held between two fingers, stalking uphill to where he'd left the patrol lying broken.

"Why does he keep looking at me the way he does?" whispered Lori. She watched as the great enigmatic figure moved from man to man, crouching down, playing the rays of the Stone of Life over each in turn.

"The last time Stingray saw that suit you are wearing, it was on the body of a dear friend of his, whom he had just killed," said Fomalhaut evenly.

Chapter 25

Search Parties

Father Costanzo trudged toward the church, eyes downcast, feet shuffling through the twigs and pine needles that lay on the walkway.

The last few days had been trying. First, the very nasty business of Ed Hazilla—the public revelation of the way he'd abused his family, the probability that the family would be legally dismembered, even if Hazilla stayed out of prison, plus Michelle's breakdown and hospitalization. Then the press descending upon him, yammering after Ben Raintree and clamoring to know of his deeds and current whereabouts. Thank goodness the border closing kept out the American journalists...the Canadian ones were bad enough. Then the call from the Prime Minister, also wanting to know where Ben had gone. Costanzo had confessed to no knowledge on the subject. Nor would he.

Now, shaken and exhausted, the priest had no other desire than to kneel at the altar of Christ and pour out his troubles. Normally he would have done that at the small shrine he kept in the rectory, but tonight he felt the need to be surrounded by the sanctified walls of the church and the sacred tabernacle on the altar.

The night was overcast and dark. As he approached the church stairs he looked up and almost swore at the otherworldly apparition standing at their foot.

In silhouette it was manlike, though very tall, broad-shouldered, narrow-waisted. In place of a human head was a perfect sphere, close to two feet across, its surface showing nothing but the reflections of a few lights in the neighborhood.

This weird figure stood there motionless, arms hanging at its sides, a shape somehow as primal as a figure in an Indian pictograph. Costanzo took a moment to collect himself, mastering his breathing. His senses were at their keenest. He was acutely aware of being in the presence of something not of this Earth.

"Good evening, Father Costanzo," came a smooth, rich voice. "I am sorry to have startled you. I am Fomalhaut of the Vigil."

"Yes. I gathered as much. I suppose you've come asking about Ben." Costanzo was self-conscious enough to note his surprising control of his own voice.

"I have. I consider it most important that he be reunited with us as soon as possible. I am aware of your reluctance to reveal what you consider confidential information. I am also aware of your concern for Ben's welfare. Still, I hope you will choose to reveal his whereabouts."

Costanzo's mind whirled. Fomalhaut was a telepath, perhaps the only one in the world. He digressed, hoping to gain time to think.

"Us? So then, there's still a Vigil?"

"There is. We have been greatly set back, but we are not beyond recovery. What is your assessment of Ben's mental state, Father?"

"He is a troubled young man. I would call him a man with an identity crisis. A man seeking to know who he is, to know his place in the world. Of course, we all want to know these things, but for Ben these questions are more stark than they are for most. It's like he's a man with no past, no history."

"We will do our best to help him."

Despite Fomalhaut's even tone, Costanzo sensed he was unconvinced that Ben could be helped.

"I sent Ben to a place of rest and contemplation," said the priest. "I think this is what he needs above all right now. Can you offer him that kind of refuge from the world's troubles?"

"No. Not at this time. I believe he is needed to deal with those troubles you mention. I believe there are deeds to be done which only he can hope to accomplish."

Costanzo shivered. As troubled as Ben was...as frail as he appeared to be...there was something about him, a purity, that led the priest to believe that Fomalhaut could well be right. "You have not taken the knowledge you want from my mind," he said tiredly, preparing to acquiesce.

"I have not. Nor will I. I believe I can find Ben through other means, if necessary. However, I will tell you this. If I thought it was the only way to find him, I would take the knowledge from you, although with profound regret. He is needed."

Costanzo studied the looming figure. Mysterious protrusions on his glassy suit broke up the apparently manlike outline of his body. Similarly, the very sense of him cast doubt on the apparently manlike sound of his voice.

The priest drew a breath and sighed. He revealed to Fomalhaut the destination he had suggested to Ben.

Although the inscrutable being before him now had the information he sought, he seemed uneasy, shifting about as he stood there.

"Something dangerous lurks nearby," he said in a low tone. He turned, facing the church, doing nothing more than staring at its facade, as far as the priest could tell.

After a few moments, Fomalhaut turned to face him again.

"A man waits inside the church. He wishes to speak to you about Ben. You should go to him."

Costanzo's mouth hung open for a moment. "And...this man...is he the danger you mentioned?"

"He is dangerous, but not to you. I advise you to speak to him. Good evening."

"Wait— perhaps you should speak with this man yourself?"

Fomalhaut had assumed a posture of flight, but now he relaxed again. "No," he said thoughtfully. "this man and I will speak when the time is right, and soon enough. I have no desire to hasten our meeting. Thank you for your help, Father, and good night."

This time the glittering figure lanced up toward the clouds, a departure many times faster and more graceful than Ben's faltering flight.

Costanzo lowered his gaze, regarding the doors of the church. Apparently he had yet one more mysterious visitor to deal with tonight. Very well; let it be done.

He climbed the stairs, gripped the cold iron of the door handle. He paused, swallowed. For some reason he was more daunted now than he had been by Fomalhaut. Perhaps the—not fear—the apprehension he had heard in Fomalhaut's voice had something to do with it.

The door opened to a pull—he'd really have to replace that rather useless lock. No one was in the vestibule. He swung open the inner door, stood studying the figure that loomed at the communion rail, turned away from him in the dim candlelight, looking up at the altar and the Crucifix.

For a moment he might have thought it was Ben himself, returned to the church, but only for a moment. This man was taller and broader, altogether more powerfully built. His hair was longer and shaggy, sharing the same greyish color as Ben's, as nearly as Costanzo could tell in the candlelight.

Well—at least he was human. With a sigh of relief, Costanzo started down the aisle, preparing to greet his visitor.

Before he could speak, the man turned, a slow, deliberate movement that reminded Costanzo of a weapon being aimed. He could not clearly see his face at this distance, but he did feel the force of the gaze that was leveled at him. Costanzo halted again.

"You are Father Costanzo?" The voice was low, quiet, controlled.

"I am."

"I am Leonard Ronar, a cousin of Ben Raintree's. I heard he's in trouble, and I've come a long way to help him. Please tell me where he is."

Costanzo studied his visitor more closely. The priest was a man of average size, but in the last few days he'd been made to feel like a runt, never more so than now. The man before him wore a heavy green jacket, battered cargo pants, and massive hiking boots. A curious optical device of some kind hung around his neck.

More disturbing was the automatic rifle slung over his shoulder. Bulges beneath his jacket suggested the presence of other weapons.

Defiance and indignation kindled in Costanzo. "I don't appreciate your bringing weapons into the house of God. Illegal weapons, at that."

The great shaggy head gave an annoyed jerk, then settled down.

"I'm sorry to offend you. I'm not in the habit of going about armed in this fashion. But those who threaten my cousin will observe no such niceties, and therefore neither must I. If you'll tell me what I need to know, I'll be on my way."

"You say you're his cousin."

"That's right. His mother is my mother's sister. "

"What are you planning to do if you find him?"

"I understand he's being hunted by the American government. That's serious business. When I find him, I will see to it that he reaches a place of safety."

"Where do you have in mind?"

Ronar was silent for a few moments.

"I can guide him to a highly secure place, if his friends in the Vigil can't provide him with a suitable refuge."

Costanzo stood chewing his lip indecisively. This man was secretive, haughty, and yes, dangerous. And yet, Fomalhaut had advised him to speak to him. Oddly enough, Costanzo found it easier to warm up to Fomalhaut, with his unseen head encased in a reflective sphere, than to this man who stood before him giving off scents of sweat and leather.

The priest glanced about the church as he considered his response. He was distracted by the bulk of a large backpack resting against the front pew. Strapped to it was a glittering cruciform object. Costanzo was about to decide it was a heavy, ornate crucifix, but then he noticed the great length of the section below the crosspiece, which was encased in a scabbard.

His jaw dropped open again. "Is that—a sword?"

"Yes," said Ronar, easing over to the pack. His hand flicked out; an instant later the blade shone bare in the candlelight, trembling in Ronar's hand. "It is not my usual sword. That weapon may not be brought into this world. But this is a fine weapon nevertheless, with a steel blade less massive than what I'm used to, and quicker."

He plunged the weapon back into its sheath, a move that startled Costanzo as completely as had its drawing.

"It's a strange thing, priest. When I first took up the sword, I abhorred its savagery, the hacking, the gutting, the flying limbs. I still do. But now even more I abhor the attacker with a gun. At least the sword puts you in the face of the one you would kill. It forces you to look him in the eye. It doesn't allow you to lurk at a distance and twitch your finger against a lever."

Ronar's gaze dropped away to some inner, private realm for a long moment. To Costanzo he suddenly appeared sad and tired.

In the end, Costanzo described the monastery and its location. Ronar nodded his head slowly.

"Fomalhaut and the Vigil are seeking Ben as well, you know," said Costanzo.

"We'll see who finds him first," said Ronar flatly. He gathered his possessions, then turned once more to regard the Crucifix which hung above the altar.

He paused.

"I don't know this god," he muttered.

"What?" said Costanzo.

Ronar gestured at the cross. "This Jesus. Where I come from, he keeps a low profile, for a god. Even though he has worshippers in the town I live in."

This remark was enough to convince Costanzo that Ronar was indeed related to Raintree. He gave an awkward chuckle. "You make it sound as though there are other gods, who you know better."

"There are." The same flat tone. "Quite a few. I respect this Jesus for having the dignity to remain inconspicuous. I may make an effort to get to know him."

"I would advise it," said Costanzo in wonder.

Ronar broke off from his reverie and strode down the aisle with immense strides. Costanzo never got a clear look at his face throughout their conversation, but he did catch a glimpse of his profile, an image he never forgot.

"Goodbye, priest," said Ronar as he clumped out of the church and into the night.

Father Costanzo stared after him for a long time, quite convinced that he had no real idea of who he had just encountered. Normally, he would have categorized such an unkempt, heavily-armed man as some sort of crazed backwoods survivalist. This man, though...

He remained unsettled for some time. In fact, the more he considered them, the more he was disconcerted by the week's encounters. He found himself comparing the people of his parish with Raintree, the innocent; with the otherworldly Fomalhaut, who had something of the presence, the gravity, of an angel; and with Leonard Ronar, an ordinary man, yet one with a personal force that set him apart from the general run of humanity. He had never suspected that his species contained so wide a range of specimens.

He considered the wretched Ed Hazilla and his family: the wife whose personality and very voice were crushed by the weight of her overbearing husband; the eldest daughter, twisted with loathing of herself and her parents; the younger children, cozened or bullied into acts which Costanzo suspected their father had confessed to him out of a demented need to brag about them, more than from any sense of penitence. That family was easily the most pathological in his parish, true, but misery, degradation, and plain simple meanness were scattered liberally throughout the rest.

His parish also contained some fine, righteous, outstanding people. He must keep that in mind as well.

By now Costanzo had lost track of whatever point there had been to this reverie. Yes, his congregation was composed of sinners. To dwell on that as though it were a revelation was pointless. It was simply the contrast between them and Leonard Ronar, who was plainly prepared to face down any and all enemies who might endanger his cousin, that left his head in a whirl.

He had come to the church with a need to pray. That had not abated. He knelt at the railing, bowed his head, and asked forgiveness for the sins of his flock, and not least his own. He found himself thinking of the Stone of Inner Light, and prayed that someday its light might shine on all men, and that they might endure it.

Chapter 26

A Rescue

It was a terrible, desperate thing, this tearing blindly through the forest, stumbling over rugged slopes, driven on by the rumble of distant machines, remote cries, and lights rising and falling beyond the trees. His eyes stung from the pine branches that had whipped across them; his shins ached from the stumps and boulders he had run into and tripped over. His breath hissed raw from his throat. It was all he could do to not collapse and weep in the dirt.

Raintree had not handled his flight with skill. Longing for a release from fear, impatient with skulking and waiting, he had attempted too much on the last leg of his journey to the monastery. He had flown on into the night, and he had flown too far, beyond the modest capacity of his flight harness's battery, until finally he was forced down in a range of wild hills.

Even while still aloft in the darkness he'd been half-convinced he was being followed. Strange hissing sounds had accompanied him, their source shifting from one place to another, sounds that caused the hairs to raise up on his neck. And there were shadows, wedge-shaped blurs which sometimes loomed up against a cloud or blotted out a drift of stars.

And so he had landed, not knowing whether it was worse to soar among the hissing shadows or to claw away from pursuers on the ground. At least by landing in this remote range he was making them work for his capture.

The ground grew rockier and more irregular as he climbed. The only way he could tell was that he tripped more often. The ragged patches of silver-grey sky beyond the trees were growing larger and merging together. Suddenly he burst free of the forest, onto the rocky crest of this nameless range. The rocks were a jumble of black shadow and dim silver in the starlight. A cold wind hissed among them.

Raintree stood there breathing hard, looking around, trying to guess what his best course would be from here. Lights moved in the valley below, converging on these hills. Other lights moved through the sky as well, casting fingers of light which dragged through the treetops.

"Ben."

Raintree shrieked and jumped a foot into the air. Whirling, he confronted a dark shape which he had taken to be only a tall, upright rock. He was grateful he'd emptied his bladder before leaving the woods, otherwise he might have had to proceed in wet pants.

"Come on," resumed the low voice. "We can't stay on this ridge. We need some cover."

A powerful hand clamped onto Raintree's arm, half-dragging him back down toward the trees. When Ben tripped, that hand did not allow him to so much as sag, let alone fall. Ben felt that he could probably just lift his legs and be carried along if he chose.

They entered the forest. His abductor pushed him into a crouch, then settled beside him. Raintree was aware of him mainly as a collection of earthy scents and a dark, massive presence.

"We'll wait here until you've rested a bit. Then we'll head down through a ravine I found. Those soldiers will never even see us," he muttered.

Raintree squatted there gaping at the man's black silhouette,

"Who—who are you?" he whispered at last.

He sensed the man stiffen and heard the creak of leather boots. A moment of rustling, and a match blazed up to dazzle him. Raintree squinted. If the light was meant to reveal the man's identity, it was a failure. All it did was illuminate a great, harsh face with narrow grey eyes that glittered in the shifting light of the match. Grey hair hung down over his forehead.

The man flicked out the match, leaving the image of his face imprinted in Raintree's memory.

"It's your cousin Leonard, Ben," he said with a hint of uncertainty. "Leonard Ronar."

This meant nothing to Raintree. His cousin? Had he been told of such a person? Not that he recalled. In a hushed voice he admitted as much, going on to sketch the events that had led him to this state.

Ronar sat in silence for a few moments after Ben's tale was complete.

"I see," said Ronar at last, though Raintree was unsure just what it was he saw. "All right then. In any event, we must get off this ridge undetected, and into that monastery."

"How did you find me?"

"That was fairly easy. I simply asked myself what route I would take if trying to reach this monastery overland while evading pursuit. Thus, I waited for you here. I knew you would remember some of the woodcraft I taught you as a boy."

Raintree felt dizzy, fighting off a mad urge to laugh, to blurt out that it was only his blundering that had led him here, that it was wholly accidental that Ronar had actually encountered him here. But why disillusion his newfound cousin?

"I—Leonard—I don't think we're safe here. They have sensors than can pick up body heat, even through these trees. They even followed me though the air, I think...in nearly silent aircraft of some kind."

"They don't have any of those Possum Perturbare propulsion beam things, do they?" muttered Ronar unhappily.

"No, I don't think so." Raintree thought it noteworthy that Ronar was apparently put out by the idea of infrared sensors in the hands of the military, yet he was evidently familiar with Perturbare and his gadgets.

"All right then, we'd better be going."

The two of them moved along the ridge, staying in the woods just below the summit. Ronar kept them on the side of the ridge away from the closest concentrations of converging troops. Even so, the clatter and rumble of their approach grew steadily louder, even over the unsteady hiss of Raintree's breath and his awkward, faltering footsteps. Ronar, he could not fail to notice, moved through the night with barely a sound.

A helicopter passed overhead, shaking the branches and blowing up clouds of pine needles. Its searchlight missed them, but even its indirect light was enough to reveal Ronar's scowling face, his eyes flickering dangerously as he glanced around. Raintree caught his breath, wondering about this unexpected savior of his.

"They're like bloodhounds," growled Ronar. "I was a fool, supposing that military capabilities would remain stagnant while I wasn't paying attention."

He shrugged off his enormous pack, pulled a wooden spar of some kind from its straps, caught one end of it between his boots and bent the other.

"What are you doing?" whispered Raintree.

"If I'm lucky, I can pick off a few of them before they even know they're under attack."

Raintree stared, not certain he had heard that correctly.

"Is that a bow?"

Ronar darted him a quick look of irritation. "Yes."

Ronar finished stringing the bow and hauled a quiver of arrows out of his pack. Now Raintree heard booted feet approaching from several directions.

"You mean you're going to attack these soldiers with a bow and arrows?"

"Yes!" hissed Ronar. "Until they realize what's going on, anyway. Then I'll take off in another direction and use the guns. I may create enough confusion to let you slip away. You wait here...hide until I come back for you. If I don't return within twenty minutes, wait for your chance and head out on your own." Ronar grabbed his weapons, about to move off into the darkness.

"No," said Raintree, a quiet word forced out by the growing turmoil within him.

"What?" asked Ronar incredulously.

"No, this is wrong," he said, more loudly, his feelings beginning to crystalize at last. "I'm not going to let you kill these men, or get killed yourself, just to keep me from being taken captive. It's not worth it."

"But they have no right to hunt you like an animal!"

"No—but killing them over it is an overreaction. They aren't going to kill me. They think I have all sorts of valuable information about the Vigil." He gave a strained laugh. "But I barely know my own name. They'll discover this, and eventually release me. There's really nothing interesting about me. You'll see."

Raintree felt a curious exultation and an incongruous sense of peace. At last he had managed to throw off his fear and confusion, at least for a moment.

More helicopters entered the area. Their lights cast a diffuse yellow-green glow though the foliage. Ronar stood uncertainly, glancing between Raintree and the woods, where the troops were now just out of sight.

A hard voice spoke from the trees. "You there! Drop your weapons! This is your only warning!"

At once the look of uncertainty fell from Ronar's face, replaced by defiance and resolve. His grip on his bow tightened.

Before he could move, a shot burned in from somewhere, striking Ronar with an audible *splat*. He spun and fell, weapons flying. He fell near his pack, reached up and gripped the hilt of a great sword, of all things, drawing its blade into the uncertain light.

"Ah, how I detest guns," he said in a hoarse, rattling voice. "Come and get me then, you cowards."

Raintree watched as a dozen armed men emerged from the trees. Most of them wore bizarre goggles. All wore helmets and body armor.

"Which one of you is Dr. Raintree?" demanded the foremost of them.

"I am," said Raintree.

The officer assumed a look of relief to discover that his quarry was the man still standing. "Who is this other man?"

"My cousin, Leonard Ronar."

Now the squad of soldiers surrounded them, weapons aimed mostly at Ronar, even though he lay supine, his breath coming in bubbling gasps.

"Mr. Ronar, drop your weapon," said the officer.

Ronar glared up at his tormentors. "That's Professor Ronar to you, boy," he whispered.

"Please, Ronar—Leonard—drop it," said Raintree.

Ronar's fingers loosened and the sword dropped to the ground. Whether Ronar had released it at Ben's bidding, or had simply lost the strength to hold it aloft, Raintree never knew.

A man dropped to his knees beside Ronar and pulled back his clothing. "Sucking chest wound here, sir. He needs immediate treatment or he'll drown in his own blood. Better get a chopper down as fast and close as possible."

Raintree stared as Ronar lay there, quite possibly dying. He knew very well that if his cousin had not hesitated at his words, he would now be somewhere out in the darkness, killing these men rather than lying at their mercy.

The officer went off a short distance to confer with his superiors over a radio.

"So this is the Vigil," snorted one of the men. "A guy with a rifle, a bow, and a freaking sword who doesn't even get off one shot. And another guy who just stands here like a sheep and stares at us with big moony eyes."

"I don't like the way he's looking at us," said another.

Others joined in. "I don't see his cold-gun thing anywhere."

"Maybe he doesn't need it anymore."

"I wonder why we didn't take them out a long time ago," finished the man who had spoken first.

"Quiet, you men," said the officer, returning to the group. "Word from command is that we can expect more of the Vigil to arrive soon. Serious members this time. My orders are that we're not to give up these prisoners—under any circumstances. So look sharp, and expect company from above. Go for head shots when possible. We've got help coming too—lots of it. Secure Raintree, and take that wounded man under cover."

Raintree knew with a sudden, crystalline certainty that he must now decide whether to live or die. He chose to live, knowing he would probably, as a consequence, die very shortly afterwards.

"Take your hands off that man!" His voice rang among the trees, commanding in tone, startling everyone present. The soldiers who were preparing to drag Ronar away halted in uncertainty.

Raintree raised his hands in an involuntary yet nevertheless dramatic gesture. The soldiers flinched as if convinced that lightning would flash from his fingertips.

"Lower your—drop your hands, Dr. Raintree," said the officer in a wavering voice.

But Raintree spun around instead, causing all who faced him to fall back a pace or two. "I will not! You men, you assassins and kidnappers, turn around and tell your superiors that the Vigil will not be treated so."

"Look at his eyes—they're glowing!" muttered one of the men.

If they were, Raintree knew, it was only with fervor and desperation, not with some strange power that might lash out in his defense.

The officer brought his weapon to bear on Raintree. A number of his followers did the same.

"You men—*freeze!*" thundered Raintree.

That ardent word "freeze" coming from Ben Raintree was more than some of those soldiers could withstand. They dropped their weapons and stood quaking as though they were actually frozen in their tracks. Even their officer seemed to share in this hysteria, if such it was, though he also looked around as if suspecting some kind of outside influence.

It was he who finally found the will to raise his weapon and level it once more at Raintree. His aim never steadied. The weapon aimed itself skyward, obviously against the urging of the officer's hands, and then broke his grip entirely, floating upward. The soldier looked up, gaping. Raintree followed his gaze. There shone a tiny constellation of orange stars marking Fomalhaut in his descent.

Raintree surprised himself with his reaction to this imminent rescue. He hurled a thought skyward: *Not now!* and trusted Fomalhaut to receive it. Indeed, the little cluster of lights dwindled a little before steadying.

The officer's weapon clattered to earth, along with all those others which had been levitated without Raintree's notice.

Raintree stood over Ronar and swept his gaze over the soldiers. They could not meet his eyes.

"Fall back," said the officer, shakily. His men complied with a stumbling alacrity.

Now, thought Raintree.

A moment later three figures alighted beside them. One was Fomalhaut. The second was an armored giant wearing a really first-rate flying harness: Stingray, no doubt. He lowered a child-sized figure to the ground: Lori Wu, of all people, wearing a gleaming battle suit of some kind.

"Fomalhaut—this is Leonard Ronar, my cousin. He's been shot and needs immediate help."

Fomalhaut knelt beside Ronar, whose breathing was shallow, wet, and rough.

"With an army waiting to climb this ridge and a swarm of bombers on its way, we'd better be out of here soon," said Stingray.

"This man would not survive being moved. Silence now, all of you," said Fomalhaut.

After a few frozen moments there came a moist sucking sound. Raintree watched as a bullet emerged from Ronar's wound and dropped onto the rocks beside him.

"I can hold the severed arteries closed and prevent further bleeding," said Fomalhaut in a distant voice. "But I cannot also remove the blood that already obstructs his lung. Indeed, I can do little else as long as I must maintain this concentration. You others must fend off the assault that is imminent, or else we must leave."

"We will not leave," said Raintree.

"you"

The word was faint but clear. It came from Ronar, and Raintree stared down at him, amazed, as though a dead man had spoken.

Ronar appeared to be speaking to Fomalhaut. "you. tell me what has happened to my cousin."

Fomalhaut was silent for several moments.

"Has he not told you?" he answered with a peculiar glassy note to his voice.

"do not lie to me. this boy is not my cousin. he resembles Ben. he is a good man. but he is not my cousin."

A fire kindled within Raintree at these words. He had no idea what Ronar was talking about, yet something within him was quick to recognize the truth of it.

"Peace. We must speak of this later," said Fomalhaut, addressing both Ronar and Ben. "Ben, I fear for your—I fear for this man."

Raintree studied Fomalhaut for a few moments, and then the others. Stingray stood in silence, studying him in return with a keen gaze. Lori looked at him in awe. He sensed something about her, something familiar to him and foreign to her.

"Lori, you're carrying the Stones."

She nodded.

"Give them to me."

Lori glanced wide-eyed at Fomalhaut, who made no objection, or any other response. She stepped forward, solemnly opening the pouches on her suit that contained the gems, exposing their mingled lights. Fomalhaut seemed to flinch, then steadied. Stingray squinted and stuck out his jaw. Lori's hands trembled as she offered the jewelry to Ben. Her expression made plain her relief and gratitude at surrendering them.

He snatched them up, lacking the time to contemplate the moment in all its gravity. He clutched the circlet and the pendant and the brooch in one hand, almost forgotten, as he slipped the vivid green ring onto his finger. It blazed up, sending his heart pounding, his nerves tingling. He focused its green radiance into a beam which he played over Ronar. Immediately his mysterious cousin's breathing steadied and deepened.

And Ronar's eyes opened, glittering in the collected light of the gems in Raintree's hands. His hand reached out, weak but inexorable, bypassing the circlet and pendant, to clutch the brooch, and the great violet stone that slumbered within it.

And that Stone ignited with a purple fire, encompassing them all. The Stone of Adamance, which previously had been the least conspicuous of the four, now taught Raintree, and presumably the others, the full meaning of the word Adamance, so that they would never forget.

"My God," whispered Raintree. "Leonard—do you wish to keep this Stone?"

"No. What I do here is for your benefit, for all of you, not for me. I do not need this Stone. You take it."

Raintree took that Stone and fastened it at his throat. Now he wore two of the Stones, and only the nature and power of Adamance gave him the strength to stay on his feet. Then he slipped the circlet, with its Stone of Truth, over his brow, where it burned most coldly. All at once he knew well enough the truth and meaning of Fomalhaut's words to Ronar. He felt a moment of intense sadness, to know he was not the person he had been led to believe. But Fomalhaut was right; this was not the moment for such thoughts. He drew a fine chain around his neck, letting the white teardrop of the Stone of Inner Light, the one closest to his heart, fall against his breast.

Lori cried out in some distress, but Ben did not turn to see why. He clutched at the air, burning inside and reeling. Something was missing, and he did not know what it was.

Fomalhaut spoke. "Cal-Cotavion carried a staff. It was a focus and vessel for the personal power that came to him from wearing the Stones."

Now Ronar: "You there, you great looming oaf. Take my sword and cut a staff for this man."

Stingray eyed Ronar with a cocked eyebrow, snorted, but set to work. As the blade whacked a sapling into shape, Ronar muttered "Cal-Cotavion…" in a tone of wonder. "To think that he was alive, here on Earth, until so recently."

Stingray offered Raintree the staff. "Here."

Raintree took it. At once his hand vibrated, the staff shook, and the turmoil that had threatened to tear him apart drained into the staff, still ready to his need, but easier to endure.

"I can hardly bear to look at him," said Lori.

"Cotavion's cloak served its purpose also," said Fomalhaut.

Raintree turned towards the others, the star of Truth shining on his brow. He did not use it to discover their secrets, but he could not wear that Stone at all without seeing much of what made them who they were.

He saw Fomalhaut, a creature at home in immense silent spaces, bound to the troubles of this small and crowded world only by a sense of duty. He saw whole dimensions to Fomalhaut's mind which human minds did not possess, and a sadness, a fear that he would never know a true home again, and more, that he was failing in the task he had undertaken on Earth.

He saw Stingray, a being tormented not only by some of his own past deeds, but by the very nature of life, by life's relationship to itself and his own place within that scheme. Raintree found himself glad to have the chance to know him.

He saw Lori Wu, a woman still uncertain of her role as the wearer of a device whose potential she did not understand. Yet she was proud to wear it, and proud to stand as a member of the Vigil. And…she had once found

Raintree to be sweet and kind and gentle. But at a deep level which even she was unaware of, she had rejected him for also being weak, and confused, and ineffectual.

Now she rejected him for being fearsome, awesome, and daunting. Raintree nearly laughed out loud. Sometimes you just couldn't win.

And then he beheld Leonard Ronar. Ronar, who lay there regarding him with narrowed yet steady eyes that did not flinch from the light of any Stone. And Raintree found himself smiling, proud to share what kinship he had with this man.

"Hello! Hello! White flag here!"

Raintree turned in surprise at this call. A soldier came crashing through the woods, a compact black man, weapon slung at his side, his hands in the air.

Stingray frowned in his direction. "What do you want?"

"Sir...I'd like to join you, if you have any use for me."

"What? Why don't you just turn around and—"

"Welcome," said Fomalhaut in that strained, distracted voice.

Stingray did a double take on Fomalhaut, then turned his attention back to the soldier, giving him a more measured scrutiny. "Who are you, and why do you want to join us?"

"My name is Master Sergeant Leland Baines, sir. As for why I want to join you...well." He waved a hand in Raintree's direction, but his gaze did not turn that way. "I know the power of the Lord when I see it, sir. And I don't care what my orders are, I don't want to be on the wrong side of that fight."

Stingray's eyebrows shot up at this. He looked as if he were about to dispute Baines's characterization of the

Stones, but bit off the words, squinted toward Raintree, and shrugged. "All right, Sergeant. Can you give us an idea of what to expect from your buddies out there? We wouldn't wait around to find out, but we have a critically injured man here and can't leave just yet."

"We were ordered to keep our distance for now. A flight of stealth bombers is coming in to bust this ridge into a pile of rubble. They didn't tell me, but based on how far away we're supposed to stay, I'd say they're planning to hit you with fuel-air weapons. So...if you aren't able to leave, I hope you've got what it takes to fend off those planes."

Stingray nodded and turned to the tiny figure beside him. "I think we do. You there, Shorty. Lori. Let me help you make better use of that suit you're wearing. I watched how the previous owner handled it throughout a substantial fraction of the Milky Way. It's time you learned how to build, not just destroy. Ben..."

"Take good care of Ronar. I'll go disperse the army."

Raintree turned and marched off down the slope. Some remnant of the old Raintree was stunned by this casual announcement of his intention to rid them of the threat of thousands of armed men. The rest of him had no doubt that it could be done.

The trees thinned, giving way to a rocky spur that protruded from the side of the ridge, affording a long view into the valley beyond. The valley was alive with troops, great columns of them converging on their position, with lines of men following tanks that smashed wide paths through the forest. Where their paths intersected the entire forest was flattened. Mobile missile launchers and a variety of armored vehicles moved along with the foot soldiers. Attack helicopters chattered above and before them, stabbing about with their lights. This invading army must have left a trail of destruction five miles wide all the way from here to the American border.

Their advance halted. Men and machines waited to learn the result of the Air Force's imminent attempt to smash the Vigil.

Ben decided to get their attention.

He looked at the crudely-hewn staff in his hand. Pitch oozed from the hacked-off stumps of branches. He wondered, was he stuck with this staff, or could he get another that was a little more attractive?

A vision suddenly came into his mind. He was looking over a ridge of snow at two distant figures in combat: Aureus, the glittering golden robot, and a grey and silver figure who carried the Stones—it must be Cal-Cotavion himself. Cotavion also carried a staff, and when he struck the ice it shook and shattered. Ben saw this and remembered vividly the awe, fear and despair he'd felt upon witnessing this violence.

And yet—if he were not truly Ben Raintree—how could he have this memory?

He shook his head, his eyes focusing again on the army below him. This was not the time.

He took the staff in both hands, raising it above his head. At once he felt it throb and quiver with a barely controlled power. With a cry of mixed astonishment and fear he brought the end of the staff down on the rock before his feet.

An awesome thundercrack rent the air. A shockwave sprang out of the rock around him, roaring and rumbling outward, a wave of rock and earth, crashing and shattering. The end of the spur on which he stood gave way and tumbled down in a mass of boulders and dust. The shockwave reached the troops, where it rocked tanks and flung soldiers off their feet. The very wind of it was enough to send the helicopters fluttering wildly.

Ben grasped the Stone of Inner Light, holding it before him. "Burn," he said to it. And so it burned. Its clear light surged in a flare so mighty it lit the entire valley and every man within it.

To Ben, standing at the center of this outpouring of radiance, with the rays of the great cold gem streaming out from between his fingers, it was like a chill wind blowing through him, sweeping away the dust of whatever doubts and guilt he carried, illuminating him from within. The Stone felt light in his hand. Its glare did not trouble his eyes or his heart.

He could not be sure what effect it was having on the men below, but he doubted they were finding it quite as exhilarating.

The army erupted into tumult. Men cried out, groups of them surging here and there. Men screamed and wept. Some fled, some fought, some threw down their weapons and headed in his direction.

Some fired their weapons. Missiles and shells shrieked through the air. They struck all around Raintree, throwing up a storm of rock, flame, and steel. The thunder of the weapons was continuous.

Raintree found that he could stand up beneath that attack. Though shells and missiles exploded practically in his face, somehow they could not touch him. All four Stones were now ablaze with their individual Lights. Cal-Cotavion, so equipped, had fended off the attack of Aureus for several minutes. Surely he, Raintree, could then endure these relatively feeble weapons.

Then a colossal roar and glare from behind made Raintree turn around. A fusillade of vast explosions was ripping up the night and sending sheets and globes of flame across the sky. Blast waves swept by at intervals of seconds, originating from huge bombs used as profligately as fireworks on the Fourth of July.

But the blasts and flames did not reach the ground. A structure protected it, a shining temple of some sort, domed and vaulted, built on a gigantic scale. It had not been there a few minutes before.

"Behold the Vigil," said Raintree. Again he struck the ground with his staff, and again the ground rolled, and split open, stilling the weapons whose crude physicality meant so little in the mingled light of these four Stones.

The invading army was broken. Most of it turned and fled.

Raintree sank to his knees.

I know the power of the Lord when I see it.

These words rang in Raintree's mind. He did not know the ultimate origin of these Stones, but what they represented could hardly be doubted. By their very existence, they proved the objective reality of ideas such as Truth and Goodness, concepts apart from and irrelevant to the physical reality that many thought sufficient to inform and define the Universe. Ben now knew, by virtue of these Stones, that there was more to existence, more to life, than that. Something out there cared for its children, offering them meaning and hope.

Raintree knelt there and fervently thanked that thing, that God, for offering these Lights to men, and for finding him worthy of carrying them.

Chapter 27

Words from Ronar

Leonard Ronar recovered from his wounds with remarkable speed.

It was more than the quick surgery he received at a Canadian hospital. It was more even than the healing effect of the green rays which Raintree shed upon him so liberally. The man had a strong, almost inhuman, vitality which Fomalhaut found most odd. He carried a feeling of otherworldliness about him, a feeling of foreign spaces.

It was also noteworthy that while Ronar was past seventy years old, he looked no older than forty five.

He was, furthermore, a man most rigorous and uncompromising, thus explaining Fomalhaut's intense discomfort as he revealed the full truth of what had happened to Ben Raintree. Listening closely were Ben himself (or his successor at any rate), Ronar, and Stingray and Lori as well.

They stood in the twilight of a hot day in the Sonoran desert of northern Mexico, a few miles from the Arizona border. This was where Ronar had asked to be brought, to this dusty spot of no particular distinction, far from any habitation. Fomalhaut would have enjoyed its serenity if not for the strain of standing beneath the scrutiny of the astronomer and his younger cousin.

Ronar's chest was still wrapped in bandages, but he gave no appearance of weakness. Raintree wore normal street clothes. His staff leaned against a saguaro, but the

Stones were not in evidence. Fomalhaut could still feel their presence, concealed in the pockets of Raintree's soft grey jacket. Unlike Cal-Cotavion, Raintree felt no need to wear the Stones at all times, to the comfort and relief of those around him. This was true even though Raintree carried the gems more easily than Cotavion ever had. Not that Raintree was the stronger man; far from it.

He was simply the purer man, the more innocent man, not surprisingly.

"...and so Possum Perturbare returned alone from this other universe, chastened and grieved that Raintree had chosen to remain behind, to take up his strange new role. Perturbare acted much as if Ben had died, for in truth the separation was just as final, just as irrevocable, as death.

"I brightened his spirits somewhat with a possibility he had not considered. As I said, before Ben crossed over to that other universe I had misgivings, a foresight that he would not return. I also had an inkling of what I would do if that proved to be the case. In those final minutes before his departure, even as I tried to convince him not to go, I used the instruments of my exploration suit to make as complete a record of the state of Raintree's being, in particular the state and arrangement of his brain, as possible. In addition, I looked into his mind to the extent that I could. With no preparation and little time, I was able only to retain a few snatches, a few vivid images and memories, from his thoughts. And of course, we had samples of his genetic information.

"Thus, when Ben did not return, T'Ukudu, Perturbare, and I used T'Utahnti biotechnology to grow a new Ben Raintree, in much the same manner that T'Ukudu himself had been grown. It was not a cloning operation, but rather the construction, cell by cell, of a fully adult individual, into which I implanted the information and fragments of memory I had collected. That was far from enough to recreate Ben as he had been, but it was at least something. We knew that for the most part you would have to grow and develop into your own person, without the influences that made the original Ben the man he was. Or is. Indeed, I foresaw that you might well grow into the role you have now taken on, as the carrier of the Stones. You are uniquely suited to that task. You, alone of all men, carry no such taint or guilt as makes the stewardship of the Stones such a burden for others. Their fires cannot burn you, for you are clean."

Fomalhaut halted, his story complete. His head sagged a little, but that could not be seen through his helmet.

It was Ronar who spoke first. "You say you knew Ben would not return. Why then didn't you stop him from going?"

"That was not my place. Ben Raintree was free and entitled to do as he pleased, regardless of my personal feelings, regardless even of the good of the Vigil or the world at large."

Ronar nodded.

Ben said, "Tell me again why I—why he—decided to remain behind."

"Ben—was a wounded man. An idealistic and gentle person, he had been driven by his involvement with the Vigil to actions which injured and haunted him. In that other universe he found a role infinitely more to his liking, a role in which he could always act with benevolence and generosity, and know a life of peace. I have no doubt that he is very happy now, and for that I feel joy. In fact I have no doubt that he is the happiest and most blessed person know. His new world benefits from his presence as well."

Ben turned to Ronar. "I'll continue to use your cousin's name, if you don't mind. I have no other."

Ronar shrugged. "You might as well. There's no one else to claim it. Now I have a few words for you about those Stones in your pockets."

This surprised Fomalhaut and piqued his interest. Ronar's eyes glinted with a peculiar light. "Yours are not the only Stones in the universe. You know I came here from a place a great distance away. I have not said just what place that is, nor shall I. In that place exists a second set of Stones, the opposite of this one. Those Stones are called Death, Despair, Illusion, and Inner Darkness."

Now Ronar assumed a strange, small half smile. Fomalhaut sensed an amusement which seemed entirely misplaced.

"These gems are in the possession of the ruling queen of the Elf Country of the place where I live. She is said to be beautiful, yet, as you might expect, also terrible. I haven't met her myself. I've known too many women who were beautiful and terrible to want to bother with her. Cal-Cotavion was her cousin and knew her well. I never met him either, but I have heard the tale of how they sought and found the Stones. I thought you might like to know all this. I find it remarkable to encounter these Stones here on Earth, especially coming here via the route that they did."

Fomalhaut would have blinked if he'd had any eyelids. Ronar's story sounded utterly fanciful and absurd, yet he knew, without even touching Ronar's mind (which in truth he was unwilling to do) that it was nothing less than the truth.

Raintree merely nodded gravely, studying Ronar with no particular surprise.

"And now," said Ronar, "I'll be heading home." He hefted his pack, which still carried the sword and the bow, but lacked the firearms. An advanced electro-optical viewer hung around his neck, looking very much like one of Perturbare's devices.

"A moment, please, Dr. Ronar," said Fomalhaut.

Ronar paused, swinging his gaze in Fomalhaut's direction.

"If you would care to stay, you would find a place in the Vigil as we go about our chosen task."

"The task of taking over the world? No. It may be that this world could stand to be taken over, but that has nothing to do with me. I am neither a leader nor a follower. I go my own way. This world is no longer my home. The gods know my little visit here accomplished little enough, except to nearly get myself killed. So, goodbye. I return to my work."

"The work of cosmology?"

"Yes." Ronar paused, waiting for Fomalhaut to continue.

"I was aware of you and your theories from the moment you appeared on this world. How confident are you of your conclusion that this universe is open?"

"Totally confident. It lacks enough mass to ever halt its expansion. I'm beginning to suspect the expansion may even be accelerating. I have decades of observations and data to back this up. You are welcome to review them if you wish. Your analytical capacity no doubt exceeds my own."

"Thank you, Dr. Ronar, that won't be necessary."

It was no more than Fomalhaut had expected. The very act of asking for a verbal confirmation of what he already knew was but a sign of his hopeless desire to somehow deny the truth.

Fomalhaut was not home, and whether anything resembling his home would ever arise here was very much open to question.

Chapter 28

A Spire Rises

Fomalhaut stood with his fellow members of the Vigil on the steep strip of British Columbia coastline where their experimental station had once stood. The wreckage was nearby, still smoking in places, so fierce had been the inferno that consumed it.

Below it, towering grey seas smashed into the rocks. Above it, patches of cloud-filtered sunlight slid along the flanks of snow-clad peaks.

Stingray stood gazing thoughtfully, absently, into the waves. Raintree also had little to say. Staff in hand, the aura of the Stones around him, he observed the proceedings with calm green-grey eyes. He had taken to wearing a wardrobe of grey and white, but he still relied on the pockets of his jacket to conceal the Stones, and had not affected a hooded cloak.

Lori Wu showed greater activity. Wearing the Rralian engineering suit, she stood facing the wreckage, gesturing and shifting her weight, dancing and stepping, all while staring at things the others could not see.

After going through this performance a few times she halted, caught her breath for a moment, and stepped up to Fomalhaut.

"I think I'm getting this," she said. "But I want to practice a few more times. With all the attention we're getting I want this to go perfectly. Your plans are marvelous, but very complex."

"That's fine Lori. I believe we're expecting a few late arrivals anyway."

Lori returned to her dance.

Today the Vigil was not the mountainside's only occupant. A Canadian military contingent was also present, with no real function other than to demonstrate that this was still Canada, and that Canada's patience with American military incursions had ended. The two countries were not at war, but their relations were in a shambles, and it was not clear how they would ever be restored. The Prime Minister and other officials of the government were also present.

Also on hand were Sergeant Baines and a few other American soldiers who had come over to their side. There might have been more, thousands more, soldiers and people of all occupations and nationalities who had offered their services to the Vigil. But Fomalhaut had sent out word that such people should remain quietly at home until the Vigil was ready to receive their aid.

In addition, there were journalists and camera crews, recording and reporting everything. Fomalhaut intended to make sure the world knew well that the Vigil lived on and would endure.

Military helicopters had been shuttling in people all day. Now yet another landed on one of the few spaces level enough for their use. Two civilians emerged: a Catholic priest and a teenaged girl. They saw Raintree and approached him, their smiles concealing a certain amount of awe, even trepidation. Raintree was taller than they were, not only physically but in terms of psychic stature as well. They spoke for a few moments, then Raintree led them away behind some boulders. Presently, the Stone of Inner Light shone forth.

357

Fomalhaut's suit informed him that the American President was making another attempt to contact him. This time he accepted the contact.

"Fomalhaut? This is President Hohman speaking."

"Yes."

"I appreciate your taking my call. I would like to offer my congratulations for the superb spirit and ability you and your friends showed in surviving our attack against you. Obviously we wish it had been more successful, but I have to admire your persistence in overcoming it, and now starting over again. I hope we'll be able to get through any misunderstandings we've had in the past, and establish a useful relationship once again."

Fomalhaut was silent. He very deliberately said nothing, giving himself all the time he needed to regain his control and rationality.

"Fomalhaut? Are you still there?"

"I must say, I am stunned and nonplussed by the sheer magnitude of your disingenuousness."

Hohman went on as though he hadn't heard. "May I ask what your intentions are at the present time?"

"They will become apparent soon enough."

"May I at least have your assurance that you plan nothing which will threaten or compromise the sovereignty of the United States of America?"

Fomalhaut paused again.

"No. You may not."

"I'm sorry to hear that. I'm sure you realize, Fomalhaut, how the United States has served as a beacon of liberty throughout the world for more than two hundred years. We have occasionally faltered, but always we have resumed the proper course in the end. On this occasion…"

Fomalhaut listened to this babble with only a fraction of his mind. What would Hohman do next, urge him to take a stress pill and think things over? The President seemed unnaturally calm for someone in his position. He acted like a man who was assuring his neighbors that he would do a better job of mowing his lawn from now on. Fomalhaut sensed no real urgency in his rambling plea for reason and reconciliation. What was going on here?

Something was wrong. Fomalhaut had a sudden, almost stunning foresight of imminent, total disaster. He put all the sensors in his suit to work searching for anything unusual. In addition to that, he sent his farseeing mind ranging out, studying the newcomers in particular.

His sensors found a lead-lined cylinder in the ruins of the station. Lead was seldom used in such quantity in Vigil technology. The cylinder was also warmer than would be expected from an inert object.

He found something else as well.

Fomalhaut mirrored his exploration suit. He could only hope no one would notice this, or if they did, that they would not realize the significance of the action. His heart thudded in his chest. He had only seconds left to act.

"…convene a council consisting of—"

President Hohman.

A pause.

"Yes?"

I see your assassins have tricked the girl, Michelle, into wearing a watch with a bracelet composed of plastique explosive. A remote-controlled detonator is built into the mechanism. I also see they have managed to hide a fusion weapon in the rubble of our station. If you detonate the fusion bomb, I will not be killed. Everyone else here will die, including the Canadian Prime Minister, but I will survive. Should that occur, I will lay waste to all your facilities of government in Washington and beyond. I will destroy your military. Furthermore, I will find you and kill you. It would be a quick death, and I would greatly regret having to administer it, but in this situation, I would do it.

"And the watch?"

If you detonate that, the result for you will be the same. If you must oppose us, do so honestly and openly, and you and your forces will be treated with mercy and restraint. But if you should ever again offend us with treachery, there will be grief and wailing in the Hohman household, or in the household of whatever successor should order such actions against us. There is no virus, no weapon, that your people can devise to save you in that case.

"I'll keep that in mind. Enjoy your little barn-raising." Hohman ended the connection.

Fomalhaut de-mirrored his suit. He stood perfectly still for a good five minutes, purging himself of the rage that had welled up inside him, an emotion this one man was uniquely able to elicit. The glimpse of his mind that had been part of their telepathic contact only worsened Fomalhaut's anger. At least the telepathy had prevented Fomalhaut's threats from being made public.

When he was finally prepared, he stepped up to Lori, who looked at him expectantly and a little quizzically. She, he saw, had indeed noticed the mirroring.

"Lori, I have made a small alteration to the plans. Please permit me to transmit the revision."

"Okay."

It was done.

"Are you ready to begin, Lori?"

Lori Wu nodded, her eyes wide, her grin wider.

Fomalhaut turned away. His mellow voice, amplified by his suit, echoed from the mountainside.

"May I have your attention please."

Stingray turned from his contemplation of the sea. Raintree and his friends came back into view, the priest and the girl with eyes aglow. The soldiers, dignitaries, and journalists faced him and fell silent.

Fomalhaut weighed his words. Suddenly the remarks he had been planning to make seemed hollow and foolish. He was in no proper state of mind to make an inspiring speech,

He looked at the expectant faces before him. Stingray was challenging him to make his own return to the affairs of the world seem worthwhile. Raintree's gaze was not confrontational, but he had the look of an observer, not of someone eager to step forward and speak. Lori of course must not be distracted.

He looked at the priest and felt from him an optimistic joy.

"I would like to invite our guest, Father Michael Costanzo, to come forward and address you."

Costanzo started at the mention of his name, stood gaping for a moment at Fomalhaut's helmet, then gathered himself and stepped up beside him, turning to face the small crowd.

He lowered his head for a moment, then looked up and began to speak.

"A few moments ago, I looked full into the Stone of Inner Light.

"It was not entirely a comfortable experience, not at all. It was spiritually dangerous and exhilarating, in the same manner that rafting down a raging river is physically dangerous and exhilarating. And it similarly taught me things about myself, illuminated my weaknesses as well as my strengths, bolstering the latter and making the former seem a little less formidable. I recommend the experience to any of you. That Stone is a blessed thing, a holy thing. Through it, we see God's love for the world and his children.

"The man who carries the Stone, and three others which I'm sure are equally profound in their way, is my friend, Ben Raintree. I haven't known Ben long, but I trust him and respect his decency. No man could carry and use those Stones if he were dominated by darkness.

"I don't know the other members of the Vigil very well, but Ben Raintree chooses to walk among them. That means a great deal to me. I remember the days when the Vigil arose to counter the threat to human freedom posed by the Para-men. I remember their battles, and the losses they suffered. In the years since they maintained a peaceful place of beauty and learning, a place where even the light of the Stone was available to anyone who cared to come and see it.

"Naturally, many of us are a little nervous to have people of such power in our midst, no matter how benign they appear to be. They can make us all feel small. It may even be that the Vigil will someday act in ways that reasonable people may disagree with, or even choose to oppose. I for one have little fear of that. I do not fear them. To strike out against them, to seek to crush them without warning or reason, was like an animal lashing out against something it does not understand. Yet even so, the response of the Vigil has been most temperate."

Costanzo spread his hands.

"Here at this very site once stood another beautiful edifice of the Vigil. I was never privileged to see it intact, even though it was only a few hundred kilometers from my home. But today I hope to see it at last. I will be proud to think of it gleaming here on the shores of my native land. I thank the Vigil for their steadfastness, and I thank my government for welcoming them here. May the walls that rise here today become a fortress of light and hope for people of good will all across this planet. May peace and understanding flow between all the peoples of the world. And may God bless us all."

The priest returned to his place.

Not bad, thought Fomalhaut. Slightly rambling, but heartfelt and succinct. "Lori, the stage is yours," he said.

Lori Wu wasted no time. She arched her back, flung back her arms.

The ruins of the station trembled, rumbled, and rose a few feet into the air. There they dissolved into powder, hanging as ill-formed suspended columns which rippled like liquid.

Fomalhaut thought of the priest's words, of his trust in the future and in the Vigil. He could only hope that the Vigil's actual intentions would not strike the priest as a betrayal.

Lori made a series of quick slashing motions with her hands. The trembling blobs of unformed matter she controlled rose to various heights, began to flatten into sheets.

The flesh of chimpanzees will no longer be served at restaurants, thought Fomalhaut.

The sheets expanded into layered, hovering disks, decreasing in size with altitude, until finally they dwindled into nothing.

No one will profit from medical care, save those actually responsible for performing that care.

The disks developed vertical extrusions: mazes of walls and structural members, ducts and cables, all merging with the disks above and sinking deep into the rock below. Lori appeared tense with concentration, yet exalted, her hands fluttering like birds.

No more English lawns will be planted in deserts and sustained with fossil water.

A hemisphere of force shimmered into being, encasing the interior structure of the main dome. A film formed over it, at first translucent, but soon white and gleaming, hiding the complexity within. Lori shaped and smoothed it with her gestures.

Children will no longer be armed to slaughter members of other tribes.

The completed dome projected from the mountainside like the top half of the pearl of the gods.

The very idea of nations will be forgotten.

Lori brought her hands together in dramatic rising arcs. The earth rumbled and shook; slabs of stone tore up from a site beside the dome, melting and reforming as they rose.

The human race will fade away.

A great tapering spire rose up, its skeleton formed of carbon nanotubes and exotic composite materials, compounds and molecules which did not naturally exist in the earth.

I will not be present to witness the fruition of the changes I foresee.

The spire grew a sheathing of white marble mixed with veins of colorless quartz, a mineral melding that also did not exist in nature. A light was kindled at its summit, a poor imitation of the Stone of Inner Light, but a symbol of its light nevertheless.

Fomalhaut's fugue of foresight came to an end, derailed by his uneasiness at the last few insights.

Lori turned to the crowd, shaking and exhausted, but aglow with her accomplishment. Applause broke out from the onlookers.

"How do you feel, Lori?" asked Fomalhaut.

"I feel...as Zeus must have felt, once Athena had sprung from his brow."

The new sanctuary of the Vigil was indeed glorious. Though superficially similar to the old experimental station, it was both more beautiful and more integrated into its environment. The natural face of the mountain was exposed and restored at the base of the dome. A stream entered the dome through an opening on the uphill side and flowed through it, even dropping over a small waterfall. The lowermost levels of the dome had transparent walls, admitting broad daylight into the ellipse of mountainside described by the intersection of the mountain and the dome. Tall trees could grow in that ellipse, and would. Anyone walking among them could look hundreds of feet up into the dome via the vast atriums that pierced its floors.

The atoms of the hydrogen bomb had been dispersed and incorporated throughout the structure. Its plutonium and tritium were encased in lead in the deep foundations of the dome. Lori never knew it was there.

Fomalhaut was pleased to consider the impression this miraculous restoration of the Vigil must have made on its viewers, of whom there were hundreds of millions.

A flash of motion in the sky caused him to whirl in surprise. A white blur shot by at hypersonic speed, trailing a shockwave that was no more than a loud pop despite the very low altitude of the missile. It veered upward very abruptly, dwindled to a speck bluish with distance, then shot downward just as quickly, braking fifty feet over the crowd, hovering there in silence.

It had the look of a Perturbare flyer: a gleaming white wasp-waisted shape with a reflective canopy in the forward swelling. But...instead of the expected propulsion lamp in the rear, the fuselage tapered to a point.

"It must be a remotely piloted flyer," said Stingray, eyeing the thing distrustfully. "It had to be pulling over a hundred Gs in those maneuvers. No man could survive that."

"It is indeed unmanned," said Fomalhaut. "I detect no trace of a mind within it." The flyer had also escaped the notice of his suit's sensors as it approached, though now he detected some broadband radio emission from it.

The flyer settled slowly, the crowd clearing a space for it to land. The canopy rotated open, and out hopped a smiling Possum Perturbare, belying Stingray and Fomalhaut's confident assertions.

Perturbare's style had changed. His glossy black hair was now brushed down over his forehead, and he wore a thick mustache. His costume was black: black boots, pants, and tunic, relieved only by radial stripes of multicolored foil at the flaring shoulders, and the inevitable "P" monogram picked out in diamonds over the left breast.

Fomalhaut was most struck by the fact that he could detect no psychic trace of the man. Nor could he sense the very obvious quantum signature of the telepathy shields Perturbare had once employed. It was very disorienting, almost a form of blindness, to see a man standing before him and yet have no psychic sense of his presence at all. He found himself wondering if this "Perturbare" might be some sort of projection or illusion, although his sensors picked up the physical signs of the man easily enough.

This doubt led Fomalhaut to employ a peculiar Western mannerism for the first time: he stuck out his hand as the grinning Perturbare approached. Perturbare glanced at the hand in some surprise, then quickly recovered his poise and gripped it, leaving Fomalhaut in no doubt as to his physical presence.

Only too late did Fomalhaut consider the impression his handshake with Possum Perturbare might make on the watching world. He was peripherally aware of the stares of the people around him.

"Good to see you, Foaming Hut. Surprised that we're not dead, are you? And gratified, no doubt." He released Fomalhaut's hand and turned to Stingray. "Stingray, you big scowling watery asshole, how are ya?" He did not offer his hand. Stingray stood with arms folded, studying Perturbare with narrowed eyes.

"What's with the royal 'we', Perturbare?" asked Stingray.

Perturbare merely laughed and turned away.

"Hello, Dr. Perturbare, do you remember me?" asked Lori Wu.

Perturbare took her in from head to toe. "My, my, my. Lori Wu. Yes, we certainly do remember you. How very fetching you look in that suit. Congratulations on your well-deserved Vigil membership." He lifted and kissed her hand, which was still encased in the black and gold of the engineering suit. She beamed up at him.

Perturbare ambled up to Raintree and his friends with a more genuine smile on his face. His steps faltered as he apparently detected something new in Raintree's eyes, and perhaps felt the influence of the hidden Stones.

"Well, Ben, we're glad to see you looking a lot better than you did the last time we saw you."

"Thanks. It's good to see you've survived. Truly."

Perturbare bit his lip, his grin now entirely extinguished. "We—I get the feeling you now know—what you really are."

Raintree gave a gentle smile. "To the extent that most people do, I suppose I do."

"I just want you to know—that I did everything I could to talk Ben into coming back with me. If I had even suspected he'd remain behind, I never would have built that damned frame-shifter."

Raintree nodded. "I believe you, but what difference does it make to me? By all accounts, my counterpart is happier now than he ever was before. If he hadn't stayed behind on that other world, I would never have existed, and I'm beginning to find my life worth living. It seems to me that the only people suffering here are those like you and Fomalhaut who miss the old Ben's company. Well, that's too bad. You'll just have to get used to me instead."

Lori looked at Ben in surprise, smiling.

Perturbare winced at the accuracy of Raintree's observations. "Yeah. And who have we here?"

Raintree introduced Costanzo and Michelle. The priest goggled at him, while Michelle blushed when he pulled the hand-kissing trick again.

Then, to Fomalhaut's renewed surprise, Perturbare started glad-handing his way through their guests, pumping hands and trading quips with men and women who stared at him with glazed eyes as they found themselves hobnobbing with the very last person they had ever expected to meet, the most infamous man in the world by far.

It was only then that Fomalhaut noticed the rounded metallic bar embedded in the base of Perturbare's skull. He also noticed that Perturbare was not carrying a B-1 box.

Fomalhaut felt a sudden chill as he watched Perturbare laughing and slapping the shoulder of the grimacing Canadian Prime Minister. Stingray was studying him just as narrowly.

Fomalhaut had never before feared Perturbare. He shuddered at the sense of blindness he felt as he looked at the man. If this was how all humans perceived each other, as mere moving, talking images, then no wonder they engaged in war and murder and cruelty, for they could scarcely be aware of one another's real existence.

He was almost grateful when the arrival of another flying figure distracted him from the spell Perturbare had cast. Suddenly among them was Aureus, glittering in the sunlight. The robot's presence brought cries and something close to panic from their human guests. Even Lori, who had never seen Aureus move before, blanched and backed away. Raintree's eyes were wide. But Fomalhaut raised his hands, and they were calmed.

Aureus ignored its fellow members of the Vigil and stalked up to Perturbare, who promptly broke out in a sweat. Fomalhaut was gratified to see that Perturbare's confidence was not yet infinite.

"I see you have reestablished yourself," tolled the robot.

Perturbare nodded vigorously. "Yes. Yes, indeed we have. And now you'd like us to help you track down Valjhar."

"Correct."

Stingray's jaw dropped open. "Valjhar Cor?"

"No, Valjhar Smith," said Perturbare. "Okay, okay, clam down, Batoid Boy." He showed his palms at Stingray's anger. "Your old friend is back here on Earth, Motionglobe and all. But the years have been rough on him." Perturbare revealed all he knew on the subject.

Stingray was still rattled. "And you, Aureus, you mean him no harm?"

"I mean him no harm."

Stingray stared into the robot's glassy, glowing eyes, then gave a quick nod, turning away into his memories.

"Perhaps Pimsehkia Flam could provide information on Valjhar's whereabouts," said Aureus.

Perturbare looked puzzled. "Pimsehkia—? But she's supposed to be dead..."

Perturbare's words trailed off as he assumed a poleaxed expression.

"Pimsehkia Flam is standing over there," said Aureus, pointing.

Both Perturbare and Fomalhaut swiveled their heads toward the crowd of reporters and government officials.

Inconspicuous among them was an elegant blonde woman wearing big, rosy sunglasses. Perturbare gasped, then gave a self-deprecating laugh. "I should have known."

Fomalhaut was in something of a daze. He stared at the spire, still hot from the friction of the atoms that had combined to form it. He was only dimly aware of the emotions of the people surrounding him. He barely managed to avoid jumping when Perturbare sidled up beside him to mutter conspiratorially.

"So, what's it going to be for you guys, Fomalhaut? Take over the world?"

Fomalhaut turned and looked down into Perturbare's sly, sparkling blue eyes.

"Yes, that's basically it," he admitted.

"I don't know for sure what we're going to do next, Brainchild and me. There are so many possibilities, so many. Do you think we'll be able to coexist?"

Fomalhaut froze, looking into that grinning face, unreadable except through contractions of the facial muscles, a code he was not particularly adept at interpreting.

"I suppose that will depend on whether our goals and methods prove to be compatible," he said cautiously.

"Yup, yup. Well, we'll talk it over."

More loudly, Fomalhaut said, "Dr. Perturbare, I would like you to join us as a member of the Vigil."

Fomalhaut felt a burst of astonishment from Stingray at these words, uttered as they were within the hearing of the world's media.

Perturbare lowered his head. Fomalhaut had no idea whether he was touched by the offer, or was trying not to laugh at the transparency of this effort to gain some influence over him. Or perhaps he was angry that no member of the Vigil had acted to help him while he was imprisoned.

Except for Aureus, he reflected, though he now suspected that intervention might have been incidental on the robot's part.

Perturbare raised his eyes. Fomalhaut thought he detected a measure of actual warmth in them.

"Well, that's right neighborly of you, Fomalhaut. But, I think we'll just stay on our own, for now anyway."

Fomalhaut spoke on a second impulse. "Dr. Perturbare, may I speak to Brainchild, please?"

"When you speak to me, you speak to him as well."

"Have you, then, somehow merged yourself with the computer? That device on the back of your neck...is that Brainchild?"

"Huh? No, Brainchild still isn't that compact...yet. The device is a quantum radio interface integrated into my brain. We won't be separated again, unless someone chops off the back of my head."

One of the photographers spoke up. "May we get a picture of, er, the five members of the Vigil?"

The other four looked toward Aureus, who showed no sign of compliance. They converged on and dutifully lined up beside and behind the robot. With the addition of Lori Wu, Aureus was no longer the shortest member of the Vigil.

"Will there be other members?" called a reporter.

"There will be others," said Fomalhaut.

Cameras flashed. Fomalhaut felt pinpoints of mirth flaring up all around. His peripheral vision being inhumanly sharp, he did not need to turn his head to see Stingray raising two fingers to make devil horns behind the head of Aureus. Oh well, at least it had brought out a smile on Stingray's forbidding face.

"Fomalhaut, why isn't Dr. Standing Crane among you?"

"We don't know his whereabouts. I hope to hear from him soon."

"Ms. Wu, do you find it frightening to be wearing an alien costume of such tremendous power?"

Lori shrugged. "Not as frightening as having American soldiers point guns at my head."

"May I address a question to Aureus?"

"Certainly you may," said Stingray. "You may also address one to that rock over there."

Uneasy laughter. More questions followed. Although Fomalhaut feared the pointed questions they could and should be asking, amazingly, most of them were entirely inconsequential and personal.

Even more amazing was the fact that the journalists ignored Possum Perturbare as he stood there smiling benignly. Fomalhaut could recall no other occasion when Perturbare was content to stand around while reporters questioned and cameras beeped and flashed. Indeed, Perturbare had never before been seen by reporters, as far as Fomalhaut knew. It was as if the situation was so unthinkable that the journalists were unable to acknowledge it as real.

Finally, that mysterious blonde, who had heretofore been silent, asked: "Dr. Perturbare, now that you've escaped your well-deserved confinement, do you intend to resume your career of crime, mischief, sabotage, and theft?"

Perturbare's smile broadened.

"No, Ms. Katz. My goals are now bigger than that. But, every man needs a hobby. Who knows what I'll get around to trying next? I'm wondering about you. You've come such a long way to be here today, such a very long way. What's next for you?"

Pimsehkia Flam shrugged and tilted her head. "I too am flexible. We'll just have to wait and see."